OR THE BULL KILLS YOU

Jason Webster was born near San Francisco, brought up in England and now lives in Spain – the setting for his Chief Inspector Max Cámara series – where he divides his time between Valencia and the mountains. The second book in the series, *Some Other Body*, will be published by Chatto & Windus in 2012.

You can learn more about Jason and his books at http://www.jasonwebster.net

ALSO BY JASON WEBSTER

Fiction

Some Other Body

Non-fiction

Duende: A Journey in Search of Flamenco
Andalus: Unlocking the Secrets of Moorish Spain
Guerra: Living in the Shadows of the Spanish Civil War
Sacred Sierra: A Year on a Spanish Mountain

JASON WEBSTER

Or the Bull Kills You

VINTAGE BOOKS
London

Published by Vintage 2011

2 4 6 8 10 9 7 5 3 1

Copyright © Jason Webster 2011

Map by Sandra Oakins

Jason Webster has asserted his right under the Copyright, Designs
and Patents Act 1988 to be identified as the author of this work

First published in Great Britain in 2011 by
Chatto & Windus

Vintage
Random House, 20 Vauxhall Bridge Road,
London SW1V 2SA

www.vintage-books.co.uk

Addresses for companies within The Random House Group Limited can
be found at: www.randomhouse.co.uk/offices.htm

The Random House Group Limited Reg. No. 954009

A CIP catalogue record for this book
is available from the British Library

ISBN 9780099546962

The Random House Group Limited supports The Forest
Stewardship Council (FSC®), the leading international forest
certification organisation. Our books carrying the FSC label are
printed on FSC® certified paper. FSC is the only forest certification
scheme endorsed by the leading environmental organisations,
including Greenpeace. Our paper procurement policy can be
found at www.randomhouse.co.uk/environment

MIX
Paper from
responsible sources
FSC® C016897

Typeset by Palimpsest Book Production Ltd, Falkirk, Stirlingshire

Printed and bound by CPI Group (UK)
Ltd, Croydon, CR0 4YY

Para Montse,
que sin tí este libro no existiría.

Bien sabe el sabio que no sabe; sólo el necio piensa que sabe

The wisest of wise men knows that he knows not; only a fool
thinks he knows

Spanish proverb

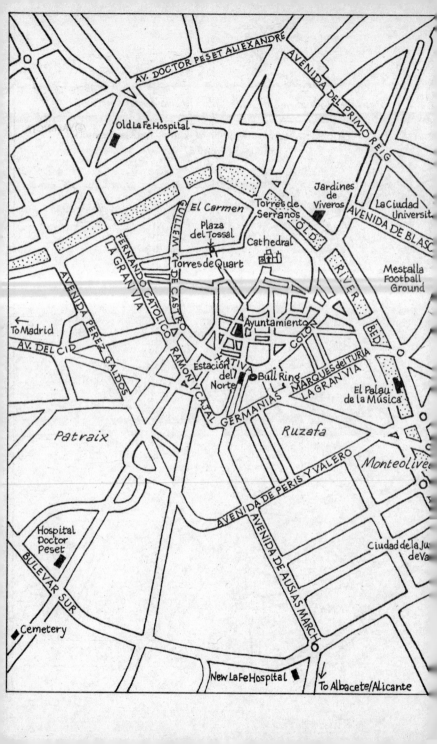

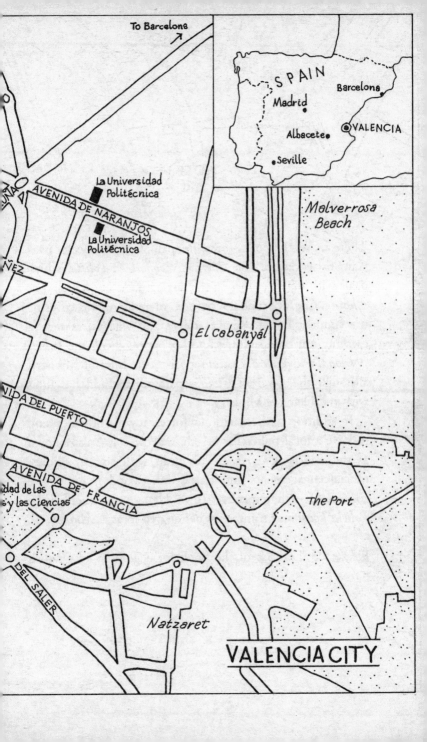

NOTE

There are several police forces in Spain. Chief Inspector Max Cámara works for the *Cuerpo Nacional de Policía*, which deals with major crimes in the larger towns and cities. The *Guardia Civil* is a rural police force, or gendarmerie, covering the countryside and smaller towns and villages, as well as carrying out border duties and sea patrols. Both the *Policía Nacional* and *Guardia Civil* report to the Interior Ministry, although the *Guardia Civil* is paramilitary and has links with the Defence Ministry.

In addition to these national forces, towns and cities tend to have a local police force – the *Policía Local*, also known as the *Policía Municipal*. This deals with smaller crimes, official engagements and traffic duties, and is under the control of each respective Town Hall. A member of the *Policía Local* may sometimes be referred to as a '*Municipal*'.

Please see the back of the book for a glossary of Spanish terms.

He watches the blood as it trickles from a wound near the back of the neck, seeps over a shoulder, thickens into a steady stream, before turning into a torrent, coursing over hair and skin, pushing its way down in thick pulses until heavy drops begin to fall on to the sand below. Unable to move from his seat, as though tied to his chair – the chair of honour, they'd called it – he struggles to breathe. Below, the killer holds his blade high and rises up on to the balls of his feet as he prepares for the final thrust, piercing his victim's back, slicing through ribs, splitting lungs.

He feels an urge to call out, but his captors are watching him: it is his duty to see this. Only he can pass judgement. Forced to be the overseer, their master of ceremonies, he stares, while trying not to see. The killer is ready, calm, the weight of a thousand previous kills evident in his poise. They say he is good, this one. Turns murder into an art.

The victim waits, bloodied, exhausted, tongue hanging heavy and dry, refusing to give in.

There is barely a sound. He hears the killer suck in air through clenched teeth . . .

And he is here again: smaller this time, lighter. How old had he been? Nine? Perhaps ten? There had been a shadow behind him – an elderly man, trying to ease his distress, patting him tenderly on the shoulder. There was nothing to fear, nothing. His grandfather meant well: a distraction, a change, something to help him forget. But this had made it worse. And so he'd run out, and his grandfather had followed, drying his tears outside in the shadows with his shirt sleeve. He'd always been grateful to him for that, coming with him rather than waiting inside to see the kill. They went home together, walking hand in hand in silence. He'd sworn he'd never watch this again.

But now he has broken his vow. Not only witness, but adjudicator.

The killer stretches up to his full height, gives a cry, and the victim lurches towards him with a final burst of life. The killer catches him on the rise, forcing his sword down to the hilt past bone and through flesh, before dancing to safety at the side. Next to him, the victim gives a deep, echoing groan.

The spectators are on their feet, cheering and waving. The drama and spectacle have reached their climax. The victim staggers for a second, then falls to the ground, legs now helpless pegs thrusting out from a steaming body. With a final breath the head slumps to the sandy floor.

The killer turns to the applauding crowd, raising his hands before crossing them over his breast as he acknowledges their adoration.

The president turns to his two advisers. They both nod, and with heavy, sick indifference he pulls out his white handkerchief and places it over the balcony in front of him. The bullfighter pretends not to notice, but the crowd erupts with joy.

PART ONE

TERCIO DE VARAS

ONE

Either you kill the bull, or the bull kills you
Traditional

Saturday 11th March

Chief Inspector Max Cámara of the Valencia *Cuerpo Nacional de Policía* cast a dark eye over the other guests at the Bar Los Toros, and sniffed.

Stopping by the Jefatura after lunch had been a mistake.

'Cámara, there's no one else around. You'll have to stand in for me.'

The idea had been to run in quickly to see if he was owed any leave. *Fallas* was coming, Valencia's pyromaniac spring fiesta, and he was hoping to get out of the city until it was over. But he could still hear Pardo's voice as the commissioner raced through the door, his wife waiting for him outside in a taxi with their three-year-old. There had been no time to remind Pardo he knew nothing about bullfighting, or that he hated it: a daughter with suspected meningitis took precedence over everything. Still, someone else could have stepped in. Maldonado, perhaps. He would have revelled in the pomp and glory.

As it was, though, he had ended up standing in as president of that afternoon's corrida, wondering to himself if there was anyone in the country less suited to the job. Pardo loved it – one of the perks of being a top policeman in a big city. Cámara had sometimes imagined him sitting up there in the balcony, the grave, unsmiling face, all the responsibility of the spectacle on his shoulders as representative of the Ministry of the Interior – the branch of government that oversaw bullfighting. He was convinced Pardo enjoyed it even more than the few times he managed to appear on TV at the successful conclusion to a case. Anyone foolish enough to go near him the day after a fight would be regaled with unnecessary detail on whether one or two ears – if any – he had ordered be cut off each dead animal and given to the matadors in recognition of their performances. Sometimes they even cut off the tail as well and presented it to the torero as a trophy, but Pardo didn't go in for that: it was rare. And a bit showy.

It could have been a disaster, but two others had sat with him in the presidential box – one an expert on bullfighting, the other, Cámara discovered to his surprise, a vet – to guide the president in his decisions. Cámara allowed himself to be steered by these stern-looking men. They made it clear they were unhappy that Pardo hadn't made it himself, sending a subordinate with no knowledge – or even apparent interest – in *los toros*.

'When did you say Pardo found out about his daughter?' one of them – the vet – had asked. His heavy, inanimate face stared out at the crowd, as if Cámara were to blame for the little girl's illness. And the two of them sucked on their cigars, veiled behind clouds of blue smoke: still, lifeless shadows on the outer reaches of his line of vision. Thank God they hadn't been invited to the Bar Los Toros.

Actually, Cámara wasn't quite sure why he had been invited himself to this award ceremony for Jorge Blanco, the star of the afternoon. All three matadors had come close to blending into one for him – each one finishing by slaughtering the bull. Only the reaction of the crowd had alerted him to possible differences. The first had been given a mixed welcome. What was his name? Cámara dug his hands into his pockets looking for the glossy programme that had been thrust at him when he arrived at the bullring. He stared into the face of a man in his mid-thirties, dark sideburns stretching down his cheeks: Alejandro Cano. The crowd had whistled at him at the end of his first fight, while his second had gone better: applause, and perhaps a trophy ear; he wasn't sure now.

The second matador had been cheered almost from the start. That one he did remember more clearly: the one they were waiting for now in the Bar Los Toros. Jorge Blanco, the man who had singlehandedly saved Spain's national fiesta from oblivion. Or at least there had been comments to that effect. His face had even appeared recently on the front page of *El País*; he was becoming a hard man to avoid. The crowd loved him, applauding every move with the cape, every triumphal swipe with his sword. He had rescued the old values of bullfighting, they said. Valour, strength, and a true life-and-death struggle with the animal. Down there, on the sand, Blanco put his balls on the line like no other bullfighter.

Cámara had pulled out his handkerchief twice for him the first time – meaning two trophy ears – then again with his second bull, the fifth of the six that made up the afternoon. His advisors had twitched at that point: perhaps he'd overdone it, but looking at the jubilant spectators – almost 13,000 people; the place was full to capacity – he'd decided to err on the side of generosity, the policeman in him considering the crowd-control options should any reluctance to award severed ears on his part lead to a riot.

At the end of the afternoon, Blanco was festooned as admirers threw flowers and cuddly toys to him. A live hen caught Cámara's eye as it was hurled down into the ring, Blanco's assistants handing it to the matador to lay his hands on before they threw it back to the crowd and, hopefully, to reunion with its owner. That night, he imagined, someone in Valencia was about to feast on chicken that had been blessed by the great man himself before having its throat slit.

Cámara remembered Blanco's keen steady eye, his slightly upturned nose, heavy eyebrows and pained, almost tortured air. There was no standing on ceremony about him, no dedicating the fight to one of the bullfighting grandees down in *Sombra* – the expensive seats. Each fight had gone to the crowd itself, and they loved him even more for it.

Cámara glanced down at the last photo on the flyer. It was the young Antonio de Mora's first proper bullfight, they'd said. At some stage before his first bull there had been a mini-ceremony of sorts down in the ring where Cano had acted as his godfather – a rite of passage from *novillero*, or apprentice, into fully fledged bull killer. The crowd was generous, applauding after each despatched animal, but there were no ears today for de Mora. Blanco was the man, and once the whole thing had finished some of the crowd rushed into the ring and carried him off on their shoulders through the main door – *la Puerta Grande* – and out into the street. That was the greatest honour for a bullfighter, his companions had told him before taking their leave, a last impassive handshake before joining their aficionado friends.

Cámara stood on his own for a moment in the presidential box, wondering how quickly he could get out of there before anyone noticed him, when the owner of the Bar Los Toros introduced himself and asked him to join them. He was president of a *peña taurina* – a bullfighting appreciation society – he said, and they were giving Blanco an award for the previous year's performance, as doubtless they would be doing next year for what had just taken place that afternoon. It would be an honour for them if today's president himself could be present. Cámara had been on the point of turning him down; he'd already made other arrangements.

'I'd be delighted.'

The words had come out with curious ease.

Now, as he sat in the grubby surroundings of the Bar Los Toros down a street at the back of the bullring, with a quickly vanishing glass of Mahou lager in his hand, he began to wonder. The owner was talking to the barman, leaning in to make himself heard above the noise of the TV set bolted high in a corner and a dozen conversations bouncing off the red-painted greasy walls. Blanco still hadn't shown up, while conversation with the two dozen other people there was proving difficult: something about the chief inspector, perhaps his clothes, just the way he was, told them he wasn't an aficionado, not one of them.

If any of them had focused on him at all, they would probably have described Cámara as an unassuming man, with short, dark, slightly ruffled hair crowning a high fore-head, a larger than average chin, dark brown eyes and a crooked, fleshy nose – the kind of person who no doubt could look after himself, and had possibly had to do so on more than one occasion. More perceptive observers of the forty-two-year-old might notice other details: strong yet thoughtful hands devoid of any rings, bracelets or watch; an observant expression in his lively brown eyes; and a vulnerability only partially masked by his broad shoulders and powerful physical presence. He was a man you would pass without a second glance down a street in broad daylight, but who might cause you some unease were the same situation repeated at night.

As he sat at the bar at the edge of the group, wondering whether to make a last attempt to talk to some of the other guests, a proverb – one of the dozens his grandfather used to repeat – floated through his mind: *Más vale estar solo que mal acompañado* – Better to be alone than in bad company. He shouldn't have come.

The last mouthful of beer disappeared from his glass and he looked around the room. The other guests looked to be *pijos* to a man – rich, well-dressed conservatives: people he might have to mix with at work on occasion, but rarely chose to spend his free time with. The other side of Spain, the other tribe. He leaned back in his chair. Five more minutes and then he'd go.

To kill time, he decided to play a game to see if he could work out who some of them were.

An elderly man sat at a table dressed in heavy tweeds, his hair slicked back and with a well-heeled country air about him. Cámara felt certain he was a bull breeder. He checked his flyer again. The bulls for the fight had come from the Ramírez farm, their symbol a large capital letter 'R' with a cross running through the lower right tail. Cámara had noticed it burnt onto the haunches of some of the bulls earlier on. Was this the man who had bred them? For a moment Cámara observed his thin, downturned mouth, large hooked nose, small untrusting eyes. His hair was almost white, and gave him a distinguished air, albeit in a slightly studied way.

Cámara moved on, scanning the room.

One face seemed familiar now – a woman standing at the centre wearing a red low-cut dress and exceptionally high, strapped silver heels. Cámara was sure he had seen her on TV, with her bee-stung lips and tightly stretched bronzed complexion. She looked like the kind of person who appeared on the gossip programmes, screaming out the intimate details of their love lives in a constant search for higher and higher doses of media attention. Carmen Luna? Wasn't that her name? If Almudena had been there with him she would have told him her life story by now. Cámara searched his memory for some reference to her. If she was here she must have something to do with Blanco. Weren't they engaged? Rumoured to be getting married soon? Blanco couldn't be more than thirty-five years old. There was no way Carmen was less than fifty. On a good day.

He watched for a moment as her eyes darted about the room clocking all the men who were looking at her.

Another woman – the only other one there – was standing on the far side of the bar. She was slightly stockier than Carmen Luna, and wore a pair of tightly fitting jeans. Her hair was cropped short and highlighted, while a pair of large brown sunglasses perched on top of her head like an Alice band. She smiled broadly as she talked to a couple of men leaning in towards her, both captured by her energy, an attractive force more powerful than mere good looks. In fact, she wasn't pretty in any conventional sense, or at least not in Cámara's mind. Her nose was a little too long and sharp, her figure a little plump, while the slight gap between her two front teeth meant she was never going to star in any toothpaste commercials. And yet it was clear from her poise that she was used to being in the company of men, and enjoyed it.

Cámara watched her for a while trying to work out who she was, but nothing, no clue, came to mind. Yet something about her was familiar. For a moment she noticed him looking her way and smiled, before turning back to her companions. Cámara stood up and headed to the bar to get himself a last quick drink. Time was beginning to drag. And still no sign of Blanco.

The door opened and all heads turned expectantly. A tall man in a dark suit appeared, and Cámara was immediately struck by his resemblance to the elderly bull breeder he'd identified earlier. A few voices called out in greeting – '*Hola* Paco!' – but he could sense the collective groan around the bar: it wasn't Blanco. After shaking a few outstretched hands, the newcomer went and sat beside the bull breeder, where the physical similarity between them was even clearer: the same hooked noses, the same small eyes. Even his hair was slicked back in the same style. This was almost certainly the old man's son. Paco Ramírez? The two of them quickly locked in conversation, the younger talking in a low voice into the other's ear.

Cámara turned away and stared up into the glass eyes of the bull's head mounted on the wall behind as the barman poured him another beer. The horns rose up in straight, parallel points from its temples before splaying out at the ends. *¿Yo también tengo cuernos?* he thought to himself. Do I have horns as well? He checked himself; where had thoughts of being cuckold arisen from all of a sudden?

He looked at the time on his mobile phone: it was already gone nine o'clock. They'd been there for almost an hour. He thought for a moment about Almudena and their plans for the evening. He'd texted her from the bullring to say he'd be running late. Come round when you're finished, she'd answered. Perhaps he should just slip out now. No one would notice.

The barman placed his drink in front of him as the sound of shouting came from the street outside.

'Those bloody *anti-taurinos* again,' the barman mumbled. 'Think they're going to frighten us off with their rallies.'

No one else seemed to be paying any attention, assuming them to be another bunch of kids setting off firecrackers for *Fallas*. But Cámara listened as a barrage of whistling and calls of 'murderers' – '*asesinos*' – filtered through the walls. Someone out there was playing a drum.

There was a kick to the door and it opened with a crash. Conversations stopped, and everyone turned to look. The doorway was empty, and across the street, election posters for the mayoress grinned back at them, while fiesta lights blazed down from their wire supports above.

'*¿Qué coño?* What the fuck?'

There was a bewildered murmuring from the guests before a huddle of people burst through the doorway and into the bar. On their chests were emblazoned drawings of a bull with a red line painted through it, while two of them were holding a banner with the words '*Blanco asesino*' painted in dark green letters which they struggled to unfurl in the cramped room. Without moving from his position at the bar, Cámara looked over and quickly counted: there were nine of them, with perhaps a straggler or two outside. Most were in their twenties, one or two slightly older. Almost all of them were wearing jeans, with walking boots or trainers, and brightly coloured shirts and jackets. No sign of any of them carrying a weapon.

Once inside, the demonstrators pulled out their whistles and started to blow, splitting the air with a tremendous sound, while someone banged a drum with a slow, stomping rhythm. Above the noise, a tinny voice echoed out from a loudhailer, the words angry and violent but incoherent in the racket. Cámara spotted the would-be spokesperson – a girl of about twenty-five, her hair in dreadlocks and pulled back in a loose bun.

Some of the guests had stood up and were gesticulating aggressively at the intruders. Ramírez, the bull breeder, sat where he was, his skin reddening. The owner of the bar was rooted to the spot, an expression of panic on his face. Cámara looked for Carmen Luna, but she seemed to have disappeared. Instead he found himself being watched by the short woman with the highlights in her hair. He felt sure she knew who he was, and her wry, knowing smile seemed to tell him that he was the only one there who could deal with the situation.

He placed his drink back on the bar and walked towards the intruders. They were now inching their way forwards with a growing group momentum, and there was a danger of imminent physical contact with some of the guests.

Cámara stepped in and quickly placed himself between the two opposing forces. The whistling intensified, as though to blast him out of the way, before finally subsiding as the intruders paused to take their breath. Cámara grabbed his chance.

'*Venga*. Come on,' he said, gesturing towards the door.

The girl with the loudhailer stood to the front and looked him up and down. She seemed curious: he didn't fit here. The absence of an expensive watch on his wrist, his uncombed hair, the short sideburns framing his face, the stubble on his chin showing that he hadn't been as careful as he might have been when shaving that morning. By the looks of it he should have been on their side.

'Who are you?' she asked.

'It's time to go,' Cámara said. 'You can carry on outside.'

From behind, Cámara could feel the eyes of the guests on him, wondering if he was capable of solving their little crisis. In front, the demonstrators decided it was time to increase the noise levels again, and the cacophony started afresh, the whistling piercing his ears like needles. Yet instinctively he could tell, as he watched them jumping and waving their arms, stamping their feet to the sound of the drum, that they had not come here seeking any more than this – a minor discomfort, a show of strength, despite their limited numbers. Their intention was to embarrass and annoy, not cause a fight or a riot.

He raised his voice.

'I'm a policeman. I want you to leave.'

The girl gave him another quizzical look.

'Policeman? So what are you doing here standing up for these murderers?' She pointed at Ramírez and his son. 'You should be locking them up.'

There was a surge in the group as she spoke, a lurching, unconscious step forwards. Cámara put out his arm and held them back. They felt his strength, like a rock. It would be difficult to get past this one.

'I need you to leave,' Cámara repeated, his voice lower this time. 'Now.'

A shout came from the back, while two of them took up their whistles once again, but the girl with the dreadlocks remained silent, flaring her nostrils as she looked into Cámara's eyes. Moments passed and neither moved, but then, with a slump of her shoulders, she sighed. The others began to read the signal and started backing slowly, very gradually, away.

'Murderers! Murderers!'

A final cry of defiance, until there was just the girl left, and a young man standing beside her; he was taller than the others, with a slim, muscular build. He grinned mockingly at the people in the bar, then turned and walked out into the street, leaving the girl on her own. She cast a disgusted eye about the room, and turned to Cámara. Tilting her head up, she blew him a kiss, then spinning round she swept her arm out over one of the tables nearby, sending glasses and cutlery crashing to the floor, before running out to join the others.

Cámara felt a powerful reflex in his leg, a desire to lunge after her and pull her in. But he held back, his jaws tight, fists clenched. The stand-off was over. Peace, albeit of an uncertain kind, had been restored.

He felt a hand on his shoulder. Turning, he saw the barman holding out a glass of brandy for him.

'You might want this,' he said.

The owner of the bar sauntered over, all smiles now the crisis had been resolved.

'We're indebted to you, Chief Inspector.' And he held out a cold damp hand to shake.

'Tonight is not the night, but those sons-of-bitches need teaching a good lesson, if you ask me,' the owner said.

Cámara returned to the main group, many pressing forwards to pat him on the back. He nodded and smiled, cursing that it would be more difficult now to leave unnoticed.

The woman with the highlighted hair was the first to break the newly found bonhomie.

'I've just called Blanco on his mobile,' she said. 'He's not answering. He should have been here by now.'

She looked over at Cámara, and this time he remembered who she was – Alicia Beneyto, a journalist on the local newspaper *El Diario de Valencia*.

'I'm just wondering if he's having difficulties getting here,' she said. 'Perhaps the demonstrators have put him off. Would it be a good idea to call for backup, Chief Inspector?'

All eyes were back on Cámara. He'd saved them once. Now it seemed he was expected to pull their missing guest of honour out of a hat as well.

Before he could say anything, the door from the street opened again and in stepped a *Policía Local* – a municipal policeman – his dayglo jacket flapping in the breeze just above the hilt of his revolver.

'Chief Inspector Cámara?' he called out.

Cámara walked over. The young policeman's breath was shallow and cold.

'Chief Inspector. There's something you should see.'

Jorge Blanco's naked body was slumped in the middle of the empty, unlit bullring. He was curled into a ball, his legs tucked underneath his body, and a pair of bright yellow and red *banderilla* darts hung from the centre of his back, their sharp fish-hook points ripping at his flesh as they flopped to the ground. Higher up, towards his shoulders, a red-handled matador's sword had been thrust into his ribcage, still swaying as the upper half of the blade caught glimmers of the street lights outside. A Spanish national flag was tied around his neck like a noose and lay mingling with congealed dark black bloodstains in the sand.

Cámara felt an icy weight sink in his guts, and a fierce, electric buzz beginning to crawl up his spine. The *Municipal* who had brought him was coughing and hacking some yards behind, trying not to throw up. Outside in the street, cars streamed past and *Fallas* music blared, the city still unaware of the storm about to break over the cold corpse curled up at its heart.

Cámara's phone bleeped. It was the duty officer back at the Jefatura.

'The *científicos* are on their way,' he told him.

'Pardo?' Cámara asked.

'He's been informed. You're the nearest officer to the scene.'

There was a pause: no need to say it, but the duty officer felt compelled to spell it out.

'It's your murder, Cámara.'

TWO

I believe that bullfighting is the most civilised
fiesta in the world
Federico García Lorca

Cámara reached out for his ivory inlaid box in its usual place by the sofa as he switched on the TV news. Most of the channels were still showing their usual programmes, but already the local station, Canal 9, was running a ticker-tape news flash across the bottom of the screen, while Cuatro seemed to have been on the story for a while already. He picked out a small dry bud of marihuana and crumbled it into the palm of his hand. Then he placed a Rizla paper on top of it and flipped it over on to his other hand in one deft movement, before pinching it into a cigarette shape, rolling it, licking it together and placing it in his mouth.

The end of the paper flamed for a second as he lit it, then dulled into a warm glow as he took his first puff and inhaled. The Cuatro newsreader was reading from the screen of the laptop at her side.

'To recap our breaking news story: Jorge Blanco Sol, the celebrated matador, has been found dead in the Valencia bull-ring. Officially the police are saying they're treating his death

as suspicious, but we understand that a murder inquiry is already underway. There is reason to believe that Blanco, who only this afternoon was awarded four ears and was taken through the main gate in triumph at the end of the afternoon's fight, was killed in a particularly brutal fashion.'

Images of the matador's life flickered across the screen, while a rapid résumé of his achievements was read out. Blanco was only thirty-four years old and at the height of his career. A year before he had come out of early retirement, many claimed in order to counter the sharp decline in bullfighting's popularity across the country. Since his dramatic comeback performance in his favourite venue, Valencia, bullrings around the country were beginning to fill again, with people talking of a Golden Age and of Blanco as a new Manolete to lead bullfighting into the twenty-first century.

Cámara pulled hard on his joint, filling his tiny living room with smoke as a shield against the barrage of journalistic clichés. The screen cut to an 'expert' on bullfighting, a man with grey hair and rectangular glasses with bright red frames, who struggled to keep his composure as the microphone was thrust under his chin. His name – Santiago Rodríguez – flashed at the bottom.

'Blanco was known for his . . . classical, fearless style of bullfighting, always insisting on traditional rituals and customs. He was the only matador on the circuit who insisted on visiting the chapel both before and after each fight. He was gored several times during his career, most famously in Seville back in 2002, when it seemed for a while we might have lost him for ever. And indeed he stayed out of the bullring for four years after that. But his comeback was the event of last season. Not everyone

was happy to see his return – he had his detractors in the bullfighting world, as all matadors do. But this is a grave, grave loss, one which we will be reeling from for years to come.'

The screen was filled with a photograph of a man wearing a trilby hat, a closely cropped grey beard wrapped around his chin like felt, and a cigar stuck firmly into the side of his mouth. The newsreader's voice blared through the speakers.

'There's been no statement yet from Blanco's apoderado, Juanma Ruiz Pastor. Blanco's relationship with Señor Ruiz Pastor had been in the headlines recently after reports of a rift between the bullfighter and his manager. There is no . . . And we're going over live now to the Valencia bullring.

The image cut to show a woman standing in front of the arches of the Coliseum-like building, a huddle of microphones and mobile phones pressed up to her mouth. The harsh white television lights reflected off a tired face, but Cámara immediately recognised her from the Bar Los Toros. The words *'Alicia Beneyto – journalist and friend of Jorge Blanco'* were ticker-taped across the bottom of the screen.

'As you can imagine, this has been the most terrible evening. Bullfighting has lost the greatest matador of this generation, and perhaps the greatest of all time. And I say that with all due respect. Bullfighting was on its knees in this country before Blanco reappeared, and there were many who were happy to see it there, perhaps even help it in its decline. But Blanco turned it around single-handedly. Bullrings are full once again. Blanco showed the way; now it is up to others, the younger generation, to take up his mantle and lead bullfighting into the future. Bullfighting is here to stay. It is the national fiesta of this country. They cannot make it go away. Bullfighting has

never been more popular, but it has never been so fragile. This is the worst night of our lives.'

For a second the camera stayed on her as a dozen questions were fired at once. Cámara wondered if she had been crying: heavy make-up dulled the skin around her eyes.

The joint squeezed between his fingers had almost gone out, and the slight tremble that had developed in his hands after seeing the corpse had begun to subside. He glanced into his box as he brought the lighter towards his mouth to fire it up again. His supplies were running out: he'd have to ring Hilario back home in Albacete to see if there was any left, and make sure he'd sowed some more seeds for harvesting in September. It was too late now, well past twelve o'clock. He'd call him tomorrow some time, if he got the chance.

The TV continued its coverage of the story as Cámara got up and strolled across his living room to the fridge in his tiny grey kitchen. The rubber seal around the door was peeling away with age, leaving a black stain in its wake: one of the downsides of having to buy second-hand white goods. The fridge contained a single limp carrot, some Manchego cheese with just the hint of a fluffy white mould around the edges, half a can of chopped tomatoes, and two cloves of garlic. But no beer or wine. Convinced he was about to leave the city to escape the *Fallas* madness, he hadn't bothered to do any shopping. He turned on the tap and poured himself a glass of water. The *maría* had made him thirsty, while if he was still going to pop round to Almudena's, as she had insisted, he'd do well to wash the taste off his tongue.

He started unbuttoning his shirt as he passed back into the living room, stubbing out the joint in a white marble ashtray he'd stolen from a restaurant when they'd first been going out together. He'd wanted her to have it, but she insisted it stay in his flat.

Cámara remembered the smell around the body back at the bullring. Had it been Blanco, or just the lingering scent of so much death in that place? He had noticed there was less blood than there might have been.

'The wounds you see were inflicted after death,' Dario Quintero, the *médico forense*, had explained back at the bullring. 'Hence the lack of bleeding. At a guess I'd say we're looking at a secondary crime scene here. You need to look for the primary, Cámara: the place where the victim was actually murdered.'

Quintero was all right as far as forensic doctors went. Others tried to keep their distance, insisting on their role as medical practitioners, associates of the investigating judge and the employees of the law courts, not the police. But Quintero had been doing this for years and didn't bother with the usual hierarchies of power and responsibility. Cámara had worked with him on the Calle Puerto Rico case a couple of years back – one of the many simple crimes of passion that had taken up most of his three years in *Homicidios*: couple splits up; husband/boyfriend loses it, grabs gun/knife/something and uses it to kill his beloved, and sometimes anyone else happening to be around, like any kids they might have, or a mother-in-law or two; then moments later, perhaps after a drink with his mates, he is filled with remorse and hands himself in at the nearest police station. Three years of taking statements from shattered men sobbing over their shattered lives.

Quintero had pulled on his long grey beard as he muttered

some more details to the *secretaria judicial*, Irene Ortiz, who was busy jotting down notes. Time of death: no more than a couple of hours before; anything much more than that and Blanco would still have been fighting bulls here on this very spot with several thousand witnesses to his state of good health. Cause of death: from the marks on his neck, and the burst capillaries in his eyes, almost certainly strangulation, probably with some kind of thong. In addition, from the small cut marks on his skin, Quintero suggested that Blanco's *traje de luces*, his shiny, colourful bullfighter's costume, had been cut from his body.

'Probably the only way he could get it off the dead body,' he said, placing his hands into the front pockets of his white coat. 'And I do think we're talking about a *he*. Just the physical effort of killing Blanco somewhere and then bringing his body here makes it very unlikely that we'd be talking about any but the most powerfully built woman.'

There had been more, though: not just the sword and the *banderillas*.

'There's a deep cut very near the genitals,' Quintero had added. Cámara had refused his offer to show him.

'As you wish,' he said. 'It's not pretty, I agree. And I need to get a closer look at it, but from the angle and depth of the cut it's possible the killer was attempting to remove the genitals completely.'

'Why didn't he?' Cámara said. Quintero shrugged.

'Perhaps he heard something. Perhaps he got frightened off. I don't know. That's more your department, I'd say.'

The *Juez de Guardia* arrived at that point and Cámara was called away. Moments later, aware of how late it was getting, and with an eye to the public aspect to the case, the judge had ordered the body be removed, and the crime scene was left in the hands of the *Policía Científica* to scour for clues.

Cámara glanced down at his notes, tossed on to the table as he'd walked in. Unsurprisingly, the overweight, balding guard at the bullring had seen nothing, too busy watching the Valencia–Real Madrid game in his little booth. (It ended in a goalless draw.) There was only one security camera, fixed on the main entrance, and there was nothing on it as they'd run out of film three months before and no one had got round to replacing it.

Not that it was much good anyway, the guard had insisted – all it showed was a grainy black-and-white image. Wouldn't even recognise himself if he appeared on it. It was only when he'd gone for a piss at half-time that he'd noticed something strange in the middle of the ring. Of course the floodlights were off, so he couldn't see, and he wasn't allowed to switch them on. Rules. Still, he'd gone out there to take a look, not that he was supposed to walk into the ring, mind. And that's when he'd found the body. Still hadn't got over the shock. Wouldn't do his blood pressure any good.

Far from being concerned that the crime of the year had taken place under his nose on his watch, he'd been more interested in complaining about the inconvenience this had caused him. Cámara had encountered this kind of thing before: one minute competing with the dead man for victimhood, the next he'd be down the bar milking it with his mates about having been there 'the night Blanco was butchered'.

The guard had called a local policeman to the scene, who had immediately contacted the *Policía Nacional*. The

Municipales were for keeping traffic moving, sorting out domestic disputes, taking direct orders from the Town Hall. Murder was for the real police – the *Nacionales* – to sort out.

They found Blanco's driver back at the Hotel Suiza, where the matador had been staying. He'd waited after the fight, but Blanco never showed up, something the other bullfighters' drivers confirmed. When Blanco failed to appear after half an hour, he left on his own, assuming that Blanco had already gone without telling him. He was fastidious about some things – like visiting the chapel – but then he had a habit of disappearing sometimes, breaking away from his entourage without telling anyone, perhaps vanishing for anything up to a couple of days before returning as though nothing had happened.

'We were never allowed to talk about it, or even ask,' he told the policeman who interviewed him. 'Just had to fit round him. The way it goes – he was the one paying the wages.'

He'd only been with Blanco for a couple of months, and had already been ticked off by the matador's *apoderado*, Ruiz Pastor, for trying to second-guess where he wanted to go.

If ever he doesn't show, you wait a bit, but then leave, Ruiz Pastor had told him. Don't ever go around looking for him.

Cámara reread the notes.

'I never asked,' the driver said. 'He'd disappeared for a couple of hours around lunchtime as well, just before getting ready for the fight. I suppose I thought it might have something to do with all those rumours about him having a boyfriend and stuff.'

There was still no sign of Ruiz Pastor himself. The hotel

staff said he hadn't returned since that morning, but he hadn't checked out, either. Other members of Blanco's *cuadrilla* – his two *banderilleros*, a couple of picadors, and his personal assistant, his *mozo de espada* – had all left the city together in a minibus after the fight to head back to their homes in Albacete. Blanco wasn't due to fight again for another month.

A change in the images on the TV caught Cámara's attention, and he looked up to see a second familiar face looking out from the screen. Pale skin, dreadlocked hair tied back in a bun. The words 'Marta Díaz – spokesperson for the *Anti-Taurino* League' flickered underneath.

'So we're against this killing. We're against all killing. But he got what he deserved. He who lives by the sword, you know, kind of gets it in the end.'

The image cut back to the newsreader.

'The Anti-Taurino League have been staging demonstrations against bullfighting throughout the week, but decided to suspend their activities temporarily on hearing the news of Blanco's death. In a statement, they said they would be resuming their rallies tomorrow, although they denied allegations of taking advantage of tonight's events to further their cause.'

Cámara made a mental note of the girl who had burst into the Bar Los Toros earlier in the evening, putting a name to the face.

On the TV, the newsreader was interviewing an overweight man in an electric blue suit, billed as Javier Flores of the Town Hall, 'right-hand man of Mayoress Emilia Delgado'.

'Of course we condemn this appalling act in the strongest possible terms. Valencia is a civilised, peaceful city, and this has

*rocked its inhabitants to the core. I cannot stress enough: we
condemn this utterly and totally.'*

Cámara saw a greasy, clean-shaven face, jowls bursting
over the edge of a tight red-and-white striped collar, a
hammed-up expression of concern shaping his knotted brow
and downturned mouth.

Newsreader: *'Will you be suspending the elections because
of this?*

Flores: *'No, not at all. That is a constitutional matter, and
completely out of the question.'*

Newsreader: *'Yet your anti-bullfighting policies—'*

Flores: *'Look, a horrendous crime has taken place tonight.
This is not the time to be talking politics. This is a time for
vigilance and mourning. Our thoughts go out to Blanco's family.
It's true Mayoress Delgado has promised to ban bullfighting in
the city when she is re-elected, but as I say, this is a tragic night
for Valencia, and it's a tragic night for Spain. I have nothing
more to say.'*

Cámara undressed and dropped his clothes on the ground
where he stood, then walked over the white tiled floor
towards the bathroom. Leaning over, he switched on the
hot tap, and the shower spluttered into life. He had one
foot inside when his mobile rang.

'*Dime*,' he said after checking the name on the screen:
Huerta from the *Científicos*. 'Anything?'

The voice on the other end was unmistakably flat and
deadpan.

'Don't be so fucking cheerful, Cámara. I've been on shift
for sixteen hours and I want to go home.'

'Not every day you get such a famous *marrón* on your
hands,' Cámara said.

'Glad to see you're treating the deceased with the respect they deserve,' Huerta said. 'I prefer the word "corpse". I take it you're not a fan.'

'Of him – couldn't really care. It was his way of making a living I wasn't sure about.'

'We're all trying to pay the bills, Cámara.'

A cold draught coming in from the door to the balcony at the back reminded him that half of his body was wet from the shower.

'So, got anything?'

'The *Municipales* made a nice mess of the place, as you'd expect. And that ape of a guard didn't help.'

No comments of Huerta's would have been complete without the usual preamble about the endless difficulties he faced carrying out his job. Somewhere in his imagination there existed a perfect crime scene, a place so unsullied by any other agent except the murderer and the victim that little more than five minutes were needed before he could stand up and point the finger with scientific exactitude at the perpetrator. He was overworked, understaffed and his equipment was mostly years out of date. His outburst years back, directed at an eager young inspector hoping for quick clues, that 'This isn't fucking *CSI Miami*,' had since become an unofficial police motto. Cámara had only ever known him like this. No one at the Jefatura could remember him having been any other way. But they accepted it: Huerta had never been known to get anything wrong. Ever.

'Still,' he continued, 'let's start with what there isn't.'

Cámara waited, but Huerta seemed to be expecting him to say something.

'Go on,' he said at last.

'We've got no obvious exit point,' Huerta said. 'I'm assuming our man got inside the bullring along with everyone else. But how did he get out?'

'The gates were locked,' Cámara said.

'Not only that, there's no sign of them being forced in any way. Either he's still in there somewhere – which I doubt. Or he managed to vanish somehow.'

'Perhaps he jumped from the outer passageway.'

'A bit high,' Huerta said. 'And a bit public. Someone would have seen him. And he's nothing if not careful, this one.'

'What do you mean?'

Cámara was beginning to shiver in the cold. He reached for a blanket flung over the edge of the sofa and did his best to wrap it around himself with one hand.

'He raked over his own tracks. We would have got some nice prints from that sand, but he went to the trouble of raking after himself.'

'Have you found the rake?'

'Of course we've got the fucking rake. But it's useless: no prints we can use. The point is I don't think our man would have been so stupid as to have left prints everywhere, either.'

'OK. I understand,' said Cámara.

'We found something else, though,' Huerta said. 'A silver man's-style bracelet not far from the body. Initials A.A. engraved on the inside.'

'Doesn't mean anything to me,' Cámara said. 'I'll have a look at it tomorrow. Any fibres?'

He knew as soon as the words left his mouth that it was the wrong thing to say.

'Fibres?' Huerta laughed. 'It's a fucking bullring. The place was packed with people and bleeding animals until only an hour or so before. Yeah, we've got fibres, hairs, bits of dry skin, you name it. Anything to do with the murderer? Probably not.'

'Quintero said the actual murder probably took place somewhere else,' Cámara said.

'I was coming to that,' Huerta said. 'We're looking at the chapel as a primary. Possible signs of a struggle there: a few knocked-over chairs. We're taking a closer look at it in the morning.'

The question remained, though: why go to the trouble of stripping the body, carrying it out to the middle of the ring and mutilating it?

'A message, that's my guess,' said Huerta. 'Either that or a sicko.'

'A sicko could pick on anyone, though,' Cámara said.

'As I say, then: a message.'

What message? Who was it for?

Cámara glanced up at the clock.

'OK. Thanks. Anything else?'

'Pardo's daughter?' Huerta said.

'Christ! I forgot. Any news?'

'Nothing,' Huerta said. 'Which probably means everything's fine. Believe me, if the commissioner's daughter had pegged it we would have heard. Even on a night like this.'

The phone went dead. In the background the TV blared on. Cámara put his phone back down on the table, then looked up in time to hear his name mentioned.

'*Heading the investigation is Chief Inspector Max Cámara of the* Policía Nacional . . .'

He reached for the remote and killed it.

Joder. Who gave a fuck what the policeman in charge was called? No one needed to know. Pardo was usually more than happy to take the applause. Or at least once a case was closed.

He stepped into the shower. By now most of the hot water from the tank had run off, and he had to rinse himself quickly in rapidly cooling water.

'*Me cago en la puta.*'

Five minutes later, wearing a clean shirt, his hair still damp, he stepped out into the brightly lit, empty street to walk the ten minutes to Almudena's flat, on the other side of the Ruzafa quarter. Lying just to the south of the old centre, it was no longer the refuge of drug dealers it had once been, but Moroccan grocery shops sat next to Chinese wholesalers of cheaply made clothes and antique dealers selling Art Deco furniture. Cámara liked it for its friendly, village-like atmosphere.

Architecturally, like much of Valencia, it was a mixture of elegant, brightly painted Eclectic apartment blocks – five or six storeys high, with tall narrow French windows and ornate iron railings – standing next to younger, more awkward siblings: ugly, brown-brick structures from the 1950s and 1960s, with bright orange awnings and aluminium doors. The Carmen area a twenty-minute walk away – the oldest quarter, near the cathedral – managed to retain a more historic feel. There the streets were narrower, windier and dirtier, giving a sense of the labyrinthine atmosphere of the medieval city, and a feeling of intimacy – in a relatively small city like this it was common to bump into friends and acquaintances.

Among the graffitied walls and abandoned houses with weeds growing out of their crumbling roofs, some of the more important buildings, like the late-Gothic *Lonja* silk exchange with its spiralling pillars and lustful gargoyles, and the *Generalitat* palace, with delicate needle-column windows and large fan-like stone arches over the main doors, were a reminder that five hundred years before, Valencia had been the richest and most important city in Spain, home to the Borgias – before they became Popes and moved to Rome – and powerhouse of the Spanish renaissance.

Fallas, the biggest fiesta in the city's year, was just beginning and some of the roads had already been cleared of parked cars for the garish wood and papier-mâché statues that the next day would be erected at every crossroads and on every street corner. The *falleros* – those Valencians actively involved in the fiesta – always took over the city for a fortnight like an army of occupation. And this year – as every year, it seemed – the authorities were boasting of a million visitors expected from abroad and other parts of Spain. When it came to *Fallas*, there was a clear division in the city between those who loved it and those who didn't and who left town to get away from the all-encompassing noise. Cámara had long counted himself among the *anti-fallero* group.

There was a sound behind him, something out of place, but he didn't feel the blow to his upper back, just an empty lost second as though for a moment he had ceased to exist; and then the sensation of falling. Awareness of what was happening came just in time for him to avoid landing on his face, and he twisted his body quickly to the side, his shoulder taking most of his weight as he crashed to the pavement. The edge of his mouth caught the cement as he turned, however, and he felt the skin of his lip tearing. A kick bore into his stomach in the second that he lay still, the first of more he sensed were to come. He retched, but before a second kick landed he was up on his knees and scrambling to his feet, lifting himself up with his hands and jerking away from the direction of the attack so as to get back upright. Never stay on the ground. In a normal street fight it paid to stay vertical.

Gripping his stomach with his left hand, breathing deeply to clear his head, he saw three forms darting around him, preparing to strike again. Despite the darkness, they were under the direct glow of a street lamp and Cámara could almost see their faces. Instinctively, he crouched slightly, rounding his shoulders and lowering his weight into his hips and thighs. Prepared.

The first one came in with a swinging haymaker punch. The dropped shoulder, the grimace, the arc of the fist as it started low around the hip and closed in on his face. Cámara blocked it easily with his left wrist and drove the knuckles of his right hand into the man's throat with a straight, short stab. A little too hard, perhaps. As long as he could still breathe once he hit the ground. Break the trachea and he might have problems.

One down, two to go.

The second attacker, enraged at seeing his colleague on the ground gasping for breath, came in next, charging with a kind of war cry and lunging with both arms as though reaching for his face. Cámara just managed to twist out of his way in time, spinning on his heel and feeling the man's breath on his skin as he brushed inches away. Then he chopped down with his right arm on the man's outstretched arms as he sailed past, tipping him off balance and forcing him to the ground, where he tripped and crashed his chin against the edge of the pavement. There he lay motionless, emitting a low, sobbing groan.

Cámara quickly looked around for the third, wondering what he would do, but already he appeared to have thought better of it and taken flight, his footsteps echoing as he raced round the nearest corner, out of sight.

The taste of blood from his split lip distracted Cámara's attention for a second. He placed his hand to his mouth and felt the cut. Not too bad, he thought, but it would make him a bit of a sight for a couple of days. The bottom of his ribs ached from the kick to his stomach, the pain spreading from his solar plexus round and up his back to his shoulders before shooting down his arms and finally into his groin.

'Hijos de puta.'

He heard a sound. The second attacker had managed to get back up on to his feet and was speeding away as fast as he could, barely able to keep a straight line as he staggered and hopped his way down the street, his hand to his chin, spitting as he reached the corner before he, too, disappeared from view.

It was over. Like so many fights, it had barely lasted beyond the first exchange of blows. Only professionals could make them continue for any length of time.

Cámara bent down to look at the first attacker, still lying on the ground with his hand to his throat. The man was motionless, his eyes wide open, staring at him in fear and pleading, his breathing steady but difficult. He'd be OK, Cámara thought, but would need some attention fast.

He shook himself as he got up to walk away, his hand gripping the throbbing in his stomach. In the circling chaos of his thoughts it was clear that they had gone for him deliberately. Any number of people had reason to have a grudge against him: people he'd put away; friends and relatives of people he'd put away. It was one of the reasons why so many policemen lived outside the city, in anonymous estates and tower blocks near the beach. Cámara had never joined them, refusing to give in to fear.

He wondered about these three, though. Others might simply have knifed him and have done with it. These guys had come unarmed – and completely unprepared. Whoever they were, and whatever they were after, it made little sense.

He tried to catch the blood dripping from his mouth, but the splashes from the palm of his hand were already scattering a shower of crimson over the pale cotton of his jacket, showing up as dark purple under the orange street lights. He leaned in heavily against a public phone booth and called 112 for an ambulance. Crossroads of Antiguo Reino and Salvador Abril, there's a man on the ground. Looks like he's having trouble breathing.

Tonight let someone else sort it out.

He caught the sound of the ambulance charging down behind him as he pressed his thumb against Almudena's doorbell. A second later the lock buzzed and he pushed his way through into the entrance hall.

Hot, silent tears splashed on to his face as she wiped at his lip with a damp cloth before reaching for the bottle of iodine. Cámara had vomited in her toilet as soon as he'd got inside, and splashes of sick were entering the cut.

'I'll be fine. It's just the shock. Thanks.'

36

Her dark blonde hair was tied back with a rubber band, her make-up already scrubbed from her face, her pre-bedtime routine already long completed by the time he arrived.

'I really need a brandy.'

She left him to dab the dark brown iodine on to the cut himself and went into the kitchen to fetch a glass. He felt the shudder through his body as the cotton pad made contact with his raw, exposed nerves, and closed his eyes. The sound of the brandy being poured brought him back, and she thrust it into his hand.

'You'll have to drink it from this side of your mouth,' she said, pointing at the undamaged part. 'I've run out of straws.'

He attempted a laugh, but she wasn't smiling, her dark brown eyes begging him for an explanation.

'I don't know who they were,' he said.

'Why didn't you ask? Why didn't you arrest them?'

He shrugged and moved towards the long brown sofa in the living room, where he flopped like a heavy bag.

'I suppose you heard about the whole thing?' he said.

'About Blanco?'

'They've given the case to me.'

She looked surprised.

'I know,' he said. 'My reaction as well. But I was the first one there. Or at least that's what they told me.'

He emptied the brandy glass and lifted it up for more. She gave him a look, reached for the bottle and took a couple of steps forwards to pour, then stepped back again, leaning her shoulders against the wall as she watched him.

'Holiday's off,' he said, 'as you'll already have worked out.' He groaned as a spasm of pain shot through his abdomen. 'Got any ibuprofen to go with this?'

'I'll drive you back,' she said. 'I've got an early start tomorrow.'

'Tomorrow's Sunday,' he said.

'We've got a big project to push through.'

'Another shop?'

'Restaurant,' she said. 'Down by the port.'

Her Audi purred through the empty streets as they sat in silence. Cámara glanced through the window when they neared the spot of the attack. There was no one there. The ambulance would have picked him up, whoever he was. By now he'd be in La Fe hospital, a couple of night-duty doctors forcing his throat back into place. Perhaps he'd call the next day to try and find out the man's name. Or perhaps not.

Almudena kept the engine running when they reached his door – this wasn't going to be a long goodbye. She cast an eye around the street.

'I think you'll be all right,' she said.

'Thanks.'

He pulled at the handle and got to step out.

'I was at the doctor's yesterday,' she said quietly.

He stopped and turned to her.

'I'm giving up the fertility treatment,' she said. He waited for a second, expecting her to explain.

'There's nothing wrong with me,' she said finally. 'Everything's fine.'

Another silence. He was being expected to work it out for himself.

'The doctor says . . .' She sighed. 'He said you might want to pass by yourself for some tests.'

* * *

Her car rolled away as he stood for a moment at the entrance of his block of flats, watching the tail lights slowly diminish, then turn away. He checked the street up and down once, then again. No movement, no sign of any attackers.

The key slotted straight into the hole, and with a click, the door opened.

THREE

The truth about bullfighting is having some
mystery to tell . . . and telling it
Rafael Gómez, 'El Gallo'

Sunday 12th March

Three boys no older than seven were huddled outside the doorway as Cámara headed down the stairs to the front door of his block of flats. Through the glass he could see the dark red glow of the fuse for the firecracker as it inched along the paving stones towards its target. The boys stood up and scattered, and a second later the inevitable BANG of the explosive filled the street. Get it wrong and some *petardos* could take a finger off. But Valencian boys were brought up with this, as though they learned the dos and don'ts through some kind of osmosis. Moments later they were back in position, another firecracker – a powerful *trueno* this time – ready to light. This would go on all day, and there were tens of thousands of similar groups all over the city, all with an uncontrollable greed for noise.

After today there were only three working days left, then

the real holidays started and the hard-core pyromaniac fun could begin.

The walk to work took him down streets lined with palm trees and acacias until he connected with the old river which led him up to the brand new police Jefatura. The Turia had once flowed this way, a tiny little stream snaking down a wide, empty river bed. Every once in a while it had filled with the flood waters from the inland mountains and become a proper river for a few short days or weeks before returning to its habitual trickle. But then, in 1957, it broke even these copious banks, and the city had found itself three metres underwater. So they had diverted the whole thing around to the south of the city, and the old river bed had been turned into a park, an arching streak of green through a densely packed city. Thank God they had made the right choice in the end – at one stage Franco had wanted to turn it into a six-lane ring road.

A clear spring sky shone overhead as Cámara neared the gleaming white of his new offices. What had been intended as a new art museum for the city had been converted at the last minute into a police station when the banks pulled the plug on the Town Hall's massive debts. The architectural masterpiece by Valencian wunderkind Jaume Montesa, designed to crown the transformation of the city from provincial backwater to Mediterranean powerhouse, was now struggling to function as the hub of police activity for the whole region. Practical considerations like places to park hadn't been at the forefront of the great man's mind, more concerned with the lines of his parallel white cement arches, and the blue crystal walls that were meant to reflect the waters of the sea just a couple of miles to the east.

Cámara caught the now-familiar smell of stale urine floating in from the side of the main entrance where colleagues unwilling to climb the stairs or take the lift to the only toilet, on the fourth floor, relieved themselves after enjoying a couple of cigarettes away from their smoke-free offices. Groups of them were standing around as he approached, some in uniform, the *Judiciales* like himself in ordinary clothes. As part of *Homicidios* Cámara was regarded by some colleagues as being near the top of the tree – where they all wanted to be if they'd admit it. And now he'd just landed himself the murder of the century. A couple of them nodded as he walked past. Maldonado was there as well, but pretended to look the other way.

Inside, people were walking quickly in all directions with expressions of frustration on their faces, still trying to adapt to this new, ill-equipped building. They'd been fine back in the old place on Fernando el Católico Avenue. No one had wanted this. But the Ministry had insisted. Millions had been spent on it, and there was nothing the government in Madrid liked better than rubbing the Town Hall's nose into the fact that it had screwed up. Bringing the police here had everything to do with political battles, not fighting crime.

Cámara spotted his boss on the other side of the hall. Commissioner Vicente Pardo, head of the *Grupo de Homicidios*, looked as lost as the rest of them, his face colouring as he tried to show Judge Jordi Caballero the way to the lifts and away from the sea of flustered people. Cámara hesitated for a second: he'd hoped for a few minutes in his office before this.

'They're over here,' he said, eventually walking over to

Pardo and pointing to the lift shaft hidden behind a pillar of more white cement.

'You don't have to show me around,' Pardo snapped.

The three of them walked over to stand before the metal doors. No one moved, until Cámara leaned in and pressed the call button. Caballero stood still, taller than Pardo in a charcoal-grey suit, a sharp expression in his eye and grey hair spouting around his temples.

The lift arrived and opened with a ping and they stepped inside.

'Well, now that we're all together,' Pardo started. He looked properly at Cámara for the first time. 'What the fuck happened to your face?' He sighed. 'Never mind. I don't want to know.'

Cámara tried to cut him off before the inevitable speech. 'I'd like Torres with me on this one,' he said.

Pardo looked up at the flashing numbers above the door as they slowly ascended.

'It's already been taken care of. I've packed him off to pull in your chief suspect. With any luck we'll have this wrapped up by the end of the day. Quintero's been on to us – Blanco's body was covered in fingerprints. He's got some special kit that can spot them. A Raman spectroscope.'

He mouthed the name like some schoolboy proud of having memorised his times tables. Cámara hoped Huerta didn't hear about it: anything more to highlight the poverty of the *Policía Científica* equipment in the Jefatura compared to what the forensics lot had over at the *Instituto de Medicina Legal* next to the law courts and he might just lose it. Huerta got to do the hard, dirty work, while the magistrates and medics, with their degrees and doctorates, got the best facilities.

Pardo placed his fist to his mouth and gave an unnecessary cough. 'You've met Judge Caballero.'

Caballero nodded towards Cámara.

'Yes, of course,' Cámara said.

He recognised the judge who had shown up late the night before at the crime scene, just in time, as the person officially in charge of the investigation, to go through the motions of ordering the body to be taken away. It was his signature that would go on the warrants; the police gathered clues, wrote reports, but in the eyes of the law he made the final decisions, even if it didn't always work like that in practice. Cámara hadn't had any dealings with him before, but everyone in the Jefatura knew each judge in the city by reputation at least. Caballero wasn't one of those old-style Francoist types who gave the police a free hand, believing in them implicitly as a force for good. Some attention had to be given to the rights of the suspects. But he wasn't an interfering type either. If anything, colleagues had put him down as an ambitious sort, relatively young in his late forties, and keen to get promoted to the national court in Madrid, where the big cases were handled.

'We'll soon be getting the whole story from Blanco's little *chapero*, his rent-boy,' Pardo continued. 'You heard about the bracelet, Cámara. I would have thought you'd worked it out for yourself.'

Pardo shared a smirk with Caballero.

'A.A.,' Cámara said.

'Antonio Aguado. Don't you read the *prensa rosa*, the gossip magazines?'

Cámara said nothing.

'You should, you know. Just because it's not in *El País* doesn't mean it's not news – or important. Anyway, those fingerprints are almost certainly going to be his. You heard it here first.'

He raised a finger as though to emphasise the point. The lift pinged again and the doors opened. They stepped out into a long white corridor, views of the city stretching across through the smoked glass on the far side of a row of offices. The squat octagonal Gothic tower of the Cathedral – the Miguelete – was just visible over the rooftops. Caballero spoke for the first time.

'It's all pointing at Aguado.'

'Might even have it wrapped up for the nine o'clock news,' Pardo said with a grin. He rubbed his hands together. 'Quintero's happy to release the body to the family. They're insisting on a quick burial. Later this afternoon, in fact. No point extending the whole thing for days. Not like they do in those cold northern countries. Keep them in the fridge for weeks, apparently.'

'Perhaps I'll get my holiday after all,' Cámara mumbled to himself.

'What was that?' Pardo said. 'I can't begin to tell you how sensitive this case is,' he said, not waiting for a reply, 'what with the elections and everything.'

A policewoman in uniform walked past carrying a sheaf of papers, turning sideways to shuffle past them. With his back to the wall, Cámara watched as their eyes lingered on the woman's buttocks for a couple of seconds as she walked away, before Pardo turned his attention back to the conversation and fixed his eyes on his subordinate.

'Aguado will be here screaming for forgiveness in a minute

45

or two. I've impressed your strengths on Judge Caballero. We're both convinced you're the man for the job.'

He'd already moved into PR speak, Cámara thought. Already with half a mind on the words he'd be using to brief journalists over another long lunch at *Torrijos*. Never had he received such praise from Pardo in all the years he'd known him.

He saw Caballero stretching his arm out towards him.

'We'll be in touch,' he said, shaking Cámara's hand.

He patted Pardo on the shoulder and turned to walk away down the corridor.

Cámara waited until he'd moved out of earshot.

'He seems to know his way around.'

'He's very good friends with the *inspector de servicio*,' Pardo said. 'I suspect he's come to pay a visit.'

'You mean he's actually come here to see *your* boss.'

'You should have your lip looked at,' Pardo said.

'I've had worse.'

'I know; I've seen them. Should I be worried about the other guy?'

'How's your daughter?' Cámara said.

'Fine. False alarm, thank God. You don't have kids, Cámara. But when you do – *if* you do – you don't ever want to have to go through what we did last night. Believe me.'

'You should have been there at the bullring,' Cámara said. 'This should be your case.'

'I heard Blanco fought quite well. Awarded him four ears, right?' Pardo shuffled as though to leave. 'Probably a little over-generous, but apt, given the circumstances.'

'I didn't know he was going to get killed minutes later.'

'Bullfighting's better off without him. Weirdo, that one. And a poof. Look, Cámara,' he said. 'It's only fair, you know: you're on probation with this one. That Bautista affair – it's not going away. People just don't like that sort of thing. Looks messy. Get this one right, though, and we'll see what we can do, eh?'

He started walking away.

'Oh, and Cámara,' he called over his shoulder. 'You might want to head down to the Town Hall. The mayoress has asked to see you ASAP.'

Piles of box files and papers were stacked in towers around the office. Cámara cursed as he cut a way through to his desk, trying not to send them crashing to the floor. No time even to work out where the coffee machine was, and already he had to be on the move.

He sat down and glanced out for a second at the apartment blocks on the other side of the river, orange and green shutters flapping over the windows as the sun moved around and shone directly on the red-brick facade. He looked back at the chaos, wondering where to begin.

A copy of the Sunday edition of *El Diario* was lying on the desk. They had just had time to get some copy in on the Blanco story before putting it to bed. A large photo of the dead matador taken the day before, holding two bull's ears in his hands in triumph, took up most of the front page. Cámara pursed his lips: he had awarded him those. Turning over the page he glanced quickly through the newsprint. Most of it was a repetition of what he'd heard on the TV the night before, with a résumé of Blanco's career, and an evaluation of his importance to bullfighting. There was also a special column by Alicia Beneyto, with a photo next to her byline looking several years younger. Shocked by the death of her friend, she'd still been able to fire out a five-hundred-word eulogy. Blanco was the best, she said. The best there'd ever been.

Cámara folded the newspaper and cast it to one side. He felt thirsty. A piece of paper tucked under the base of the lamp caught his eye. He picked it up and read in familiar thick black handwriting: 'It's behind the last filing cabinet. Call me when you read this.'

Cámara stood up and walked to the filing cabinet, then bent down and slid his fingers over the back until he felt something. Unpeeling the sticky tape that held it in place, he pulled out a stainless steel hip flask. He gave it a shake: it was still half full. Looking around, he spied a used plastic cup sitting on the windowsill. He shook out the dregs, staining half a dozen of the report papers lying on the floor, then poured himself a *dedo* – a finger's width of brandy. He paused for a moment, smelt the alcohol tickling the insides of his nose, then made it a double. In two gulps it was gone, the warmth shuddering down his insides, a tingling where it had caught the still-raw cut on his lip. With a sense of satisfaction he crumpled the cup in his hand, feeling it crush under his fingers.

An image of Almudena flashed in his mind: her expression as she'd cleaned him up the night before. And how she'd leaned back against the wall watching him as he lay in pain on the sofa. Strange that that was the enduring image from the previous night, he thought, and not the scene in the car when she'd dropped him off. Still, Pardo had picked something up about that, he'd noticed, with his sixth sense for other people's weaknesses.

Thinking better of pulverising an innocent plastic cup,

he relaxed his hand and began trying to push it back into shape. A crack had developed on one side, though; it was useless. He looked for a rubbish bin, but there was none to be found. With a sigh he opened one of the drawers in the desk and dropped the cup in.

The phone whined in his ear as he beat out a flamenco rhythm with his fingers on the desk: SEVEN EIGHT nine TEN. There was a click and Torres's heavy voice came on the line.

'Morning, chief.'

'I take it you've found Antonio Aguado.'

'He was at his home in El Cabanyal. On his own.'

'Saying anything interesting?'

'Not at the moment. Bit cut up.'

'Makes sense.'

'Pardo told us to bring him in,' Torres said.

'Go easy on him,' Cámara said.

'We'll sort out one of the duty lawyers. And of course, it's a Sunday, so until he or she arrives . . .'

Torres paused for a moment. Cámara could hear the sounds of El Cabanyal – the old fishermen's quarter – from the other end of the line: cars honking, a Gypsy woman shouting out for her kids.

'I'll catch you later,' Cámara said. 'I've got to go out.'

'Got a date already?'

'Kind of. Bit of a hot shot, actually.'

'Ho ho. Emilia's given you the call already, has she?' Torres said. 'I thought she might. Give her a kiss from me.'

Avoiding the lifts, Cámara walked down one flight of steps and along a corridor to the control room. This was the one functioning section of the building, the bit that they'd had to get right before anyone could move in. One wall was taken up by a giant screen with a colourful interactive map with little symbols of *zetas* – squad cars – dotted in half a dozen places, slowly moving around the city streets. In front of the screen sat four uniformed policemen and women, leaning back in their chairs and chatting. Things were quiet.

Cámara stepped into the small booth-like office adjacent to the control room.

'I thought they'd got rid of you years ago,' a voice said. He looked up and caught sight of a familiar, smiling face.

'They're still working on it, Beltrán,' he said.

'Taking their time, are they?'

'They think they've just found the perfect excuse,' Cámara said.

'Don't tell me . . . ?' Enric Beltrán slapped him on the shoulder.

'First officer on the scene,' Cámara said, rubbing the back of his neck. 'No escape.'

Beltrán gave him a knowing look. He was ex-GEO (*Grupo Especial de Operaciones*), the elite force within the National Police; small, with closely cropped black hair, a prizewinning marksman, and usually regarded as the toughest man in the Jefatura. Not that he boasted in any way; he didn't have to: men like Beltrán gave off an air of physical strength and ability that was unmistakable. He and Cámara had been on a training course together a couple of years before – 'confidence enhancement'; the usual, irrelevant bullshit – and naturally gravitated towards each other. Neither man was given much to toeing a line that was increasingly corporate in tone; alone among the others – all greasy-pole specialists – they had found they could communicate.

'Who was on duty here last night?' Cámara asked.

'I was,' Beltrán said. 'Doing an American shift.'

Cámara had worked enough of those himself, bunching up your hours as much as possible to get a longer weekend. Except that for a few days it meant you ended up virtually living at the Jefatura.

'What happened last night?'

'You mean with the Blanco killing?' Beltrán said. 'The *Municipales* called it in. One of theirs found the body and got on to us. I thought he'd gone and found you himself.'

'Just wanted to hear it from you,' Cámara said. 'What about the demonstration by the *Anti-Taurino* League?'

'Again,' Beltrán said, 'the *Municipales* were on it. I've seen their report. The usual bunch. We've come across them before a couple of times. That Marta Díaz seems to be the leader, along with her boyfriend, Angel Moreno. Trained to be a torero himself years back, before he turned against it.'

'Can you get it to me?'

'It's already been sent. It should be there.'

'OK.'

'There were a couple of ours at the bullring,' Beltrán said, 'as there always are for a fight, but they'd gone by the time all that was happening. Why? You wondering about that breakaway group that went down to the Bar Los Toros? Heard you did all right looking after that lot yourself.'

Cámara cast an eye over the control room to the side, and the flashing screen on the wall.

'If there was anything else to tell me—'

'I'd have told you already,' Beltrán said. 'Nothing. Nothing strange or out of the ordinary. It was pretty quiet until that call came in from the *Municipales*.'

'And you got in touch with Pardo?'

'We put it straight through to *Homicidios*. I didn't talk to Pardo personally. Why?'

Cámara shrugged.

'Nothing.'

Beltrán gave him a friendly, if bruising, punch in the arm.

'Big case,' he said, raising his eyebrows.

A phone started flashing a yellow light from the other side of the office.

'Maldonado again,' Beltrán said with a sigh.

'What's up?'

'Been calling me all morning. Trying to make up for the fact that he skived off yesterday afternoon to go to the bullfight.'

Cámara sniffed.

'He was there?'

'Loves his bullfights,' Beltrán said. 'He only goes because he dreams of taking over from Pardo as president of the bullring one day.'

He turned and went to pick up the phone.

'All part of his scheme for taking over the world,' he said.

FOUR

The history of bullfighting is intimately linked with that of Spain,
such that, without understanding the first it is impossible to understand the other
José Ortega y Gasset

One of the *zeta* cars was heading into the centre and Cámara hitched a lift as far as the *Estación del Norte* train station. Crossing the road he stepped into the small square – not much more than a widening of the pavement – at the entrance to the bullring. The bullfight scheduled to take place that afternoon had been cancelled out of respect for Blanco, and notices to the effect in large black lettering had been hurriedly plastered over the bright posters announcing the usual *Fallas* bullfights; only the traditional banner – *¡6 Bulls, 6!* – was still visible at the top. A few people – a solitary man wearing a flat, blue corduroy cap; and a middle-aged couple, the woman leaning heavily on her husband's arm – were standing in front of the building with vacant, lost expressions on their faces, as though trying to understand what had just happened, how such a great bullfighting figure had been taken away from them – and in a manner which they struggled to comprehend.

53

Cámara was surprised to see that the *Anti-Taurino* League were in their usual spot near the entrance, with their trestle table and their leaflets and posters. He recognised some of their faces from the night before – Marta Díaz, the girl with the loudspeaker, Moreno, her muscular-looking boyfriend, straightening everything up as the papers got caught in a breeze, tidily placing them back into neat piles. They all looked a bit smarter today.

It was strange that no one had objected to their being there on this day. Not that they weren't allowed to be, but he would have expected them to have eased off for a while. Either that or be heaved from their pitch by irate Blanco supporters. Or a *Municipal* more interested in social decency than the demonstrators' constitutional rights. Perhaps people were still in a state of shock.

He showed his ID and badge to the policemen guarding the door and stepped into the cool shade of the bullring. Avoiding the passageway down into the arena, he walked around the outer corridor to the entrance through which the bullfighters themselves entered the ring – the *Puerta de Cuadrillas*. There he saw a couple of Huerta's colleagues from the *Científica*. They nodded at the open door of the chapel nearby and Cámara walked in.

Huerta was standing on his own near the altar, pinching his nose and pursing his lips – his usual habit when trying to concentrate. Cámara waited, taking in as much of the surroundings as he could. The altar was very much like any other in Valencia, with a large statue in the niche of *La Virgen de los Desamparados*, Our Lady of the Helpless, the patron of the city. A deep red carpet extended along the floor and up the steps. More noticeable, however, was the positioning of some of the oak benches lined up in front of him: one was lying face down, while another two had been forcibly pushed out of place. Close to where Huerta stood, pieces of broken ceramic were also scattered on the floor.

Huerta looked up and nodded at Cámara.

'The chaplain's told us there was a statue here of San Pedro Regalado as well. The patron saint of bullfighters,' he explained. 'Got smashed to pieces in the struggle, is my guess.'

Cámara took a tentative step forwards.

'It's all right,' Huerta said. 'We've done that bit.'

'So it was here, then?' Cámara said.

Huerta lifted up an evidence bag containing what looked like a thin black strap.

'Almost certainly. Found this under one of the benches.'

'You'd better get it to Quintero soon if you want to check it against the marks on his neck,' Cámara said. 'He's releasing the body to the family this afternoon.'

Huerta rolled his eyes, then called over one of his team. Handing him the transparent bag, he gave him some instructions and then turned back to Cámara.

'But Blanco wasn't an easy kill, by the looks of it,' Cámara said, looking at the damage to the chapel.

'You saw him,' Huerta said. 'They're not musclemen, those bullfighters. But they're no weaklings either.'

'Blanco fought back, then?'

Huerta pursed his lips.

'Struggled, yes. Not sure about fighting back. If our man knew what he was doing with that thong then Blanco didn't stand much of a chance. The brain gets starved of oxygen in seconds.'

Cámara looked around the chapel. To one side there was

55

a small wooden confession box, with a purple curtain over the central section. Huerta signalled to him that it was all right to have a look. Stepping over, Cámara flicked the curtain open: white powder marks dotted the side panels where Huerta's team had already been searching for fingerprints.

'It's clean,' Huerta said as Cámara pulled his head back out. 'Although someone's been in there: the polish on the wood has been smudged.'

'Nothing?' Cámara asked.

'Not even any fibres.' Huerta allowed himself a half-smile. 'I'm telling you, our man was very careful. Did he use the confession box to hide in, though, before pouncing on Blanco? Yes, that's a fair assumption.'

Cámara looked from the confession box to where Huerta was standing, imagining the killer coming out, catching Blanco unawares from behind as he – what? Prayed? Perhaps. Huerta read his mind.

'A quick struggle as Blanco fights to stay alive. A bench or two get knocked over, the statue smashes to the floor.'

'And then?' Cámara said.

'And then he cuts off his *traje de luces* – we've got signs of that here.' He pointed to a space on the floor near where the benches had been pushed to the side.

'Small bits of Blanco's suit,' he said. 'Hard to see against that carpet. But they're there. Then he carries the body out to the centre of the bullring along with a matador's sword and a couple of *banderillas*.'

'Puts the body in place,' Cámara continued, 'mutilates it, and then disappears.'

'Mutilation certainly didn't happen in here,' Huerta said. 'Not a single bloodstain or spatter. Even though he was

56

already dead when it happened, he was still fresh enough to ooze blood, even a small amount.'

'What about his point of exit?'

'Still a mystery,' Huerta said. 'As I said, no sign of any forced gates or locks. Our man must have climbed out somewhere.'

'Carrying the *traje de luces* with him,' Cámara said. 'I take it there's no sign of it here.'

Huerta shook his head.

'Of course,' he said, 'if half my team hadn't taken time off for fucking *Fallas* I could have someone working on finding that as we speak.'

Cámara waved a hand as he turned to leave.

'Forget it,' he said.

A dayglo-orange tour bus was circling around the Plaza del Ayuntamiento, the top deck brushing against palm tree fronds, as the driver explained to the bemused tourists why the large paved open space in the middle was fenced off at this time of year. Preparations for the lunchtime *mascletà* – the ear-splitting firecracker display – were at an advanced stage, and already some of the noise junkies were hovering around the entrance to the post office on the other side of the square, hogging the best places next to the Red Cross van in case the excess of decibels made them faint, or their eardrums burst. The usual TV truck from Canal 9 was there to televise the event, but so too were a couple from international news channels. They were clearly not here for *Fallas*, but for the high-profile murder that had put the city unexpectedly in the public eye.

Cámara dodged the traffic to cross the road and stepped

inside the Town Hall, where he was directed upstairs to the mayoress's assistant.

The girl behind the desk was no more than twenty-five, and very pretty, he couldn't help noticing, with dark brown hair curled behind her ears, large gold earrings and thickly painted full lips.

Cámara introduced himself.

'Chief Inspector Cámara. The mayoress wants to see me.' He placed his hands on the desk and leaned in.

'I know it's a Sunday, and it's *Fallas*, but I've got rather a lot to do today.'

'Mayoress Delgado is busy,' the girl said. 'You'll have to wait.'

Cámara glanced at the clock on the wall, then over again at the girl behind the desk. Back straight, head down, she seemed strangely lifeless.

A text message came through on his mobile. Cámara fished it out of his pocket; it was from Torres: the prints on Blanco's body had been confirmed as Aguado's. He sniffed and flipped the phone shut.

Pacing over to some of the noticeboards on the far side of the hall, he tried not to think of the time that was being wasted, or of what was probably happening back at the Jefatura. A photograph of a bull on one of the posters caught his eye. It was black, with magnificent white horns curling up from its head: a *toro de lidia*, a bullfighting bull.

The text underneath explained a policy that was now so familiar to everyone that he could almost recite it with his eyes closed. Mayoress Delgado's regionalist party was proposing a ban on all bullfights within the municipal boundaries, hoping to beat the hated Barcelona to the north to become the first city in Spain to do so. Valencia, host to the America's Cup, and now the Formula 1 European Grand Prix, was reinventing itself as a venue for international sporting events. There was no place in this grand scheme for archaic and barbaric activities such as bullfighting. The age of cruelty to animals must come to an end. Valencia, rich, clean and prosperous, wanted to put forward a different face to the new wave of visitors, usually exploring the city for the first time. The bullring, that temple of death at its heart, would be converted into a shopping complex and open-air concert hall for some of the world's top rock bands, front-men with bug-eyed spectacles and spiky hair all too happy to promise an appearance in the name of humanity once the killing had officially been stopped.

Of course it had been easier to make this promise a couple of years back, when the policy was first presented. Bullrings across Spain appeared to be in terminal decline then; ticket sales had never been so low. Some bullrings were even talking of closing for good. Back then some had seen Mayoress Delgado's move as bold and cutting edge, a certain vote winner among those most lethargic of voters, the under-thirty-fives, whose support she would need if she were to hold on to power. Others commented that she was merely killing off an already moribund tradition.

But all that had changed when Blanco made his dramatic comeback. Seats high up in *Sol* – the sunny part of the bullring, and hence the cheapest – usually sold for around twenty euro. Now they were changing hands on the black market for as much as six hundred.

Cámara only read newspapers once in a while, and he avoided the TV news if he could, but the proposed ban on bullfighting had been one of those stories that was hard to miss. Would the plan work to help Mayoress Delgado win a record fifth term?

Cámara glanced at the slowly moving hands on the wall. It was almost one o'clock. The girl was tapping her fingers on the desk and sucking at a biro while concentrating on her papers. A fly had found its way up to the hall from outside and was buzzing above their heads with a steady, monotonous drone. Cámara watched its triangular flight pattern as it stayed in a central patch of space, never moving from an invisible cage it seemed to have constructed for itself, flying and flying around the same point: following a straight line for a second or two, then turning sharply and cutting back – the same pattern repeating itself again and again. It was odd: neither food, nor water, nor searching for other flies appeared to be on its mind, preferring instead to remain trapped in a world of its own making.

Cámara moved towards a small sofa nearby to sit down; he felt his body sink into the cushions, the weight easing from his back as he crossed his fingers over his stomach and stared up at the high ceiling. As he relaxed he realised that for a moment he had almost allowed himself to be rushed, as though much depended on him getting through this and heading back to the Jefatura as fast as he could. In fact, when he thought about it, he was sure that was far from true. Seeing how late it was now, and how close to lunchtime they were, he allowed himself to slip into a late-morning lull, listening to the sound of the Town Hall clock bell as it chimed. Torres could take care of things with Aguado. If Pardo was right, he'd be singing his confession in full any time now. Just another crime of passion, like the others.

He closed his eyes as a door opened and the sound of footsteps came from across the hall.

'Chief Inspector?'

He stood up and saw the familiar face of Emilia Delgado beaming at him, with just the slightest of reactions when she caught sight of his split lip. Her face was blotchier than in the photos, Cámara noticed. Perhaps the rumours of her heavy drinking and smoking were as true as the ones about her private life.

She stood where she was, waiting for him to walk over to her, then held out a hand framed by heavy gold bracelets; Cámara shook it, and they gave a self-satisfied rattle.

'I'm so glad you came, Chief Inspector,' Emilia said, her voice deep and husky. 'This is my campaign manager, Javier Flores.'

Flores looked the same as he had on the TV news the night before: heavily overweight, the kind of man who hadn't seen his own penis without the aid of a mirror since the age of twenty-five. He was wearing a black suit with a pale green shirt and bright pink tie with a wide knot. His clean-shaven face was covered with a thin film of grease. He gave Cámara a limp handshake.

'I hope we didn't wake you,' he said.

Ever since she'd been in power there had been stories about which one of her underlings the famously single Emilia was sleeping with. All part of an image that the former cabaret singer never seemed at pains to play down. These days her bed partner was Flores. Allegedly.

'Step inside,' Emilia said.

Cámara was shown into a large room with high windows looking out on to the main square outside. A Valencian flag

– red, yellow and blue – was draped on the back wall, while photos of Emilia with visiting dignitaries were placed on all available tabletops and shelves: Emilia with King Juan Carlos, Emilia with the Pope, Emilia towering over the boss of Formula 1. Next to them were other shots of girls in traditional Valencian eighteenth-century costume, their hair in tight flat rolls on the sides of their heads, a golden comb placed at the back: the *fallera* beauty queens for each year Emilia had been mayoress of the city.

Emilia walked round to behind her desk. Cámara sat down in one of the green tapestry chairs. Flores remained standing, his arms crossed.

'Drink?' Emilia asked as she placed her large, skirted behind down on her black leather executive chair. She waved an arm at a cabinet where Cámara caught sight of at least a dozen bottles of malt whisky. He tried to make out if there was any brandy.

'1866,' he said. 'If you've got it.'

Emilia motioned to Flores, who uncrossed his arms and paced over to the drinks cabinet. He poured a large measure, then brought it over, the brandy sloshing inside the glass as though desperate to get out.

Emilia cleared her throat.

'Chief Inspector, I suspect you've guessed why I asked you to come.'

Cámara nodded.

'The situation is . . . delicate,' Emilia said.

'Because of the elections?' Cámara asked, momentarily surprised at how innocent he could sound when he wanted to.

Emilia smiled.

'That's part of it,' she said.

'Surely Blanco out of the way makes things easier for you,' Cámara said more sharply this time. 'He was, after all, the main reason behind the recent rise in bullfighting's popularity.'

There was a pause.

'Chief Inspector,' Emilia started, 'I hope you're not insinuating—'

'You misunderstand me, Mayoress,' Cámara said. 'But perhaps we can clear something up: am I here to talk about the police investigation, or the politics of Blanco's murder?'

From the side of the room Flores seemed to twitch.

'You're right,' Emilia said after a pause. 'We need to make ourselves clear.'

She stood up and walked over to one of the windows, pulling back the blinds to gaze at the crowds quickly filling the square outside.

'We've got television crews here from CNN, the BBC, and channels I'm ashamed to say I've never even heard of. All sitting on our doorstep, all desperate for news about this killing,' she said. 'And while we appreciate the coverage the city is getting,' she turned back to face Cámara, 'this is hardly the image of Valencia we're trying to get across. I'm sure you understand.'

Cámara took another mouthful of brandy, and felt the ache in his ribs from the night before losing its edge for a few precious moments. The perfume and delicacy of an 1866 put it above the ones he usually drank – a Carlos III, or a Torres 10 – but it felt wasted here; it was best savoured alone, at home listening to Enrique Morente singing a *Seguirilla*, finding gaps between notes that no one else even knew existed. For Cámara he was still the greatest flamenco singer alive – one of the very best there'd ever been.

Emilia continued.

'All eyes are on whether we – or rather *you* – can resolve this as . . . painlessly as possible.'

Cámara stared down into his brandy, not wanting them to see into his eyes. Did they know that Aguado had been picked up? If so, why all this?

'Reputations are at stake,' Emilia said.

From his position near the drinks cabinet, Flores spoke up.

'All we're asking, Cámara, is that you don't screw it up.'

Cámara looked at him. He'd been trying to work out what kind of animal the man reminded him of, and now he could see it: an overfed bull terrier.

'I appreciate your concerns, but there seems to be some mistake,' Cámara said, turning to Emilia. 'This is a *Policía Nacional* case. We take orders from the Ministry, not the Town Hall.'

'It's my job to think about what's best for Valencia,' the mayoress said, 'and it's yours to solve crimes, Chief Inspector. What we're hoping for is a degree of . . . harmony between those two objectives. I know I can count on you. I am a very good judge of character.'

'We're watching this case,' Flores barked.

'Now I would offer to refill your glass,' Emilia said, 'but we are rather busy, as you'll appreciate.' She looked at the gold watch on her wrist. 'The *mascletà* will be starting soon.'

Cámara got up to leave: he had a murder case to solve; she had to oversee the lunchtime firecracker display. Emilia stood up, smiled and shook his hand firmly from behind her table. Flores stayed where he was.

Cámara walked to the door and let himself out.

FIVE

A bullfighter is never a coward, although, sometimes, he can experience an indescribable sensation of fear
Victoriano de la Serna

Cámara walked down the white cement steps to an annex section of the building. When Montesa had been designing the place, this area had been intended as storage space for the art museum. Now it served as the interrogation rooms of the new Jefatura.

Aguado was being interviewed in Room 2/N. Cámara peered in through the small, wired glass window at the top of the door and saw a youngish man, perhaps in his late twenties, slightly built with a pale face and straight black hair, wearing jeans and a white shirt, a black belt with a silver eagle buckle shining from the reflection of the strip light above. He looked wounded, but resolute.

Torres had his back to the door. From the shape of his shoulders, Cámara could tell things weren't going well. He knocked twice, and without looking round, Torres got up and came outside.

'I need a smoke,' Torres said, stepping into the corridor and closing the door behind him. 'What the fuck happened to your face?' he added, catching sight of Cámara's lip.

'Nothing.'

Cámara grabbed Torres's arm as he tried to step away.

'Wait,' he said.

He reached over to Torres's hand and took his packet of cigarettes off him. Then he unlocked the door and stepped into the interrogation room.

The place already stank of lost, rotting humanity despite only having been in use for days at most. Instead of leaving the walls bare, as they had been in Fernando el Católico, these had originally been painted in a soft off-white. Now they were scarred and scraped, the marks from backs of chairs, dirty shoes and occasionally rougher interrogation techniques already mapped out on the smooth surfaces.

Aguado didn't look up as Cámara walked in, keeping his gaze fixed on his hands pressed between his knees. His hair was falling over his eyes, the fringe cut at an angle so that it almost covered one half of his face. Cámara observed his slim build, the rising and falling of his chest as he breathed; his shirt looked one size too small and it seemed to stick close to his skin. Cámara had seen others wearing a similar style recently: it must be the fashion.

Pulling out the chair on the opposite side of the desk, Cámara sat down and pushed out the lighter tucked inside Torres's packet of cigarettes. Then he loosened one of the cigarettes and held it close to Aguado's face.

'Smoke?' he said.

Aguado kept his head down.

Slowly, Cámara withdrew the packet and took the cigarette for himself, then he placed it in his mouth and lit it. The smoke danced in the air above them as he inhaled and exhaled a couple of times. Smoke alarms had still not been installed in this area. Aguado didn't move.

When half the cigarette had been smoked, Cámara leaned in and slid the packet over the table towards Aguado, almost forcing it on him.

'Are you sure?' he said.

Aguado lashed out with his right hand, sending the packet back over the table towards Cámara.

'I don't want your cigarettes,' he said, momentarily looking up, before resuming his previous position.

Cámara finished smoking and got up, stubbing the cigarette out on the floor with his toe.

He stepped outside and rejoined Torres.

'Come on, let's go,' he said.

They climbed up the stairs and found an emergency exit half hidden behind a buttress wall. Torres pushed on the bar: after the second go the door opened out on to a wasteland at the back of the building. From the amount of cigarette butts dotted on the ground, it seemed they weren't the first to discover this addicts' refuge.

Torres pulled his packet of Habanos back from Cámara, placed a cigarette in his mouth and lit it. Smoke drifted out of his nostrils and filtered down through his thick black beard. Cámara grabbed his hand and took another one out for himself before he could put them back in his cardigan pocket.

'I thought you'd given up,' Torres said.

'I have.'

Smoking *maría* when he got home after work, he told himself, didn't count. Torres's Habanos were one of the strongest brands you could buy, like a mini-cigar wrapped in white paper – guaranteed to leave a coating of tar on the back of your tongue for at least a week afterwards. He was amazed they were still on sale these days.

'So what do you think?' Torres asked.

'About Aguado?' Cámara paused. 'He's a smoker. I saw the stains on his fingers. Yet he refused a cigarette.'

'Perhaps these are a bit too much for him,' Torres said with a grin.

'Maybe,' Cámara said. 'But it was a lifeline of sorts, and he turned it down.'

'So?'

'Ah, I don't know,' Cámara said, waving the idea away. 'But a guilty man might have accepted – have leapt through the door that had just been opened for him.'

Torres shrugged.

'What do we know about him?' Cámara said.

'Sculptor. Got a little workshop at his place in El Cabanyal. Lives on his own, no job, no pets, not much of a life, as far as I can see.'

'How does he make a living?'

'The sculpture, I suppose.'

'Any exhibitions? Is he known?'

Torres sucked on his cigarette.

'I'll get on to it,' he said.

'What's he saying?'

'About the time of the murder?'

Cámara nodded.

'At home, on his own, not doing very much,' Torres said.

'He said that?'

'More or less.'

'Did you sort out the lawyer?'

68

'I put in a call for a duty one to come down.' Torres exhaled deeply. 'Or at least I think I did. It's a Sunday, anyway. No one'll be showing up for a while.'

'How long has he been here?'

'Three or four hours,' Torres said under his breath. 'There's a bar round the corner I wanted to try for lunch.'

'Any good?' Cámara said.

'All right. Bit expensive. Nice waitress. Redhead.'

They both finished their cigarettes.

'What's he saying about him and Blanco?' Cámara asked.

'Just good friends.'

'Well, at least he admits to knowing him. Nothing else?'

'What do you want me to do? Ask him if he and Blanco ever did it?'

Torres started playing with his wedding ring, rolling it around his finger with his right hand.

'What did he say when you mentioned his fingerprints being found on Blanco's body?'

'Nothing. Just sat there.'

'And the bracelet?' Cámara asked.

'That was a bit more interesting. Claimed he didn't know what I was talking about, but when I pulled it out to show him . . .'

'Yes?' Cámara asked.

'Well, there was definitely a look of recognition there.'

Cámara waited for a second.

'Is that it?'

Torres nodded.

'Fantastic,' Cámara said. 'Caballero's going to love this. No confession, but we did get a strange look when we showed him Exhibit A. Open and bloody shut case.'

'All right, you *gilipollas*. Give it a rest,' Torres said.

'What's Pardo got against this guy anyway?'

'You know what he's like about *maricones*.'

'Are we even sure Aguado and Blanco were lovers?' Cámara said. 'What are we basing it on? Gossip magazines?'

'The fingerprints?' Torres said. 'It would explain that. Perhaps he and Blanco, you know,' he jerked his head to one side, 'just before the bullfight.'

'In which case they can hardly prove he killed him as well.'

A group of eight-year-olds had arrived on the far side of the wasteland and were throwing firecrackers at one another's feet, dancing and laughing as they popped around their ankles.

'Still,' Torres went on, 'the mutilation. It's . . .'

'What?'

'Well, you don't try and cut the balls off a dead man for no good reason.'

Cámara gave him a look.

'It's a crime of passion, chief. Got to be. Who else is going to do that but a jilted boyfriend?'

'Was he jilted?'

'Might have been.'

'We need more on Aguado,' Cámara said. 'Who are his friends, people who know him? Has he got any family? Can someone confirm for us that at least he and Blanco were an item, albeit in secret? At the moment we're not even treading water. Who's with us?'

'Sánchez and Ibarra,' Torres said through his teeth.

'Send them back to El Cabanyal. Get them talking to people, neighbours, anyone.'

'And me?'

'Stick with Aguado. It'll keep Pardo happy at least.'

They turned and headed back to the emergency exit. Behind them, the group of children were trying to get louder and louder bangs by simultaneously throwing as many firecrackers to the ground as they could. Squeals of laughter came from the girls watching as the boys took turns to set off the mini explosions.

'So how was Emilia?' Torres asked as they got back inside.

'Well, she didn't get fresh with me, if that's what you mean,' Cámara said. 'Her lapdog got quite friendly, though.'

He turned to leave.

'So Flores was there as well, was he?' Torres called after him. 'They really did want to put the thumbscrews on.'

Cámara headed out of the building, crossed the former river bed, and slipped into the Carmen district. Something was on his mind, something he had to do, but his thoughts were moving in several directions at once, and he couldn't remember what it was. Just keep going, he thought. Whatever it was had something to do with coming this way.

More *fallas* were being erected: caricature statues over five metres high made of wood and plaster then painted in bright colours. Cámara had often thought they looked like rejects from a 1950s Walt Disney film, characters that hadn't quite been drawn well enough, or were deemed too ugly or too obscure to make the final cut and which had been sent here into a kind of cartoon exile world. They were usually three-dimensional satirical comments on politicians, or people who'd been in the headlines over the previous twelve months. With half an eye Cámara looked out for any *ninots*, or images, of Blanco. The man who had revived bullfighting would certainly have caught the attention of some of the *falla*-builders, working away for months so that their colourful structures could be given this briefest of displays before being ceremoniously burnt on the *Cremà*, the night of 19 March. Would any references to him be taken down now out of respect? Something in him doubted it.

The sound of explosions came from further ahead, and the smell of gunpowder filled his nostrils as he wound his way through the alleyways. It would be good preparation for war correspondents to come to Valencia at this time of year, he thought: a quick intensive course in how to train your nerves. He kept moving, past walls with graffiti paintings, nineteenth-century blocks of flats slowly crumbling and sinking into the soft, watery earth, but still he couldn't remember why he was here, or what he'd meant to do. The afternoon sun reflected off a high window and into his face.

He closed his eyes . . .

. . . and saw the sea, the smell of salt waves as they crashed against the rocks below. Formentera, his favourite corner of the Mediterranean. The two of them had gone the year before to escape the *Fallas* madness, stripping naked on the beach, feeling the sun on their skin for the first time that year. Cámara braved the freezing waters to look for cuttlefish. Even Almudena dipped her toe into the sea for a few minutes, screaming as the waves licked up her knees before she ran back to their suntrap beneath the rocks. And when he emerged from the water she told him she wanted to try for a baby. After two years together she said it was time. They ran along the waterfront together in the shade of the umbrella pines, calling out names to one another for their future child: Enrique for a boy;

Susana if it was a girl. Perhaps they should live together, he said. But no. She insisted. This was how they would do things. The child would bring them together. She'd stopped taking the pill a couple of weeks before. It was only right he should know. And he held her in his arms, her nakedness against his, and made love to her, lifting her up on to him with his powerful hands, resting his back against the trunk of a tree.

At the end of the week, just before catching the ferry back to Ibiza to fly home, she gave up smoking. Better for the baby, she said. And he'd crumpled his last packet and dumped it in the ashtray as well – they'd do it together.

And for a while, back in Valencia, the magic of the island had stayed with them. Sex every day for two or three weeks, perhaps more. They'd meet at lunchtime and catch a taxi to his flat, barely able to restrain themselves before opening his door and throwing themselves on to the sofa. And she came so strongly that she wept.

Weeks passed; lovemaking became less frequent as they both landed with a jolt in their respective lives, sucked into a whorl of long hours, paperwork and plastic grocery bags. Her periods continued with their clock-like consistency. Again he suggested moving in together: sex would be easier, more spontaneous. There'd be a greater chance of her getting pregnant. But again no. Things would stay as they were.

They'd only done it once over the past month. Was it his fault? Perhaps, he thought, if they could get away again, head back to Formentera, away from the suffocating blanket of their jobs and rediscover the passion that had vivified them back then.

Then Blanco's body had been dumped in the middle of the bullring.

Infertility – just the thought of it weakened something in him. One of Hilario's proverbs filtered through from some part of his mind: *Quien al mear no hace espuma, no tiene fuerza en la pluma* – He whose pee doesn't foam has no lead in his pencil. In the past it had brought a smile to his face. Now it seemed to crush something in him. Did it apply to being infertile as well? He'd have to check next time.

He looked around: cars were streaming past along the road in front. Somehow he had come out of the labyrinth of the Carmen and arrived in the centre of the city again. His eyes widened as he looked up: he was in front of Almudena's office, standing on the pavement opposite. A knot formed in his stomach as he wondered about crossing over and ringing the bell. With all her ideas about Fate and letting things happen of their own accord, she might appreciate his appearing like this, unexpectedly. Perhaps there was still time to fix things.

Waiting for a gap in the traffic, he looked up at the office window and caught sight of her face staring out. She hadn't seen him, but was laughing. Breaking out into a spontaneous smile himself, he was about to put his hand up to wave at her when he realised she was talking to someone. A client? She might be in the middle of a meeting, explaining her ideas about the designs for that new restaurant.

The smile had already dropped from his mouth when he saw. With a last chuckle from her, a hand – a male hand – was placed around her waist from behind. She turned and took a step back inside the office.

There was a lull in the traffic. The way across the street was open to him. Cámara looked down at his feet, images flashing in his mind of running over, dashing up the stairs, crashing the door down and then causing intense physical damage to the other man. A storm raged within him, but he stayed where he was, slowly sinking into the concrete paving stones where he stood.

He took a deep breath, swallowed and looked up the street. His fingers dug into his pocket and he felt around for how much cash he had on him. The reason – the real reason – why he had walked out of the Jefatura had come to him. A little green light on the roof of a white car caught his eye and he stuck his arm out. If the taxi-driver hurried he could still just make it.

The city cemetery lay on the outskirts of the city. Cámara ordered the driver to swing over and drop him on the opposite side of the road from the main entrance, next to a line of small florist stalls.

He bought a bouquet of white lilies and looked over towards the red-brick gateway. To the right the *Municipales* were policing a large group of people held behind some hurriedly erected barriers. There were as many as five thousand people there, he guessed, lined up six or seven deep along the route leading back into the city, paying their respects to Blanco in what seemed like near silence. All the while cars and buses were bringing yet more, and the police were having to turn many away, letting the odd one through as it brought what he assumed to be members of Blanco's family or his friends.

To the left of the entrance, a dozen TV vans were squeezed into a tight corner at the end of the boulevard, all aerials and cables and bright lights shining on microphone-wielding reporters performing to camera. Cámara wondered if any of them had managed to get into the funeral itself.

He crossed the road and moved towards the main gate. An elderly porter with three days' stubble on his chin and a blue peaked cap was sweeping with a straw broom, dropping ash from his cigar on to the marble floor where he'd just cleaned up. Cámara identified himself and the man nodded him through.

A wide avenue led through the centre of the cemetery, with ostentatious graves and mini mausoleums on either side, stone angels with giant wings casting their eyes down on fading black-and-white photos of the deceased placed in small iron frames. The chapel was at the far end, and from the crowds of well-dressed people pouring out of its doors he guessed the mass had already finished. The clicking of several dozen paparazzi cameras sounded like the chatter of hungry sparrows at sunset.

A group of five *Municipales* stood to one side watching the crowd. One of them caught Cámara's attention, a plastic brace around his neck, his pale brown sunglasses only partially disguising the swelling around his eyes. He seemed to sense Cámara's presence, and for a second they looked straight at each other, before the crowd surged between them. Cámara felt a cold sweat breaking out as he dodged around the bobbing heads, trying to get another look, yet when a break in the throng came, the other *Municipales* were still there, but the man with the neck brace was nowhere to be seen. One or two of the others glanced in Cámara's direction, then pretended they hadn't seen him.

Cámara looked around for a moment, wondering whether

he was imagining things, a heavy thudding in his brow. First Almudena, now this?

He decided to ignore it; it was time to go to work. He moved in towards the crowd, looking for faces he recognised. In the centre, surrounded by a small group of very tall, slim and well-dressed women – none of them in black – was Alejandro Cano, the bullfighter. He had appeared in the ring the day before with Blanco, the first of the three matadors to face a bull.

Cano looked small and slight in the middle of his harem, with his sideburns and his thick chestnut hair carefully swept back, just the hint of a quiff. The suit and black tie took something away from the man Cámara had last seen in the bullring, yet he was smiling and nodding at the other mourners, his face animated and cheerful: an incongruous beacon of light in a sombre sea.

Cámara passed around the edge of the mourners, watching as white handkerchiefs fluttered among the swell of black cloth. Shoulders were patted, hands shaken, cheeks kissed. A cloud seemed to hang over them, threatening to rain, yet never quite managing to, as it slowly evaporated in the sunshine.

He felt a tap on his arm and he spun round to look into a face he felt he already knew well. Short, highlighted hair, a slight gap between her front teeth. There was an expression of anguish in her eyes, yet also of strength. It reminded him of Aguado back at the Jefatura. Aguado – something inside him told him he should have been here instead of in the interrogation room. That is, if he'd have come at all.

'Chief Inspector Cámara,' the woman in front of him said. 'I'm Alicia Beneyto.'

They shook hands, Alicia glancing approvingly at the lilies Cámara had bought. He waited for a second for the recoil the sight of his broken lip seemed to cause in people, but it never came.

'I'm sorry we're having to meet again in circumstances such as these,' Cámara said, casting a glance at the crowd in front of them. None knew that he, too, was in his own private moment of mourning.

'I understand you were quite close to Blanco,' he said.

'We had . . . We were close,' she said. 'He trusted me.'

'With his secrets?'

There was a pause.

'Blanco almost never gave interviews,' she said at length. 'On the two occasions in his career when he did, it was with me.'

'Why was that?' Cámara asked. 'Because you're a woman?'

'There aren't many female bullfight journalists, you're right. In fact, I'm the only one in this city. But I like to think it wasn't only for that reason.'

She gave a heavy, chesty cough.

'Two outsiders in a closed, traditional world,' Cámara muttered to himself.

'You saw the body,' Alicia said. 'Was it really as bad as . . .' She stopped.

Cámara nodded.

'They'll be building a mausoleum of black marble over the grave once the burial is finished,' Alicia said. 'The Ramírez family have paid for it all.'

Applause broke out as the final group of mourners emerged from the chapel and the pall-bearers appeared with the coffin. Behind them, weeping and being led out into the sunshine, was Carmen Luna. Vast sunglasses shaded most of her face while a black veil cascaded from the top of her head. She wore a tight black miniskirt with a slit up the front, black stockings, black shiny leather heels, a black jacket with a single button, with only a black bra underneath, and heavy gold chains set against her deeply bronzed décolletage. The cameras clicked wildly as she vainly held up a pleading hand to be left alone in her grief.

'Drawn like flies to shit,' Alicia said under her breath.

'Tell me,' Cámara said. 'Did Blanco ever wear any necklaces or anything?'

'A silver bracelet,' she said without looking up. 'He'd take it off immediately before a fight, then put it back on again as soon as he'd finished. It was one of his funny little habits. Why?'

'Nothing,' Cámara said.

They set off behind the crowd of mourners away from the chapel to the grave site. Burial was rare in modern Spain, cremation being the norm, but Blanco was being treated like a hero of the nineteenth century.

Alicia pointed to a group at the front of the procession, and Cámara recognised the men he'd put down as bull breeders at the Bar Los Toros the evening before.

'Francisco Ramírez and his eldest son Paco,' Alicia explained. 'Blanco was very close to them.'

Cámara got a better look at Paco. He was very similar to his father, but there was a greater physical strength there, he thought. Although it was hard to tell: the mourning Francisco bore only a superficial resemblance to the man he'd seen the night before.

'That's Roberto, the second son,' Alicia said, pointing at a taller man with jet black hair walking beside them.

Cámara watched him for a moment: he looked both rougher-edged and more urbane than his father and elder brother; less country gentility, more city sophistication. While Francisco and Paco both wore brogues, Roberto sported black slip-ons with a golden buckle at the side.

'Blanco was brought up on the Ramírez farm,' Alicia said.

'Tell me more,' Cámara said, keeping his eyes on the Ramírez family group.

'His father was an employee there,' Alicia continued, 'but died in an accident when his horse threw him before Blanco was born. Blanco's mother still lives on the estate. Francisco Ramírez brought Blanco up almost as one of his own sons, and when he began to show promise as a torero, they paid for him to go to Mexico to train – underage bullfighting is allowed there. When he returned to Spain he fought as a *novillero* for about four years before taking his *alternativa* here in Valencia fighting Ramírez bulls. That's when he became a fully fledged matador. It was the perfect combination: Ramírez's bulls and now being championed by one of the best toreros to emerge for generations.'

'What about Ramírez's sons?' Cámara asked.

'Paco is the spitting image of his father, as you can see. He'll take over once the old man dies. Roberto is different. Hates bullfighting. Broke away from the family years ago. He's an investment banker.'

'But he's still come to the funeral.'

'Blanco was like a member of the family, as I said.'

The crowd reached the graveside and formed a circle. Cypress trees shot like needles into the sky around them.

The pall-bearers eased the coffin down. The priest said a few more words, shook some water on to the coffin lid, and then the box was finally lowered into the sharply cut pit. A wail came from some of the mourners: Cámara turned in time to see Carmen Luna drop the flowers she was holding in her hand and faint into the arms of a strategically placed assistant. The journalists moved in.

Alicia stayed at Cámara's side.

'You're holding Aguado,' she said.

'What do you know about him?' Cámara asked, turning to watch her expression.

She shook her head.

'Why?'

'The ritual nature of the killing – going to all those lengths with the *banderillas* and . . .' She swallowed. 'I think it's too clinical; it might look like one but to my mind it doesn't fit with a crime of passion.'

'So they *were* lovers,' Cámara said.

'I didn't say that,' she corrected herself quickly.

'Many people do.'

'Has Antonio said as much?'

'I'm not sure if he has to, now.'

She turned her gaze towards the other mourners.

'Where's Blanco's manager?' Cámara asked.

'Juanma Ruiz Pastor? He's here. I saw him speaking to Roberto earlier.'

'Is it true?'

'About Blanco and Ruiz?'

She seemed about to say something, then fell silent.

'Had they fallen out?' he asked more seriously.

'You should ask Ruiz Pastor himself,' she said.

81

They joined the line of people waiting to pass in front of the grave and throw their flowers on to the coffin. Cámara caught sight of Santiago Rodríguez, the bullfighting expert with the red-framed glasses who had appeared on the TV the night before. He was talking in low tones to what looked like a group of fellow aficionados.

'Blanco always insisted he should be buried in Valencia,' Alicia said absent-mindedly. 'It was his favourite bullring.'

'Why's that?'

'It was where he had his first great triumph as a matador,' she said. 'Also, the *Fallas* bullfights are the first big ones of the season to be held after the winter break. It's a kind of showcase for the bullfighting to come over the rest of the spring and summer.'

'Where was Blanco from originally?' Cámara asked.

'Albacete. Just like yourself, Chief Inspector.'

'*Albacete, caga y vete*,' Cámara quoted the joke about his ill-loved home town: Albacete, have a shit there and get out.

She giggled.

Ahead of them an elderly woman was being helped along by Roberto Ramírez. Frail and delicate, she struggled to move forwards as her walking stick caught in the stones underfoot. Roberto guided her along, placing his hand under her arm and helping to take some of her weight. The woman's hands were trembling, her face pale and fraught, an expression of disbelief in her eyes.

'Blanco's mother,' Alicia whispered.

Ramírez and Paco looked on as the woman threw flowers on to her son's coffin. Then she turned and quietly shuffled away, her face buried in Roberto's shoulder. On the other side of the Ramírez family group stood another woman, her back straight, dark blonde hair tied back in a bun on her head, her face set like granite. Cámara looked at Alicia.

'Ramírez's wife,' she explained. 'Aurora Palacios.'

The line moved forwards, until it was their turn to throw flowers into the grave. Cámara nodded his head in respect, then cast his lilies into the pile of other flowers. Behind him Alicia lingered a little.

Standing on his own, he looked around again for Juanma Ruiz Pastor. Perhaps he wasn't wearing his trademark hat this afternoon, and Cámara simply hadn't recognised him. He sensed a presence behind him and he turned to see Francisco Ramírez staring him straight in the eye, beads of sweat forming in the thinning lines of his carefully combed near-white hair.

Cámara offered his condolences.

'That boy was like a son to me,' Ramírez said in a shaky voice. His eyes seemed to flare.

'Get whoever it was who did this.' He spat violently to the side. Next to him, Paco tried to usher his grieving father on.

'Just get him!' Ramírez repeated as they stepped away.

Paco nodded at Cámara as he passed. Behind him Roberto approached and held out his hand.

'You have to understand, it's a difficult time,' he said. His voice was firm and confident.

'To lose him in a bullfight – I think he could have coped with that. But not like this. Not this way.'

Cámara nodded in understanding and Roberto headed back to console Blanco's mother, momentarily standing on her own.

As the mourners began to disperse, Cámara walked with

them down the avenue to the main gate. Small groups had formed along the way as people said their goodbyes, hugging and kissing one another. Cámara pulled out his phone and called Torres.

'Make a note,' he said. 'I want information on the following people by tomorrow.' And he read out a list of names: 'Francisco Ramírez father, Francisco Ramírez's son – Paco, Roberto Ramírez, Aurora Palacios, Carmen Luna, Alejandro Cano, Juanma Ruiz Pastor, Marta Díaz, Angel Moreno . . .' He paused.

'That it?' Torres asked on the other end of the line.

'And Alicia Beneyto,' Cámara said.

'OK,' Torres said. 'Where do you want me to look? *Webpol*?'

'Not just the police network,' Cámara said. 'Get on to the internet as well. I need an idea of who these people are, and anything interesting that catches your eye.'

'OK,' Torres said. 'Aren't you going to ask me how it's going with Aguado?'

'Is there anything to tell?'

'Not really.'

'Well no, then.'

Cámara flipped his phone shut. A group of TV journalists came running down behind him and pushed their way through, heaving their cameras out to the waiting vans. Cámara walked on in their wake. The porter was still there, watching the people passing through his little domain with a heavy frown. Cámara approached him.

'Who let them in?' he asked, jerking his thumb in the direction of the journos.

'I wouldn't have it,' the old man said. 'But they insisted.'

'Who?'

'Big bloke.' The porter pulled his arms out at his sides to denote bulkiness rather than height. 'Wearing a hat. Said he was Blanco's *apoderado*.'

'When was he here?'

'Earlier on, at the start.'

'Have you seen him leave yet?'

The porter shrugged, the frown deepening on his face.

'People have been flying in and out of here all afternoon. Can't keep tabs on all of them, can I?'

Cámara thanked him and stepped out into the street. For a moment he wondered about heading back inside, having a last check to see if Ruiz Pastor was still with the rest of the mourners, but he knew it was pointless. The man had already gone.

He glanced around in the vague hope of finding a taxi. There was a rank just a bit further along, near the crowds still holding their own vigil, but it was empty. A car sounded its horn from the other side of the road. He looked up and saw a woman waving at him from a tiny Smart car.

'Chief Inspector,' Alicia Beneyto called over. 'Do you need a lift?'

SIX

Apoderados, *comedians and bullfighters are the biggest liars*
Traditional

Near the San Miguel market in the Carmen she parked on
a piece of wasteland that was still to be barricaded off for
Fallas. A table by the window was free inside the Cafetín
bar. They sat down and a waiter took their order: gin and
tonic for Alicia; a large beer for Cámara. Groups of foreign
tourists already looking for somewhere to have dinner at
this early hour strolled by in the street outside, smiling and
laughing in amazement as clouds of smoke drifted along the
cobblestones. Inside, they were partially sheltered from the
incessant noise of the *petardos*, and could talk.

The waiter brought their drinks, along with a small metal
dish of salted almonds. They both started speaking at once,
then stopped.

'You first,' said Cámara.

'I was wondering why were you president of the bullfight
yesterday?' Alicia said. 'I was going to ask but then . . .'

'The commissioner's daughter was ill. It was an emergency.
He asked me to stand in at the last minute.'

'You mean Pardo?' she asked.

He nodded.

'Is she all right?'

'Yes, but . . . This is off the record, all right?'

'We're just having an informal chat, Chief Inspector.'

'From past experience with journalists I'd say there's no such thing,' he said.

'From past experience with policemen I'd say the same,' she countered.

Cámara laughed at his own pompousness. She gave him a generous grin.

'So why did *you* stand in? Someone else could have done it. Someone less . . .' She paused. '*Anti-taurino.*'

Cámara smiled. 'Is it that obvious?'

'It was obvious you don't have a clue about bullfighting. And for someone to reach the age of – what? forty-two? forty-three? – in this country without knowing even the basics can really mean only one thing.'

'There was no one else in the Jefatura at the time. I was the only officer available.'

As the words left his mouth he realised how strange they sounded. Had that really been the case? Surely Pardo could have found someone else at that moment if he'd tried. It was a big building. But in the rush and panic of his daughter's suspected meningitis there'd been no time to think.

'It was a last-minute thing,' he tried to explain. 'I . . .'

'Didn't have anything better to do?' Alicia finished the sentence for him.

'Something like that.'

'I hope she's forgiven you.'

'Tell me more about the Ramírez family,' Cámara said quickly.

'The Ramírez farm is based in Albacete province.' She looked him in the eye as though wondering if the information meant anything to him. 'Top breeders,' she went on. 'No Ramírez bull has ever killed a torero. They're very proud of that. They're always *bravo* – strong and eager for a fight. It's the *manso* ones, the less aggressive bulls, that are dangerous. Non-aficionados rarely understand that.'

'Does it make much of a difference?' Cámara said. 'They all end up dead.'

'The whole species of *toros de lidia* would be dead if it weren't for bullfighting.' Alicia put her glass down with a clunk on the table. 'These animals aren't good for anything else – certainly not for meat. They'd be extinct.'

'Now you're going to tell me they live like kings, have wonderful lives in the country with as many cows as they can manage, and then go out in a moment of glory at the end. And all the while we're protecting an endangered species.'

Alicia took out a packet of Fortuna cigarettes and lit one. Cámara felt the surge of desire, but stopped short of asking her for one.

'Chief Inspector,' Alicia said. 'You're supposed to be investigating the murder of the greatest bullfighter who's ever lived. Are you sure which side you're on?'

'There's the thing,' Cámara said. 'You see, unlike the bull, I have a choice.'

'Do you eat meat? I notice your shoes are made of leather.'

'It's not the same,' Cámara said.

'Have you been to an abattoir lately? I have,' Alicia said, not waiting for an answer. 'And I know how I'd prefer to die.'

'Does that make it all right? Just because we set up factories to kill animals for us for meat, we can torture them to death in public?'

'Only a vegetarian can criticise *los toros* without being a hypocrite,' Alicia said. 'And then only just.'

'It sounds,' Cámara said, finishing the last of his beer, 'as though you've been rehearsing this for some time.'

'I'm a bullfight journalist. It's my job to defend one of this country's great cultural institutions. Especially in these ridiculous times, with all this talk being *politicamente correcto*.' She spat the words out.

Cámara called the barman over. Alicia asked for another gin; Cámara ordered a brandy. She pulled out her cigarettes again and offered him one. After the briefest of pauses, he accepted.

'My second of the day,' he said. 'No, my third. I gave up a year ago.'

Alicia smiled. 'I hope I'm not being a bad influence on you, Chief Inspector.'

'Cut the Chief Inspector, will you? Max is fine.'

The barman brought their round. Alicia raised her glass.

'How does Ruiz Pastor fit into Blanco's relationship with the Ramírez family?' Cámara asked.

'A rift developed between Blanco and Ramírez once Ruiz Pastor appeared,' she said. 'Until then Francisco had done everything for him. But Ruiz came along and took over as Blanco's *apoderado*. He'd been Cano's manager until then – the matador who fought yesterday with Blanco,' she explained. 'He was at the funeral.'

'I saw.'

'It was a big story at the time. Caused great frictions.'

'When did this happen?'

'About seven or eight years ago.'

'So before Blanco's temporary retirement?'

'Yes, about a couple of years before. Ruiz Pastor was furious when Blanco said he was pulling out for good. Tried everything he could to get him back in the ring. But Blanco wouldn't be pushed. He was badly gored in Seville. I think he lost the will to carry on.'

'Tell me about him and Cano.'

'More's been made of it than is actually there, if you ask me,' she said. 'It made for good copy – a great rivalry between the two top bullfighters of the day. Cano has his band of followers, who don't have any time for Blanco's more traditional, classical style. Some of the newspapers took sides. But Blanco always told me he had nothing but respect for Cano. Even that was part of his old-fashioned approach: no one used to go in for the kind of back-stabbing you get nowadays.'

She paused for a moment as she realised what she had just said. Cámara signalled for her to go on.

'There was always a code of honour among bullfighters,' she said, breathing deeply. 'Never criticise anyone who's got the balls to go out there and stand in front of a bull. It's being lost, though, and you get comments now from someone saying that so-and-so hasn't got a clue what he's doing, and that kind of thing. But Blanco was very strict about that. If ever he commented on another bullfighter – which was extremely rare – it was only ever to praise him.'

'And Blanco's relationship with Ruiz Pastor?'

'I honestly don't know how bad it was. Or even if it was bad at all. I think it was something to do with money. Blanco never told me, although I've wondered . . .'

'What?' asked Cámara.

'I don't know. Blanco called me the night before the fight. He said he wanted to talk to me about something. I wondered if it might have something to do with Ruiz Pastor. Thought maybe he was thinking of getting another *apoderado*.'

'Did he say that?'

'No. It was just a hunch.'

'Did Blanco say anything else?'

She paused.

'No. Sometimes he gave the impression that things weren't quite right at the Ramírez farm. But he never said what, exactly.'

'Did he often ring you up like this?'

'Sometimes every day,' she said. 'Then weeks, months go by and nothing. It's how he is.' She checked herself. 'Was, I should say.'

Cámara looked down, his eyes resting on the large, man's watch on Alicia's wrist. It was gone nine o'clock. His thoughts turned to dinner – and who to have it with. He frowned as Almudena's face flashed momentarily in his mind. What about Alicia? A quick bite round the corner? He smiled to himself. Was he really thinking of having dinner with a bullfighting aficionado?

'What was Blanco like?' he asked suddenly.

'The best,' she said. 'As I said—'

'No,' Cámara interrupted. 'I mean as a person.'

'He used to give money regularly to an orphan's charity,' she said. 'Gave his entire bullfighting fee to them on one occasion.'

She hesitated, as though searching for the right words.

'But?' Cámara prompted her.

'He could be an arrogant shit,' she said with a deep sigh, her shoulders lowering as she spoke.

'He'd often call me in the middle of the night. Any time. He didn't care. *He* wanted to have a chat, so that was that.'

She drew hard on her cigarette.

'I'd see him sometimes, if we were out together,' she went on. 'People – kids – would come up to him to ask for his autograph and he'd just push them away. He could be very sulky and moody, but he didn't care what people thought about him – at least not outside the bullring.'

Cámara leaned in.

'What about Antonio Aguado?' he asked. 'What about him and Blanco?'

He glanced to the side; something had caught his eye. A white taxi was slowly cruising past, emerging from the end of Calle Caballeros, braking to pass through the crowds of *falleros* gathered in the middle of the road. Cámara leaned in closer to get a better look. The back window of the taxi had been partially wound down and he saw a trail of thick smoke drifting out into the night air. The passenger had a short-cut grey beard and was smoking a large cigar, his head crowned with a dark trilby hat. Ruiz Pastor.

Cámara got up with a start and burst out into the street. The taxi had already pushed through into the Plaza del Tossal and was about to pick up speed as it headed down into Calle de Quart. Cámara made chase, but the car accelerated away, moving out of the crowds and into the street. Frustrated at having been momentarily held up by the fiesta, the taxi-driver sped off, Cámara sprinting after them as fast as he could.

He was strong, but had never been quick. Struggling to

keep up, he ran down the centre of the road, deliberately avoiding the tiny pavements on either side of the ancient street. He had to talk to Ruiz Pastor.

A group of teenagers making their way to the bars of the Carmen for the night leered at him as he puffed past.

'Go on, Grandpa! You can do it!' And they laughed hysterically.

Cámara sped on. Grandpa?

The taxi was nearing the end of the street, and the tall dark bulk of the Torres de Quart that marked the edge of the old city. Soon the car would be out on to Guillén de Castro Avenue, and then away. Unless it got held up at the lights, in which case there was just a chance . . .

He sprinted along, his lungs straining. A honk came from behind. Cámara turned his head round and saw a red bus behind him, the driver annoyed that he was slowing them up. The Torres de Quart were closing in fast. Just a few more yards. He turned the corner to see the lights turning back to red. Jumping on to the pavement he emerged at the front of the old gate and quickly looked up and down Guillén de Castro. There were at least half a dozen taxis heading up towards the river, all too far off now to catch. Ruiz Pastor could be in any one of them. Panting heavily, Cámara glanced to his left: the street was empty save for double-parked cars and kids setting off yet more firecrackers.

He stood on the corner for a moment trying to catch his breath. A bead of sweat had formed at the back of his neck and was trickling down his back.

A couple of *Municipales* were standing on the other side of the road, supposedly guiding the traffic, but clearly marking time until they could clock off. Cámara glanced over at them, wondering for a second whether to ask if they'd seen the taxi, which way it had gone.

One of them turned round. Night had fallen at least a couple of hours before, yet he was wearing sunglasses. Around his neck, catching the light of the street lamps, was a plastic brace. Cámara dodged into the shadows of the Torres de Quart before they could see him, his breath suddenly quick and shallow. He closed his eyes in disbelief. The same one from the funeral? A heavy pulse thudded in his stomach as the bruise where the kick had landed seemed to come back to life, like a dog sensing the presence of its owner.

Cámara forced himself to think more clearly. There was no good reason why a *Municipal* should want to attack him in the middle of the night. It made no sense. Besides, there were a dozen other ways a man could hurt his neck. But the pain was insistent: he'd seen that face before, and it spoke to him of violence.

From behind the stone wall of the old city gate, he took another glance: the two policemen had their backs to him and were strolling away down Guillén de Castro. Outside a bar they stopped and slapped each other on the shoulder before shaking hands. One of them was going inside for a drink. The one with the brace shook his head, turning down the offer, and carried on, his right hand briefly stroking the handle of the gun hanging from his belt as he walked away.

Cámara slipped again into the shadows of the old city gate. Questioning Ruiz Pastor would have to wait: he'd pitch up sooner or later. Yet the image of the *Municipal* with the neck brace played on his mind. If that had been the one who attacked him – and part of him was already convinced, despite his attempts to reason otherwise – then there could be only one person responsible. The only question was, why?

The table was empty when Cámara returned to the Cafetín. The barman told him the woman had paid and left after he'd run off. He thought for a second about giving her a call, before realising he didn't have her number.

His route home took him past the market, back through the Plaza del Ayuntamiento, where the preparations for the next day's *mascletà* were already underway. He checked his phone: there was a message from Torres: they were holding Aguado in the cells overnight. He was calling it a day and heading home, just on the off chance that his son remembered who he was.

Cámara crossed over to the Calle Ruzafa. An edition of one of the evening give-away newspapers was lying at the edge of the street, waiting for the road-sweeping machine to come along and gobble it up.

Emilia calls for swift conclusion to Blanco case, the headline read. '*The world is watching.*'

Arriving home, he threw his jacket over the sofa and went to put some music on. An Ojos de Brujo CD was already inside and he hit the play button, the edgy, jerky sound of Flamenco-Rap filling the flat as he scoured his collection of empty wine bottles looking to see if he had enough dregs to pour himself half a glass.

The phone rang. He lowered the volume and walked over and checked the number before answering, half-hoping, half-dreading that it might be Almudena.

'Hello,' he said, picking up the receiver.

'It's me,' said a voice.

'Yes, I know.'

'How?'

'Your number was on the little screen.'

'Don't do that to me: you give me the creeps.'

Cámara eased himself down into the sofa.

'How are you?'

'Fine,' Hilario said. 'Saw you on the telly.'

Cámara sighed. 'Blanco.'

'Best bullfighter since Manolete.'

'That's what they tell me.'

'When are you coming over? You've yet to pick up the last of the crop. New ones already beginning to shoot.'

'Are you watering them?' Cámara said, opening up his ivory marihuana box to see how much was left.

'Not much else to do,' Hilario said with a sigh. 'Pilar won't touch them. Thinks she'll go to hell if she does. She says she's given up on me already, although I know she lights a candle for my soul every Sunday. So it's up to me.'

Cámara could hear his grandfather's difficult breathing from the other end of the line. His housekeeper could do many things for him, but while age had brought some physical limitations, the old anarchist's bloody-mindedness had resisted all assaults from either her or his increasing frailty.

'They like a bit of sunshine at this time of year,' Hilario continued. 'Helps them get off the ground. I suppose you're going to be busy what with all this lot. Still, you could drive up and back in a day. Bring what's-her-name. Almudena.'

'I don't know about that.'

Cámara felt the pulse in his temple where he was holding his head.

'Like that, is it?' Hilario said. 'Never mind. Get as much

as you can while you can, that's my advice. You only regret it when you reach my age. When I think of the amount of skirt I could have had and didn't.'

Cámara laughed silently to himself: the phrase had become something of a motto for his grandfather in recent years.

'It was your grandmother, never took her eyes off me, that was my problem. *Mujer con celos, los diablos tiene en el cuerpo* – A jealous woman has devils in her.'

'I've got to go,' Cámara said. 'I'll come up soon. Promise.'

'I know you will,' Hilario said. 'Must be close to running out, I'd say.'

SEVEN

The only important muscle in bullfighting is the heart
Agustín de Foxá

Monday 13th March

Torres was already in the office the following morning when Cámara walked in. First at the entrance, then in the hallway, Cámara had noticed one small group, then another, huddled over what looked like photocopies of some pictures, lifting their heads and giving him furtive glances. Torres had his head buried in what appeared to be the same material.

'Something to brighten up your morning, chief,' he said as Cámara threw his coat over some box files. Cámara sat down amid the debris and Torres leaned over to pass him four sheets of paper stapled together.

The photocopies appeared to show what looked like a dummy of a magazine article, with bright colourful photographs and blocks of text. The first thing that Cámara noticed was a logo in the top corner. *Entrevista* was a well-known title, one of the batch that had emerged in Spain in the wake of Franco's death offering a best-selling combination of sensationalist investigative journalism and photos of topless women. The bare breasts on its front cover might not have shocked now quite as much as then, but it had a more than respectable circulation, and was a staple of doctors' and dentists' waiting rooms across the land, along with the usual gossip magazines of the *prensa rosa* and a comic or two for the kids.

In the centre of the front sheet, however, dominating his line of vision, was a shot of a person who only the day before he had seen in mourning.

My tears for love of my life Jorge Blanco, Cámara read next to an image of Carmen Luna kneeling down, a bullfighter's hat – a *montera* – on her head, and a blue and pink *capote* with Blanco's name printed on it draped over her naked shoulder, leaving exposed one proud, rounded breast.

Large red letters across the bottom encouraged would-be readers to read the full 'story' inside. Cámara turned the page. The next photo showed Carmen in a vaguely religious setting, a black veil pushed back off her face, approaching what appeared to be an icon of some sort – perhaps a statue of the Madonna, although it was out of focus. Her eyes were slightly downcast, a look of sadness etched into her face, while in her hands she held a candle, whose soft light cast down on to her exposed breasts. The caption read: *Carmen has been praying night and day for Blanco's soul since his untimely and brutal death.*

Cámara's eyes passed down to the next shot. Here Carmen had her back to the camera and was holding out one of Blanco's *capotes* to the side of her body, as if pretending to fight an imaginary bull. On her head once again was a bullfighter's cap, while on her feet as she stood in the middle of a sunny, sandy practice bullring, was a pair of very red high heels. She was wearing nothing else. Cámara read the caption: *Carmen has been an aficionada of bullfighting since she was a child.*

He looked up at Torres pleadingly.

'Keep going,' Torres said. 'There's more.'

Cámara sighed and turned over the page to see yet another naked image of Carmen taking up the entire A4 sheet of paper, this time raising a couple of bright red and yellow *banderillas* in her hands as about to bring them down on the lens of the camera.

'Pretty impressive camera work, don't you think?' Torres said. 'Almost makes you feel what it's like to be the bull.' His face fell when he saw the expression on Cámara's face.

The last photo, in an act of uncharacteristic modesty, showed Carmen wearing a bullfighter's *traje de luces*, the shiny adornments – the *alamares* – reflecting the studio lamps surrounding her like a thousand suns. The front of the suit had been left partially open as Carmen gazed up at an image of Blanco on the wall, almost in an act of devotion, the curve of her breasts and just one tasteful nipple visible this time. The caption read: '*Jorge is like a god for me*'.

'That's it, no more,' Torres said, attempting to put Cámara out of his misery. 'She certainly doesn't mess about, does she.'

'I take it this is a piss-take,' Cámara said. 'Someone's made the whole thing up with some computer program.'

Torres shook his head.

'It's real,' he said.

Cámara looked up in disbelief.

'Sánchez brought them,' Torres went on. 'Says he's got a mate who works at the magazine – marketing side, apparently. Sent him this in an email. They're publishing it tomorrow. Special edition.'

'And Sánchez made some printouts.'

'First useful thing he's done for weeks. The whole Jefatura will have seen it by lunchtime.'

'I notice there was a scattering of text in there,' Cámara said, casting an eye back over the photos. 'Say anything interesting?'

'She and Blanco were going to get married this summer. The engagement, you may remember – or not – was announced around Christmas time.'

'Anything else?'

'Not really. Just that Blanco was the best lover she'd ever had. No small claim, given her track record. Still, doesn't necessarily rule him out as gay.'

He leaned out to pick up the photocopies, flicked over a page and started reading: '"*My Jorge was all man. I never loved anyone as handsome or as virile. He taught me what true love means. My life has been destroyed by this cruel, tragic event. I will never forget him. Once we were married we were going to try for children, the one thing that has been missing from my life. But now this dream lies in ruins.*" Laying it on a bit thick, don't you think.'

'When would these have been laid out?' Cámara asked. 'This morning?'

Torres nodded, his black beard brushing against the collar of his shirt. 'Finish it off today, print all night, rush it out for dawn tomorrow.'

'So the shoot would have been yesterday, almost certainly before the funeral. Could they really do the whole thing so fast?'

'Makes you wonder, right?' Torres said.

'Where's Aguado?'

'Downstairs. Nothing doing. I was going to start on him again in a minute or two.'

'Has he seen this?'

'Chief!'

'Forget it,' Cámara said. He stood up and looked about the room. 'Have you got those reports I asked for?'

Torres leaned over and tapped a finger on the small pile of brown folders at the side of Cámara's desk.

'Oh, and Ibarra came back with info about Aguado at El Cabanyal,' Torres said.

'And?'

'He puts on exhibitions at a local art centre sometimes, but keeps pretty much to himself. A couple of mentions in the local press over the past five years, but he's not exactly a big player in the city's art scene.'

'All right,' Cámara said. 'It's still not clear how he makes a living. Anything else?'

'One of his neighbours said he occasionally had a visitor. She only noticed because it was so rare. Says she never saw the face, but that it was definitely a man. Went round late in the morning the day Blanco was killed.'

'That it?' Cámara asked. Torres shrugged.

'Right, I need to do some studying,' Cámara said. No need to rush; Spain had some of the harshest laws in Europe regarding detainees' rights: they could keep Aguado incommunicado, with only access to an appointed lawyer, for up to five days. 'Forget about Aguado for a minute and put out a search for Junama Ruiz Pastor, Blanco's *apoderado*. I want to speak to him and he's doing a good job of making himself scarce.'

Once he was on his own, Cámara flicked through the information files looking for the one he'd wanted to read first. *Alicia Beneyto*, he read, and immediately opened it up. The photo was the same as the one he'd seen by her newspaper column, the face a little younger, the eyes harder than he remembered them. From the top he read the basic information: date of birth – just a couple of years younger than himself; place of birth – Madrid; ID number; marital status – divorced; children – none.

The rest of it was as he had expected: a degree in journalism from the Complutense University in Madrid; worked for a series of regional papers across Spain before settling in Valencia on the staff of *El Diario*. Her ex-husband, Cámara had correctly remembered, was the editor. They'd separated after the night editor found him having sex with one of the summer internees on top of the sports desk. The scandal had been bad enough for him to lose his wife, but not his job. That had been a year and a half ago. The official date for the divorce was the previous October.

Cámara stood up and walked over to the filing cabinet, where he felt his hand down the back looking for the hip flask. His fingertips found nothing. Cursing, he tried the other side, but came away empty-handed. He glanced around the office for a second, his eyes assaulted by the piles of still-unsorted paperwork lying around like mini siege towers. But still no sign of the hip flask. Defeated, he slumped back in his chair and started reading through the other files.

The next one that came to hand was the one on Carmen Luna. For a second Cámara hesitated to open it, wondering if Sánchez had placed one of his photocopies inside as a mugshot. He flicked the cover open and was pleased to see there was no image at all – clearly, none was thought necessary.

Cámara read the story of Carmen's life, information filleted out of the pages of gossip magazines over the years. She was actually fifty-one, although she sometimes claimed to be only forty-three. Born in Malaga, she used to be a singer of *coplas*, or traditional Spanish folk songs, and became famous at the age of seventeen when she won the Benidorm Song Competition. The ageing Franco had invited her for tea at the Pardo Palace. She quickly married her manager, Juan Casillas, although he had died a couple of years later of a heart attack, leaving her a mansion in Puerto Banús and enough money never to have to work again. Despite that she had carried on singing, and over the years had several high-profile love affairs with, among others, Pedro Llorens, the famous golf impresario, and Jesús Cabra, the lead singer of the punk rock band Los Hijos de Puta. An Arab banker and half a dozen minor celebrities had also been 'romantically linked' to her over time. She'd had her own popular TV show for the past three years, but had given it up on starting her relationship with Blanco, which had officially begun six months before. Carmen, Cámara read, had said she now wanted to devote her entire life to the young 'god' of the bullring, hoping that one day she would be mother to his children.

No mention was made of how this unlikely couple were expecting to make children, particularly given her advanced years, but doubtless, Cámara reasoned, it had something to do with test tubes. Part of his imagination was already wondering if samples of Blanco's sperm weren't already in the deep freeze in some fertility clinic somewhere, waiting to be injected into Carmen's womb. A dead man fathering children. He let out a sigh. Carmen was of the old-fashioned school, at least as far as public image was concerned. Marriage would almost certainly have had to come first. Still, the possibility niggled inside him as he put Carmen's file down and reached for the next one.

The files on the Ramírez family members didn't tell him much he didn't already know from Alicia. Ramírez himself was seventy-eight, while Paco, the elder son, was forty-nine, and Roberto, the second, was forty-five. Ramírez had married Aurora Palacios when he was twenty-five and she was eighteen, and they'd lived on the *finca* ever since, Ramírez inheriting it from his father, who had got it from the grand-father, the founder of the bull farm back in the late nine-teenth century. Paco was due to inherit and continue the family business in turn, while Roberto, who had split from the family ten years before, was a successful banker in Madrid, with investments around the world concentrating on biochemicals. He was the major shareholder in the German firm Hauptmann und Fischer GmbH as well as having important stakes in the US firm Technochemical Inc. and the Italian logistics company Malatesta Servizi Logistici S.p.A. The news of his break with the family had been a big story at the time, given the high reputation of the Ramírez breeders, and particularly given Roberto's well-publicised rejection of bullfighting as a cruel activity unworthy of a modern country like Spain. And it appeared that these weren't empty words: he was a major backer of Mayoress Delgado's campaign, with strong links to her right-hand man, Javier Flores. According to the information Torres had gathered, he'd been spending considerable time in

Valencia in recent weeks for this reason, in between business trips to Hamburg, Vienna and New York. The last one had been cut short by Blanco's death, and he'd immediately flown over to be present at the funeral.

Cámara spent slightly more time studying the next file, on Juanma Ruiz Pastor, staring closely at the photograph of the man with the trilby hat, cropped grey beard and habitual cigar in his mouth. At the time he had been certain it was the man he saw in the back of the taxi the night before. Hours later, and after an albeit fitful night's sleep, he was less sure. He remembered Alicia's comments about the frictions between him and Blanco. Something about money, she had said, although she hadn't been more specific. Cámara had an urge to speak with the man, a feeling almost like a physical hunger. And the more elusive he was proving, the stronger it got.

Ruiz Pastor (age – sixty-four; married, no kids) had been in the bullfighting world since he was a boy. He'd wanted to be a torero himself, but had soon found he had greater talents outside the ring. Becoming Cano's *apoderado* had been his first big move, and his fortunes had risen alongside the flashy young matador's. The two had been a kind of double act, Cano often making the headlines as much for his personal life as for his bullfighting, Ruiz Pastor acting as his spokesman to the press when scandal and impropriety came knocking at the door again.

But then Blanco had appeared, and Ruiz Pastor moved in on him. He'd set out to become Blanco's manager before he'd even told Cano he was leaving him. Cano had always blamed Ruiz Pastor, never Blanco, although there were those who claimed Blanco had been the one who went out aiming to hook Ruiz Pastor for himself.

Cámara opened the file on Cano. It told the same story, and tallied with what he'd heard from Alicia. What was new, however, was that when the split occurred, Cano had made jokes about Blanco being a *maricón*. Later he'd denied the comments, but in some ways they accorded with the respective public images of the two men: Cano the womaniser always happy with the cameras on him, especially when snapped coming out of a bar or a flashy brothel; Blanco the more private man, an enigma in many ways as far as his life outside the bullring was concerned. The only woman who'd even been seen at his side was Carmen Luna, but even that very public relationship hadn't been enough for the rumours about his homosexuality to go away.

Cámara took a last glance through the Cano file: he was a couple of years older than Blanco, known for a more showy, more modern style of bullfighting. If Blanco's focus in the ring had all been on the bull, Cano's was on the audience.

The two remaining files were on Marta Díaz and Angel Moreno, of the Anti-Bullfighting League. Moreno was twenty-seven and had formerly trained, as a teenager, at the Valencia bullfighting school. There was no official record of why he had left, but on the league's website he explained that he'd rejected the world of *los toros* after seeing the horrific suffering of the animals at close hand. Since then he'd campaigned to have it banned, and had become a leading member of the organisation. In a handwritten note Torres added: *Moreno's former maestro at the school, Emilio Valdés, alleged that Moreno attacked him in the street some time after Moreno had left the school, and that it was a revenge attack because he'd actually been expelled for 'activities not in keeping with the ethics of bullfighting', whatever that means. Nothing ever came of it – lack of proof – so it was dropped. No police records of the incident, but one of the guys in Violent Crime remembers it.*

Cámara read on: Marta Díaz was twenty-five and had been involved in anti-bullfighting causes since she was a child. Her parents had been active among the earlier campaigners back in the seventies, but kept out of things now. Considered to be relatively eloquent and experienced, she'd been an unofficial spokeswoman for the league for the past three years. It wasn't possible to date the start of her relationship with Moreno exactly, but it was thought they'd been together for at least two years.

Cámara looked up as Torres opened the door.

'Put out a call for Ruiz Pastor,' Torres said. 'No one seems to know where he is. His office haven't got a clue, he's not answering his mobile phone, while the Hotel Suiza are saying he checked out early this morning, around six o'clock.'

Cámara put his fingertips together and thought for a moment.

'What about his family?' he said. 'Do they know anything? Get in touch with his wife.'

'Straight away, chief.' Torres hesitated at the door.

'What is it?' Cámara asked.

'I don't know. This . . . this Carmen Luna woman,' he said.

'What about her?'

'Well, isn't it just a bit weird? These photos, I mean. Doesn't it make you a bit suspicious? Getting them out so fast. It's as if she already knew it was going to happen.'

'She was at the Bar Los Toros with me, remember?'

'Yeah, I know, but . . . perhaps she got someone to do it for her.'

'Who? Aguado?'

'Chief, I'm serious. Someone you say is the love of your life gets chopped up, and the next minute you're flashing your tits to the camera claiming you'll never get over his death. It's a bit quick, right? How do you do that? How do you—?'

'What is it that as soon as you think someone's fucked someone, they're immediately a suspect in their murder?' Cámara said. 'First Pardo with Aguado, now you with Carmen Luna.'

'Chief,' Torres said, giving him a look, 'you know how it is. The odds are stacked that way. Sex and violence – they go hand in hand.'

The phone rang. Cámara made no move to pick it up, so Torres walked over and grabbed the receiver. Cámara rubbed his eyes for a second, his head spinning. Still blinding himself to the outside world, he breathed in and out slowly, trying to make his brain work more clearly than was its habit before lunchtime. He thought longingly about his hip flask: he could do with a quick shot right now.

He heard Torres put the phone down, then gave his eyes a final rub, opened them and tried to focus on Torres's face. He looked paler than usual.

'They've found Ruiz Pastor,' Torres said. 'He's in the Albufera. Dead.'

PART TWO

TERCIO DE BANDERILLAS

EIGHT

A bull always goes for the lame man
Traditional

A *Guardia Civil* in dark green uniform with a Heckler & Koch G-36K assault rifle in his hands was standing by the side of the road and directed them off down a dirt track heading towards the banks of the Albufera lake. A large, shallow, sweet-water lagoon, the Albufera had been used for centuries to water the rice-paddies lining its banks, home to the traditional short-grain rice used for making paellas. Passing through a clump of pines and thick mastic bushes, they spied the peaked thatched roof of the *barraca* in the distance. Symbols of the area, these were traditional fishermen's cottages, shaped like an upside-down letter V, with whitewashed walls and a little cross on top; there was only a handful of them left these days.

A second *Guardia* was standing near the entrance to the small garden that led up to the *barraca*, and he indicated a spot for them to park. They were just outside the boundaries of the city; this was the *Guardia Civil*'s patch, their crime scene, and if they allowed members of the *Policía Nacional* to come and visit, it was made clear that it was only as a courtesy.

The *Guardia* saluted as Cámara and Torres got out of the car. The black shiny leather *tricornios* they had traditionally worn on their heads were reserved for formal occasions now. But the corporal who escorted them up towards the *barraca* and his colleagues taking photographs and collecting video evidence, were no less military looking, with their green caps and golden insignias on their arms. It was a good job Huerta wasn't there, Cámara thought: in general the *Guardias' Criminalistas* had a better reputation than the Police's *Científicos*: better equipment, better discipline.

In the distance Cámara could make out the wide expanse of the Albufera stretching away to the west. White egrets were flying low over the water as they sought shelter in the high reed beds. The far side of the lake was invisible that morning: heavy, humid air was blowing in from the sea just a few hundred yards behind them creating a pale, milky haze.

Cámara had been to the Albufera dozens of times – one of the few natural beauty spots near Valencia, lying to the south of the city. He and Almudena had come for Sunday outings, stopping off at the village of El Palmar just across the water to eat seafood and rice dishes laced with thick, garlicky *allioli* mayonnaise. But that day El Palmar, like the other villages on the fringes of the lake, was out of sight, smothered in the mist. The *barraca* felt isolated from the outside world, as though this patch of earth and water existed in a space of its own.

As they approached, a *Guardia Civil* officer stepped forward and saluted before holding out a hand, introducing himself as *Teniente* Castro.

'Of course,' he said, 'given the connections with the Blanco case, I thought it best you came along.'

Cámara looked up and saw Quintero's familiar figure in the shadows inside. He was pulling on his beard as he leaned forward, dictating his observations to Irene Ortiz, the *secretaria judicial*, as he had done in the bullring only a couple of days before. Whatever lay at his feet was out of view from here. The building itself had clearly long since been abandoned: the thatch was thin and patchy, the doors and windows had gone, the whitewash peeling from its walls.

'The *médico forense* is deputising for the judge,' Castro said.

'Who found the body?' Torres asked.

'Corporal Pelayo,' Castro said, pointing at the *Guardia* who had escorted them up from the car and who was now returning to his post.

'There was a robbery reported early this morning – some German campers parked near the beach,' he explained. 'Personal effects. The local teenagers often come and use this *barraca* for all-night parties. Corporal Pelayo decided to pay a visit to see if he could find anything related to the robbery.'

'He thought the kids might have done it,' Torres said.

'It was a possibility,' Castro answered.

Cámara looked down at the ground leading up to the doorway: it was littered with cigarette butts and empty beer cans, with a few shards of glass glistening in the dirt.

'But he didn't find any kids, obviously,' he said.

'No,' Castro said. 'They weren't here last night. We've checked.'

'What time did your man arrive?' Torres asked.

'At 11.04 this morning.'

'And that's when he found the body.'

'Correct.'

Cámara looked at the time on his phone: it was gone twelve thirty.

'Would it be all right if we . . . ?' he asked, looking in the direction of the *barraca*.

'This way,' Castro said, and he indicated for them to follow him. A camera from one of his colleagues from the *Unidad de Criminalistas* was clicking feverishly around the entrance. They paused for a moment to allow the woman to finish, and then Castro nodded for them to enter.

'I hope you have strong stomachs,' he said as they passed through. Torres gave a dismissive snort.

The inside of the *barraca* smelt of blood and stale urine. Cámara's eyes took a moment to adjust to the lack of light. In the gloom a figure approached him, a man pinching his nose.

'Huerta!' he said with surprise. 'I didn't . . .'

'Why should you be the only *Nacional* they called?' Huerta said. 'Asked me to come in and observe as well. Bit like you, I suppose.'

He leaned in and spoke confidentially into Cámara's ear.

'I've come across this *Teniente* Castro fellow a couple of times before. He's all right. A lot better than some of the others.'

'I bet you'd like to get your hands on some of his kit,' Cámara said.

'You see that thing over there,' Huerta said, rising to the bait. Cámara saw a kind of box with a lens supported on a stand. 'You can make 3-D images out of the photos that thing takes. Reconstruct everything in virtual format back in the office: a perfect replica of the crime scene at the moment of discovery.'

'Perhaps you could nick it while no one's looking,' Cámara said.

'It's not just the equipment,' Huerta said. 'They're just so much more disciplined. Comes from them being paramilitary, I suppose. Not a bunch of disobedient civilians like us. I wish I could give orders like this lot can.'

'Have you seen the body?' Cámara asked. He could see that it was on the floor not far from where he stood, but it was shielded by some of the other *Guardias* standing in the way.

'It's Blanco all over again,' Huerta said. 'Worse, even.'

Torres was already making his way out, having had a look. Cámara caught the look of horror in his eyes as he dashed to get some air. With a sense of dread he moved over and crouched down to see for himself.

Ruiz Pastor's body was lying in the middle of the floor of the *barraca*, naked. A pair of *banderillas* lay scattered nearby, their points bloodied, while a matador's sword had been pushed deep into his broad, hairy back. It appeared that the killer had tried to curl the body up into a foetal position, as with Blanco, but Ruiz Pastor was a bigger and much heavier man, and the corpse had slumped on to its side. As his eyes grew sharper in the half-light, Cámara saw how the top leg had fallen straight, exposing a bloody hole between the man's thighs where his genitals should have been. A dozen flies were already buzzing around the wound.

He felt a hand on his arm: Quintero nodded to him to join him outside.

'I won't be needing much longer here,' he said. As ever, the sight of violent death seemed to leave him unaffected, his voice calm, his manner as serene as it had been at the bullring.

'Caballero's tied up, and there wasn't any point bringing the *Juez de Guardia*, so I'm standing in.'

Cámara nodded.

'You'll need to liaise with *Teniente* Castro, but Huerta will be able to fill you in on much of what's gone on here.'

'What's your idea on time of death?' Cámara asked, breathing deeply as he tried to steady himself.

'We're looking at somewhere between six and seven o'clock this morning,' Quintero said. 'The man's been stripped naked, so body temperature is more complicated as a gauge. But the lividity is pointing to around five hours ago. Give or take.'

'And we're looking at the same M.O.'

'The similarities are clear,' Quintero said. 'Stripped naked and mutilated with *banderillas* and a matador's sword. This time he managed to take the genitals too, as I'm sure you noticed.'

'Was he strangled?' Cámara asked.

'There was an attempt at strangulation,' Quintero said. 'But I'm inclined to think it wasn't successful. There are marks around the neck, as with Blanco. But Ruiz Pastor was a big man, and from the cuts and damage on his hands and fingers I'd say he fought back. We'll be analysing the material we found under his fingernails later. Also, there's bleeding, so my conclusion at the moment is that mutilation was carried out before actual death.'

Cámara twitched.

'The sword?'

'That's what probably killed him in the end,' Quintero said. 'Yes, I think so.'

'And the genitals?'

'From the lack of blood spattering I'd say they were severed after the heart had stopped pumping. But Huerta will also have an opinion on that.'

Huerta was stepping out of the *barraca* at that moment. Quintero explained the point.

'From what I've seen that fits,' he said. 'Haven't analysed it myself, obviously. Just here to observe. But that's what the *Guardias* are saying, and I think they're right.'

'Any prints?' Cámara asked.

'This place has been used for kids' parties,' Huerta said.

'Yes, *Teniente* Castro explained.'

'There are prints all over the place. I doubt any will be any use, though.'

'And no sign of the missing . . . ?'

Huerta shook his head.

'There is something, though,' he said. 'There's a chance our man came and left by water.'

He pointed at the lake, just a few yards from where they stood.

'There are impressions in the grass leading in and then out. Sadly, there's nothing there to tell us about the kind of shoes he was wearing, but he's almost certainly a size forty-three.'

Cámara turned and started walking up the grass verge that led away from the *barraca* along the edge of the garden towards the lakeside. Torres fell in behind him.

A pair of ducks heard their steps and started splashing forwards, paddling and pushing their way into flight until they too disappeared in the mist. Cámara leaned up against a willow tree and stared at the still waters as he reached out to grab the cigarette Torres was offering him.

'Any other *barracas* round here?' Cámara asked.

'Not many,' Torres said. 'Most have been left to rot or been pulled down. One or two have been converted into restaurants.'

'Does anyone live out here? Any fishermen?'

Torres shook his head. 'I don't think so,' he said. 'Not any more. The nearest people these days are in El Perellonet, about a couple of miles away. But even then, at this time of year there's hardly anyone about.'

'And the kids who come here?'

'Mostly from El Saler, according to the *Guardia*. Some from El Perelló.'

They both fell silent for a moment, gazing out at the lake. In the distance a *mata*, one of the reed islands, was just visible in the haze. The area was a labyrinth of channels and waterways: it would be easy to disappear in a boat out there early on a misty morning. Wherever the killer had gone, there were a hundred little inlets where he could have disembarked, dumped the boat and then reappeared on dry land as though nothing had happened.

Torres finished his cigarette and flicked it into the water below them.

'You don't think we've got a serial on our hands, do you?' he said.

'It's too early,' said Cámara.

'I mean, just the same M.O. and all that.'

'Perhaps he needed to shut Ruiz Pastor up,' Cámara said. 'Perhaps he knew something.'

'So why do all that?'

Cámara inhaled deeply on his cigarette.

'We still don't know how he got here,' Torres said. 'Ruiz Pastor, I mean.'

'Get Sánchez to talk to the taxi firms,' Cámara said. 'See if anyone was brought out here – or anywhere near here – some time early this morning. Any time between five and seven. And check if anyone called to be picked up here, too. You never know.'

Neither of them moved, heavy with the weight of what they had just seen. Out on the lake a fisherman's boat was leaving a silk-like trail in its wake as he headed home.

'The *Guardias* will take care of talking to him,' Torres said, nodding towards the boat. 'And any others who might have seen something. They're a suspicious lot, though, Albufera people. Don't like talking to the authorities, no matter what colour their uniform.'

'Know the area, do you?' Cámara asked.

'My dad used to bring me here a lot when I was a kid,' Torres said. 'We used to have a flat in El Perelló during the summer. Used to go fishing with some of the local lads.'

'Here?' Cámara asked. 'Not out at sea.'

The Mediterranean was less than a five-minute walk in the other direction.

'Sometimes,' Torres said. 'But less often. People here live *espaldas al mar*, with their backs to the sea. It's on their doorstep, but it's almost as if it wasn't there. The Albufera lake is their thing – shallower, less dangerous. Doesn't claim so many lives.'

There was a pause. From the direction of the *barraca* behind them they could hear the sounds of men hauling away Ruiz Pastor's body. Quintero must have given the order.

'Don't suppose there was much water round Albacete for you to go fishing as a lad, right?' Torres said, attempting a smile. 'Still, I bet your dad took you—' He stopped, cutting himself short. 'Sorry, chief,' he mumbled. 'I forgot.'

'It's all right,' Cámara said.

'I'll get on to Sánchez,' Torres said. And he edged away, pulling his mobile out to dial.

Cámara walked along the bank, looking down at the water. He'd come boating himself once or twice near here. Once with Almudena, another time some years before that, with a girl whose name he struggled even to remember now. Some of the fish had a strange habit of leaping out of the water and landing in the boat: you hardly had to put a line out for them at all.

A sharp movement at the edge of the water caught his attention. Something was bobbing about near the edge of a bunch of reeds. Turning to look he saw it again; it looked as though a fish of some sort was reaching up, trying to get at something, like an eel taking a bite out of some food. He walked over to get a closer look, stepping down the grassy verge of the bank as far as he could without slipping into the grey-brown water himself.

Even from this distance, however, he struggled to see what it was: a pale, shapeless object about the size of a fist was floating near the surface. There was something curious and foreign about it, something that told him it shouldn't be there.

He held on to the grass near his feet, then grabbing a floating reed nearby he poked at the object. It was soft, like a piece of meat, bits around the edges already floating away where the eels had taken chunks out of it. Cámara stared more intently, moving his head to the side to avoid the reflections partially obscuring his view.

Then he saw clearly what it was. His eyes closed and he swallowed hard once, then again, strongly fighting the urge to throw up.

Below him the missing piece of Ruiz Pastor bobbed up and down under the ripples of the lake.

NINE

Just as a few passes with the muleta in a bullfight can make the whole afternoon worthwhile, so it is in life with certain achievements
Doménico Cieri Estrada

'Two *fiambres* already, Cámara? It's turning into quite a case.'

Cámara stretched out a hand and patted Maldonado on the shoulder.

'Glad to see you're up to speed as usual.'

He brushed past him, heading towards the lifts, hoping like hell the doors would open as soon as he pressed the button, and whisk him away to solitary seclusion. But the great Montesa hadn't designed elevators for a busy office environment, expecting them to be used only by sedate art-lovers, and the numbers flashing on the wall above the shiny aluminium doors showed that Cámara would have to wait for his deliverance.

'You think it's strange for a policeman to know what's going on?'

Maldonado was standing close behind him.

'Oh, of course,' he continued, 'you prefer to just muddle through, waiting for one of your hunches. Don't you always say that's your way of doing things? Some might say it's unprofessional, but hey! It's working a treat this time. What are you hoping's going to turn up next? Another dead body? Why not? Go for the hat-trick.'

The day before, perhaps even only a few hours ago, Cámara might have thrown the case away. He'd never wanted this, still dreaming that he might get some time off, head out of the city with Almudena, try to rediscover some missing, dying element in their relationship. But now . . . For the first time he realised he cared about the case, that he wanted it, that it had absorbed him. Something – what? Losing Almudena? Seeing what he had just seen in the Albufera? – had hooked him and pulled him in. The realisation seemed to paralyse his tongue, and while normally he would have snapped back at Maldonado, almost relishing their rivalry for the ridiculously childish game that it was – although he knew his adversary failed to see this lighter side to it – this time all he could do was turn and stare at him.

Maldonado seemed almost perturbed by his silence.

'Some fucking angel passing overhead, or something?'

The lift pinged and Cámara walked in, keeping his back to Maldonado until he heard the doors finally close behind him. Then he let out a sigh, his shoulders dropping as he reached behind for the button to take him to the second floor.

Perhaps it was the shock, he thought. It could come in waves like this, a delayed reaction as the various layers of him registered the violence of what his eyes had seen. He never hardened against this, not really. He'd always thought that a day would come when the sight of murder would cease to drain him so, would leave him unaffected, like a surgeon happily chopping away at his patients then going back to his family undisturbed by the blood and broken bodies that had filled his day. But the moment had never come. Perhaps it never would. The wounds from the past refused to heal over, ready to open up and bleed afresh whenever he witnessed the violence and horror that men could inflict on each other.

Torres was already back in the office when he entered. Cámara walked over and slumped down in his chair, pushing his hands through his hair. The fuzziness in his brain refused to clear, and wasn't helped by the sensation that he had forgotten something – something important.

'We could do with some more manpower,' Torres said, screwing up a ball of paper and launching it towards the empty space on the floor where he expected a litter bin to be.

'A proper incident room,' Cámara said. 'Get working on it. Pardo will give us the green light.'

Both of them fell silent, until Cámara spoke.

'You still think Carmen Luna's behind it?'

'You can laugh.'

'Can you see me smiling?'

'What . . . You think—?'

'What else have we got?'

The sound of the phone ringing brought them both up with a jolt. Cámara closed his eyes, breathed in deeply, then exhaled.

'That'll be Caballero,' he said.

'It's time I found that bloody coffee machine,' Torres said, getting up and walking to the door.

'Where's the hip flask got to?' Cámara called after him.

But the door slammed behind him and he was left on his own with the ringing phone. He cleared his throat and picked up the receiver.

A couple of minutes later Cámara went in search of a release form and headed down to the basement. He took the keys from the duty policeman and walked down the narrow corridor in search of Aguado's cell. The key turned in the lock and the door opened on to a tiny grey space with a double strip light hanging from a flex in the middle of the ceiling. Aguado was lying on his cot with his hands behind his head, one leg pulled up. He looked up at Cámara without moving.

'Another delay?' he asked with a sneer.

'What?' Cámara asked.

'My lawyer was supposed to show up again today. I suppose you've come to tell me there's been another delay.'

'You're free to go, Señor Aguado,' Cámara said. He half-turned to the door, to make way for Aguado to leave.

From the corner of his eye he watched as Aguado reacted to what he'd said. First a pause, the confusion, as the words registered. Then the hands sliding back from their position behind his head to reach down on to the cot as he slowly pulled himself up, dropped his feet to the floor, waited again for another instant, as though trying to decide what to do or say next, then sharply stood up as the anger kicked in. Some people simply walked out wordlessly at this stage, others needed to give voice to their feelings.

'That's it?'

Cámara nodded.

'Just like that? Guilty one minute, innocent the next? No charges?'

'You're free to leave,' Cámara repeated. 'Although,' he added before Aguado could say anything else, 'we may want to speak with you again at some point. You were close to Blanco . . .'

Aguado stepped towards the open door, pushing past Cámara as he did so.

'*Que te jodan*,' he spat. Fuck you.

'You may have information relevant to the investigation,' Cámara said. 'Something that might help us.'

'Help you?' Aguado said. 'What, like I'm supposed to thank you for your hospitality, or something?'

He stepped out into the corridor and headed towards the exit.

'You're all cunts.'

Cámara followed after him as they climbed the stairs to the ground floor. He passed the form to the duty officer and they stepped towards the main doors. Through the glass a group of journalists was visible, huddling and smoking under the jacaranda trees by the side of the road in front of the Jefatura: two or three camera teams, half a dozen newspapermen and radio journalists with their brightly coloured microphones. Cámara caught the hesitation in Aguado's step.

'I can get you a car,' he said as Aguado stared out at the prospect of being pounced on. 'You can leave by another door. No one will have to see you. Take you wherever you want.'

Cámara watched as Aguado faltered, caught between a wish to storm out in defiance, and what was almost certainly a long ingrained desire for anonymity. He had tried to keep his relationship with Blanco a secret for so long.

'Very neat,' he said.

'Listen,' Cámara said. 'If it makes any difference to you, I didn't let them know. I didn't ask them to be here. It's just how this place works – information gets out. Now look . . .'

He paused for a moment as he looked Aguado in the eye. His face had gone pale with anger, his jaw clenched tightly, lips screwed tight.

'They don't know who I am,' Aguado said in a low voice.

'On the contrary,' Cámara said. 'They know *exactly* who you are. Why do you think they're out there waiting?'

Aguado was beginning to breathe heavily as rage and panic seemed to grip him. Cámara nodded in the other direction, towards a different exit. Aguado gave him a look, then finally agreed.

'All right.'

They stepped away from the smoked-glass doors and back into the centre of the entrance hall as Cámara went to order a car to take Aguado away. Aguado stood still, his hands in his pockets, eyes staring down at his feet.

'You haven't told me why you're releasing me,' he said as Cámara beckoned him to follow.

'Ruiz Pastor was killed early this morning,' Cámara said. 'We found his body out in the Albufera.'

He watched for a reaction, but Aguado stared straight ahead as they walked down the white corridor to a back entrance.

'Did you ever meet him?' he asked.

'Never,' Aguado replied quickly. 'I never mix in bull-fighting circles. In fact, I loathe bullfighting.'

'Well, if you did remember hearing something that could help . . .'

'There you are again. You seem to think I enjoy being in your company.'

'This is a murder inquiry, Señor Aguado. For the death of someone you were very close to.'

This time there was no attempt at denial.

'The fingerprints on Blanco,' Cámara said. 'How else could they have got there? The bracelet? You gave him that, didn't you?'

Aguado stared back at him, then cast his eyes down to the ground.

'The morning of the fight,' he said after a pause. 'He came round. It was the last time I saw him.'

'Did he say anything?' Cámara said. 'Any comment that suggested he felt in danger in any way?'

Aguado kept his eyes to the floor, breathing heavily.

'Where's this car, then?' he said, looking up with a start. 'Or am I going to have to wait for that like I did for the lawyer who never showed up?'

Cámara ushered him along to the back exit. A uniformed police officer was sitting at a desk nearby. He looked up as they approached. On the desk in front of him were Sánchez's photocopies of the pictures of Carmen Luna. Clearly, there wasn't a single policeman left in the entire city who hadn't seen them. Aguado leaned forward to see, shuffling the sheets of paper round to get a good look.

'Good old Carmen,' Aguado said.

The metal door buzzed loudly and swung open, revealing an unmarked patrol car.

'Still doing her bit.'

TEN

Bullfighting is a mysterious art form – half vice, half ballet.
Those of us who dream of one day becoming bullfighters live in
a vibrant, intimate and colourful world of caricature
José Camilo Cela

Tuesday 14th March

Road sweepers were coming to the end of the night shift
when Cámara stepped out into his street and started the
ten-minute walk to Almudena's door. A handful of labourers
were drinking brandy-laced *carajillo* coffees in a working
men's bar on the other side, while the smell of fresh bread
from the baker's oven around the corner filled his nostrils
with the promise of croissants and *coca de llanda* cake. The
light was pale and lemony still, the sun low on the horizon
as it began to arch up from the sea. The first blossom on
the Judas trees was appearing, brightening up the dawn with
powerful shades of lavender-pink. Within another couple of
hours or so shops would be opening, the closely packed
apartment buildings reflecting the rattle of their metal shutters as they were raised for another day. In general, Cámara
was not at his best early in the morning, but when there

was a sense of peace, like now, of calm before the city fully awake, he almost felt like getting up at dawn every day of the week.

Brandy and the last of his *maría* had helped smooth over the night before, to the point where the images of a mutilated Ruiz Pastor had lost some of their sharpness, and he had eventually slipped into a heavy, dreamless sleep. Yet he had woken with a start in the early hours, and despite trying to will himself back into unconsciousness, he had lain restless for over half an hour before realising it was pointless. He was early enough not to have to rush back to the Jefatura, and whatever Pardo had waiting for him there. Would he be taken off the case? For some reason he thought not: there was a danger at this point that it might reflect badly on Pardo himself, suggesting incompetence in his managerial abilities. No, for now he'd hold back.

He knew her morning routine well enough to predict almost exactly what she would be doing. The alarm always went off at a quarter past seven, and after pulling up the shutters at the front and back, she'd slip out of her pyjamas and into the shower. After which came her regimented breakfast rituals: hot coffee with three splashes of semi-skimmed milk with added omega-3 – always served in a glass, never a cup. Then she'd carefully peel a kiwi, cut it up into slices, place them on a saucer and eat them with a teaspoon. At this point she would switch on the radio, listening to *La Ser* while she decided what to wear. By about now, Cámara reasoned, looking at the time on his mobile phone, she'd be putting the last items into her handbag and about to head out the door, picking up her bicycle from the cupboard at the bottom of the stairwell before going to work.

He turned the corner and her building came into view, the morning sun shining brightly on it now. A smile played on his lips as he thought of catching her by surprise at the door. She had loved it when he'd done this, years ago at the start of their relationship – rushing over after a night spent apart to see her and make love hurriedly and urgently in the doorway of her flat before she'd pull away, never wanting to be late. He'd been amazed that someone could be so set in their routines. He'd almost admired it then, seen it as a sign of self-discipline. Even when they'd been up most of the night, sweating and breathless in a pile of ruffled bedclothes, her morning rituals had never changed. The alarm always waking them at a quarter past seven . . .

He drew closer to the front door of her apartment building and looked up. On every floor he saw open windows, light glinting off the glass, even a curtain blowing in the breeze where someone was letting in the fresh morning air. Yet on the third floor, on Almudena's floor, the shutters were firmly closed.

He knew at once what had happened, and could see clearly in his mind the unslept-in bed inside, but where violent thoughts and images had filled his brain outside her office the day before, now there was nothing: a tired, strained silence which gave no indication of what he should do next. Should he ring the bell, just to make sure? Call her up, to see if she was all right? Perhaps she'd gone to stay with a friend. But all this was as dead skin lingering after the life of their relationship had slithered away in front of him. What had he expected? Why had he come here? A last attempt to save things, fuelled by some kind of blind optimism? He'd seen enough.

After a few seconds he remembered to breathe, and the air cut into his lungs like shards of glass.

No, clearly they weren't simply business partners; it had gone further than that.

He turned and headed up the Calle Ruzafa and struck into the city centre, blind, unfeeling, shock tightening around him like a cord.

The central *falla* statue in the Plaza del Ayuntamiento was already half-built. Traffic had been blocked next to the central isle and a gigantic, brightly painted figure six storeys high rose up from the ground, a female torso with plump, sharply pointed breasts and a smiling, heavily made-up face with a flame of strawberry-blonde hair cascading down her voluptuous shoulders. In one hand she held out a mirror to get a better look of herself, while in the other she was pointing a camera at her face as though about to take a self-portrait. Beneath her, dwarfed by her colossal size, *ninots* representing TV cameramen and technicians jostled about, pointing up at the starlet above them. Doubtless it was meant to be some message about the modern obsession with physical beauty and becoming famous at whatever cost, Cámara mused, but in the meantime the men of Valencia – and the foreign visitors as well, of course – were content to ogle at the oversized mammary glands which had now become the main attraction in this focal point of the city.

Something at the side of his vision stopped him. He turned his head and glanced across at the newsagent. The now familiar photographs of Carmen Luna in *Entrevista* were staring out from copies of the magazine clipped on to a rack with clothes pegs. He took a step closer: something else at the kiosk had caught his attention. A man with a grey hat had stepped forward and was looking at the head-lines, momentarily blocking Cámara's view, but after pausing for a second he pulled out a copy of *El Diario* and headed to the cashier to pay. The headlines of half a dozen papers stared up at him.

Second murder in El Caso Blanco

Blanco's apoderado *found dead in Albufera*

Bullfighting world in mourning after slaughter of Juanma Ruiz Pastor

Those were just in the national, Madrid-based papers, the ones with less stake in the local politics. But soon Cámara's eye fell on the Valencia publications, with their more emotional take on the story.

Emilia calls for renewed police efforts to solve Blanco murder

That was in the relatively sedate *La Veritat*. Its rival *El Diario*, however, was more forthright.

Blanco investigation in chaos as fresh corpse discovered

Flores slams police methods

Cámara had always liked to assume that he was never the kind of policeman to worry too much what the news-papers said. Many journalists simply repeated the press releases that the Jefatura put out, barely troubling to examine the facts. But a more aggressive journalistic style had emerged which liked to consider itself more rigorous in its approach, but concentrated on raising the emotional pitch, tickling its readers with stories of secret 'plots' and 'conspiracies', or corruption and gross incompetence in government, while stroking their egos by claiming to be high-brow and a cut above the other rags. This combina-tion of frightening, enraging and flattering the public had been a commercial success. Now barely a headline could be written without there being a sense that, each time, they were designed to bring down the authorities or at least make heads roll.

Cámara thought again about Pardo, about how he would react to all this. That – not how people in the street might view him – was of concern.

It was all horse shit, though, he thought as he stepped away, dismissing the idea from his mind. What had he realised almost the first day he'd joined? Promotions and demotions came and went like flu epidemics. Sometimes you were lucky, and sometimes you weren't. Worry about all that stuff too much and you ended up like Maldonado: reason enough never to think about it again.

Still, the realisation was there: he had a few days only, perhaps a week maximum, to sort this case out. After that he'd be shunted out somehow, in some manner that saw him fully screwed, yet with the image of the police force itself miraculously untarnished. The Bautista case gave them the excuse they needed. Pardo had already flagged it up, as though he'd seen this eventuality coming.

Torres looked at him blankly when he walked into the office.

'We're to use the broom cupboard down the corridor as an incident room,' he said. 'Three policemen from the pool on shifts manning the phones. Apart from Ibarra and Sánchez, we've got Vargas and Montero full-time. Anyone else, we just have to ask.'

Cámara grunted.

'Pardo wants to see you.'

He held up the hip flask and shook it consolingly in Cámara's direction.

'Got a refill.'

'Later,' Cámara said.

A pile of the morning's newspapers were heaped on Pardo's desk, but the commissioner had turned his back on them and was staring out at the open sky.

'Sit down, Cámara,' he said without swivelling his chair round.

'Must I?' Cámara answered.

'Look, just sit the fuck down, will you.'

Cámara removed some of the papers stacked on the only other chair, looked in vain for a place to put them, then finally slid them into the wastepaper basket behind Pardo's back. He sat and waited.

'Judge Caballero,' Pardo said at last, spinning his chair round towards Cámara, 'is not very happy.'

'He seemed all right yesterday.'

'I don't care,' Pardo said. 'The fact is he's not happy now.'

Cámara cocked his head towards the newspapers lying on the desk between them.

'It's because he reads all that shit,' he said.

'Yes, that's right,' Pardo said. 'Like everyone else in this city – except for you – he reads the morning papers. And like everyone else in this city, he's going to think we've got a bit of a problem on our hands.'

'It's a police investigation. Who do they think I am? Sherlock fucking Holmes?'

'*Por el amor de Dios*, Cámara. We've got two stiffs on our hands, one of whom just happens to be the most famous person in the country after King Juan Carlos, and we've released our only suspect.'

'Caballero gave me specific instructions to release Aguado.

Seemed a bit miffed I hadn't done it sooner, to tell the truth,' Cámara said.

'*Me suda la polla* – I don't give a sweaty cock what he said yesterday. Understand?' Pardo brought his hand down on the desk and the newspapers gave a jolt; the top ones dislodged themselves from the rest and started to slide off and cascade on to the floor. Pardo thought for a moment about trying to stop them, but hesitated. Cámara watched as the stinging headlines flew in all directions, only to be smothered by the sports sections of the other newspapers falling on top of them.

Cámara looked back at Pardo.

'So what am I supposed to do?'

'Look,' Pardo said, 'we're just having one of those chats, *¿vale?* Things aren't going too well in the investigation, looks like it's actually going backwards rather than forwards. So the big boss – that's me – calls in his subordinate – that's you – to have a talk about where things are going and how they might improve. You know how it works.'

'Are you recording this conversation?' Cámara asked, leaning in and looking for signs of a microphone somewhere.

'*¡Joder!* Just reassure me, will you?' Pardo raised his hands as though trying to reach Cámara's neck and strangle him. 'We've got the fucking *Guardia Civil* involved now. We're going to look really bloody good if they catch the killer before we do, coming in late in the day as they did. Let me know you've got some leads, even one of those fucking hunches of yours, whatever. I need to know things are on track, that this isn't actually a fucked-up investigation – despite the evidence to support that – and that you know what you're doing. Got everything under control. That kind of thing.'

'How about a proper team?' Cámara said. 'Ibarra and Sánchez are a couple of piss-heads not fit for directing traffic, and I haven't even heard of the other two goons you've given me.'

'Do you want me to take you off the case?'

'And leave Torres on his own?'

'Listen.' Pardo paused, took a breath and lowered his voice. 'We've got to start putting out some chickenfeed on this, something they can fill tomorrow's papers with, because believe me this is not going to go away.'

'I wish Flores could hear you,' Cámara said under his breath.

'Fuck the Town Hall. Look, just tell me anything. Give me something I can tell them.'

A buzz of crashing thoughts and images passed through Cámara's mind: the dark empty hole between Ruiz Pastor's legs; Flores's shining, scowling face; the closed shutters at Almudena's flat; the slight gap between Alicia's front teeth; the *Municipal* with the neck brace . . .

'We've got some leads,' he said at last. 'Tell them we've got some promising leads.'

He felt ashamed to hear himself come out with such empty words, but he looked up and saw a smile playing at the corner of Pardo's lips. It was enough: it was the kind of vacuous language Pardo himself used every day.

Pardo put his fingertips together and leaned forward.

'Then I suggest,' he said softly, 'that you go out there and follow them up.'

Cámara put his head back round the door.

'Did Sánchez find anything out from the taxi firms?'

Torres picked up his notes and glanced over them.

'*Teletaxi*. Said they picked up a large man from outside the Torres de Serrano at five thirty yesterday morning. Dropped him off at the *embarcadero* near Les Gavines at around ten to six. Not much traffic around at that time, I suppose.' He glanced down again at the notebook. 'No tip.'

Cámara pursed his lips.

'There's something else,' Torres said. 'Huerta called. Blanco's *traje de luces* has been found – at the rubbish tip. One of the dustmen picked it up. Huerta reckons it would have been dumped in one of the containers near the bullring.'

'All right. If he finds anything on it he'll let us know,' Cámara said. 'I want you to go back to the Albufera. Where the hell are Ibarra and Sánchez?'

Torres looked up.

'Probably outside having a smoke.'

'Take them with you. Talk to the *Guardia Civil* again, see if they've got anything from the fishermen down there. This is our murderer as well. They're early risers in the Albufera. Someone must have seen something. Bring them here, if you have to – the sight of this place will loosen them up if they don't want to talk to you.'

Torres took up a pen and started scribbling.

'And get . . . the other two . . .'

'Vargas and Montero,' Torres said.

'Yeah. Get them to check out Cano's movements yesterday morning. Is he still in the city? I want to know what he's been doing since Blanco's funeral.'

ELEVEN

The bullfighter is still a mythical figure, and when he becomes an expression of human valour against brute force, people can become enflamed and the old passions reappear.
Enrique Tierno Galván

A *zeta* squad car dropped him in front of Albero's hat shop, across the wide boulevard from the bullring. Cámara waited for the high-pitched pinging of the traffic lights to begin and then started to cross carefully, watching the white flashing countdown of the seconds left to get to the other side. Valencian drivers showed little mercy to any foolhardy enough to be caught in the middle of the road. Halfway over he caught sight of a small group of people huddled around a table with posters taped to the front. The *Anti-Taurino* League were at their stall again, handing out leaflets and buttonholing as many people as they could along this busy walkway. You didn't get a spot like this without some kind of permission, he thought, otherwise the *Municipales* would be all over them in seconds. Somehow, he felt sure, he could detect the hand of Flores. Get this lot to do some free electioneering for them in these last few days of the campaign.

Cámara spotted Marta Díaz, with her tied-back

JASON WEBSTER

dreadlocked hair, trying to catch the attention of a woman passing by with shopping bags and a pram.

Cámara circled for a moment, watching, then dived in, arriving just as a gap appeared in front of them.

'*Hola.*' Marta gave him a smile which quickly turned into an exaggerated frown once she recognised him.

Cámara glanced down at one of their flyers.

'I'm surprised to see you here,' he said. 'No hostility towards you lot?'

'You gonna be our saviour now?' She gave him a teasing, testing grin.

'A few nutters come and spit at us,' she said. 'Think we're being disrespectful. But we try to remind them that we're showing respect to all the animals that get killed in there.' She cocked her head towards the massive brick walls of the bullring behind them.

'Most people are just interested in hearing what we have to say,' she said.

'We've got a petition!'

A man with short dark blond hair butted in from next to Marta, clutching a piece of paper which he thrust in Cámara's face.

'Sign it for us?'

'Angel, this is—'

'Oh, I know you,' Moreno said, cutting Marta off. 'You're the cop doing the Blanco thing. Saw you on the TV.'

Cámara pulled a face.

'Must be hard being a policeman during *Fallas*,' Moreno continued with a chuckle. 'All the noise from the firecrackers and stuff. Perfect time to shoot someone, right? BANG! Ha, ha!'

He lifted his arm and pretended to shoot.

'BANG!' he repeated. 'No one would even hear.'

Cámara shrugged.

'Come to check us out, then?' Moreno smiled.

Cámara picked up a second leaflet from the table between them and flicked through. Scattered throughout the text were photographs of dying, bleeding bulls. For a second he was taken aback by how gruesome the images were.

'What do you reckon?' Marta asked him. 'We've had these new ones printed out. Much better quality paper and stuff. I thought we could catch people's attention more.'

'My design, actually,' Moreno said with a sneer directed at Marta. 'My idea, not yours. Got it?'

'All right.' Marta rolled her eyes. 'I was only saying . . .'

'Yeah, well don't. You know I don't like it.'

Marta fell silent.

'Got to shock people, see?' Moreno said, turning to Cámara. 'Otherwise they don't get it. So you gonna sign our petition, then? It's only if people like us really get together that we can stop the bloodshed. Put our names down, get a new law passed banning bullfighting. We can do it, we really can, what with the election coming.'

'I'll think about it,' Cámara said.

'We can come round to your house and pick it up there, if you prefer. Might not want people seeing you join us in public, that kind of thing.'

'No, that's all right,' Cámara replied.

'At least sign it while you're still in charge of the case.'

'Angel.' Marta gave him a look. He leaned forward and gave her a wet kiss on the cheek.

'Sorry, babe.'

In an instant he had turned his attention on a group of English tourists who were confused by the pictures of bulls on their placards and the words they didn't understand.

'Take the leaflets with you if you want,' Marta said.

'Thanks,' Cámara said, folding a couple and putting them into his jacket pocket.

He looked around at the crowds pouring out of the *Estación del Norte*. A train had arrived, one of the local services bringing people from the outlying towns and villages to take part in the *Fallas* fiesta. Soon, in a matter of days, it would be almost impossible to move in the city.

He turned back to Marta.

'That little show you put on at the Bar Los Toros that night,' Cámara said. 'What was that all about?'

Marta hesitated for a second.

'The main demo was here, outside the bullring,' she said. 'But we wanted to take it into the lion's den, I suppose.'

'Did you all go?'

'No, just a smaller group of us. Perhaps we got a bit carried away.'

'What did you do afterwards?' Cámara asked.

'What, after you'd kicked us out?' She smiled. 'Well, we went home. What with Blanco's death we just decided to pack it in for the night. Respect and stuff.'

'They weren't very pleased with you in the Bar Los Toros.'

'They're bloody murderers, those people. Sitting there, drinking expensive wines, with their plush cars. And they have a go at us!'

'It was you who smashed the glasses off the table, remember.'

'Well, as I say,' Marta said, her chin rising defiantly, 'you get a bit carried away sometimes, but we're talking about criminals. They should be locked up. Someone's got to take a stance.'

'Are you a vegetarian?' Cámara asked her.

'What?' she said.

'Oh, nothing.'

'Look, they're not gonna do us for the damage in the bar, are they?'

'Plenty of witnesses, passions running high,' Cámara said. 'The club will probably report you.'

Marta's face fell.

'But then people have got a lot on their minds at the moment,' he added. 'Chances are it's already been forgotten.'

The red-painted, greasy walls gave off a dull shimmer from the late morning light as Cámara walked into the now familiar space. The bull's head mounted on the wall behind the bar looked out with its heavy, black-eyed stare. Well, my friend, Cámara thought as he spied it, you were right: it looks as though I do have horns, I am cuckold.

The barman made a solitary figure at one end, smoking a cigarette and flicking through the newspaper, not bothering to look up at the sound of the door and Cámara walking in.

Cámara had been mildly surprised to see it open. It wasn't beyond a place like this to close for a week in mourning after what had happened, but the bullfights had restarted after a day's suspension in Blanco's honour, and the aficionados would want a drink at their usual place before and after the spectacle.

Cámara went up to the bar and looked over expectantly in the barman's direction, but his host's head remained buried in the pages of the sports section, just waiting long enough to show that he was servant to no man. Eventually, after drawing hard on the end of his cigarette and then stubbing it out thoroughly, taking as long as he could – all rituals one expected in an established bar, where mild rudeness to customers was the prerogative of the staff – he stood up straight and as nonchalantly as possible sauntered over in Cámara's direction, not as though Cámara mattered to him at all, but in a manner which suggested he had other business to attend to at that end of the bar, and that if he took Cámara's order while he were at it he would be doing him a favour. When finally he glanced at his customer's face and recognised him, however, his body language changed instantly.

'*Hombre*, Chief Inspector,' he said. And without waiting to hear Cámara's order, he immediately reached for a glass and started pouring Cámara a complimentary Mahou.

'There,' he said, bringing it down on to the chrome top in front of them with a clink. Some of the foam on top spilled over the edge and started sliding down the side of the glass.

'Not going to have one with me?' Cámara asked. The barman raised an eyebrow, frowned, then poured himself half a *caña*.

'The boss hasn't been here since you-know-when. Depression, he says. Can't face coming in. Don't think he'll grudge me quenching my thirst a bit on the job.'

'I was a little surprised to see you open,' Cámara said, raising his glass now that the barman was joining him and taking his first cold gulp. The Mahou was on tap here, Cámara's favourite.

'Things have been a bit rough, as you can imagine,' the barman said. He put his glass down, walked back to the end of the bar, picked up his cigarettes and lighter and then strolled back to Cámara's end. He nudged a cigarette out with his finger and offered it to Cámara. *Fortuna*: he preferred something stronger, but it was becoming more and more difficult to call himself a non-smoker, so he reached forwards and took it.

'We kind of feel tainted by it all, you know? The boss feels guilty, somehow, as if he was responsible – inviting Blanco over here for the award ceremony and all that. Seems to think that if he hadn't, Blanco would still be here today. I told him, it's nothing to do with you. I told him. Whoever it was would have gone for him anyway. But he says no, Blanco would have probably left straight after the fight if he hadn't been coming round here. Instead he stuck around in the bullring and . . . well, I don't need to tell you.'

Cámara nodded and inhaled deeply.

'I mean, I know there are people who are pleased to see the back of him. To tell the truth, we all thought he'd get it in the ring one day. But from a bull, of course. The way he used to stand there, bulls running past him centimetres away. No one fought like that. He was a hero to ordinary folk – putting his balls on the line like that. Why he was injured so often? 'Cause he fought like you're supposed to. Life and death, like the old ones used to. Nowadays the rest of them are just happy getting the cheque at the end of each fight. Not Blanco. He wasn't doing it for the money. Strange that – haven't honestly been able to say that about any bullfighter, for, ooh, I don't know how long. Not since I was a kid, probably. Antonio Ordóñez's time. But that's why people respected him, see? You can tell, you can just tell when they're doing it for real. We've had nothing but fake bullfighting all these years, and then along comes Blanco and whoosh, it's like a breath of fresh air. And for lots of people it's the first time they're seeing the real thing, and they're just blown away by it, never seen anything like it. And some people come along saying it's just *morbo* – people just going to see him 'cause they're hoping to see him gored and all that. But that's bollocks. People went to see Blanco fight 'cause he was the greatest bullfighter around. Probably the greatest there's ever been. I know there are people think it's blasphemy saying something like that, but I reckon it's true. I saw the greats back in the sixties, I saw Ordóñez and Dominguín. And they were special, believe me. And Blanco was up there with them, I swear. People loved him, they respected him. And they can't take that away from him. Ever. No matter what they do to him, no matter how they humiliate him. Alive or dead. That was Blanco all over. Once you've got people's respect, that's the most important thing. Money, women, the cars, all that bollocks, you can forget that. It's the respect that lasts, what'll make him immortal.'

Perhaps deprived of the usual clientele over the past days, the barman could finally express his feelings and thoughts about the murder. For the time being, Cámara was happy to sit and listen.

'What about all that stuff about him being gay?' he asked simply.

'Pah! What's Carmen Luna, then? Does she look like a bloke to you? They were going to get married, have kids and stuff. It was all in the papers. Gay? Well, even if he was, so what? He was the best bullfighter there was, and that's what counts. Reckon it was just people trying to talk him down saying he was a *maricón* and all that. They feared him, that's what. They didn't like it. Not the poncy politicians 'cause they're trying to ban bullfighting. But not the grandees in bullfighting neither. Man like Blanco's dangerous, see? Too popular. And he's doing it the old-fashioned way, the real way. And there's all these businessmen running bullfighting now. It's all about money. They don't want to see someone like Blanco coming along, 'cause then everyone's expected to be like him. And you can't fight a bull the way he did without talent. Raw talent, that's what I'm telling you. Any other matador, one of the ordinary ones, tries to fight like Blanco and he'll end up in A&E before you can blink. That Cano – fought the same day as Blanco. Great bullfighter, don't get me wrong. But he couldn't do what Blanco did. That's probably why he hated him so much. 'Cause it wasn't just fearlessness in Blanco, see? It was skill, talent. Yeah, he got gored, but that's because he was so good. Anyone else does it like him and forget it. But Blanco was exceptional. And people loved him, and they flocked to see him. You couldn't get tickets for love nor money round here. I know – did a nice little business in some of the spares I managed to get my hands on, know what I mean? But the businessmen running bullfighting these days, they're not overly impressed with all this. I mean, of course they love the ticket sales and all that, and bullfighting's back on the front pages, but they've got interests. And Blanco's coming along and he's upsetting the apple cart. Shaking everyone up. And they don't like it. Had his enemies. Course, not that I'm suggesting any of them could have, well, you know, gone as far as that. Must have been some madman or something. What about them *anti-taurinos*? Suppose you checked them out.'

Cámara drank steadily through all of this, his glass emptying. Without batting an eyelid, the barman picked it up and refilled it, then placed it back on the bar in front of Cámara, reaching for a small tray from the other side, filling it with a handful of almonds and placing them next to him. A spare copy of *El Diario* was lying nearby; Cámara glanced over and caught the inflammatory headlines barking out their faux concern.

'Don't want to look at that,' the barman said. 'Don't take any notice. Just trying to sell more copies.'

Cámara sniffed and took another gulp of beer. His cigarette had finished.

'Have you got a tobacco machine in here?' he asked.

'Over there.' The barman nodded at the opposite wall with his head. 'I'll unlock it for you. Got to keep these stupid remote controls now, to stop kids from buying fags. Machine doesn't work unless I flick the switch. Stupid EU bloody rules. Started smoking when I was twelve, me, and it hasn't done me any harm.'

Cámara fished for some change in his pocket, then walked over and bought himself a packet of Ducados.

'Prefer black tobacco, I see,' the barman said respectfully when he saw the blue-and-white packet in Cámara's hand. 'Stick to the blond stuff myself.' He lit Cámara's cigarette, then pulled out another for himself and fired it up, leaning in to continue their conversation as though they'd been friends since childhood.

'You know what sticks in my mind from that night,' the barman went on. 'After you'd left, I mean, and we'd all found out about what had happened.'

'When *did* you find out?' Cámara butted in.

'Must have been about fifteen minutes after you left,' the barman said. 'That journo woman, Alicia What's-her-name, got a phone call.'

'How did she react?' Cámara lifted the delicious cigarette up to his mouth but kept his eyes on the barman.

'Horrified. Like the rest of us. Looked like she was going to be sick, or something. Quickly told us what had happened then ran out the door.'

'But you were saying,' Cámara said. 'What sticks in your mind from that night.'

'Yeah, I mean, you know, the image that kind of stays in my mind, like what I see when I close my eyes and I'm trying to go to sleep, is the face of old Ramírez. When he heard what had happened.'

'Go on,' Cámara said.

'Well,' the barman frowned. 'He just went all white, as though the blood had gone from him completely. I thought for a second he might be about to have a heart attack or something. That can happen, you know. A bit of a shock and the old heart just packs in. His face just went grey, as though he was already dead. Never seen anything like it. It chilled me right through. Everyone else was wailing and crying. Shed a few tears myself, I'm not ashamed to admit it. That Carmen Luna was a right mess – started throwing things around, screaming and tearing her hair out. But old Ramírez just sat there, not moving, his face like stone or something.'

'How did his son react?' Cámara asked.

'Paco? Yeah, he was cut up as well. Not as bad as his father. He was there helping to sort out Carmen, I remember. Stopping her from trashing the place – made her sit down and shut up. Talked to her like a little girl, if you want my opinion. Don't think the boss is going to chase her up for it. After all, it was her fiancé just got murdered. Still, she's not short of a peseta or two.'

Cámara wondered for a moment if in the confusion of the traumatic evening the barman had confused Carmen Luna for Marta, the *anti-taurino* girl who had smashed a table clear in front of Cámara's face. He wasn't shy of elaborating a story, by the sounds of it. If he'd left coming round till the next day Cámara might have ended up hearing a slightly different, perhaps even more dramatic account of what happened.

'How long was Ramírez like that?' he asked. 'In a state of shock, I mean.'

'About ten minutes, I reckon.'

'What happened then?'

'Then he suddenly stood up, as though he'd come back from the dead, or something. Called Paco over and the two of them just left right through that door there. Never said a word. First to leave, probably. After yourself and the journo girl, Alicia.'

Cámara had a flash of her smiling at him at the second mention of her name. Had he dreamt about her last night? He couldn't tell. But some image of her seemed to jump out at him from his subconscious.

'Do you know where they went?'

The barman gave him a conspiratorial look, proudly aware for a moment that he might be doing his bit to help the police investigation.

'Can't say for certain,' he said with a pronounced frown. 'Didn't say where they were going, see? But I reckon they went off to their house off Blasco Ibáñez Avenue. Always stay there during *Fallas*. It's their official Valencia base. Just for when they're down for the bullfights. Ramírez bulls traditionally start the *feria* off on the first day.'

'The best bulls around, I hear,' Cámara said.

'Oh, yes.' The barman closed his eyes, as though bringing to mind the image of a Ramírez bull. 'In my opinion, at least. One of the longest established breeders. They produce strong, angry bulls. Always *bravo*, a Ramírez bull. Not to everyone's taste. Some people don't rate them. But you'll never see a *manso* Ramírez bull. Or at least . . .'

The barman tailed off and looked down at the shiny bar top separating them. Cámara cleared his throat.

'Well,' the barman said, 'a few people – I'm not saying I'm one of them – but a few people have been commenting recently that the Ramírez bulls might not be what they used to be. Not quite so strong, not quite so powerful.'

He stopped and glanced around the empty bar again before continuing.

'It's a difficult one this, 'cause some people won't even hear such a thing, see? It's like blasphemy or something even to suggest that Ramírez isn't producing them like he used to. But you want my opinion? You take a Ramírez bull from ten years ago, and you pit it against the ones they're breeding now, and the old feller would beat the young one every time. Course, it's hard to prove this kind of thing. We always like to think things were better when we were younger. Bullfight aficionados more than anyone else. But the Ramírez bulls, they're different. Not the same as they were, at least. The *casta* – the genes, the breeding, the blood – it's all there. You can't ruin a bloodline like that overnight. But are they doing things to them that they didn't in the past? Ah, well, that's the question, isn't it.'

Cámara picked up some of the almonds the barman had placed out for him and tossed them to the back of his mouth.

'Look, I'm not saying anything, right?' the barman went on. 'To accuse someone of bad breeding practices is about the most serious thing you can do. But we all know it's going on. ¡Por Dios! You don't need to be an expert to see how the bulls' horns have been shaved down. Just look at all the splinters around the tip. You can see that with the naked eye. Sometimes they get carried away and then the horn starts bleeding, 'cause that's flesh inside there. It's not just a hard bit on top of the bull's head. It's got blood and nerves and everything running up there.'

He jerked his thumb up at the bull's head mounted on the wall behind him.

'It's bloody criminal. Everyone's doing it. But that's not all. They're having to find ways round it, see, 'cause there's checks and stuff, to see if the bull's all right or been tampered with. The bullring employs a couple of vets – they get to check the bulls the day before the fight, and then again a couple of hours before going into the ring. But you can get round that easy. There are injections you give them just before – that way it doesn't show. The first ones are a bit livelier, maybe, but by the time you get to the last one of the afternoon he can barely stand up from the dope, let alone run around the ring. There's some new chemicals they're coming up with all the time to get round the tests. But then best of all is these new trucks they've got where they keep the bulls on a slope, with all the weight on their back legs. That way when they come out into the ring there's not so much strength there, see? 'Cause they've been standing at an angle, bearing all their own weight for an hour or two before the fight. And how are you going to detect that? Some people don't even bother with the trucks and just park on a hill for a couple of hours before delivering the bulls. Does the same trick.'

It had gone ten o'clock when his mobile phone woke Cámara up. His head hurt from where it had been lying on the pile of interview notes on his desk, and a small puddle of saliva dribbling from his mouth had smudged some of the ink of the reports. He reached for the desk lamp and switched it on, trying to make sense of the muddled images of Almudena flashing across the back of his eyes. Still half-asleep, he couldn't remember where he'd put the phone, and as he flailed around, trying to locate it by sound alone, he stood up sharply and banged his head on the corner of the metal shelf above his desk.

'¡Joder!'

Collapsing to the floor, he let out a sharp, low grunt. Whoever was trying to reach him would have to wait.

The blow to his head seemed to clear something in his mind, however, banishing thoughts of Almudena to allow memories of where he was and what he had been doing that afternoon to filter back in: Torres's reports on the interviews with the El Perelló fishermen; a possible identification of the boat the killer might have used. Cámara stumbled back to his feet and his eyes fell on the note he'd written to himself: 'El Perellonet *barraca* – Old Pere's place. Rope cut, boat found floating nearby.'

Old Pere, it seemed, hadn't been too worried by it at first. The boat, after all, hadn't disappeared completely or anything – he'd found it in the reeds just a few yards downstream. Though it was probably just someone messing about. It was only when he'd heard about the murder, and police being round, that he'd thought he might mention it to someone. The *criminalistas* from the *Guardia Civil* would be analysing it and would probably get word to them the next day. Although perhaps nothing would come of it. Torres hadn't seemed that convinced.

He thought the voicemail would have kicked in by now, diverting the call, but his mobile still chirped away at him. Ducking his head so as not to repeat the same trick as before, he went round to the other side of the desk where his jacket had fallen to the floor from the back of a chair. Inside he searched for the vibrating plastic box and pulled it out, flicking it open without checking first to see who it was.

'Cámara,' he grunted into the end.

'Max.' It was a woman. Cámara didn't respond. The fact that it wasn't Almudena's voice hit him like a physical force.

'I can still call you Max, can I?' came the voice again. 'Or do you prefer Chief Inspector?'

Cámara cleared his throat.

'Is this a bad time? Perhaps I should call back later.'

'Alicia?' Cámara grunted.

'Ah!' came the voice. 'Thought I'd lost you there for a moment. Are you all right?'

'I'm fine. Fine. Er, nice of you to call. How did you get my number?'

'I know it's late,' she said. 'It's been a long day at this end as well. Just finished actually, and I was wondering if you fancied popping out for a drink. I'm round your way. Just in a little bar near the Torres de Serrano. Across the river from you.'

Cámara rubbed his hand through his hair, his mind still grey from sleep and the aching that had now replaced the sharp pain where he had hit his head.

'Look, I . . .'

'It's all right if it's not a good time. I understand.'

Another couple of reports on the desk caught his eye – a note from Sánchez about Ruiz Pastor's body: Quintero had released it and it had been flown back to Madrid for burial. Then one from Vargas on Cano's movements. According to his *mozo de espadas* – his right-hand man – he hadn't left Valencia since the night of Blanco's death. All his movements, however, were accounted for: parties, dinners, girls; it seemed the man almost never spent a moment alone.

'I'd love to, really,' he said. 'It's just . . .'

'Fine. Don't say any more. I take it you're coming to the bullfight tomorrow. A commemorative corrida to honour Blanco's memory.'

'I, er . . .' Still struggling to think straight, Cámara reached for a pen. 'Will Cano be there? Fighting, I mean?'

'Yes,' she said.

'I'll be there. What time does it start?'

'Six o'clock. Look for me at the entrance. We can watch it from the side of the ring. You get a better view, a better understanding there than from up in the president's box.'

'Quite.'

'Then we'll go out afterwards,' she said. 'I can accept a refusal now. But you can't turn me down two nights in a row.'

TWELVE

Yes, there is death in a bullfight, but as an ally, as an accomplice to life: death has a walk-on part so that life can be affirmed
Fernando Savater

Wednesday 15th March

The house stood back from the road, down a recently asphalted track lined with tall, mature cypress trees. Antique, cast-iron street lamps arched over the green-painted metal gates at the far end, while the drip irrigation system watering the crown daisies and blue lupins between the trees hissed as moisture leaked out into the fox-coloured soil underneath. Having parked his old Seat Ibiza around the corner, Cámara walked down the middle of the tunnel-like driveway wondering if anyone was at home.

He buzzed the intercom panel by the side of the gate and waited. There were no sounds from inside, but he had been informed that this was her habitual place of residence, and that there was no information of her being anywhere else at the moment. At least not according to *Webpol*, the police intranet, or even to a probably more reliable source, the gossip magazines and their websites. Cámara had expected to find a group of paparazzi gathered here, waiting for more shots of Blanco's would-be bride. But either they'd moved on to new prey, or else he'd caught them napping down at the nearest bar.

He cast an eye up at the cypress trees pointing like accusing fingers at the deep blue sky above. He didn't know what he expected to see – some signal of mourning, perhaps? Some sign of the loss that had been suffered behind these gates. But there was nothing, no black ribbon tied around the railings, no message to the world. He remarked at the lack of birdsong. Although the splash of waves caressing the rocks not far below was just audible. He could smell the sea strongly from here: salty air and the promise of a seafood lunch. There was a new little place in the Carmen across from the Jefatura that he might try if he got time. One thing Valencians had got right was how to mix rice and fish. No one else in the world could beat them at that. Except, of course, for those funny Japanese guys who came over every year and won the International Paella Competition hands down. But they didn't count.

The intercom crackled and a male voice answered.

'¿Quién?'

A moment later the electric motor on the gate buzzed, the doors swung open, and Cámara walked through into a green, luscious garden. In front of him a red Mercedes sports car was parked under a carport, while a gravel path led off towards the front door of the house. A young Moroccan man appeared from behind a large oleander bush wearing a white shirt and black trousers.

'Chief Inspector,' he said. 'Would you come this way?'

Cámara followed him into the house, a modern building constructed mostly of cement and glass. Had Montesa had a hand in this? Cámara doubted it – it was far too small and the cement wasn't quite white enough. Still, he might have inspired it in some way – a house built more for looking at than for living in.

They passed through into a large living room with tinted glass walls that gave out on to the Mediterranean. In the distance, to the right, he could make out the Montgó mountain above Denia marking one end of the Gulf of Valencia, while to the left the coastline stretched far beyond Valencia port up towards Sagunto and beyond into the neighbouring province of Castellón. Ahead there was nothing but a vast expanse of shifting, rippling, threatening blue.

'Please, have a seat,' the Moroccan said. And he indicated the large white fluffy sofas forming an L-shape. Cámara remained on his feet.

'The Señorita won't be long.'

Cámara was left on his own, smiling to himself at the use of 'señorita' to describe his hostess. Not only her age, but the fact that she had been married before made the use of such a word unexpected. Perhaps she was still trying to play the role of the young bride.

Cámara scanned the room: photos of Blanco were everywhere, placed in silver frames at the side of the room in the built-in bookcases: in his *traje de luces*; in a suit with a shiny blue tie; with Carmen, holding her hand as though it were a precious object and gazing into her eyes. Was that love? Intensity, perhaps.

He heard soft footsteps behind him and turned. It was the Moroccan again with a cocktail glass in his hand. He bent down and placed it on a small white table by the side of the sofa along with a white paper napkin and a tiny tray with a handful of nuts.

'*La Señorita*'s compliments,' he said with a smile and walked away again. For a minute Cámara had the feeling of having stumbled into an airport executive waiting lounge. But the call of a passing gull – the first sound of real life that he'd heard since arriving – brought him back to where he was. He looked out over the sea again. Below, the garden sloped down to a swimming pool surrounded by outsized olive-oil jars and a couple of reproduction Greek statues.

Cámara checked the time on his mobile phone. He didn't usually drink so early, he told himself. No, that wasn't strictly accurate. To tell the truth he'd had a few morning drinks in the past. In fact, now he came to think about it, it was actually a fairly common occurrence. And if he counted the surreptitious gulps from the office hip flask he had to admit that morning drinking – even early-morning drinking – was a regular pattern of his day. He shrugged as the realisation sank in. Perhaps he should just accept it.

He edged towards the cocktail glass, picked it up and had a sniff. The Moroccan hadn't said exactly what the Señorita's idea of a 'compliment' was. Poison? His nose was tickled, however, by the unmistakable scent of an Agua de Valencia cocktail, the orange juice, cava, vodka and Cointreau making his mouth water as he breathed in their fragrance. He pulled out the slice of orange that had been placed in the glass, flicked it into a nearby plant pot, and then drank the thing in one.

He waited, savouring the flavours on his tongue, the roaring sensation down his gullet as the mixture burnt its way down to his stomach. No, he thought, still convinced that the first stiff drink of the day was best served before ten in the morning, that was clean. Or at least if they had tampered with it there was nothing he could detect.

An alcoholic flush had just reached his cheeks when he heard a clipping sound on the floor behind him. Turning, he found himself face to face with Carmen Luna. Or rather face-to-bosom with Carmen Luna, as it took the tiniest fraction of a second for his attention to rise above her cleavage.

'Chief Inspector Cámara,' she said slowly, smiling blandly at him.

The last time Cámara had seen her in the flesh had been at Blanco's funeral. Since then he'd seen most of the rest of her flesh thanks to the revealing photographs in *Entrevista*. Now, as the Agua de Valencia kicked rapidly into his bloodstream, thanks to the lack of anything else in his stomach to delay its progress, it was challenging to keep those powerful images from his mind. The black attire of their last encounter was still in evidence, but there was possibly even less than before. A black, filmy negligee was covered only by a black satin dressing gown tied very loosely and expertly around her waist. Both these garments were short, barely descending to her thigh, and revealing tanned naked legs and high-heeled slippers with fluffy feathers bunched up just above the toes. The effect was to suggest that she'd only recently risen from her bed, although Cámara noticed that her face was fully made up, her skin smooth and free of blemishes as though she'd spent some time at least in front of a mirror before appearing.

'If you'd given me more warning I wouldn't have to receive you like this,' she said, waving her hand.

'Did you enjoy your cocktail?' she said, beaming at the empty glass still balancing in Cámara's hand. 'Cyril makes them specially for me. It's his own recipe. A secret. He refuses even to tell me. I've threatened to fire him and send him back over the Strait unless he tells me. But he never gives in.'

Cámara tried to recall the face of the Moroccan who had brought him the drink. Cyril?

'Oh, I know,' Carmen said, waving her hand. She brushed past him and went to sit down on the white sofa, crossing her legs delicately as she looked out towards the sea. 'His real name's Abdul . . . Abdul Something. I can't remember right now. But he prefers Cyril. It's the name I gave him when he joined me.'

Cámara walked over and sat on the opposite sofa. Carmen crossed her legs a little tighter and turned to him.

'Of course, as a Muslim he's not supposed to drink at all, never mind mix cocktails for unbelievers like me. But I found him at this wonderful little *riad* hotel in Marrakesh and simply had to bring him back with me. And he's been loyal ever since. Even if he can be a bit naughty sometimes. Just like those cocktails he makes.'

Cámara wondered to himself how long someone like Carmen Luna could keep up the performance. Did she spend her whole life talking like this? Or did moments of clarity occasionally shine through?

'Before I ask you some questions,' Cámara said, 'I would just like to say how sorry I am for your loss.'

She looked blankly at him for a moment. Cámara had wondered if she would break down at this point, or at least perform something of the kind of display he had seen at the funeral. But instead she simply gazed ahead with an expressionless look on her face.

'Are you, indeed,' she said at last.

'Forgive me,' Cámara said, trying to back-pedal. Perhaps the cocktail was affecting him more than he realised. 'I simply . . .'

'If there were no murders, Chief Inspector, you'd be out of a job. So unless you're looking to be unemployed, I fail to understand how you can be sorry for what has happened. This is, after all, what you do.'

Cámara fell silent; words failed to come to his dulled brain.

'Unless, of course,' Carmen went on, turning away from him and staring out at the waves again, so that he couldn't see her eyes, 'you only say these things to test the other person's reaction.'

A smile played on her lips and she raised her eyebrows.

'Am I right?'

'I've spoken out of turn, perhaps,' Cámara said.

'Not at all. You said what anyone is expected to say in these circumstances. Only the fact is you're a policeman and you've come here unannounced to speak with me, all of which makes me wonder quite what your motives are.'

Cámara rubbed his eye, trying to feel his face, his skin: everything seemed to have gone numb.

'Do I surprise you?' Carmen said, finally turning back round to face him. 'I've had people trying to catch me out all my adult life. You develop a sixth sense for it.' She closed her eyes for a second before reopening them. 'If not always for ways of dealing with it.'

It wasn't hot, but almost instinctively Cámara reached up

to his throat to loosen his collar and tie. For some reason he'd thought it appropriate to wear a suit for this meeting, but now that he thought about it he wasn't entirely sure why. A shirt and jacket was his usual dress. Something about her celebrity, perhaps? It was curious how these things affected you, even when you were convinced they didn't.

'Perhaps you'd like to take a stroll outside,' Carmen said, standing up. 'You need some air.'

Not waiting for him, she walked up to the glass doors on the far side of the living room and slid them open, stepping onto a wooden portico that surrounded the house and out into the shade of a tall palm tree. Cámara followed, half-expecting some yappy little dog to appear and gnaw at his feet. A few minutes ago he would have assumed Carmen was the kind of woman who kept a fluffy little companion, something to cuddle on those lonely, cocktail-fuelled nights. But now he was less sure.

Carmen sat on a low stone bench down by the pool, dangling her hands in the water.

'Jorge used to love it here,' she said, watching as the mid-morning sunlight caught the ripples she was creating on the surface. 'One of the few places he felt safe. He told me that many times. "Carmen," he'd say. "*Aquí tengo paz.*" Of course, he's peaceful where he is now; no one can get him where he is now, no matter how hard they try.'

Cámara felt the urge for a cigarette kick in, and his hand was already caressing the plastic cover of the packet of Ducados in his pocket. But he hesitated. Carmen, he felt sure, would allow him if he asked permission, but instinct told him not to interrupt her train of thought.

'He was a good man. I hope you understand that,' she

said. 'Some people deserve their death, the way they die. But not my Jorge. He was never meant to die like that. I could never watch him in the ring. I'd go, of course, to the fights, to be with him sometimes. But I always made an excuse not to have to watch. It's hard for a woman to do that, to see the man she loves placing himself so close to death. I know we're expected to sit there obediently in the stands, drape our finest *mantón de Manila* shawl over the side like those ladies in the stories of knights of old. It's what the man wants, after all, displaying his strength, his valour, in front of the whole world. Look at me, look at this man pitting himself against the worst that the world can throw at him. But that's for future conquests, the ones to come. For the woman already in a torero's life it is the worst thing imaginable to see him out there.

'Oh, don't get me wrong,' she said, glancing up for a second, 'I never worried about other women. Not with Jorge. He was a one-woman man. I knew, from the moment I met him. I've been jilted in the past, believe me. And a woman can always tell. But Jorge was pure, which was why our relationship was pure, why I wanted to make myself pure for him.'

Still standing some distance away from the pool, Cámara slowly took a couple of steps forwards and sat down on a wooden lounger at right angles to Carmen. She looked up at him, as though trying to gauge whether he understood her or not.

'Did you ever argue?' Cámara asked.

'Ah, of course. *The* question,' she said. 'I wondered when you'd get to it. Well, can you believe it? But no, we never did. Not once. Oh, Jorge had a temper; I know that. A man needs anger to do what he did. But he took his anger, his violence, and turned it into art. Jorge could be sharp with people sometimes. But you have to understand – he was under a lot of pressure. He risked death daily; he was the best: everyone was watching him, waiting for the tiniest error, anything just to bring him down, say that he was finished as a bullfighter. We live in a strange country, always beating down our heroes, the best of ourselves. Or at least while they're still alive. If you want to be a great Spaniard, better to die first, then let them mourn over what they have lost. Only then can you really be appreciated.'

Cámara lifted his head as she spoke, looking back at the living room above them where they had been sitting a few moments before. The Moroccan had appeared at the window and was looking down on them. When he saw that Cámara had seen him he pulled back and disappeared.

'It doesn't matter to those people what you do,' Carmen said, resuming. 'Once you've reached the top everyone wants to pull you down. Not even all of Jorge's charity work could make them realise he was a good man. You know about his work with orphans?'

She looked round; Cámara nodded.

'I know that most people in the street adored him. But they adored him as an image, as an icon. They didn't know him, never saw the man behind the *traje de luces.*'

She sat up, lifting herself up with one arm, and opened her legs slightly before crossing them again.

'You mentioned his temper,' Cámara said. 'Did you ever see him angry at anyone else? Did he ever talk badly about anyone? About tensions with anyone?'

She paused, bending down again to run her hand through the water.

'There were always tensions,' she said at last. 'Jorge was an artist. An artist has to be a perfectionist, and demands perfection from those around him. Yes, there were tensions with Ruiz Pastor, if that's what you're interested in, and with the Ramírez family, with some of the other bullfighters on the circuit, with the media, with the businessmen and their mercenary attitudes towards bullfighting, busy trying to make it into just another *negocio*, like football, or the cinema. And of course all these stupid politicians with their talk of banning bullfighting. Nonsense, all of it. But he never spoke about any of it. I was only ever aware of it from how he was, how he behaved. I was here to protect him, to give him love, to help him forget the rest of the world. And it worked, to an extent.'

'Any specific examples?' Cámara asked. 'Anything in the past couple of months, perhaps?'

'Since the beginning of this year?' she asked.

'*Por ejemplo.*'

'There were some comments of Cano's in the press during the run-up to the new season,' she said. 'I don't know what they were. Cyril told me, in fact. Not Jorge at all. Just some silly spat. I never believed they were really rivals like people said. Just some story made up for the newspapers. That happens a lot, you know.'

She gave him a look, then pushed her hand deeper into the water.

'Did Blanco – did Jorge say anything about it?'

'About Cano?' she said. 'No. I'm sure it was nothing, as I say.'

'Anything else?'

She thought for a moment.

'We weren't together every day. You know that. We were waiting to get married before moving in together.'

'But you spoke on the phone?'

'Oh, yes. He called me three, sometimes four times a day when we were apart.'

'And did you ever notice anything wrong during the calls?'

'Wrong? Oh, did he ever seem angry over anything, you mean? No. Maybe. He didn't seem very happy the last time he went up to see Ramírez at the farm. Furious, really. But I told him he shouldn't have gone. He wasn't feeling well that day. The whole world could be against him some days from the way he spoke. It was his genius, you see?'

'When was that? When did he go to the Ramírez farm?'

'A couple of weeks ago. He always went just before the *Fallas feria* started, to check up on things, see the bulls they were going to send down, that kind of thing. Or at least that's what I think he did when he went up there. I never visited the place.'

'Did he tell anyone else about his visit? Ruiz Pastor, perhaps?'

'If it was anything to do with his art then I suspect he did, yes. They spoke often on the phone when Jorge was here. Always something to arrange or organise.'

'How do you get on with the Ramírez family?' Cámara asked.

She pulled her hand out of the water and straightened up, swinging her legs tightly underneath her as she sat up.

'Perfectly well.'

'Have they been here to see you? Since what happened, I mean?'

'I prefer to mourn in solitude,' she said.

She got to her feet.

'The sun's getting too strong out here,' she said, and started walking back up the slope towards the sliding glass doors. Cámara got up and followed her back into the house. The Moroccan was nowhere to be seen.

Carmen stood at the window looking out at the sea.

'Cyril!' she called out. There was no reply.

'Cyril?' Still nothing.

'He must have gone out to do the shopping,' she said after a pause. Cámara watched her closely as she turned round to face him again: something about her seemed to quiver slightly. As she raised her arm to her hair to push it behind her ear he could see her hand was shaking.

'Are you all right?' he asked.

She smiled.

'It's been so nice to have some company,' she said. 'To talk about things. I have struggled all my life to find happiness. And with Jorge I found it. My time with him was the best period in my life, and I give thanks to God every morning for what He allowed me to have. Our life together as man and wife was going to be just the start – a new life, a pure life. I wanted it so badly.'

She sniffed, her hand swiftly wiping away a tear that had formed at the edge of her eye.

'I'd even had my virginity restored for him. That's how much I wanted it. Did you know that? No, of course, nobody knew that. There, you can go and tell the newspapers now, if you want. They'd pay you well for that. Or are you one of the honourable ones? Yes, perhaps you are. But they can do that, these days, you know. A specialist in London. Works a lot with girls from Arab countries, as you'd imagine. But also from Latin America. Very good, very discreet. Some Spanish women had been to see him in the past, he told me. He was a kind man.'

She shook her hair loose, the belt around her dressing gown coming undone and falling to the floor where she stood.

'He said I had the prettiest vagina he'd ever seen.'

THIRTEEN

*Bullfight critics, row on row, crowd the enormous
plaza de toros, but only one is there who knows,
and he's the one who fights the bull*
Robert Graves

'Why are you going to the bullfight? I thought you hated
it.'

Torres pulled hard on his cigarette, the bright end glowing
brightly against the black of his beard.

'Worried that someone else is going to get it in the neck?'

Cámara breathed out a plume of smoke and looked out
over the empty wasteland behind them: no kids with *petardos*
today.

'The best police work, my dear Torres,' Cámara said,
flaring his nostrils, 'is often done by adopting an oblique
approach, to come from a direction where the criminal least
expects . . .'

'Fuck off!' Torres said. 'You just want the afternoon off.
Leave me here with all the boring stuff.'

Cámara coughed.

'Well, that's part of it as well.'

'*Cabrón.*'

'I could always have you transferred to Maldonado's team, if you prefer.'

Torres smiled.

'You're the one who has a problem with him, remember? Not me.'

'I don't know what you're talking about,' Cámara said. 'I only have the greatest respect for Chief Inspector Maldonado.'

'Is that why you hit him, then?' Torres asked.

'What?'

'Oh, come on. Everyone knows. Just because he didn't report it, you think the whole building didn't find out about it? Half the guys gave you a cheer, it has to be said.'

'And the other half?' Cámara asked.

'Too scared.'

They both finished their cigarettes, but hovered at the door, not wanting to go back in. The lull from a late lunch weighed down on them, while the sun on their faces brought images of being elsewhere: for Torres, sitting out at a terrace bar, drinking beer and watching the girls go by; for Cámara, lying on the beach at Formentera, where he should have been. With Almudena? He examined the image for a moment. He was no longer sure.

'Why did you hit him, anyway?' Torres asked more seriously.

'Ancient history,' Cámara said. 'I've forgotten. Anyway, I didn't really hit him. Not *really*. His chest just got in the way of my fist.'

'Some say it was because Maldonado was in charge of the pay review that year. Recommended you for a pay cut.'

Cámara frowned.

'I'm sure there were other reasons as well.'

Torres was the one to make the first move back inside. Cámara's limbs felt leaden, as though his body were rebelling against the idea of having to work. He still had half an hour or so before heading over to the bullring.

'The *criminalistas* had a look at the boat they pulled in,' Torres said, jerking the door open where it caught on the floor.

'Anything?' Cámara asked.

'Not much. The *Guardia Civil* called Huerta: said that whoever had been in there last was probably wearing blue overalls, like the kind workmen use. Found some fibres.'

'Ah!'

'Yeah, Huerta said you'd be pleased to hear that. I've checked. Old Pere, the boat's owner, doesn't own any blue overalls. Fishermen in the Albufera wouldn't be seen dead in them, apparently.'

'Anything else?' Cámara asked.

'Nothing,' Torres said, shrugging his shoulders. They passed into the shade of the building.

'She said I'd be happy that Blanco'd been killed,' Cámara said absent-mindedly as they walked up the white concrete emergency stairway back up to their floor.

'Who?'

'Carmen Luna. Said murder was what I dealt in, so Blanco's murder was just more grist to my mill. Or something like that.'

'Well,' Torres said, beginning to pant as they climbed up, 'I suppose she's right.'

Cámara stopped where he was and Torres looked at him. They both knew what the other was thinking: the scene back at the *barraca* and Ruiz Pastor's bloodied, mutilated body. Things like that weren't easily erased from anyone's mind.

'Or maybe not,' Torres said.

'We could always ask to move to Personnel.' Cámara started walking up the stairs again, this time taking them two at a time as he tried to kick himself into gear.

'Yeah,' Torres said, heaving himself up behind. 'You'd be good at that.'

He'd broken his vow once. Now that he'd done it again he felt almost worse, but coming to this bullfight, he knew, was important: politically because it showed the *Policía Nacional* was still concerned about the appearance of finding Blanco's killer; for the investigation because the chances were significantly high that the murderer would be present, revisiting the scene, enjoying the spectacle of a bullfight in his victim's honour, and it behoved Cámara to be there as well; and emotionally because Alicia had invited him. No, if he was honest with himself, whatever he felt towards her was only physical at this point; his emotions were in a state of paralysis.

The bullring was packed. Few tickets had made it on to the open market as grandees and aficionados from all over the country had hustled for a place at this, what had turned out to be one of the most important events of the year. There had been a rumour at one stage that Mayoress Delgado herself might turn up, declaring a truce in her war against bullfighting. But the idea had been scotched by her team; Flores himself had written in the morning's copy of *El Diario* to deny it, and insisted that their anti-bullfighting policies were still a major plank of the manifesto. There was to be no back-pedalling at this late stage, with only four days to go until the election. Blanco's murder might have been an embarrassment for the Town Hall, and bullfighting might have been given a martyr figure, but the Delgado team had decided on a show of strength.

Cámara pushed through the crowds, his eyes darting from face to face, his senses alive and sharp. The sound of the beating drum from the *Anti-Taurino* League was barely audible above the din of the thousands of people streaming through the gates and into the portico walkway that circled the outside of the bullring. Moreno caught his eye as he walked past their position.

'Come to check it out again?' he said, cocking his head. 'I wouldn't bother – the bulls are all doped up to their eyeballs anyway.'

Cámara moved on. Next to Moreno, Marta was pulling her megaphone up to her mouth to begin a new tirade.

Alicia wasn't at the entrance waiting for him as she'd promised, and in the end he had to wave his badge at the ticket girl and force his way in – something he could have done anyway, but he preferred the idea of slipping in just like any other member of the public. Word would get out eventually that the policeman heading the Blanco case was there.

A hand grabbed his arm and jerked him to one side.

'You found it, then?'

Alicia was wearing a low-buttoned cream blouse with a high collar, and a tan suede jacket. Gold earrings with shiny red gemstones dangled around her exposed neck. She smiled at Cámara.

'Our seats are just here. We need to go: it's about to start.'

She led Cámara by the arm down a wide tunnel before they came out into the sunshine of the bullring. Stepping up a small stone staircase, they passed through a gate of painted wood and into the very first row of seats, just above the *callejón* passageway where the bullfighters moved around the ring before stepping out into the arena itself.

'We certainly couldn't be any closer,' Cámara said.

'Not unless you wanted to jump in there and have a go with the bulls yourself,' said Alicia.

They squeezed in among the other spectators and sat on a wooden bench with a proper back and armrests. Not only the best seats for viewing the spectacle, but the most comfortable as well: a few rows higher up this level of luxury came to an end and people had to make do with stone benches, softened only by plastic-covered cushions hired from one of the stalls near the entrance.

Many of the men were wearing jackets and ties, while some of the women, Cámara noticed, had come in black, or sombre-coloured dresses, taking advantage of the below-average temperatures to take out their fur coats for one final outing before being mothballed till the following winter. The ubiquitous cigar smoke, hanging thickly in the air above their heads, was mingled with sweet-scented perfumes and rich colognes.

Yet despite there being a seriousness about the afternoon, the atmosphere was anything but solemn. A woman sitting next to him carefully placed her *mantón de Manila* – a flowery, embroidered silk shawl – over the barrier in front of them, as was the custom, and then pulled out a black-and-white photograph of Blanco from her bosom and pinned it to the top. She smiled as she did so: she was here to commemorate the life of a great bullfighter, more to remember him than to mourn for his loss.

Cámara wondered aloud about Carmen Luna coming. He'd forgotten to ask her that morning.

'She made a statement saying she wouldn't be here,' Alicia said. 'I'm glad. This is for the bullfighting world to pay its respects to one of its greatest artists. She's had her moment.'

Cámara took in the rest of the faces around him, sweeping across the bullring to the other sections, glancing up and down: in the cheaper seats, in *Sol*, he detected a similar ambience: more men wearing hats than might otherwise be the case; the women taking more care to make themselves up for the event.

And all the while he was thinking, Was *he* here, their man? Somewhere, among the thousands, he might be close by at that very moment.

The last spectators were taking their seats as the trumpets sounded and the *Puerta de Cuadrillas* – the main doors to the bullring – were opened. The first to ride out were a couple of men dressed in black velvet eighteenth-century-style costumes, with white ruff collars and long, elegant feathers quivering in their caps. They rode to just below the president's box, saluted him and then circled around the arena. Cámara glanced up expecting to see Pardo's face there, in his usual spot as overseer of the event. But he was surprised to see the city's Civil Governor in his place. Perhaps a mere police commissioner had been deemed insufficient for this special bullfight: only the top representative of the government in Madrid would do.

At his side, Alicia leaned in, pressing her body against his.

'These horsemen,' she explained, 'are the *alguacilillos*.'

'I've never quite understood what this bit is about,' Cámara said.

'It's a throwback to the past when bullfights took place in public squares,' she said. 'The city authorities – the *alguaciles* – had to clear the public away, push them back to the sides to create a space, before the event could start. So this is an echo of that.'

Cámara pulled out his packet of Ducados and lit one.

'Are you going to turn this into a lesson in how to watch a bullfight?' he said. 'I have a strong suspicion that you're trying to convert me.'

Alicia grinned.

'There's always hope,' she said.

Once the *alguacilillos* had finished, the main procession of bullfighters into the ring commenced. In the lead, their right arms wrapped in brightly coloured capes, came the three matadors, then behind them the members of their *cuadrillas* – *banderilleros* and picadors – followed by the *monosabios*, the picadors' helpers, the *areneros*, whose job it was to rake the sand after each fight, and finally the *mozos* with the mules used for pulling the dead bulls out of the ring.

Each detail of this was explained to Cámara by Alicia, but he had become more interested by one of the matadors at the front of the procession. Alejandro Cano was standing to the left of the trio.

'He'll be the first one,' Alicia explained to him. 'He'll take the first bull, as the most experienced bullfighter here today.'

Cámara pulled on his cigarette.

'Are you surprised?' Alicia said.

'Blanco took his *apoderado* away from him – a man who is also dead, but I notice no one seems to be remembering him this afternoon.'

He glanced at the spectators behind them – all eyes were on the bullfighters in the ring.

'All I've heard about the two men is that they were great rivals.'

'Blanco and Cano were opposites in many ways,' Alicia said. 'But that's probably what links them so strongly. Cano the socialite, womaniser, very much a public figure. And a showman in the ring. He's aware of the audience in a way that Blanco wasn't. With Blanco there was just him and the bull. I think that's what made him so special: you felt, when you were watching him, that you were somehow present at a private, almost secret act of communion between him and the animal. He fought for himself, set himself against his own high standards, and that's where the spark for him came from. And it was reflected in how he was outside the bullring – never showy, always preferring to keep to himself.'

Cámara thought of Aguado for a moment; he wondered how he was coping with a life without Blanco.

'But bullfighting in some ways is about opposites coming together,' Alicia continued. 'The man and the bull, the brute strength of the animal pitted against the intelligence of the human.'

She placed a hand on his arm.

'Things that are apparently opposite are not always working against each other,' she said. 'Besides, Cano was there at Blanco's last fight: he's part of the Blanco story.

Without him here this afternoon Blanco's memory would be ill served.'

A familiar face in the crowd drew Cámara's eye.

'I take it the bulls today are Ramírez ones as well, then,' he said.

'Yes,' Alicia said. 'It's all been arranged in a hurry. Other bullfighters, other bulls were meant to be here today. But under the circumstances . . .' She paused, then smiled. 'You're learning fast, I see.'

'Not so much that,' Cámara said. 'I've just spotted Ramírez and Son over to your right.'

Alicia turned her head. A few yards from their seats Francisco Ramírez and his son Paco were sitting, like them, in the front row. Paco was glancing down to one of the *mozos* in the *callejón* below, while his father stared blankly out at the ring.

'No sign of Roberto, then,' Cámara said.

'It's unlikely he would come to something like this,' Alicia said, giving him a look. 'Besides, I heard he jetted off back to New York the day after the funeral.'

The procession had ended by this point, and their conversation was interrupted by the sight of Cano passing through the barriers into the *callejón* and making a beeline towards them, brushing aside with nods and smiles the people who were trying to attract his attention.

Alicia leaned over as he stepped up to where they were sitting and they kissed each other on the cheeks.

'Chief Inspector Max Cámara,' she said, introducing the two men. 'Alejandro Cano.'

Cámara felt a warm, welcoming hand shaking his: no cold sweat, no apparent nerves in a man about to fight an enormous, violent beast to the death. Cano was dressed in a deep burgundy-red *traje de luces*.

'I wanted to thank you for your generosity the other afternoon as president,' Cano said. 'The ear you presented me was perhaps only partially earned.'

Cámara paused before answering: was the man making fun of him, or was this genuine humility on his part?

'I'm a poor judge,' he said at last. 'I followed my advisors that afternoon as best I could.'

'If you've come to learn more then you couldn't be in better hands,' Cano said with a smile for Alicia. 'There are few people – men or women – with a greater knowledge of bullfighting than Alicia.'

He reached out and grasped Alicia's arm in what appeared to be a naturally affectionate gesture.

'I'm still not sure how much about our national fiesta the chief inspector wants to know,' Alicia said. 'I suspect he's here more as a policeman than a potential aficionado.'

'Yes,' Cano said, the smile dropping momentarily from his face. 'I understand. Bullfighting is cruel. But for a person of sufficient sensitivity it can also be something else. Given the right moment – the right bull, the right torero, the right day.'

His *mozo de espadas* stood behind him holding his pink and yellow *capote* for the first part of the fight. Cano turned to him and allowed the man to open it out and then hand it to him.

'If there's anything you need, Chief Inspector,' he said before stepping away. 'Anything at all. Blanco was very dear to me. Ruiz Pastor as well. I feel their loss as intensely as anyone here. More so, even. We need to catch the madman who did this.'

He shook hands with him again, and then strode off, glancing out at the ring as the horns blew once more: the first bull of the afternoon was about to appear.

The first two sections of the bullfight passed without incident. In the *Tercio de Varas* the bullfighters tested the bull with their *capotes*, executing elegant *verónicas* and *chicuelas*, getting a sense of its strengths and tendencies. The more *bravo* the bull, Alicia explained in Cámara's ear, the more it would stand near the centre of the ring, dominating, challenging the bullfighters to take it on. A more *manso* bull would tend to stay on the outside of the arena, or close to the gate from which it had entered – the *Puerta del Toril* – as though trying to escape. All this would have a bearing on how the matador would fight the bull at the end.

This initial section ended quickly, however, the bullfighters retreated and the picadors came out on their well-padded horses and the bull was urged to charge at them. This part had always seemed the most meaningless and cruel to Cámara, the heavy picador pushing his lance as deeply as he could into the bull's shoulders, while around him the audience whistled and shouted loudly in protest.

'I agree, it isn't always very attractive,' Alicia said. 'But it's for two reasons. First to get a sense of how strong the bull is: does he charge headlong at the horse, or does he have to be coaxed to do so? And secondly, you have to take some of the bull's strength away, to make him lower his head. Otherwise it would be virtually impossible to fight him.'

The whistling from the crowd intensified as the picador went to thrust at the bull for a second time.

'But the crowd don't want the bull to be weakened too

much,' Alicia went on. 'That's why they complain at this point.'

'You aficionados talk about this being about a man pitted against a mighty beast,' Cámara said. 'But it seems the odds are always stacked against the bull.'

But Alicia wasn't listening, standing up out of her seat along with most of the rest of the crowd as the picador went for a third, and highly unpopular, thrust. Everyone looked up at the president, waiting for him to give the signal for this *tercio* to end. Cámara remembered having to place the white handkerchief over the edge of the balcony himself at this stage, but he'd merely been taking orders from the two sitting next to him, understanding little of what was actually going on.

Finally the sign was made, the horns blew, and the picadors walked their horses out of the ring, leaving the bull on his own. Time for the next section, the *Tercio de Banderillas*. This was the one part of the event that for Cámara seemed to have some kind of artistry to it, even if it meant further torture of the bull. With brightly coloured darts in their hands, about a metre in length, the toreros seemed to carry out a kind of dance in front of the bull, finally planting the *banderillas* in its back as they dodged within inches of its horns. This, according to Alicia, was designed to bring a bit of life back into the animal, the *banderillas* acting as a colourful spectacle meant to spur the bull on after the punishment of the picadors, before the final section, when the matador would face him alone.

The *banderilleros* came and went, and the bull stood in the middle of the ring, with their red, yellow and blue darts hanging from his neck almost like a Red Indian's headdress.

Voices were lowered as the final moment approached, the *Tercio de Muerte*. Cámara watched as Cano was handed his red *muleta* cape and *estoque* – the same kind of sword with a slight curve at the end that had been used in the killings of both Blanco and Ruiz Pastor – and stepped out on to the sand. He stood for a moment in front of the president's box, with his *montera* cap in hand, asking for permission to begin, and then once that had been given, he started walking towards the section of the ring where Cámara and Alicia were sitting.

'This is when he dedicates the bull to someone,' Alicia said. 'He can do it either to an individual, or to the entire crowd.'

Cano crossed the sand and stood at the edge of the *burladero* just in front of them, looking in their direction. Cámara glanced around him to see who Cano was about to dedicate the bull to, wondering if it might be for Alicia at his side. He smiled, but as Cano stood there expectantly, he felt Alicia nudge him in the ribs.

'Stand up,' she ordered. 'It's for you.'

He felt several thousand eyes turn towards him as he got to his feet.

'You honour us by being here, Chief Inspector,' Cano called out from the arena, stepping through the *burladero* and handing his *montera* to him. Cámara felt the hat's tight curly astrakhan fabric rubbing against his fingers as he reached down for it.

'It is my honour to be here,' he said, uttering the first thing that came into his head. Then Cano held his arms out towards him and the two men embraced.

'I loved Blanco as a brother,' Cano said in his ear as the

audience around them broke into applause. 'And I will fight this bull in his name.'

Cámara's attention was fully on the fight for the first time now as Cano crossed the sand again and focused on the bull. The burgundy of his *traje de luces* stood out against the bright yellow of the sand and seemed to echo the blood that was dripping off the bull's back and falling in dark patches at its feet. Cano arranged the *muleta* and his sword and took a few steps towards the animal's horns. He gave a cry and thrust the cape in the bull's direction. At first it didn't move, pausing before pawing the ground in anger. Again Cano flicked the red cape. This time it responded, lowering its head and suddenly charging at him. Deftly, Cano swept the *muleta* to one side and the bull passed within inches of his body. Turning on his heel, Cano flicked the *muleta* towards the bull on his other side, and again the animal charged, pushing forwards with his horns, passing even closer to the man this time as Cano gracefully passed the cape in front of him, slowing the bull down, never allowing the horns to actually touch the cloth. Again a turn, and again the bull thrust itself against the *muleta*.

The first shouts of *olé* were being heard from the crowd by now and Cámara could feel how the concentration of the entire audience was fixed upon the dance that the man and the bull were performing in front of them. What was most extraordinary was that Cano had barely moved from his spot, keeping his feet planted firmly on the ground as the bull was made to pass him first on one side and then the other, circling around him as though the man had become a pillar in the sand, dominating the bull, making it move wherever and whenever he pleased, in total control.

And as he watched, for a second, for a moment that was lost almost as soon as it came, something extraordinary happened. It was as if the division between Cano and the bull had disappeared, as though for a fleeting instant they had become one single being out there on the sand, unified by their fight and struggle: one entity separated not by their mutual wish to kill each other but almost as if by a kind of tenderness, a passion. It was as if, for a brief time, matador and bull were brought together and joined through something that felt almost like love. But it was not any kind of love that Cámara had ever sensed or been aware of before, nothing he had ever known. And yet it was there, binding them and making them one.

It came in a flash, one exceptional moment, and then was gone. But the entire crowd had captured it as well, and a roar went up. Many were on their feet, clapping already, shouts of *olé* echoing around the ring. At the other side of the arena the band started up on a paso doble. People shouted and cried out: the maestro had come and shown them his best; up above, Blanco would be smiling.

The bull had come to a standstill, its energy seemingly gone, and Cano stood as close as he could before its once powerful and feared horns, thrusting his chest out, before spinning around majestically and making a sweep with his *estoque*. The audience cheered: the beast had been beaten.

Cámara felt as if he were in a trance. Something had just happened, something he struggled to identify or explain, but which had gripped him for a moment and then gone. It was absurd: the bull and the man were intent on killing one another; how could anything that was happening down on the sand have anything to do with love? Yet he failed to find any other word accurately to describe what he had experienced.

He watched as Cano went through a few more passes, wondering if it would come back, if he would feel the same, but although the atmosphere inside the bullring was now alive in a very special sense, it failed to reappear quite as strongly. By the time Cano pulled out his sword to finish the bull off, Cámara had turned his head. Something magical had occurred, but he didn't need to see this.

Minutes later, with two trophy ears in his hands, Cano re-entered the *callejón*. He handed the ears to his *mozo* and then walked back to where Cámara and Alicia were sitting. Hands reached over the barrier from the audience in order to pat him on the back.

'I'm glad you got to see that,' Cano said as he paused in front of them. 'Those moments are all too rare.'

Alicia reached out and touched his arm.

'Blanco deserved nothing less.'

FOURTEEN

When you choose to put your life on the line,
you also earn the right to choose other things
José Tomás

A roar from the crowd inside the bullring hurtled down the stone steps and bounced off the brick walls as Cámara paced the empty corridor behind the seating area, smoking and enjoying a cool breeze. The smell of *buñuelos* – hot, sweet, battered pumpkin purée freshly fried, a *Fallas* delicacy – was inescapable now, with half a dozen stalls lining the sides of Xàtiva. This was one of the few main roads still fully open. Elsewhere, in the remaining streets that hadn't been cut off completely, the cars had to steer carefully around *falla* statues like multicoloured kerbs of a chicane. Yet here the great city fiesta was still overwhelmingly present: teenage boys were throwing exploding *chinos* at each other, while most people were wearing the blue-and-white chequered neckerchief of the *falleros*. Occasionally a *fallera* beauty queen would appear, walking hurriedly in her flowery period dress as she dashed to some official ceremony. For a part of the world that had thrown away so much of its architectural heritage, the city went to great lengths to hang on to its traditions when it came to fiestas and folkloric costumes.

Inside the corridor, a middle-aged woman with an overhanging gut was sweeping up behind one of the bars that had been serving drinks and cigars. Cámara had seen enough for one afternoon and had decided to go for a stroll. Leaving Alicia, he'd found refuge in the emptiness of the passageway. Briefly, when he was in his late teens in Albacete, he'd worked as a gatekeeper at a football stadium, and he'd enjoyed the sensation of being close to some great emotional event taking place just a few yards away, yet being separated from it at the same time. It was, he'd realised, a moment for savouring the calm which, curiously, seemed to exist at the edges of so much passion.

The woman with the broom lifted her head and gave him a look as he stood there pondering. Without realising, he'd been staring at her for a few minutes, his mind drifting. He sniffed and turned to walk away.

The floor was littered with the blackened butts of home-made *caliqueño* cigars as he made his way to the upper level and the next corridor above. From here he had an even better view of the street outside.

Cámara pulled out his cigarettes, but shaking the packet he realised there were none left. Cursing, he screwed it up. Alicia would have some back inside, but the fight was still going on and once he'd squeezed past all those people to get to her he'd be obliged to stay. Better to remain out here enjoying the sensation of being set apart from the crowd. Silence was an impossibility in Valencia at this time of year, yet caught between the bullfight inside, and the fiesta outside, he felt that he'd found a temporary home – neither one nor the other. A no-man's land.

He began scouting around to see if any of the bars were still open and if they sold tobacco. The corridor led around the side of the building until he came to the west side flanked by the Calle Alicante. Was that an opening in the wall he could spot further down? He continued for a few more yards then slowed to a halt: there was nothing here. Perhaps downstairs again. The woman with the broom at the bar might be able to help.

He drifted to the edge of the passageway, looking out over the street before heading off. Hundreds of people flowed backwards and forwards below him like tight currents in a troubled sea.

Something caught his eye. Below, in the triangle of space between the outer edge of the bullring and the road, sat a lorry. It was blocking almost the entire space, but there was room just to slip past, as he could make out from where he was standing. To the side was a building set at right-angles to the bullring. At the edge of its outer wall, running very close to the bullring itself was a drainpipe – one of the older metal ones, square rather than rounded and with sturdy brackets every metre or so supporting it. Above it, where the top of the building touched the edge of the outer bull-ring wall, was a fan-like metal structure just over a metre across made up of steel spikes thrusting out horizontally, designed – it appeared – to dissuade any would-be intruders from trying to climb in. Cámara stepped in closer to have a look: the 'spikes' were no more threatening than the monkey bars he'd swung on as a child in the school play-ground, while the drainpipe made for an easy route both in and out of the bullring. Slip down there, invisible at this time of year thanks to the lorry blocking the view, and you

191

could emerge into the street without anyone noticing you at all. While across the street were a couple of green plastic rubbish containers – ideally placed.

The sound of piercing whistles penetrated through from inside the bullring: the picadors must have made a return. He took a last look at the drainpipe and walked off to find some more cigarettes, flicking his phone open and dialling Huerta's number.

The back of her hand brushed against his as they walked towards the Plaza San Agustín: it felt warm, smooth. Tonight was the *Plantà* – the official start of *Fallas*. But that was no more than a formality these days – almost every statue and street bar had been set up and in place for at least a week beforehand.

'I know a place in the Barrio Chino,' Alicia had said as they left the bullring together.

They stopped at one of the stalls and ordered half a dozen *buñuelos* to share, licking their fingers clean of the sugar as they lifted them into their mouths, laughing.

'I used to love these when I was a girl,' Alicia said. 'Eat hundreds of them every year. That was when I could afford to, though.' And she patted her thighs.

'I was the *fallera* beauty queen of our street one year,' she said. 'My elder brother was president of the panel. I think he fixed it so that they would choose me. Of course, as a thirteen-year-old it was the best moment of my life, putting on all those dresses and make-up. My mother spent four months solid sewing so it would all be ready on time.'

They turned off the square and started heading down

Barón de Cárcel Avenue. It was almost dark, and the usual night workers were starting to appear, waiting for the early-evening customers.

'It was when I had my first kiss,' Alicia went on. 'Ramón Martínez. He was fifteen, the leader of our group.'

'What happened to him?' Cámara asked.

'He married my best friend.' She laughed. 'A few years later, of course. They had a boy – he's at university now; can't remember what he's studying. I saw Ramón for the first time in years only a month or so back. He told me what he'd been up to.'

'And what did you tell him?'

'Not much.' She sighed.

A dark-skinned woman was watching them from the side of the pavement as they walked slowly forwards. Standing under the harsh light of a street lamp, she wore black shiny platform boots that laced up to her knee, above which torn fishnet stockings barely covered her thighs. The black leather miniskirt seemed little more than an afterthought, while her breasts bulged over the top of a red plastic basque. She smiled at Cámara as he caught her eye, her teeth brilliant white against the heavy tan of her face.

'¿*Buscáis algo*?'

They walked on, pretending they hadn't heard. From her accent Cámara suspected she might be Caribbean.

'The bull represents male sexual energy,' Alicia said as they slid back into the shade, away from the burning fluorescent of the street lamp. 'In the bullfight. I'm sure you've already worked that out, though.'

'So why kill it?' Cámara asked.

'I didn't manage to convert you this afternoon,' she said.

'No wonder you went off wandering about on your own. Did you find anything?'

'Secret,' Cámara said.

'Ooh, how exciting. The answer to your question, my dear,' she said without pausing for breath, 'is that the matador is supposed to absorb the potency from the bull he kills; he takes on the animal's fertility.'

Cámara felt a weight crushing him like a rock. Instinctively the hand in his pocket pushed down and over to feel the edge of his testicles, useless sacks hanging between his legs. Had he really forgotten about all that? For a moment he thought he had, but he knew that part of him was always dwelling on it. Somewhere inside him a fundamental reason for living had been taken away.

'I found out a secret about you the other day,' Alicia said. The first cars were beginning to kerb-crawl. Valencia had one of the longest traditions in Europe for taking a more liberal attitude to the sex trade – a red-light district had been in existence since the fourteenth century. But some morally outraged civil governor during Franco's time had decided to ban it. So the girls had simply walked out on to the streets below their brothels, not even bothering to change *barrio*, and here they had stayed ever since. Cruising at this festive time of year had become something of a tradition, and instead of *falleras,* the working girls were sometimes referred to as *folleras* – women who fuck.

Cámara already knew the answer, but he felt compelled to ask.

'What did you discover?'

'Allegations of misconduct in an interrogation, going too far,' Alicia said with open eyes and an expression of intrigue.

Cámara frowned.

'I hadn't thought it warranted a news story.'

'Oh, I didn't get it looking through back copies of *El Diario*, if that's what you mean.'

Then: 'You shouldn't worry about it,' Alicia said, trying to defuse the sudden tension. 'I suppose things can get heated when you're dealing with a vicious murderer—'

'I got caught,' Cámara interrupted her. 'That's what counts. It's not because of what I did; they don't care about it for any moral reason. It's because I got caught.'

'What was the guy's name? Pedro Bautista? Stabbed his wife to death. Brutal case. How did you know they were filming the interrogation?'

'Yes, all right.'

'I suppose you thought those cameras never got switched on.'

Cámara pretended he hadn't heard.

'Broke his jaw, I heard.'

'OK, so you've done your research!' Cámara raised his fist to his mouth. 'Congratulations. Is that why you asked me out to—?'

She pulled his arm down, stopping him as they walked, then leaned over and kissed him, her lips wrapping quickly and delicately around his mouth, tongue flicking gently against his.

'Let's go and get a drink,' she said.

She took him deep into the Barrio Chino – no longer the drug-filled haunt it had once been, but still an edgy, slightly decrepit part of the city. They stood at a grubby bar with broken green-and-white tiles on the walls and floor, waiting for one of the tables in the booths on the other side of the room to become free. Alicia ordered a sweet *anís*; Cámara a Carlos III. For a moment their fingertips played against each other beneath the bar, until an elderly couple got up to leave and they were able to sit down.

'What were you saying about all that symbolism of the bullfight?' Cámara said, trying to find something to say: neither had said a word since their mouths had touched in the street. He noticed a silver ring on the little finger of her left hand, the figure of a dolphin curling itself around her knuckle.

'You should talk to an expert about that,' she said. 'I don't know too much about it, but there's a woman at Castilla-La Mancha University. Margarita de la Fuente. Written a couple of books about it.'

She seemed businesslike with him all of a sudden. For a brief moment they had come close, and now had retreated. Cámara watched her face closely as she spoke, his vision coming to rest on her lips. Would he like her to kiss him again? Did he want to kiss her?

'Are you listening?' she asked with a smile.

'Yes, of course,' Cámara said.

'They do good food here,' Alicia said. 'I know it doesn't look much, but we can stay and have a bite if you want. Perhaps a quick dinner?'

Cámara looked over at the woman behind the bar, with her lank dyed-blonde hair and greasy blue-and-white apron, staring up at the TV on the wall above the door. She could make them some *tortilla a la patata* perhaps, with maybe some cuttlefish and garlic shrimps. He nodded.

'Looks like the best kind of place,' he said.

'Good. Then we'll get some wine. The heavy stuff,' she

pointed down at their drinks, 'is all right on its own but not with food.'

She got up to talk to the woman behind the bar, and came back with a bottle of local Valencia wine. Cámara picked the glass up and took a sip, expecting a sharp and unpleasant taste, but the wine flowed smoothly over his tongue, strong and rich.

'It's time I mentioned the secret I found out about you,' he said. She glared back at him.

'About your divorce.'

She frowned.

'These things happen,' she said. 'Javier's a *golfo* – got an eye for the girls. But that's why I liked him.' She took a last drink of *anís* before pushing the glass to one side and pulling the wine glass closer to her. 'Or at least at the beginning.'

'No kids,' Cámara said.

'Are you asking me, or telling me?' she said.

'Well, I know you don't have any. At least, that's what the report said.'

'There you go, then.' She forced a smile. 'Let's not talk about that.'

Cámara's thoughts wandered for a moment, images of Almudena appearing unbidden in his mind which he tried to banish with only partial success.

'Do you still see your husband?' he asked.

'He's my boss,' she said. 'Indirectly, I suppose. At *El Diario*. Well, you know that already. I try to avoid him inside the office as best I can, but sometimes he comes to my desk, seeks me out, says he just wants to chat and that kind of thing.'

'Is it just that kind of thing?'

'You sound jealous.'

'Just asking,' Cámara said.

'I'm not in love with him any more. Not for years. A long time before all that business with the girl. I'm not kidding myself, though. I know he'd jump back into bed with me again if he could. But I closed all that off long ago. No return.'

'Did you see him this morning?'

She smiled at him, pushing a stray hair behind her ear.

'Is it the man I just kissed asking, or Chief Inspector Cámara?'

Cámara didn't answer.

'No,' she said at last. 'The last time I saw him was the day Blanco died. He came to my desk just after Blanco called me. You know, saying he had something to tell me, about doing an interview.'

'Did you mention it to Javier?'

She sighed.

'Yes, Chief Inspector, I did. I thought he should reserve some space for the next day's edition. I knew it was going to be a big story. Any interview with Blanco was a big story because he never gave any.'

She swallowed a large mouthful of wine, then uncorked the bottle again and filled their glasses.

'In the end they used all that space to cover his death. And more; I think they cut some pages that night from the international section to make it all fit in.'

The woman came round from behind the bar and placed a basket of bread on the table in front of them, cutlery clattering on the oilcloth top as she dropped them from underneath her arm.

'Don't worry,' Alicia said as she sorted them out, pushing a knife and fork in Cámara's direction. But the woman wasn't apologising.

'There,' she said, banging a plate of potato omelette down and turning to walk back to the bar. 'The rest is coming.'

The tortilla had already been cut up into squares and Cámara picked up his fork and started. Alicia was already grabbing at the bread.

'*Bon profit*,' she said.

'All that bloodshed has given me an appetite,' Cámara said.

The tortilla was perfect, made with onion as well as potato, and still just a little moist where the egg had yet to cook all the way through. Cámara's eyes rolled with pleasure.

'*Riquísimo.*'

'I told you,' Alicia said.

He reached over and took a sip of wine.

'Thank you for bringing me here. I had no idea it existed.'

'Blanco brought me here the first time,' she said. 'Must have been over ten years ago. When he was still a *novillero*. I'd seen him fight a couple of times before, but the evening we came here was special. The way he'd fought that afternoon told me – this kid has got something. And I wrote about it that night. The review was picked up by everyone. No one had spotted him before. But here was I, this female bullfight correspondent saying we had a new genius of the bullfight on our hands. Many laughed – they thought I didn't have a clue. But Blanco always remembered that article – it's why he was more open with me than with any other journalist. He trusted me because he knew I could see what he had. Long before everyone else joined in and started to realise. That article put us both on the map.'

'You sound as if you were half in love with him,' Cámara said.

'I was, but not in any way you'd understand. I was in love with the bullfighter, the person out there in the ring. Not with the man himself. There was never anything like that between us. Not even a spark. But when he was in front of a bull, I could have followed him for ever. There was something so strong, so determined about him that I admired. Almost bull-like himself, in some ways. Stubborn. Once he'd put his mind to something . . .'

Cámara stretched his leg over under the table and pressed it against hers. She stopped talking.

The air was cool on their faces as they stepped out into the street a few minutes later. A brief play-scuffle over who should pay had given them further excuse to press their bodies against each other. Alicia tried to push him out of the way as she insisted that as a regular she should pick up the bill, but Cámara put his arm around her and held her tight against him, preventing her from reaching her purse as he whipped out a handful of notes with his free hand and placed them on the counter of the bar. The woman with the lank hair had finally smiled at them as she handed over the change.

'Great place,' Cámara said, filling his lungs. 'We should come again.'

They took a few steps away from the entrance and found themselves in the shadow of the doorway of an abandoned building.

'Oh,' Alicia said, pulling up towards him. 'I'm sure we shall.'

Desire pulsed heavily under his skin as he slipped a hand

into the small of her back and lifted her closer to press his mouth against hers. He felt her teeth nibbling at his lips, her fingers pressing into the flesh of his shoulders as she allowed herself to be enveloped in his embrace.

'I want you,' she whispered as their lips parted for a second. He wrapped his arms tighter around her waist.

With his eyes closed, at first he thought the flash had come from the headlights of a car trying to wend its way up the narrow, uneven street. When it burst again, however, he looked and turned instinctively towards the clicking noise coming from just a few yards away.

'¿*Qué cojones*? What the fuck?'

He pulled himself away from Alicia's embrace as the photographer took one more snap of them and began to back away.

'Hey!' Cámara shouted.

'What's going on?' Alicia was still lost in the kiss, hardly aware that their moment of passion was being recorded.

'Son of a bitch.'

Cámara took a few steps in the direction of the footsteps now running away down the alley. It was dark and he hadn't been able to see who it was. Should he run after him? By the time he asked himself the question it was already too late. The photographer appeared briefly in the fluorescent lights of the avenue at the end of the street, then disappeared as he turned away from view.

Alicia was standing behind him, her hand slipping across to grab his arm.

'Was that guy taking photos of us?' she asked incredulously.

Cámara breathed heavily, his blood racing.

There was no sign of the photographer when they reached the avenue: just a new set of whores working the later shift. They stood silently for a moment under the light of one of the lamps, Cámara wondering to himself what happened now. Before he could answer, he heard a car pull up behind and turned: Alicia had hailed a passing taxi.

He leaned over and opened the door for her to get in. She kissed him on the cheek and then stepped inside.

'Tomorrow,' she said. 'Not tonight. Not now, after this. I want it to be—'

'It's OK,' he said.

'Come to my place,' she said. 'I'll fix us something.'

'I'll call you.'

She closed the taxi door and wound down the window, smiling at him as the taxi indicated to pull away.

'I didn't know you were such a celebrity,' she said.

FIFTEEN

For bullfighting, as for marriage, the secret is getting up close
Traditional

Thursday 16th March

The slapping of domino pieces on the hard tabletops created a pattering sound inside the bar that seemed to echo the splashing of heavy raindrops on the pavement outside. Cámara shook the water from his coat, causing a small puddle to form for a moment around his feet before being absorbed by the dirty sawdust that was quickly forming into earth-like clods on the floor. He ordered a *carajillo* and turned to look around, double-checking that he had arrived first as the coffee machine gave a high-pitched scream before the barman smacked it with his hand and it shuddered back into life. Just the usual groups of old men, waiting their turn to clap their little black-and-white rectangles down with all the bravado they could muster. The roads had been clear and he had got there early: Margarita should be arriving in the next five or ten minutes.

It had been the first place that had come to mind when she asked where they should meet. Only after he'd put the phone down did it seem an odd choice. He hadn't been back to Albacete for three or four months now. And when he did come he usually went straight to the flat, not bothering to waste any time in the centre of town. So it must have been years since he'd last seen this place, perhaps even a decade or more since he'd been inside. It had been a regular haunt of theirs when he was younger, Hilario joining in some of the domino games, Cámara wandering around the tables, receiving the occasional consolatory pat on the head from some, a cold shoulder from others. Those were the ones Hilario never spoke to – or even about. Cámara had tried a couple of times to get his grandfather to explain, but the old man had always clammed up. Forbidden territory.

He'd left his car in an underground car park. His Seat Ibiza was nearing the end of its natural life, and an hour-and-a-half journey like this was about the most it could manage these days. It was almost fifteen years old, and the clutch cable – already its third – didn't feel as tight as it should. He'd have to get it changed, but somehow he felt that if he used it for anything more than pottering around Valencia, or the odd trip up here, it would let him down. It felt like an elderly donkey or mule, with set habits. Make it divert from the routine and it would probably breathe its last.

Albacete didn't have much in the way of monuments. When they were boys, Cámara and his friends had dreamt of moving away. For anyone with any spark about them, life happened elsewhere, that much they understood. Some set their hearts on reaching Madrid, others Valencia on the coast. And at least half of them had made it in the end.

If anyone from outside had heard of Albacete it was either for the knives that the city made, supposedly the finest in all Spain. Or for it being the headquarters of the

International Brigades during the Civil War. As a boy Cámara had often wondered if they'd only been sent here in order to keep them out of the way, although he'd heard later that they had suffered the highest casualty rates in the whole conflict. Doubtless many had wondered what the hell they'd come here for once they'd seen where they were to be billeted.

From the corner of his eye he spotted a movement near the door. He turned to see a stocky woman in a raincoat and wide-brimmed hat trying to shake herself dry. The cut of her short grey hair and the half-steamed glasses pressed high up her nose gave little room for doubt who she was. He took a step in her direction and she spotted him, walking towards him with small, delicate footsteps and a wide smile on her face.

'*Profesora* de la Fuente.'

'Margarita, please.'

'You'll be wanting something hot,' Cámara said.

'They do a very good *carajillo* here,' she said.

Cámara smiled.

'A proper one. Not just a *café solo* with a splash of whisky or cognac in it.'

He lifted his half-empty glass, the toasted coffee bean still floating around the top.

'Ah,' she said. 'I see you've beaten me to it.'

Cámara signalled to the waiter that they were going to go and sit down at a small table in a quieter part of the bar, and they shuffled through the steaming, smoky air, hanging their coats up on a couple of hooks on the wall.

'So,' Margarita said as they sat down. Her face looked brighter without the hat, Cámara noticed. There was a playful curiosity in her eyes. Probably in her late fifties, unmarried, if the absence of a wedding ring indicated anything. He'd been concerned she might be a dry, pompous academic, but there was a liveliness there. 'Are you any closer to finding your killers?'

The use of the plural was clear and deliberate.

'Of course I've been following it in the newspapers,' she continued. 'Who hasn't? And once I received your phone call this morning I spent the whole time going back over the news reports. Of course I don't know how much information you're giving out.'

The barman came over with her *carajillo* and placed it down on the table in front of them along with a couple of biscuits on a small plate.

'Thought you might like those to go with it,' he said.

Margarita smiled at him.

'They treat me well,' she said. 'Not many women come in here – it's a bit of a man's bar, as you've seen. But my father was a bullfighter in his time and he and a group of aficionados used to come here regularly for the *tertulia* after the fight – talking and analysing the afternoon's bullfight well into the early hours. So they have a soft spot for me.'

Cámara tried to remember if there had been a girl there when he had come in with Hilario all those years before. But Margarita would have been a grown woman by then, probably exploring worlds other than this.

'This conversation and our meeting,' Cámara said with a lowered voice, 'are not entirely official.'

'Oh, I gathered as much.'

'Not that there's anything wrong in it, but some of the people I work with are sticklers for doing everything by the book. You understand.'

Margarita nodded.

'So I have to be confident that what I tell you here doesn't go beyond this table.'

'I give you my word.'

'I'm sorry to have to be so circumspect, but it's just the way things are.'

She raised her *carajillo* in salute.

'However I can be of assistance to you. Really.'

'Thank you,' Cámara said. 'I appreciate it. Now what's been appearing in the newspapers is, as you've guessed, just part of what we know. But it seems to have been enough for you to reach your own conclusions about how many murderers we're talking about.'

'It was the mutilation of Blanco's *apoderado* – Ruiz Pastor – that got me thinking,' Margarita said. She took a sip of the *carajillo* and then put it down on the table. 'It is true, isn't it? What they say? That his genitals were removed?'

Again the image of the misshapen form floating in the Albufera lake flashed through Cámara's mind. He lowered his eyes.

'It is.'

'Yes, it's a delicate subject,' Margarita said, sensing his discomfort. 'And not just for a man, believe me.'

But more than you can imagine, Cámara thought to himself.

'This detail caught your attention, then,' he said aloud. 'Why?'

Margarita leaned in.

'I don't know how much you know about the symbolism behind bullfighting,' she said. Cámara shrugged. 'I assume that's why you're here, to pick my brains,' she went on. 'You

207

were lucky to catch me, in fact. I'm supposed to be speaking at a symposium on religious iconography in the Bronze Age in Rome. Except that the airline went bust at the last minute. There's a car coming tomorrow to drive me all the way to Madrid to catch another plane from there. They know how to treat their academics, those Italians.'

Cámara took out his packet of Ducados and offered one to Margarita. She smiled, then refused. Cámara lit his cigarette and blew out a stream of smoke. Another ex-smoker, he thought to himself.

'Anyway, you've got me here today, which is the important thing,' Margarita went on.

'I was told you were the leading expert,' Cámara said. 'And when I realised you were based in my old home town . . .'

'Look, this is a huge subject. You really can't understand the culture and history of this country without knowing something about bulls and bullfighting.'

Perhaps just a few days ago Cámara might have rejected her comment out of hand as just more pro-bullfighting rhetoric. Now he sat and listened.

'Great national writers and artists have recognised the truth of this,' Margarita continued, 'from Picasso to García Lorca to Ortega y Gasset. Something about bulls and the lore of bulls runs deeply in us. In folklore they often refer to the Iberian peninsula itself looking like the hide of an ox. While the tenth labour of Hercules – taming the bulls of Geryon – took place here, not in the lands of the Greeks.'

'OK,' Cámara said, trying to catch where this was all going.

'What I'm trying to get across,' Margarita said, 'is how

deeply rooted bull imagery and stories are in our culture. The Mesopotamians, Egyptians, Greeks and Romans all had important bull rites of one kind or another. You remember the pictures of the famous Minoan bull rituals in Crete, I'm sure.'

Images of scantily clad women jumping somersaults over bulls' backs passed through Cámara's mind. They must have made up some of the very first erotic visual representations he had ever come across.

'The point is,' Margarita said, 'that Spain is the only country to retain this contact with the ancient Mediterranean culture where bull rituals formed a part of everyday life. Yes, there's bullfighting in southern France and in Portugal, but here in Spain is where you find the real thing.'

Cámara was wondering when she was going to get to the point and explain how all this tied in with Ruiz Pastor's genitals being cut off. Not that it wasn't interesting. But the policeman in him was thinking about the investigation going on without him back in Valencia. He hadn't mentioned to Pardo he was disappearing for a while – effectively taking the morning off. Torres could keep things going for the time being. He'd give him a ring later on. As long as Margarita didn't take it too slowly he should be able to get back to Valencia by just after lunchtime. Perhaps even earlier.

'So I like to think of bullfighting as a rear-view mirror for human existence,' Margarita was saying.

Cámara raised his eyebrows. He was talking to an academic who specialised in symbolism; metaphors were her stock in trade. But this one went right over his head.

'I'm sorry.'

'Bullfighting tells us where we've come from, culturally.'

Margarita picked up one of the biscuits, broke it in two and then dipped the corner of one half into her *carajillo*.

'When you go to a bullfight,' she explained, 'you're allowing yourself a moment's communion with the Heroic Age – the world of Hercules, Theseus and the rest. So a bull represents where we come from, a world we left behind many, many centuries ago. But it also represents something deeply Spanish. And perhaps that is why Spain alone has retained this connection with its ancient bull rituals. Think about it: the stubbornness of the bull, its unwillingness to give in, even as more pain and suffering is laid upon it. And yet still it keeps running, keeps charging at the matador. Any other animal would crawl away and hide in a corner somewhere. That's why the spectacle is unique. You couldn't do this with any other beast. Not even an ordinary bull. It has to be a *toro de lidia*, a direct descendant of the ancient aurochs. But this is why I think we Spanish feel a connection with bulls – because we see ourselves in them, in their behaviour. The stubbornness, the pride, the unwillingness to give in, even if we're driving ourselves to our own deaths.'

Cámara smiled as he recognised the truth of what she was saying. Wasn't that a good description of himself? Didn't he ask himself often enough why he kept going? And yet somehow he believed deeply in the rightness of his police work. And so he went at it again, and again, doggedly, ignoring the obstacles that got in his way. Wasn't that him right there now with the Blanco case? Yet he carried on. He might have no interest in bullfighting, but the bull in him – his Spanishness – seemed inescapable.

'This really is fascinating,' he said, stubbing out his cigarette and leaning back in his chair.

'But what's it got to do with Blanco and Ruiz Pastor?' Margarita interjected. 'Yes, I'm getting to that.'

She drained the last of her *carajillo* and wiped her mouth with the back of her hand. There was a certain masculinity about her, Cámara realised, which made him feel at ease with her.

'Part of the ancient origins of bullfighting has to do with matters of sex, fertility and gender roles.' She marked the three elements off with the fingers of her right hand. 'In almost the entire ancient world bulls were associated with the sun. It's common in ancient cave paintings to see bulls portrayed with solar discs in between their horns. This bull–sun link is particularly evident from Mithraism – an ancient faith which was competing with Christianity to become the state religion of the Roman Empire at one stage. Like Christianity, it was a hotch potch of different ideas, but essentially for the followers of Mithras their god had to sacrifice a bull every morning to ensure the sun came up for another day. In that you have the elements of the bull, the sun, sacrifice and a kind of key for engaging with the cosmic order. All these are present in some form in the contemporary bullfight: the circular bullring, much like a solar disc; the death, or sacrifice, of the bull; even the bullfighter's costume is called *el traje de luces* – the suit of lights. So what we're probably dealing with here is the remnant of an ancient sacrificial ritual relating to sexuality and fertility, the bull being a symbol of male sexual potency.'

Cámara pursed his lips.

'You think there's some symbolic significance in the mutilation of Ruiz Pastor,' he said. 'Something to do with all this. He was emasculated.'

'I think there's a significance in what happened to Jorge Blanco,' she said. 'Am I right that something similar happened to him?'

'There was a deep cut near his genitals,' Cámara said. 'The murderer may have intended to remove them.'

'Look, there are various theories about gender roles in the bullfight,' Margarita said, 'but I subscribe to the theories of Julian Pitt-Rivers on this. Essentially he says that for the first two sections, or *tercios* of the corrida, the bull represents the male sexual role and the bullfighter the female. The bull is obvious, I think – all that power and aggression, the phallic symbolism of the horns etc. The bullfighter is less obvious, but the elements are there. Firstly, how many bearded bullfighters have you ever seen? None, exactly,' she said before waiting for a reply. 'The bullfighter is a paragon of masculinity in our culture, but for the first part of the bullfight at least he shows some decidedly feminine characteristics. In some ways you might even describe him as a femme fatale. His hat, the *montera*, looks very much like a female wig, while the *capote* – the pink and yellow cape he uses at the start – is very much like a skirt. Have you noticed how he always holds it at waist height and seems to use it to flirt with the bull? Then there's the rather odd way that he wears his trousers: so tight that you might see it as a way of emphasising his genitalia, and hence his masculinity. Yet to press them to one side and force the seam high up into the groin creates something resembling a vagina, does it not?'

Cámara tried to picture a bullfighter with his absurdly tight pants. A vagina? Perhaps it was pushing the point a little, but he could see what she was driving at.

'These feminine aspects are discarded, however, for the final act – the *Tercio de muerte*,' Margarita continued. 'Here the bullfighter discards his skirt-like capote, throws his wig-like *montera* to the ground and reaches for his *estoque*, thus transforming himself from feminine into masculine. And in that moment the roles are reversed. From now on the bull represents the female and the bullfighter is the arch-male, dominating and finally penetrating the bull-woman with his phallic sword.'

Margarita pressed her fingertips together and looked Cámara straight in the eye.

'Am I going too fast?' she asked. Cámara shook his head. 'The point is,' she went on, 'that when a bullfighter performs well he is awarded the bull's ears and perhaps its tail as a prize. Of course what is really meant by this are the bull's testicles and his penis. By overcoming the bull he turns it first into a female being, and then finally emasculates it, thus absorbing its sexual potency for himself. There is an overt sexuality about bullfighting. El Cordobés admitted openly that he used to ejaculate whenever he killed a bull.'

Cámara laughed.

'I thought that was just an urban legend,' he said.

'Other bullfighters have made similar comments.'

'So, forgive me, but to bring it back to our murders.'

Margarita sat back in her chair and for a second Cámara felt almost like the slow schoolboy, trailing behind the rest of the class. He still couldn't quite see the connection.

'Well, you see it makes sense with Blanco,' Margarita said. 'Blanco was a bullfighter, the best there's ever been. So to remove – or at least try to remove – his genitals has a deep symbolism: the emasculator is being emasculated. The great super-male being is having his gender literally cut away from him.'

'But at the beginning you were talking about more than one killer,' Cámara said.

'Exactly.' Margarita's face lit up, as though she sensed Cámara was finally about to understand. 'Whoever killed Blanco – it seems to me, at least – must have a good knowledge of bullfighting and its inner significance.'

'But with Ruiz Pastor—'

'Yes, you've got it,' she said, clapping her hands together with joy. 'Why mutilate poor old Ruiz Pastor? It doesn't make sense. He's not a bullfighter. Yes, he's involved in the world of bullfighting. But symbolically speaking, mutilating Blanco made total sense, disturbing though the idea might seem. To do so on Ruiz Pastor lacks the same coherence. When I heard that he too had had his genitalia removed my first thought was that you were dealing with a copycat murderer.'

She scratched her nose.

'Or perhaps with someone who wanted you to think it was the same person who killed Blanco' she said. 'Nothing else really makes sense. Or at least not to me.'

The rain had stopped and he decided to walk to Hilario's place. The sun was casting an intense streak of light over the city through a break in the thick clouds and the smells of lunch were beginning to drift out of the kitchen windows of a thousand red-brick apartment buildings: fried fish, meat stews, boiled beef with chickpeas and potatoes. Cámara pulled out his phone and dialled a number.

'Huerta's lot have had a look at that drainpipe, chief,' Torres said as soon as he picked up.

'Anything?'

'Someone's been up and down it; they can tell by the scratch marks. But no prints and no DNA. Could be just kids messing about, but they reckon whoever's done it was there quite recently – hardly any oxidisation underneath where the paint's been scraped.'

'All right. Anything else?'

'No, pretty quiet here today – apart from the *Fallas* racket outside, that is. Pardo's doing his disappearing act again. Ibarra's working through the statements we got from the Albufera fishermen. Sánchez is on his day off, and I've got Montero and Vargas talking to members of Blanco's team – see if there's anything we've missed.'

'All right. I want you to look into the Ramírez family business. And the other top bull breeders in the country while you're at it. I'm particularly interested in any suggestions of dodgy breeding practices.'

He could hear Torres scribbling notes at the other end.

'What, like nobbling the bulls?'

'That kind of thing,' Cámara said. 'You'll probably hit a wall of denial if you ask people directly. Just see what you can come up with.'

'Right you are. Thinking of going round there yourself?'

'What? To the Ramírez farm?' Cámara paused. 'I'll be back later on,' he said, and rang off.

The keyhole had all but been worn away after decades of use, and where once a sharply defined space had been, there was now a gaping amorphous hole. A lock-picker's dream, Cámara thought as he felt in his pocket for the key that he had slipped in and out of this door so many thousands of times, before deciding against it and ringing the bell instead. There was a lengthy pause before the lock finally clicked and he pushed it open. Inside the dark, musty entrance hall he could hear Hilario's door on the first floor above being unlatched. The old man would be standing there, waiting.

'You should ask who it is, first,' Cámara called up. 'You never know who you might be letting in.'

'Who else is going to show up here unannounced on a Thursday lunchtime?' Hilario's voice echoed down the stairwell. 'And besides, you'll be running out of *maría*. I told you you'd be round here soon.'

Cámara reached to grab the iron banister and pulled himself up the final couple of steps.

'You might be just a little more discreet,' he said as he kissed his grandfather's closely shaven cheeks, looking around at the other doors leading off the stairwell.

'Don't worry about them,' Hilario said, turning and walking back down the corridor towards the living room. 'They're all too ancient to know what we're talking about. Probably think you've joined the Opus Dei or something.'

Cámara closed the door and followed him in. He'd grown used to the eighty-two-year-old dismissing his contemporaries as 'ancient' or 'stupid'. In Hilario's mind – as well as his spirit – he was still a man in his thirties or forties, despite the increasing reminders from his body that he was somewhat older than that. He might not be able to get around as nimbly as before, but there was a defiance in him which refused to accept that age was anything other than a gift. Let the others moan and complain about this and that, about stiff knees and aching joints, dicky hearts and high blood pressure. For Hilario, life had to be lived to the full.

Not in the thrill-seeking way of youngsters wishing they'd been born in a more adventurous time, but through a combination of a relentlessly positive attitude with a stubborn refusal to ever be beaten down. He'd suffered enough as a boy, first losing his father in the Civil War, then keeping himself and his mother alive through ingenuity and luck during the depression and famine of the 1940s. You get through something like that and you can get through anything, he always said. If you can't learn from the experiences you've had, you might as well give up and die. *Hombre que el bien no agradece solo el desprecio merece*, he'd say: A man who doesn't appreciate the good in life deserves nothing but contempt.

'There's some spinach still in the pot,' he said as they passed the doorway into the kitchen. 'And a few scraps of *pollo al ajillo*. Pilar made it. Help yourself.'

Although Hilario was still virtually independent, ever since Cámara could remember, the dark shadow of Pilar had been a part of their lives in this flat, cooking meals, tidying the place up, ironing his grandfather's clothes and sewing for him. Dressed in permanent black, she'd moved around the dark passageways like a ghost, coming and going as she pleased, always there when you least expected it; never around when you needed her. She must have been quite young back when Cámara had first moved in, taken under his grandfather's wing as the only family remaining to him, yet she was always old in Cámara's mind, the stuffiness of widowhood sticking to her like a spider's web. Not old in the way he thought of Hilario – that had more to do with experience, and stories and proverbs. Pilar seemed to be cast in stone, petrified like one of the victims of Medusa in

217

Cámara's childhood books on Greek myths. For a while he had resented her, with her death-mask face. There were no secrets for a pubescent boy from Pilar, and the soft-porn magazines he occasionally managed to get his hands on, spreading like mushrooms across the country in the wake of the Generalísimo's death, would mysteriously disappear, no matter how carefully he thought he had hidden them. Pilar, the home help, a token female presence in their all-male environment, ruled over them with a silent, disapproving tyranny. It had been another reason to leave Albacete.

With his plate piled with Pilar's food, he picked up a fork and went into the living room to sit next to his grandfather. Hilario leaned forwards and hit the mute button on the remote control, and the TV news fell silent, the lights from the screen flickering in the background.

'Should be nice and dry, this lot,' Hilario said as Cámara began to eat. 'Been hanging up all winter. Packed it into plastic bags for you. Keep you going for a while.'

Cámara smiled to himself. The old anarchist was patting himself on the back again, ensuring that his wayward grandson – who'd joined the *police* of all things – kept one foot at least on his side of the law. In Hilario's mind, the marihuana plants were there to prevent Cámara from falling completely into the arms of the state, a small act of defiance to remind himself of his roots. Hilario and Cámara's great-grandfather before him had both been activists in the anarchist CNT trade union, although Hilario hadn't been able to join up officially until the political amnesty after Franco's death. This militancy had bypassed a generation with Cámara's father, but for the son there had been high hopes that he would follow the family tradition. Instead he had taken a law degree and joined the forces of oppression. Hilario hadn't spoken to him for three weeks afterwards and Cámara had been on the point of moving out before his grandfather had found him sitting on a doorstep nearby smoking some grass with a couple of friends. In that instant he found the gap, the chink, he had needed to hang on to his grandson.

And so had begun a new phase in their relationship. No longer was Hilario his surrogate parent, now they quickly became smoking buddies. At first it was easy to get hold of – riding a wave of anti-authoritarianism in the early 1980s, the Socialist government of Felipe González made possession legal. Things tightened up later on, though, and it became necessary to find other sources, which was when Hilario redesigned a portion of their patio – a private corner where the neighbours couldn't see what they were up to – into a mini marihuana jungle. After a couple of years of failures – during which he learned to separate the male from the female plants, and not to harvest them too soon, before the THC had been formed in the leaves – they had managed to produce a nice little amount, enough to keep them going all year at least until the next plants were ready.

Hilario had stopped smoking so much in recent years: a chest infection had given him a bit of a shock, and now he limited himself to an occasional puff on one of Cámara's *porros* when he called round, the two of them pulling up their chairs on to the balcony over their street, looking out towards the ochre-coloured fields that surrounded the city and letting the world turn quietly around them.

Never once did Hilario realise, though, that for Cámara smoking was never about turning his nose up at the system. It was – and had always been – purely about survival.

There was only one family photo in the flat. They'd burnt the rest. Hilario had insisted: it was important to keep moving forwards, never to get stuck. The remaining specimen had been placed in a simple metal frame and left in the corner of the room. But for Pilar it would have been lost, or smothered in dust, yet it managed to survive, resting at the end of a shelf next to a handful of books – translations of Steinbeck and an old book on sex education. For years Cámara hadn't looked at it at all, obeying his grandfather's command to forget the past. But over recent years he had found himself taking it down on more than one occasion – perhaps every time he came up here now. He wondered who these people were, who they would have been had they survived. Cámara himself stood at one side, pressed against his mother's legs and holding on to his father's hand. His father had been younger, then, much younger than Cámara was now. That was another family tradition Cámara had broken: both Hilario and then his son had had children early on: it was difficult to have an active sex life back then and not end up with a crop of kids, despite the Anarchists' long-held support for birth control. Growing up in a different, more liberal world, Cámara had decided, like most of his contemporaries, to wait. Waiting for what, though? If he'd known earlier what he'd now discovered he could have avoided years of passion-quelling fuss over condoms and diaphragms.

At the other side of the photo the figure of his sister drew his attention, as it always did: she looked so happy, so cheerful, her long chestnut hair falling over her shoulders and young breasts. Had it been those fresh new curves that had caught her killer's eye in the first place? Cámara looked away and concentrated on his food.

'Heading back to Valencia later?'

Cámara put his fork down and leaned over to put his hand on Hilario's arm.

'Just a flying visit. I needed to come up anyway.'

'This Blanco business, is it?' Hilario said, not expecting an answer. 'He was the best; I'm sure they've told you that.'

'Several times.'

'Course,' Hilario said, watching Cámara closely, 'I should never have taken you that time, when you were a kid. If I hadn't you'd probably know all about Blanco already, be an aficionado. Perhaps even a bullfighter yourself. But it put you off bullfighting for life, that did. Instead you've been landed with working out who murdered him. And we're not talking about a bull, neither. If I believed in a God – and I don't, let's make that clear – but if I did I'd say that right now he's having a bloody good laugh.'

They both smiled.

'Sure you can't stay for a quick smoke? You know I don't like doing it on my own these days. It's a lovely crop this year. I get the giggles just walking into the drying room from the smell of it.'

It had long been a mystery to Cámara how the severe Pilar, whose word was final on most things in the household, had ever managed to let this one crime of theirs pass without comment or reproach. For a while he suspected she simply didn't know what it was and had decided it was nothing but a harmless hobby of his grandfather's. Until one day, when he'd asked, Hilario explained that he'd caught their black-robed saint short-changing him on the grocery money.

'She had nothing on me after that. She was either out on her own, a lonely widow, or stay here and shut up. She chose to stay, not surprisingly. At which point I decided to try my hand at becoming a drug baron. I have to water them myself, of course. She won't go near them – thinks she might catch something if she did. But I know she'll never say anything to anyone.'

Cámara finished his lunch in silence, his mind wandering over details of the case, circling and probing Margarita de la Fuente's theory about there being more than one murderer. Instinctively he'd known all along – had done so since the morning they'd found Ruiz Pastor's body at the *barraca*. Now Margarita's comments seemed to confirm a previously unworded suspicion. From now on he'd work on that assumption, but would keep it to himself at least for the next day or so. Nothing would make things worse with Pardo than to tell him they might be looking at two killers rather than one. The obvious question to ask, though, was whether they were linked. Had someone held a grudge against Ruiz Pastor and then decided that this was the perfect time to murder him while making it appear that Blanco's killer was responsible? Or were the two actually working together? If so, why kill Ruiz Pastor as well and go to the trouble of making the two murders appear to have been committed by the same person?

Hilario got up from the table and wandered off down the corridor then returned a few moments later with half a dozen semi-transparent plastic bags filled with dry green leaves.

'Here,' he said, placing them on the table next to Cámara's empty plate. 'You going to the cemetery?'

Cámara shook his head. 'Not this time.' He could never make it for the first of November, the day when traditionally people tended the graves of their dead, and so he would pop over whenever he could, on the odd times when he jumped in the Seat and drove up to his home town. The flowers where his sister lay at least were changed once, sometimes twice a year. Those of his parents less often.

He picked up the plastic bags and got up to leave. Hilario walked with him to the door. It was a short visit, but it was worth popping round, just to see how the old man was doing, Cámara told himself. Sometimes they didn't need to talk too much: just being in the same space was enough.

'It's got to you,' Hilario said as Cámara opened the door and stepped out back into the stairwell.

'What has?' Cámara looked down at the marihuana he was clutching in his hand. The light was poor where they stood, but he caught a glimpse of his knuckles gleaming white where he gripped hard. He wondered for a moment about telling him about being infertile. This particular Cámara line, at least, would soon be dying out.

'This Blanco business,' Hilario said. 'I can tell. Something about this is bothering you. Are you getting enough?'

Cámara sighed. As ever, his grandfather's solution to most problems was a full and active sex life.

'That Almudena'll be giving you problems again, I'll bet. *Es una rosa pero pincha como un cardo* – She's as sweet as a rose but as prickly as a thistle.'

Cámara turned and went to switch on the stair light before heading back down into the street.

'You'll come through it,' Hilario called after him. 'You always did.'

SIXTEEN

He's got more balls than a blind bullfighter
Traditional

The road out of Albacete headed south for a mile or two before arriving at a junction. Cámara reached the round-about and stared for a moment at the large blue-and-white sign pointing the way east back down to Valencia. Ahead of him an old trunk road passed through a dusty indus-trial estate before breaking out into the open countryside and the hills of the Sierra Alcaraz in the far distance, smothered that afternoon by a heavy haze. He checked his watch: if he drove fast he could be back in the Jefatura by half past five, leaving plenty of time to go over Huer-ta's notes. Some thought was struggling at the back of his mind: a worry or concern he had managed to forget about for a while, yet an echo of it remained. What had that been about?

The lights of the car behind flashed in his rear-view mirror and he heard a horn blast: he was holding everyone up. He pushed a CD of Camarón de la Isla into the stereo, slammed the car into gear and pressed down on the accelerator, carrying on straight and ignoring the slip road heading down to the Valencia motorway. There was a place up in those hills he needed to see.

He found the village easily. In these underpopulated parts of the country it was difficult to get lost, with so few roads and a small town dotted only every ten or fifteen miles. The rest was a wash of green and yellow, stunted oak trees dotted over the hillsides, with an occasional flash of brilliant black as a small group of bulls came briefly into view only to disappear again as the gritty, unpainted road curved away. Cámara slowed to a virtual standstill as he cruised through the one street looking for signs of life. The houses were mostly old and small, the contours of their stone exteriors softened by centuries of annual whitewashing. A bar stood at the side, its presence signalled by a Coca-Cola sign in incongruous red hanging over its front door. But the iron gateway was firmly closed: the owner wasn't expecting any customers at that time of day.

He knew that the farm was another couple of miles beyond the village. Not spying anyone in the street, he slowly pressed on the accelerator and began to pick up speed. There was a risk that he might catch people during their siesta if he arrived now, but he wasn't prepared to hang around until a more sociable hour.

A small house was set back slightly from the road on the outskirts of the village. As he drew nearer he caught sight of a figure in black pouring a bucket of water out over the flagstones by the front door. He braked and brought the car to a stop. He remembered the old woman clearly: the black hair tied back in a bun; a small, frail frame; delicate, yet bony hands. He got out of the car and crossed the empty road. Hearing the sound of his footsteps, she slowly lifted her head to look, but the eyes that stared back at Cámara spoke of someone elsewhere, a spirit already moving in a different space.

'Señora?' Cámara asked. She didn't reply.

'Are you the mother of Jorge Blanco?' He tried again. At the sound of her son's name something seemed to stir inside the old woman. She placed the bucket by the side of the door and turned to head inside. Cámara followed.

A fire was burning in the stone hearth, the scent of wood smoke filling the air. Cámara stood by a dark wooden table as he watched the old woman head into an old-fashioned kitchen, with a marble sink and tiny gas stove. Did she remember wearing anything other than black, he wondered? Blanco's father had died before their son had been born. Doubtless he would have seen his mother dressed in mourning all his life.

She emerged again carrying an unlabelled bottle of wine and a glass tumbler. Not asking if he wanted any, she poured a full measure and handed it to him. Cámara took it and sat in the armchair she pointed to near the chimney.

'*Le acompaño en su dolor*,' he said, repeating the usual phrase of condolence. She waved his words away as though flicking away a troublesome fly.

'It's all dirt,' she said. '*Todo sucio.*' And she sat down opposite him, her hands wrapping over one another. Signs of forgetfulness, perhaps despair, were captured in Cámara's mind as his eyes flickered over the room: rotting fruit in a bowl on the table; firewood that had fallen from its shelf near the fire and was now perilously close to the flames; a purse spilling its contents over the floor where it had fallen and been left. He looked again into her eyes, but they appeared to be covered in a grey film.

226

'I'm investigating the death of your son, señora,' he said, reaching into his jacket to look for his badge.

She gave the golden shiny metal the minimum of attention as he showed it to her. In the silence Cámara took a sip of the sharp, vinegary wine and swallowed hard, then looked for a safe corner of the hearth and placed the tumbler down.

'There's some cheese, if you want.'

Getting to her feet, she disappeared into the kitchen. Cámara took advantage of her absence to put the firewood back on its shelf, and leaned over to pick up the purse and its contents, placing them on the table. The purse flicked open as he did so, revealing the woman's dated, old-fashioned blue-and-white ID card. Her name caught his attention for a second: Josefina Blanco Sol.

She was standing in front of him again, a plate of moulding cheese in her trembling hand. Cámara took it from her and they returned to the fire.

'Did you meet Jorge's friend?' she asked, her face brightening up for a second before seeming to cloud over again, her eyes turning to the flames.

'He had a friend,' she said. 'A special friend, he always told me he was. He called me when . . . when . . . He couldn't make it to the funeral. He said . . .'

Whatever it was he had said, she seemed to have trouble remembering it now. Cámara thought of Aguado. Had she met him?

'Señora Blanco,' Cámara said. She lifted her eyes again at the sound of her name. 'Do you remember the last time you saw your son?'

'You were there,' she said. 'I remember you now. You spoke to his . . .'

JASON WEBSTER

'I was at the funeral,' Cámara said as she tailed off again. 'I was there. But I mean when he was alive, the last time you saw him alive. Could you tell me about that?'

The greying eyes began to drift again, her chin drooping as she seemed to fall into some dark reverie. He watched her for a few moments, trying to gauge whether he'd pushed her too quickly. Perhaps he was wasting his time anyway. If there were any clues about Blanco's death in his personal life he doubted his mother would be able to cast any light on them. Although she did seem to know about Aguado.

His eyes started to wander around the room again. If he had needed a clearer example of age being more about a state of mind, then it was here. The woman had just lost her only son, it was true, but she must have been twenty, perhaps thirty years younger than Hilario. The same age his grandfather had been when he lost his own son, or there about. Yet there was no comparison. How badly had Hilario been affected by all that back then? He had hardly asked himself, so wrapped up in his own grief had he been. He must have hidden it well, though.

A tiny spark of colour seemed to flash from a corner of the room and he looked up at an image of smiling people. Another framed family photo, another reminder of a happier moment. He squinted his eyes to see better: the younger figure was clearly Blanco, his hair longer, his hips clad in tight jeans that flared down below the knee. And his arms were wrapped around a woman wearing a brightly coloured floral dress, a pair of oversized sunglasses perched on top of her flowing auburn hair, a more reserved smile on her face as she looked with suspicion at the camera. A holiday snap, perhaps. There was an air of summer about the image, of tanned skin and late nights near the beach. But who was the woman? Cámara stared in the gloom, then looked back at the broken figure now seated in front of him. Blanco's mother had raised her face again and was looking him in the eye. It was her, the same woman in the photo. In a different time and a different world, but it was the same person.

'It was two weeks before they killed him,' she said. Cámara swallowed. A sharpness seemed to have returned to her all of a sudden. 'He came up here to see me. There was . . .' Drifting again.

'Jorge came here?' Cámara said, trying to jog her along.

'Afterwards,' she said after another pause. 'Perhaps before as well. I can't remember too well. Things just get so . . . He came after he'd been up to the farm. Dirty, it's all so dirty.' She put her hands over her eyes, perhaps to hide, perhaps to see more clearly what she was struggling to recall.

'He went to the farm,' Cámara repeated. 'To talk to someone?'

'Francisco was there,' she said. 'He told me that. Roberto as well.'

'Did he say what they'd talked about?' Cámara persevered.

For a moment she seemed to fade again, then returned, like a radio capturing and losing a signal.

'Jorge was always so clean. Always insisted on being clean. Clean bullfighting. Honest bullfighting. There was no other way with him.'

'How did he seem when you spoke to him? After he'd been up at the farm.'

'He never showed it. Oh, he never showed it,' she said quickly, as though animated all of a sudden by their conversation. 'But I knew. I could tell. His mother. I always knew what was going on with him. He said there was nothing wrong, but he was angry. Angrier than I'd ever seen . . .'

She tailed off again.

'Do you know what he was angry about?' Cámara tried, leaning in towards her across the open space of the hearth in front of them.

'Not like his father,' she whispered under her breath. 'I've never understood him the same way.'

'*Señora* Blanco,' Cámara called. He wanted to reach out and hold her hand, as if to hang on to her, to keep her from slipping into the other world that was pulling at her.

'Dirty,' she said at last, her eyes lost in the last flames now flickering from the untended fire. '*Todo sucio.*'

Cámara was greeted at the front door of the Ramírez farm by a slim woman in her late sixties with pale blue eyes and white-blonde hair. Aurora Palacios bore herself with the same hauteur as she had at Blanco's funeral, her back stiff and straight, and with a mild yet seemingly permanent frown.

Cámara introduced himself, standing in the shade of a well-established bougainvillea that had been trained over the doorway, its budding purple-red flowers set against the yellow walls of the *finca*. The rain that had found him in Albacete had blown away, and an afternoon sky of brilliant clear blue now arched over the hilly landscape.

'My husband isn't here,' Aurora said simply once she'd established he was who he said he was, examining his badge and ID with a schoolmistress's scepticism.

'Can you tell me where he is?' Cámara asked.

She gave a snort.

'What are you asking me for?'

A noise came from nearby, the call of what sounded like a bull or a cow. Cámara turned.

'Don't be alarmed,' Aurora snapped. 'You're quite safe here.'

'I take it someone is with the animal, however,' Cámara said. 'It sounded quite close by.'

'Paco's here,' she said, already backing into the house. 'You'll find him.'

And the door was firmly closed behind her.

Cámara turned and started walking in the direction of the animal call. Box hedges formed a pathway along the side of the house, and his feet crunched on white gravel underneath. Pines stretched high overhead, giving more shade to the garden with a sunken pool and a small stone fountain. Black-painted, ornate iron railings were bolted over all of the downstairs windows while a burgundy stripe had been painted along the bottom of the outside wall, perhaps a metre high, the same colour as the painted frames around the doors and windows. The house itself was large and square, with two storeys, although Cámara could make out a tower with a mirador in one corner, looking out towards the peaks of the Sierra Alacaraz. It all spoke of relatively old money, of a long-established family business. Perhaps Ramírez's grandfather, the founder of the breeding farm, had had this place built. It looked to be well over a hundred years old.

Beyond the garden the pine trees came to a stop and Cámara could see some outbuildings sitting in the strong sunlight. He guessed that they were close to a thousand metres above sea level here – enough to notice a thinning in the air, and a blanching, all-powerful glare of the sun. Passing out from the shade he made out a low, ring-shaped wall, again with a burgundy stripe around its base. It was almost certainly a practice bullring, and over the top of the wall he could see the figure of a man.

Paco didn't seem to notice him at first, watching carefully as one of his farmhands flashed a cape in front of what looked like a small bullock skipping aggressively on the dirt floor of the ring. Both men were giving guttural calls, egging the animal on as it charged at the cape, stopped, lost its concentration momentarily, then focused on the cape once more and charged again.

'¡Eh-he!

'¡Toro!

Paco was wearing a flat woollen cap, with a dark green jerkin slung over a checked shirt. His sleeves were rolled halfway up his forearms and smoke rose from a cigarette clutched between his fingers as he leaned on the edge of the wall, his concentration never wavering from the centre of the ring. When Cámara walked up to him he nodded to acknowledge him momentarily before turning back. After a few moments he gave a low whistle and the farmhand promptly stopped, leaving the animal breathless and perplexed, vapour streaming from its mouth and nostrils.

'I've seen you before,' Paco said, finally giving Cámara his attention. 'The policeman, aren't you?'

Cámara nodded.

'You've come all the way here?'

There was a roughness about him, in contrast to the studied disdain of his mother. Was Ramírez the father responsible for giving him that? Or did living and working on this

232

land have something to do with it? Breeding deadly animals in this empty, underpopulated landscape, the pasture barely clinging to the thin grey soil, demanded a harsh simplicity of being, Cámara thought. It had a certain beauty, perhaps, but he found himself longing for the complexities of the city in environments such as these.

'I was told your father isn't here,' Cámara said.

'Was it him you wanted to speak to?' Paco pulled on the cigarette then exhaled. 'He's in Valencia still. Hasn't come back since Jorge was killed.'

Inside the ring the farmhand was folding his cape over his arm, keeping a distance.

'If you're here I suppose it means things aren't going too well with the investigation.'

He put the cigarette back in his mouth and stepped away, beckoning towards the farmhand.

'Give me that, Morales,' he called. 'We haven't finished with this one.'

The farmhand passed him the cape and Paco leapt over the wall to join him inside. A strong scent of earth and manure was kicked up from where his feet landed and scuffed the surface. Wordlessly, the other man pressed his back against the wall and Paco started walking towards the centre.

'The *bravura* – the fighting spirit – of a bull comes from the mother,' he called behind him to Cámara. 'Did you know that? This little cow here is showing some real character. Might use her for breeding a new generation of Ramírez bulls. But we need to test her first.'

The white horns of the cow twitched as he stubbed the cigarette out on the floor and unfolded the cape, spreading it out in front of him and allowing it to drape over the ground. What had Margarita de la Fuente said? That the *capote* represented a skirt? What happened now, he wondered, when the bull was actually a female? But then this was just practice, he told himself. The symbolism of the corrida probably broke down if you applied it to the breeder's farm as well.

With a low cry, Paco flicked the *capote* in the cow's direction. After a moment's pause, the animal charged at him, lowering its head in an attempt to catch him on its horns. But with an effortless *verónica*, Paco turned to the side, allowing the *capote* to pass in front of the cow's eyes before flicking round and slapping the animal on its haunches.

'*Venga, va,*' he called out, shouting to catch the beast's attention. It was much smaller than the bulls that appeared in public bullfights, Cámara thought, and much lighter on its feet, but it had a wiry energy, like a wound-up spring. There was no doubt of the risk involved by standing there next to the thing.

After a few more passes Paco stopped and walked casually over to where Cámara was standing by the edge of the wall. He held out the cape, a joyless smile beginning to curl at the corner of his mouth.

'Tempted?'

Cámara took the cape and spread it out as best he could in front of him, feeling its weight, the fall of the cloth, the stiffness of the material. Best not to think of it as a skirt at that moment, he thought. Whatever was about to happen, this was going to be a very male moment.

Paco was still standing on the inside of the wall, watching him as though trying to decide whether the policeman had it in him to face the horned and highly nervous cow. Taking off his jacket and hanging it on a nearby wooden stake, Cámara vaulted the wall and started walking to the centre. Both Paco and Morales were silent. In his mind's eye Cámara tried to recall images of what he'd just seen Paco do. He had seemed to be simultaneously rooted to the ground and yet light on his feet. A combination that was probably impossible to master the first time round, but something to aim for, at least.

To his relief, the cow seemed uninterested in him, and was gazing in the other direction, giving Cámara a few more seconds to compose himself. He'd fought humans often enough; to fight a small, horned and highly dangerous quadruped would be a novelty. He felt he was walking on uncertain ground: would his instincts serve him well for this?

From the side, Paco's henchman Morales beat the side of the wall with a wooden stick. The cow's attention was distracted and as it turned its head it seemed to become aware for the first time of the new presence in the ring. The breath stuck in Cámara's throat as a cool rush of adrenalin was released into his bloodstream. The cow looked at him with black shiny eyes, its left hoof scraping the ground in anger. Cámara spread the *capote* in front of him, suddenly aware of the vulnerability of his legs. The cow's horns were at thigh height; if he got caught on them they could easily pierce through his flesh. There was an artery down there, an important one that could drain you of all your blood in seconds if it was severed. For the life of him he couldn't remember what it was called, yet it seemed to be calling its presence up to his brain in a high-pitched, sustained scream. When they attacked you, men used fists, knives, guns. He knew about those threats. This, however, was different.

As the cow launched itself at him, two images flashed powerfully in his brain: Hilario holding his hand as they walked away from the bullring; and his sister's smiling face on the old photograph at the end of the bookshelf.

He only just managed to suppress the urge to turn and run. Instead, his arm holding the *capote* shot out as far away from his body as it could as he tried to draw the fierce little cow away from him, his hips arching in the opposite direction as thighs and genitals sought to distance themselves from the incoming danger. The effect made him almost lose his balance but the cow sailed past him in a black-and-white blur, a deep groan echoing from its throat as it emerged from its lunge frustrated at not finding Cámara on the ends of its horns. A strong smell of straw and animal sweat filtered up into Cámara's nostrils, but he was already preparing himself for another pass: the cow had him in its sights and was coming back for more. His cape-work might not have been the most elegant ever executed, but Cámara was aware that he had managed to emerge unscathed from their first encounter, and with pounding heart, the fear in him began to tip just slightly towards excitement.

The second pass was much like the first – Cámara's legs seemed to disappear from underneath him as he held the *capote* as far away from his body as he could manage. Again the cow ran past him without managing to make contact, and again Cámara felt something like a surge of success beginning to flow inside him. His mouth was dry, but there was a strong taste on his tongue, hot and earthy like blood.

One more. One more pass and he would walk away. It was only a cow, after all. His earlier fear, he began to realise, had been based on ignorance as much as on anything else. Bulls weighing over half a tonne were another matter, but a little cow? He could manage this. Still, an iciness seemed to sit in his lower abdomen. Don't get too close, it said. Keep a distance.

The cow itself seemed to sense the change in Cámara, and before he could prepare himself properly for another pass it had turned and was bearing on him once again. He struggled to place the *capote* cleanly between himself and the animal, but it was too late. Perhaps he should jump, he thought, like those topless Cretan women in the frescoes, leaping to safety over the cow. And for a second it seemed as though his legs had made the decision for him as he rose sharply in the air; a moment came when he seemed to be looking down on the cow rather than at it face to face. Could he make it to the other side, and safety?

The pain in his thigh registered as he hit the ground: a simultaneously sharp yet dull sensation above his right knee. Then all was a flash of pinks and yellows. He thought he heard voices. Feet – human feet – appeared near his face as he lay on the ground. Then hands seemed to grab him from under his arms and he was being hauled away, the soil seeping into his shoes as his feet dragged over the ground. Had he been cut? He tried to shove a hand down there to feel if there was any blood, but his arm movements were restricted by the person pulling him clear.

'You're fine,' a voice was saying. He couldn't tell, but it sounded like Paco. Fingers started probing around his leg to feel the extent of the damage.

'Nothing. Just a knock. You've been lucky.'

There was a brief hiatus in which Cámara seemed to rediscover the ability to breathe, sitting with his back to the wall. Then Paco was standing next to him again, holding out a small metallic cup.

'Drink this,' he said.

The brandy burnt and soothed Cámara's insides.

'Right,' Paco said. 'Let's get you on your feet. You'll be fine.'

The hands were under his armpits again and he was being hauled up.

'It's OK,' Cámara said, suddenly resenting the fact that they were treating him like an invalid. 'I've had worse.'

He stood on his own for a moment or two, pressing down on to his right leg to get a sense of how damaged it was. It wasn't too bad, like a nasty kick to the shins playing football, perhaps. But it was going to hurt later, he thought. Tomorrow he'd need some full-strength painkillers and anti-inflammatories to get the swelling down.

'Shame,' Paco said, patting him on the shoulder. 'Traditionally, if you complete three passes with a bull or a cow you can call yourself a torero.' He gave a hollow laugh. 'You fell one short. No ears or tail for you.'

'I suppose this never happens to you,' Cámara said.

'You get better with the years,' Paco said, turning away. 'But it takes time.'

He called over to Morales to take the cow away.

'We're finished here now for the day,' he said. 'You can walk, right? Come on then,' he said, not waiting for an answer. 'We'll put some things away.'

Cámara tried his best to disguise the limp in his walk as he followed him from the bullring to a one-storey outbuilding nearby. Again it was decorated with the burgundy stripe around its base.

'It was my grandmother's favourite colour,' Paco explained when Cámara asked him. 'My grandfather turned it into a kind of emblem. Every time you see something to do with the Ramírez farm it has to have some burgundy in there somewhere.'

He opened a steel door and flicked on the lights. In the storeroom, everywhere were the materials for training bulls, from *capotes* folded neatly in bags on some shelves on the far wall, to horse saddles, spare pairs of *campera* boots, *muletas*, and coat rack with waterproofs. Along one wall a row of lances were placed in a circular hoop.

'We use those when we're riding on horseback, to keep the bulls moving where we want them to go,' Paco said.

Next to the lances was a wooden rack with red-handled *estoques* used for the final killing of a bull. Cámara counted space for half a dozen, but could see only five.

'Is there anyone else out working on the farm today?' he asked.

'No,' Paco said. 'Why do you ask?'

Cámara nodded at the place where the missing *estoque* should have been.

'Things disappear,' Paco said. 'It's probably lying around somewhere.'

He folded up the *capote* they had been using and placed it on the shelf with the others.

'How's your leg feeling?' he asked. 'Seriously, I can have someone come over to have a look at it for you.'

'That's very kind,' Cámara said. 'There's no need.'

'You'll be all right to drive?'

He shrugged.

They walked out of the storeroom and back up to the main house, where Cámara had parked his Seat.

'Just a couple of questions,' Cámara said. 'I take it you came back here from Valencia after the funeral.'

'That's right.'

Their feet crunched on the gravel as they emerged from under the pine trees and passed the sunken pool. Cámara could sense a pair of eyes watching them from inside the house. Aurora Palacios might put on certain airs, but she wasn't above peeking out the window at their unexpected visitor.

'When did you get back?'

'The day after the funeral.'

'And your mother?'

'She stayed with my father for a couple of days more, then came up on her own.'

'Your father decided to stay.'

'I don't know where he would suffer more – there or here. Both places have such strong associations with Jorge for him. I suppose it was inertia in the end.'

'And he's on his own there?'

'He prefers to be alone. Especially if something's going wrong.'

Something told Cámara that Jorge's death hadn't been the only thing to 'go wrong' recently for the Ramírez family.

'How would you describe the relationship between the family and Ruiz Pastor?'

There was a pause, during which a noise, like fluttering feathers, seemed to come from nearby.

'I didn't have many dealings with him personally,' Paco

said. 'My father mainly took care of that business side of things. I'm more a man of the soil. I like to be up here, on my farm, working with the livestock. Ruiz Pastor, *que en paz descanse*, was a businessman, through and through. I can't really say any more.'

The fluttering noise had got louder, and Paco's attention was diverted. Stepping away from Cámara he walked in the direction of a nearby tree.

'That bloody cat,' he said.

Lifting one arm up to a branch, he reached up for something. It was only then that Cámara made out where the noise was coming from: a small brown bird was beating its wings helplessly, as though unable to fly. Paco grabbed it as a cat jumped down and ran off. With his hands in the air, Paco's shirt lifted momentarily out from his trousers and Cámara caught a glimpse of what looked like scratches and bruising on his lower back.

'My mother's cat,' Paco explained. 'It never actually kills the damned things. Just tortures and maims them.'

He brought his two hands together over the wretched bird and with a sharp motion broke its neck. Then he tossed it to one side before wiping his hands on the back of his trousers.

'Been in the wars?' Cámara asked, patting his own lower back to show where he'd seen the marks underneath Paco's shirt.

Paco's nostrils flared and he looked Cámara hard in the face.

'A similar accident to yours just now,' he said firmly. 'You can still find one that catches you out now and again, even after all these years.'

SEVENTEEN

The more punishment a bravo *bull receives,*
the stronger it grows
Traditional

'They've already got the photos,' she said with a grin. 'So we might as well.'

Her skin was firm and sweet.

'You won't need one of those,' he said.

'We can't be too careful,' she said.

'There's nothing to worry about.'

She came. And his body burst into a million pieces.

Later, after she'd washed, Alicia went into the kitchen for a few minutes and returned carrying a tray.

'Dinner in bed?' she said.

'Does this mean I won't be getting breakfast?'

'We'll see.'

She placed a couple of plates on the sheets beside him with some slices of smoked salmon and pieces of ready-made toast smothered in cream cheese.

'When did you find out?' she asked.

'About being infertile?' He paused. 'Not long ago. Except

that it's one of those things you later feel you've known all along.'

She leaned over and kissed him fully on the mouth, her breasts brushing against the hairs of his arm.

'Perhaps you should put something on,' he said. 'You'll get cold.'

'Don't you fancy warming me up again?'

He lifted the sheets on the other side and pulled her over to join him.

'I'm sorry,' she said. 'About . . .'

'It's all right,' Cámara said. 'For a while I'd convinced myself I was up to becoming a father. Now I don't have to pretend.'

He got up and closed the window in an attempt to soften the crashing noise coming from the fiesta outside, and turned back to face the room. Alicia stood up on tiptoe and kissed him, then walked over to the bed to find some clothes to put on. The flat was open plan – an old place that had been renovated in the past five or ten years, with walls ripped out and new windows put in. It was small – a studio flat, the kind of thing estate agents referred to these days using the English word 'loft', as though to give it some added, New York chic. Only the bathroom – little more than a cupboard, with a sink, shower and a loo – offered any privacy.

'I got this place after the separation,' Alicia said. 'For a single woman it's perfect.'

She picked up the plates of food she'd left on the bed and took them over to a table in the kitchen area.

'Come on,' she said. 'Let's eat. I always get hungry afterwards.'

'I always get the urge to have a smoke.'

'Eat first, smoke later.'

Taking his cue from what she was wearing – a jumper and the pair of knickers which earlier had been pulled off her with his own hands – he placed a shirt over his shoulders and went to put his underpants on before going to sit down with her at the table. He'd always found it curious how the levels of intimacy in a relationship were never static, always shifting. At the beginning the changes were acute as surges of erotic energy brought a fleeting, ecstatic breakdown of all barriers only for them to be replaced instantly once the moment had passed. He himself would have sat down with her as naked as they had been just a while before, but her being half-dressed as she was had little to do with the ambient temperature and more to do with how comfortable she felt with him then.

'Tell me about the Ramírez farm,' she said as her teeth crunched on a piece of toast.

'Have you ever been?' he asked. She shook her head. For some reason the words of the barman back at the Bar Los Toros flashed through his mind, his comments about the Ramírez bulls.

'Do you think they're still what they were?' he asked her.

'What's that?'

'The Ramírez bulls. Do you think they're still producing them as they always have? I mean, is there any sign of the quality decreasing in any way, producing weaker bulls?'

He felt sure that if anyone could answer this question it was her. It was inevitable that they should talk about the case at some point, although he hadn't wanted to bring it up so soon.

'I don't know what you're talking about,' she said.

'Look, I know they're legendary, the best in the whole

country and all that. All I'm asking is if people have noticed that they're perhaps not quite as good as they once were.'

'Ramírez bulls are the best in the world, and that's all there is to it,' she said. 'I would hardly expect someone like you to understand.'

'You make it sound like an article of faith,' he said.

'Come on, let's not talk about all this,' she said. 'Even I get tired of bullfighting sometimes.' She leaned over the table and slipped her fingers in between his.

'Here,' she said, getting up and walking over to the fridge. 'We need some wine with this.'

After they'd finished she took him back to bed. This time the sex was slower, stronger, more joyful. Cámara had the sense of finally falling into an open void he'd been afraid of for some time. What awaited him at the bottom, he couldn't tell. But for the moment he was happy simply not to have to cling on to the edge any more. There was something magical in the way she took pleasure in him.

Later they shared a *porro*, Cámara pulling out one of Hilario's plastic bags from his jacket. And to the sound of shuddering explosions and thudding pop music outside, they slipped into sleep, arms, legs, hair, breath all wrapped in one another.

Friday 17th March

The vibrating hum of his mobile brought him back into consciousness. Outside he could hear the brass band of the *despertà* passing through the nearby streets as dawn rose over the city. Sleep was all but forbidden during *Fallas*, and each neighbourhood made sure that none should offend even unwittingly by sending a musical band out to play as loudly as possible during the first hours of daylight. 'Come out and take part in the fiesta,' they seemed to say. 'Or we'll drag you out of bed ourselves.'

Cámara removed Alicia's hand from his belly and crawled over to where he'd hung his jacket over the back of a chair. As he reached for the phone he caught a glimpse of her naked body, the rounded curve of her hip, her arms and hands pressed up against her face as she lay on her side almost as if in prayer.

He flipped the phone open.

'*¿Sí?*

Seconds later he was dressing as fast as he could, searching the new, unfamiliar environment for pieces of his clothing that had been scattered over the floor. Without opening her eyes, Alicia reached out and pulled the sheets back over her skin, mumbling in her dreams. She'd find out soon enough, Cámara thought. No need to wake her now.

The door barely made a sound behind him.

There was no traffic at that time of the morning, and it took him less than half an hour to get there. Huerta's Audi was one of the half-dozen already parked outside the metal gate when he arrived. The same flowers and plants decorating and shaping the garden, the same house, the same view over the sea. There were no waves that morning, however, and the water stretching out towards the eastern sun shimmered a deep, tranquil blue. Cámara had rarely seen it so calm and still.

Quintero, the *médico forense*, shook his hand and led him wordlessly down to the swimming pool. Huerta was instructing his photographer on where to take his shots.

'She was in the pool,' Quintero said. 'Tied the head of

a marble statue to her wrist with a piece of rope and then threw herself in. Suicide, almost certainly, but Huerta's having a check round just in case, as you can see.'

He turned to where Carmen Luna's body lay on the paving stones at the edge of the water. The grey colourlessness of her face seemed incongruous with the brightness of the morning and the rising sun. Her eyes were almost fully open, but were now nothing but balls of unseeing jelly.

He walked over and crouched down to see more closely. She was wearing a black nightdress, her hair tied up in a bun, no make-up, the golden rings on her fingers shining more brilliantly against the pale, bloodless skin. Quintero would have checked already, but he scanned her all the same for any signs of violence or struggle. There were none. But for the death mask that now occupied her face, and the marks around her wrists where she'd tied the rope, she was the same as when he'd come to see her here himself. Nothing then in her behaviour, in her manner, had given any warning of this. He racked his brain for a clue, for something she might have said which seemed relevant or had a bearing on what he was now seeing, but his mind was blank.

'The head came from that statue over there.' He saw Huerta's feet approaching from where he was crouching, and stood up. 'She must have been pretty strong to have removed it in the first place,' he said. 'But I suppose she just wanted to be sure.'

Cámara looked over and saw a headless marble statue of a naked man.

'What did she tie it on with?' he asked.

'Got it from the gardening shed.' He held up a length of

yellow nylon plaited rope. 'It's been cut cleanly. The rest is inside, along with the knife. Prints on the cutter, but almost certain to be hers.'

'No foul play, then?'

'Unlikely. And to be honest, Cámara, you hardly look like a man who needs another stiff on his hands. It's a suicide, plain and simple. Nothing to reflect badly on you.'

'That's not really what I'm thinking about.'

'I know you're not.' Huerta pulled out a pack of Marlboros and offered him one.

'Others might, though,' he said as he fired his lighter. Cámara inhaled deeply. 'You know what I mean. This isn't your fault, though.'

They both looked over at the figure of Carmen Luna's dead pale body next to them.

'*A veces los muertos hablan,*' Cámara said. 'Sometimes the dead talk.'

He stood on his own for a few minutes, trying to remember as much as he could of his conversation here by the pool only two days previously. A few scraps and half-sentences came to mind, but there was no overall picture there, no coherence to the images, as though his memory of the occasion had been damaged in some way. He'd check his notes when he got back to the Jefatura, but then it might be too late. An instinct dulled by little sleep and the new emotions of the night before told him there was something here, something he should be doing now.

He walked around the pool and found Quintero standing beside him again.

'We're pretty much finished here,' he said. 'Judge Caballero won't be coming in. He said for me to stand in for him on this occasion. Again. So we can carry out the *levantami-ento del cadaver* now if you're ready.'

'Fine by me,' Cámara said. He drew on the last of his cigarette and looked for somewhere reasonable to stub it out. Leaving it at the scene of a suicide seemed unaccept-able, somehow. But in the absence of any alternative, he pushed the burning end out against the side of a plant pot and kicked the stub into the undergrowth.

Quintero was speaking to him again.

'It must be hard for you, this,' he was saying.

'I'm sorry?' Cámara asked.

'A death, like this. Something so connected to the case you're working on. I mean, in the end you must start taking it almost personally.'

Cámara looked him hard in the face to see if the man was trying it on, but found nothing but a look of genuine concern.

'I'm all right,' he just managed to say. Why was everyone feeling sorry for *him* that morning?

'Listen,' he said, leaning in to speak to the *médico forense* more privately. 'Is there any way, in your opinion, that Ruiz Pastor's killer might not be the same as Blanco's?'

Never an over-demonstrative type, Quintero's eyes gave just the slightest indication of surprise. He held Cámara's gaze for a moment before seeming to cast his mind back to what he knew of each murder and its victim.

'You do realise,' he said at last, 'what the implications would be if it got out that we were looking for two, rather than just one?'

At that moment the *secretaria judicial* called Quintero over and Cámara found himself on his own again. In the reflection on the water of the pool in front of him he could make out the trees swaying gently overhead, the increasing light in the sky, and the house a little higher up the slope of the garden, with its large windows stretching almost all the way around. For a moment he thought he saw a movement, a face staring down at them. He looked up, but there was no one there.

'Just one thing,' he said as Quintero and Irene Ortiz went over the final paperwork. 'Who called this in?'

'There was a call from the emergency services,' Irene said. 'There should be an ambulance arriving now to take the body away.'

'Yes, but who made the call?'

Before she could answer Cámara was striding up the garden slope and towards the sliding glass doors that led inside the house. One of them was partially open and the white curtain was flapping gently in the breeze. He pulled it aside and stepped in. The house seemed just as it had the first time he'd been round – the same neatness, the same smell of perfume.

'Cyril!' he called out. There was no reply. 'Cyril! I need to talk to you.'

The living room was empty, so he tried some of the doors leading off a corridor that led to the other end of the house. The first opened on to a bathroom, the second was locked. Cámara banged on the door.

'Cyril! It's Chief Inspector Cámara.'

He heard a sob from inside, then the shuffling of feet. Eventually, after a few minutes, the lock clicked open. Cámara waited, but when the door remained closed, he pulled on the handle himself.

Carmen's young Moroccan butler was lying on the floor of his bedroom, curled up into a tight ball.

'Cyril?' Cámara took a step into the room and then closed the door behind him. There was another sob. Cámara knelt down and placed a hand on the man's shoulder.

'I need you to tell me what happened.'

Quicker than Cámara had expected, Cyril began to uncurl himself and placed a hand on the floor to push himself up.

'This is the end for me,' he said as he got to his feet. Cámara led him to the edge of the bed and then sat down on a nearby chair.

'Carmen was my life. Now I have nothing. No papers, nowhere to go.'

'Cyril,' Cámara said. 'Listen to me. I work in homicides, murders. I don't care how you got here or if you stay. Understand?'

Cyril looked down at the floor.

'Now you must have friends, someone you can turn to.' The Moroccan was silent. 'But right now I need you to tell me exactly what happened. It was you who put the call through, right? You called the emergency services.'

After a pause, Cyril nodded.

'When was that?'

'I don't know,' he mumbled. 'Perhaps an hour ago.'

'Did you find Carmen?'

'Yes,' he said. 'I found *La Señorita*, then I made the call.'

'Did you hear anything?' Cámara asked. 'How did you find her? It must have been dark.'

Cyril held his head in his hands and began to sob. Tears streamed through his fingers and down on to the floor by his feet. Cámara looked for a handkerchief or paper tissue, but his pockets were empty. He got up, went into the bathroom opposite, pulled out some toilet roll and then went back into the bedroom.

'Here,' he said, thrusting it under Cyril's face. 'Here, take this.'

Cyril grabbed it and blew his nose. His eyes were burning red, his slim brown hands shaking as he gripped at the tissue paper.

'Last night,' he said, '*La Señorita* received a phone call. She could receive a lot of phone calls, but this one was different.'

Tears were still falling from his eyes and he dabbed at them before carrying on.

'I could not hear what was said. *La Señorita* herself said almost nothing during the entire call. It was perhaps ten, fifteen minutes long. I don't know for sure. But afterwards she shut herself in her room. This was not normal with her. Normally she liked to stay up and eat, enjoy my cocktails. Then, since Jorge died, and if no one came round, then sometimes we would stay up just me and her for hours, talking. She liked people, being with people. But last night was different. She just went to her room and closed the door. Didn't even say goodnight or anything. So I knew something was very wrong.'

A shudder seemed to pass through him, and for a moment Cámara thought he was about to break down again.

'I stayed up later than usual,' Cyril eventually continued. 'I thought *La Señorita* was perhaps ill, or would come out of her room at some stage and would need me there. So I stayed up, waiting. But eventually I fell asleep on the sofa.'

He brought his hands to his face for a second, covering his eyes as though with shame.

'If I'd managed to stay awake I could have stopped this,' he said. 'I could have stopped her. But I fell asleep, I fell asleep.'

'It's all right,' Cámara said. 'Please, go on, tell me what happened.'

'Something made me wake up. I don't know what. I heard nothing, I swear. No sound. But suddenly I woke up, as though some hand had reached out and grabbed me.'

'Something didn't feel right?'

'Yes, that's it. I don't know, but I just knew.'

Cámara had heard words to this effect often over the previous years. They had become so common in the murders he had dealt with that he had come to expect them. A sense of something not being right in the moments before the body – or bodies – were found, as if the person already knew, at some primitive level, that something awful, something horrific, had taken place. An intuition, perhaps? Or just the mind playing tricks, creating powerful false memories after the shock? It didn't really matter which – the experiences were all too real for those who went through them.

'What happened then?' Cámara asked.

'That's when I looked out the window and saw *La Señorita* in the water,' Cyril said.

'What did you do then?'

'I don't know. I ran out. I went down to the pool. I cried. I . . .'

'How long before you called the emergency services?' Cámara asked him.

Cyril thought for a moment. 'Maybe, I'm not sure, five minutes. Ten minutes? I was very upset.'

'Did you see anything else? Anything strange, out of the ordinary?'

The Moroccan shook his head. His lips had hardened, a white, fearful look in his eye.

'I need you to show me Carmen's bedroom,' Cámara said. 'It's very important.'

Cyril got to his feet shakily and headed towards the door, Cámara following close behind. Out in the corridor, they turned right and walked to the door at the far end. Cámara stepped forwards and opened it himself. The room gave on to the east side of the house and the morning sun was streaming in through the large single-pane windows. One of them was partially open and from the garden below came the sound of Huerta's team. Beyond the palm trees the sea still lapped the shore unusually gently.

The room was simpler than he had expected. A double bed, a dressing table, a couple of chairs, and just a couple of photographs on the walls: one of Carmen when she was younger, the other of Blanco in his *traje de luces*, holding up a couple of ears he had been awarded at a bullfight. A door to the side led off to an en-suite bathroom. Cámara poked his head through: a collection of large starfish had been mounted in a glass cabinet above the bath, but he saw nothing untoward. He turned his attention back to the bedroom. Cyril was leaning against the doorway, fresh tears streaming down his face. The bed was covered in a simple white bedspread, and although someone had lain on top of it, it had not been slept in. Cámara began to open the drawers of the bedside cabinet: old magazines, a box of tissues, underwear. Then he turned to the dressing table, with its collection of hairbrushes, make-up and perfumes.

Again, the drawers held no secrets, but Carmen's mobile phone was there. He scrolled through the received calls: the last one came from a number marked 'private'.

It was something: they could check later where that call had come from. Yet he felt sure there would be something else here, something that he needed to find. He glanced about the room again. The edge of the bedspread, near the top, had been pulled back. He darted forwards and began to feel under the pillows. Almost at once his fingers found something.

He pulled out the note by the corner and held it up to the light: thin writing paper that had been folded twice. He knew he should call Huerta at once and get them to open it up and study it 'scientifically', but his curiosity got the better of him. There were no other prints on the paper than Carmen's: of that he was sure. The importance of the paper was what was written inside. He unfolded it as carefully as he could. From the doorway, Cyril seemed to come back to life.

'A note?' And he rushed forwards.

Cámara held out a hand to hold him back as he studied the writing. Just five lines, in purple ink. The handwriting reminded him of how girls at school had written – all rounded, short, squat lettering.

'*I have been drowned in the lies of others,*' Cámara read. '*I am a lie, my life has been a lie. I am nothing. By doing this I shall wash myself clean as others never can. For Cyril, I love you. I'm sorry.*'

Cámara looked over at the Moroccan, then back down at the final sentence of the note.

'*For the others, for all of you,*' Carmen wrote, '*but especially for Jorge Blanco, I have nothing but hate.*'

EIGHTEEN

If our national fiesta were the national fiesta of Britain, half a dozen matadors would be sitting in the House of Lords
Antonio Burgos

The first batches of story-hungry media vans came screaming down the road from the city as Cámara drove along the pine-clad banks of the Albufera lake. The biggest story of the moment was about to get even bigger still, and no gossip journalist in the country would want to be anywhere else except Carmen Luna's villa at that moment. Usually they would have got there sooner, and he was surprised when he left the place himself that no one had arrived yet. A suicide caused people to react slightly differently, perhaps, out of a sense of respect, or shock. He wasn't quite sure. But now the news had got out and the house would be under siege for the next few days. He'd tried to warn Cyril as he'd left, but the poor man was still inhabiting a deep, aching emptiness. Eventually he had shut the gate behind him himself, hoping that it would keep the journalists at bay long enough for the Moroccan to gather himself and deal with them.

Cámara dialled a number in El Cabanyal district as he

drove away and took the road back towards the city. After listening to the ringing tone for over a minute with no response, he hung up. No one at home. But he had an idea of where he might find the person he was looking for.

The road crossed a tributary to the lake and ran alongside the few tower blocks that developers had managed to build in this picturesque corner before it was turned into a national park. Les Gavines was another stain on the local coastline, but it was almost admirable if only as a symbol of how bad things could have become if the project to continue building on the narrow strip of land between the beach and the lake behind hadn't been stopped in time.

At the roundabout, instead of heading back towards Valencia, Cámara turned into the maze of pot holed roads that circled around the twenty-storey-high blocks of flats. On the beach front he followed the road northwards for as far as it went, past a handful of beach houses with rusting iron railings over the doors and windows leaving dark streaks down the greying white paintwork of the facades. After a few yards the tarmac ran out and he parked the Seat in a sandy area at the edge of an umbrella pine forest. There was no one else in sight, but six other cars were already parked nearby, while a couple of motorbikes had been chained to wooden posts marking the edge of the beach area. A path cut through the undergrowth seemed to lead the way and Cámara headed off into the trees.

The smell of hay and dung brought back powerful memories of the Ramírez farm from the previous day, and instinctively he put a hand down to feel his thigh. The skin was hard and tight where the cow's forehead had made contact with his leg, but if he didn't put too much strain on it he could walk without too much difficulty, certainly without any outward sign of a limp.

In a clearing in the trees ahead he could make out the yellow walls of the corrals. This was where they brought the bulls during *Fallas* week, and during the summer bullfighting season, as a kind of way station between the farms and the bullring. For the bulls, this gentle sea breeze, heavily scented with pine, would be the last air they breathed before being plunged into the violent world of the city.

But Cámara wasn't there for the bulls, nor for the sea. Because of the relative privacy the trees offered, and because the nearby beach was quiet and out of the way, this had become one of the biggest gay cruising grounds in the area.

Pushing on into the forest he began to catch sight of figures and faces up ahead. In a small clearing a man with closely cropped greying hair and a cyclist's outfit was leaning with one arm against a tree, basking in the sunlight as it broke through the branches above. He gave Cámara a hard stare as he approached, but his shoulders hunched when Cámara pulled out his ID.

'Antonio?' he said when Cámara asked him. 'I don't know. What's he done?'

'I'm not here to bust anyone,' Cámara said. 'But I need to speak to him. Urgently.'

'What makes you think he's here?' the man asked.

Cámara looked back in the direction of the bull corral. 'Just a hunch,' he said.

The man seemed to size Cámara up for a moment, then said, 'If you can promise me you're not going to bust anyone . . .' Cámara opened his hands as if to show he was clean. 'Then listen. There's some guy been coming round recently. New, haven't seen him here before. Someone told me his name was Antonio. I don't know if it's the one you're looking for, but if he is then just keep walking.' He pointed in the direction of another path leading out of the clearing where they were standing and along through the trees in the direction of the beach once more. 'There's an old abandoned factory up there.'

Cámara headed up the path and before long came out of the trees and into a scrub area with a concrete floor and piles of broken brick scattered about the place. It smelt strongly of stale piss, with empty wine bottles and beer cans strewn about, scribbled graffiti with illegible words and names, or crude phallic drawings, etched on to the few remaining pieces of wall still standing vertically. Everyone knew about the place – an old plastics factory that had been abandoned some thirty years earlier and which had crumbled over the intervening period thanks to the harsh sea air. A legal dispute over who actually owned the land it was built on had meant nothing had been done to pull it down once and for all, and so at first drug users, and now gay men, frequented it – out of the way, next to a long stretch of nudist beach. Occasionally some local councillor kicked up a fuss about it, condemning the moral horrors that were said to take place down there. It was a threat to all, a danger to children. But nothing ever got done, and in the meantime the men kept cruising, and coming.

Cámara heard footsteps behind him and turned on his heel. Antonio Aguado was standing in front of him, unafraid and unbowed.

'Hello,' he said. 'What a surprise.'

'Yes,' Cámara said. 'I need to ask you some more questions.'

Aguado sighed.

'All right,' he said. 'I'd rather hoped we'd said it all earlier on.' He glanced over his shoulder. 'Let's go down to the beach. You never know who's watching or listening round here.'

Cámara followed as they walked away from the concrete and brick rubble of the old factory and through the dunes which banked up against it. Small green rubbery plants poked through the sand at the edges of the path next to broken shards of glass and shredded tissue paper. Over the low peak of the dunes they were suddenly hit by the breeze blowing in off the sea. Waves a foot high were breaking on the shoreline just ahead of them.

'It's picking up,' Aguado said. 'It was as still as I've ever seen it when I got here.'

He found a more sheltered corner in the fold of one of the dunes, and sat down in the sand. After a pause Cámara sat next to him.

'You been coming here quite a bit recently?' Cámara said.

'Drowning my sorrows, you might say,' Aguado replied, forcing a smile. He dug into the sand beneath him and pulled it up in handfuls, letting it filter back down through his fingers. 'The bull corrals just over there . . . they remind me of him.'

'I need you to talk to me about Carmen Luna.'

'Come on,' Aguado started. 'I've told you—'

'Carmen was found dead this morning,' Cámara interrupted him. 'I've just come from her house.'

Aguado closed his eyes and slowly let his head fall.

'She committed suicide,' Cámara went on. 'Tied a weight to her wrist and then threw herself into the swimming pool.

There's something you didn't tell me last time. Whether it was to protect her, or to protect Blanco – perhaps yourself. But I know there's more.'

Still slumped forwards, Aguado's head began to nod softly as Cámara spoke.

'What happened? What was it about Carmen, about her "doing her bit", as you said?'

Aguado gave a low moan and then lifted his head again.

'Carmen was a cover story,' he said, his eyes still closed. 'She was useful. For Jorge. For us.'

'You mean the relationship?' Cámara asked. Aguado nodded. 'It was a sham.'

'Of course,' Aguado said. He opened his eyes and looked Cámara in the face. 'We needed to do something. All the rumours, all the stories.'

'But she didn't know, did she?' Cámara said. 'You used her, but she wasn't in on the game.'

Aguado rubbed his eyes and dropped his head again.

'I know.' He sighed. 'We thought about telling her. Perhaps at the start. She seemed the kind who might understand. Might even help her play her part even better. But how could we know if we could trust her? Then, I don't now, after a while it seemed to be going so well, so why bother. You know what I mean?'

'*We?*' Cámara said. 'Who's the *we*? Who came up with this idea? You?'

'Good God, no,' Aguado said.

'Jorge?'

'No.'

'Ruiz Pastor?'

'Ruiz Pastor didn't know.' There was something

approaching a smile playing on Aguado's lips. 'He bought the whole story, the Carmen Luna thing. He was there helping with the wedding plans, talking to all the journalists, who was going to get the photo rights, that kind of thing.'

'So who was it?' Cámara got up off the sand and grabbed Aguado by the arm, pulling him to his feet.

'Carmen Luna is dead,' he barked into his face. 'As dead as Blanco, as dead as Ruiz Pastor. Stop trying to hide your little secrets and tell me what was going on.'

'All right,' Aguado said, trying to shake himself free. 'Look, I don't know. I don't know whose idea it was or who set it up. But, look, the Ramírez family. They're powerful, right? They had a lot riding on Jorge. He was their big star, the greatest bullfighter, and all that. And he was theirs, championed their name. As long as things were going well with Jorge they were going well with them. So, I don't know, but I always assumed they were involved in it somehow. They'd known Jorge since he was a kid. If anyone else was going to know about him being gay it was them.'

Cámara let his hand fall away from Aguado's arm.

'They're rich, they've got contacts,' Aguado said. 'They could have set the whole thing up.'

'Francisco?' Cámara said. 'You think the father was behind all this?'

'I don't know. I told you. I have nothing to say it was them. I'm just guessing. But who else was it going to be?'

Who else was it going to be? That was the point. But if the Ramírez family had set the whole thing up, who'd called Carmen up that night and told her the whole thing? That her love story with Blanco was nothing but a play, carefully staged and orchestrated, where everyone except her understood that they were just reading the lines they'd been given.

'Someone called Carmen Luna last night,' Cámara said. 'Explained the whole thing to her. I'm convinced. That's why she killed herself.'

'Oh, my God.' Aguado looked suddenly shocked. 'Oh, my God,' he repeated, barely able to draw a breath.

'She left a note,' Cámara said. 'Cursing Blanco. But what I want to know is who told her? Who made that call?'

The anger in his voice took him by surprise, but Aguado was crumpling in front of him, his face pale, eyes red, a look of fear and desperation in his face.

'I don't know about the call,' he said under his breath. 'I don't know anything about that.'

He fell back down into the sand again, burying his head as he wrapped his arms around his knees. Remorse, self-pity, guilt. Cámara had seen it so many times, the moment when a suspect or a witness broke. Sometimes they looked to him in those moments as a redeemer, someone who could cleanse them of what they had done just by hearing them out. Others simply vanished into themselves. It was too late for Carmen Luna, however. She'd been useful to them while she'd been alive, and 'done her bit'. Had anyone really had a thought for her in all this, though? Not Aguado. Nor Blanco. But someone had been thinking about her. Which was why they had made the call.

Back at the Jefatura, Cámara picked up the phone and dialled a number.

'Gómez?'

'Cámara? *Hijo de puta*. Son of a bitch. Didn't think I'd

263

be hearing from you all of a sudden. Got your hands full at the moment, right?'

'Something like that.'

'Or don't tell me. You've just worked out who killed Blanco and you wanted your old friend to be the first to know. You're a sweetheart, you know that?'

'All right. Cut the crap.'

'Hey! I'm just glad to hear your voice. Don't get much to talk about down here. Just the usual Chinks and Moros filling up the corridors with their dodgy paperwork. You know how it is.'

'Thankfully, I don't. But I can imagine.'

'Listen, strictly between you and me, you might not have to do any imagining soon if things carry on the way they are. People are talking, Cámara. This is a high-profile case you've got. And if they don't get someone nailed for it soon the chances are you'll be down here with me in Foreign Nationals within a week. Unless you prefer the *Depósito*, of course, the impounded goods depot.'

'Right.' Cámara sniffed. 'I'll worry about that when I get to it. In the meantime . . .'

'What's on your mind?'

'There's someone who needs some help.'

There wasn't a great deal they could do. But at least by flashing Cyril's case up first it might mean he didn't get roughed up and deported as soon as some uniformed thug got his hands on him.

'Abdel-Krim Rifai,' Gómez repeated his full Moroccan name. 'But he goes by the name of Cyril, you say?'

'He did, at least when Carmen was around. Listen, just keep an eye out for him, will you?'

'Will do,' Gómez said. 'And you keep an eye out for yourself, Cámara. Much as I'd love your company, I don't want to see you down here. I really don't.'

Cámara rang off, then picked up the phone again and called Torres.

'Where are you?' he asked.

'Right now I'm having a piss,' Torres said. 'In the toilet on the fourth floor, to be precise. Ever tried pissing and talking on the phone at the same time? It's a nightmare, believe me.'

'All right. I'm in the office,' Cámara said. 'I'll wait for you here. And make sure you wash your hands.'

He stood up and poked his head out into the corridor. Ibarra and Sánchez were huddled at the far end looking at a list pinned to the wall giving details of who was to receive decorations at the next medal ceremony.

'You two,' he barked. 'Get over here.'

The two men started walking in his direction. Their body language, the hesitation, the scuffing of their feet as they leisurely strolled towards him, all spoke of what Gómez had just been saying on the phone: the perception was that Cámara was on the way out. If the rumours had already got as far as Foreign Nationals, then he probably only had hours – days at best – left in *Homicidios*.

'Get the paperwork out,' Cámara said to Sánchez. 'We're going to need Judge Caballero to give us access to Carmen Luna's phone records. Do it right. I don't want any fuck-ups over some stupid mistake. You,' he turned to Ibarra. 'Just make sure he spells everything correctly.'

They turned and headed down the corridor again. Cámara didn't stick around to hear the backchat. He opened a door;

the incident room was empty except for a duty policeman manning the phones. He looked up as Cámara walked in, then quickly averted his eyes, pretending to stare at his computer screen.

'Chief,' Torres said as he came in moments later. 'You might want to hear this.'

Not waiting for a reply, he reached up to a shelf and pulled down a small radio set. Cámara sat and watched as he switched it on and started scrolling through the stations. At any normal time of day pop music of some kind would be taking up most of the airwaves, but today it was all talk, and it didn't take long for him to work out what the topic of conversation was. Carmen Luna's name was being repeated endlessly, it seemed, in half-garbled flashes as the dial was turned. Eventually Torres settled on a station and placed the radio down on the desk, turning it to face Cámara to make sure he heard.

. . . in the light of recent events. You're listening to Channel 4 radio, on 97.4, bringing news, news, news to Valencia City and beyond. To recap on our main story – our only story – at this hour: Carmen Luna, the singer, celebrity and fiancée of the murdered bullfighter Jorge Blanco, has been found dead at her home. Sources say she was drowned in her swimming pool after a weight had been tied to her ankle. Police have been on the scene all morning, and while there is no official word yet, there is surely going to be a lot of speculation over this latest in a string of deaths since Blanco was found butchered in the middle of the bullring only six days ago. Was Carmen Luna murdered, just like Blanco before? And let's not forget Juanma Ruiz Pastor, Blanco's apoderado, *also found dead near the Albufera lake just two days after Blanco was killed. Is there*

some kind of feud going on? Has someone got it in for anyone associated with Jorge Blanco? Is anyone safe? Have the police got a handle on this? From here it doesn't seem so. They had one suspect and they let him go. So what's going on? Are we any closer to getting to the bottom of this? Or is Carmen Luna just the latest in what will prove to be a long list of bodies in the world of bullfighting and the rich and famous? Call us now with your thoughts. We want to hear what YOU have to say. Perhaps you were connected with Jorge Blanco in some way yourself. Do you feel safe? Dial 902 974 974 and tell us what YOU think . . .

Cámara leaned over and switched the machine off.

'Flores is on the board of directors of that radio station, but they're all saying pretty much the same thing,' Torres said, pulling his hand through his beard. 'Don't you think we should put a statement out? Make it clear it was suicide? They're treating it like another murder.'

'We've got more important things to do,' Cámara said. Not that it would make any difference if they did put out a press release, he thought. Normally he wouldn't even have thought about such a thing – the press office dealt with that. Doubtless they were taking their time, just as everyone else around him, already anticipating the carrion that his dismissal from the case would provide.

'Come on,' he said. They left the incident room and went back to their own office.

Sitting down behind his desk, Cámara reached into his jacket pocket and pulled out a packet of Ducados, stuck a cigarette in his mouth and lit it.

'Er, chief,' Torres said. 'You know you're not supposed . . . You'll set the smoke alarm off.'

'You'd better open the window, then,' Cámara said.

Torres walked over to the other side of the room and wrenched one of the windows out as far as it would go.

'You know what?' he said. 'I reckon that's the first time anyone's opened these. Bit of fresh air will do us good. I might join you.'

And he pulled out his own packet of cigarettes and lit one using Cámara's lighter.

'Fill me in on the Ramírez family,' Cámara said, putting his feet on the desk.

'OK,' Torres said. 'Not a lot on anything untoward in the breeding area. Like you said, bit of a wall of silence there. I talked to a few people in the bullfighting world, but they all said the same – Ramírez bulls the best there's ever been, etc. etc. Seemed to be offended by the very thought that they might be anything else.'

'Yes,' Cámara said. 'I've been hearing something similar.'

With something of a jolt, he realised it was the first time he had thought of Alicia since he'd hurried out of her flat in the early hours of the morning. He could imagine her annoyance at his not telling her straight away about Carmen Luna, but there would be time for sorting that out later. She'd have heard all about it by now, just like the rest of the country. And in the meantime he'd allowed her to get a good night's sleep. Still, it was strange she hadn't called, if only to confirm the story and the police version of events.

'So, nothing, then,' he said.

'Well, not quite,' Torres said. 'No one's talking about this, but I went through the press reports for all the bullfights I could find over the past eight years where Ramírez bulls had been involved.'

'Bloody hell!'

'Yeah, took a bit of time, but I was just trying to see if there were any patterns, right?'

Cámara placed his fingertips together and nodded.

'Look, bullfighting's an art, there's no official score, like in football. Or at least there's not supposed to be. So it's not easy for people to be objective about it, to say whether a bullfighter – or a breeder's bulls, for that matter – are better or worse than they were the year before. And there's always a bit of a tendency to say that things aren't as good as in the past, and what-have-you. But listen, there is a kind of score we can look at.'

'The press reports,' Cámara said.

'Yeah, and the number of ears and tails handed out at the end of each fight. So assuming that you need a good bull to produce a good bullfight . . .'

'A good bull, and a good bullfighter,' Cámara said. 'But I take your point.'

'Right, well listen. Eight years ago, which is as far as I went back, Ramírez bulls only took part in six bullfights in the whole country.'

'Doesn't sound much.'

'No, but they managed to be at the big fiestas – Madrid, here, Seville, Pamplona, etc. But get this: six bullfights, that's thirty-six bulls, OK? But guess how many ears were awarded to matadors fighting their bulls that season?'

Cámara shrugged.

'Twenty-one,' Torres said.

'To my ignorant ears that sounds quite high.'

'You're right,' Torres said. 'I had a quick look at some of the other big farms at the time and no one even comes close, not even with twice the number of bulls on the circuit.'

'So that was eight years ago,' Cámara said. He'd finished his cigarette and leaned over to throw it out the open window. Above them he noticed that a small white plastic dish on the ceiling – the smoke detector, he assumed – had a little blinking red light. Had it always done that? He looked away. 'What's been going on more recently?' he said.

'OK, this is interesting,' Torres said, his cigarette still clutched between his fingers. 'About five years ago the number of fiestas the Ramírez bulls were involved in started to rise. Nine for that year, then ten the next, then twelve, until last year Ramírez bulls were taking part in fifteen bullfights across the country. For this year's *Fallas* fiesta they were providing bulls for both the first and last fights. That's pretty much unheard of, but what with them sending bulls for the Blanco tribute fight as well, it means their bulls will appear three times in the same bullring in the same fiesta.'

'I'm amazed they can even do that,' Cámara said. 'What about the ears and tails over those years?'

'They actually started to go down at first,' Torres said. 'Only ten one year. Then they picked up again. Last year matadors fighting Ramírez bulls were awarded twenty-seven ears and two tails.'

'Out of a total of . . .'

'Ninety bulls over the season.'

'So we're talking about a huge drop in the number of ears per bull, as it were.'

'If we can take this method as a legitimate way of measuring how good the Ramírez bulls are – and I admit it's probably got more flaws than advantages – then we're look at a fifty per cent fall off in quality over the past five years.'

'Yet this is coinciding with a massive increase in the number of bulls they're putting out for fiestas,' Cámara said.

'Which means greater revenues.'

A gust of wind from outside brought the window crashing back into its frame. Torres jumped. Cámara stood up to close it tight, then looked up at the smoke detector again. The little red light appeared to be flashing even faster than before.

'Does that mean something?' Cámara asked, pointing up.

'*Joder!*' Torres quickly stubbed his cigarette butt out on the inside of the waste-paper basket. 'Open the window again!' he said. 'The fucker's about to go off.'

Cámara opened the window and grabbed his jacket.

'Come on,' he said. 'Let's go for a stroll.'

They'd made it downstairs, across the large, glass-and-cement entrance hall and were just passing through the doors out into the street when the high-pitched scream of the alarm finally pealed out.

'I don't know about you,' Cámara said. 'But I need a drink.'

Realising at the bar that he hadn't had any lunch yet, he ordered a *sandwich mixto* and some *patatas bravas* – fried potatoes laced with spicy tomato sauce and garlic mayonnaise – to go with his beer. Outside they could hear the sirens as the first fire engines began to arrive.

'Make it a *doble*,' Cámara told the barman as he reached for a glass to pour the beer. 'And give me a brandy as well to follow up.'

'So how was your day trip into the country?' Torres asked.

Cámara told him about what he'd learned.

'If there was anything dodgy going on with the Ramírez bulls,' Torres said once Cámara had finished, 'softening them up and all that, making them less aggressive, I can't imagine Blanco being too happy about it.'

An hour later they headed back over the road and up the stairs to the office. The fire engines had gone and everything appeared to be returning to normal.

'I wonder if they had to evacuate the cells in the basement,' Cámara said.

'Probably just leave them there to fry,' Torres said. 'If it's a real fire, I mean.'

The office looked much the same as when they'd left, but Cámara was the first to notice the change.

'Oh,' Torres said when he saw it too.

Someone had placed a 'No Smoking' sticker almost a foot wide on the window pane, blocking out much of the daylight.

'Something tells me we've been rumbled.'

Although it was late by the time Cámara left the Jefatura, a group of journalists was camped on the other side of the road from the front door, TV cameras pointing at them to catch any sign of movement from inside. Usually it was only the hotshot judges who got this kind of media attention, but this was turning into an exceptional case. He left through the back door and started circling the neighbouring streets trying to remember where he'd parked the Seat.

Surprisingly, Judge Caballero had offered no resistance to the idea of looking at Carmen Luna's phone records. Cámara had expected some kind of questioning, evidence of a direct link between her suicide and the murders they were investigating. But he'd called up as soon as he'd received the request and given his approval. Almost too easily, Cámara thought. Perhaps he thought there was nothing in it.

He put his hand into his jacket pocket and felt his phone nestling at the bottom. He thought for a moment about calling Alicia. They still hadn't been in touch since the night before. Was that all it was, all it was going to be? The phone seemed to tingle between his fingers as he rolled it around, then he let it fall back to the bottom and pulled his hand out once more, reaching into his other pocket for his packet of Ducados.

Cars were rammed into every available space – on the pavements, across the zebra crossings, as many as five deep in a mini-square where two roads converged. At last, turning the corner of another street, the flash of fireworks lit up the dark red of his Seat just a few yards ahead. Inhaling deeply, he strolled towards it, feeling for his keys in his trouser pocket. It was only when he sat down behind the steering wheel that he noticed the broken glass covering the passenger seat.

'*Me cago en la puta.*'

He checked the radio set, but it was still there. Then he reached for the glove compartment: it was locked, as he had left it, with no sign that anyone had tried to force it open. Switching on the inside light, he finally saw: in the footwell of the passenger seat were three A4-sized photographs. They were slightly out of focus, but lifting them to have a look, Cámara could easily make out the images of him and Alicia kissing outside the restaurant in the Barrio Chino quarter from a couple of nights before. In the first two their faces were partially concealed by being pressed against each other, but in the third, both were looking in the direction of the camera, in Alicia's case with an expression of bewilderment, in Cámara's of blazing anger. There was no mistaking who they were.

He put the key in the ignition and started the engine. First thing in the morning he'd take it round to Alejandro, his mechanic. For the time being, Hilario's gift would help him get through the night. Revenge would have to wait.

NINETEEN

Women, bulls and melons – how they appear is how they are
Traditional

Saturday 18th March

'*Escucha, tío.*'

Alejandro was being even friendlier than usual that morning. The garage was filled with broken cars and oily, rusting parts lying around like the diseased, discarded innards of an ailing patient, but even though he clearly had a lot of work on, he immediately agreed to fix the Seat window. After what felt like a sleepless night thanks to the *Fallas* noise, Cámara had dragged himself over as Alejandro was opening up, catching him climbing into his overalls, with his fourth or fifth cigarette of the day clamped between his lips. Alejandro didn't believe in health and safety, and the more smokers there were in his highly inflammable and explosive environment the happier he was. He wasn't a great believer in *Fallas* either, which was why he tended to stay open during the holiday period when everyone else shut down, even working Saturday morning.

Alejandro had said he'd park the car himself once he'd

finished, probably be done in half an hour if he wanted to wait. But no, Cámara had to get going; he didn't mention the clutch cable: that could wait till another time. It was only then that it became clearer why Alejandro was being so nice to him.

'Listen, mate,' he said. 'I know you don't like to get too much into all the media stuff. At least that's what you've always said.'

'What is it?' Cámara asked.

'Look, no one likes to be the messenger of bad news, right? But I don't know if you've seen today's *El Diario*.'

Cámara shook his head.

'Do I really want to?'

'I don't know, *tío*. I really don't but, well, you'll probably find out about it sooner or later.'

'You got a copy here?' Cámara asked.

'No. Saw it in the bar this morning. I can go and get it for you if you like.'

'That's fine. Thanks, Alejandro. I'll pick up a copy on my way in.'

Cámara turned to leave.

'Don't worry about the car,' Alejandro called after him. 'I'll sort it out for you.'

The morning editions were stacked up on a shelf below the news-seller's green metal booth on the corner of the street. Carmen Luna's name screamed out from a dozen headlines alongside some of the last pictures taken of her next to Jorge Blanco. No one appeared to have got wind of the suicide note, he saw. He'd handed it over to Huerta once he'd read it; it seemed his colleague had managed to keep its contents to himself for the time being. Cámara scanned the headlines; they didn't have to make an effort to sensationalise the story: it was big enough on its own. Of all the newspapers on display, however, only *El Diario* went for a more sinister angle: *The black holes of the Blanco case*, Cámara read. *Police investigation ridiculed as Carmen Luna found dead at her home.*

He gave the man inside the kiosk €1.10, picked up a copy and walked away with it. Just as on the radio the day before, the fact that Carmen Luna's death was a suicide was largely glossed over. There was a third body now linked to the Blanco affair: that was all that seemed to matter. And the police were being given the blame.

But it wasn't just the police as a whole, as Cámara realised when he turned the page and looked inside. Staring at him from the middle of page 3, with a little photograph next to his byline, was an editorial by Javier Gallego entitled *Why heads have to roll in Blanco case*. Cámara took a breath and glanced back at the article. When he saw his own name in the very first line he closed the paper shut: there was no point going on.

At the next kiosk further down the road he saw an elderly man wearing a heavy coat and scarf against the cold morning air shuffling towards the stacks of newspapers.

'Here,' Cámara said, thrusting his copy of *El Diario* into his hands. 'Save yourself the money.'

For some reason Flores's face kept flashing in his mind. He couldn't say exactly why, but part of him felt sure he had something to do with this: a sense, like a lingering stench of rancid lard. He and Gallego were friends, Alicia had said. The connection was there.

He'd barely got any sleep the night before since the

open-air disco beneath his bedroom window had belted out endless pop 'classics' until five in the morning. Most people were sleeping off the excesses of the night before, preparing for another two days of hard-core fiesta before the final explosion – literally – the following night.

It was election day the next day, Cámara remembered. By now all the campaigning would be over and voters were allowed an official 'day of reflection' before casting their votes. Not that there'd be much reflecting going on, if truth be told. If anyone actually went to vote the next day they'd probably be doing so pissed out of their skulls. Which may have been what Mayoress Delgado's team was banking on.

He listened in vain for the brass-band sound of the *despertà*. Perhaps even the musicians were too hungover to get up that morning.

At the corner of the block he came across another *falla* statue, one of the smaller ones that dotted the entire city, perhaps only three or four metres high. He hadn't seen it before. The central theme appeared to be bullfighting in general: the main figure at the centre was a gigantic bull breathing fire out of its nostrils and with an angry expression on its face. Standing next to it, and almost as high, was a skinny matador raising his *muleta*, encouraging the bull to charge. There was something effeminate about him, though. Cámara walked closer to have a better look. Was it possible? Had someone really built a *falla* about Blanco and kept it up, even in the wake of his murder? Perhaps even hinting at the rumours about Blanco being gay? Circling around the *falla* to see, he was relieved to discover that the face of the bullfighter was definitely not meant to be a representation of Blanco.

Cámara had no idea what the 'message' of this particular statue was meant to be. Standing around the central figure were the lesser statues – the *ninots*: a fat picador on a horse with a lance, a handful of *monosabios* with their blue-and-red uniforms. At their feet were scraps of verse painted on to pieces of board. He leaned forwards to get a closer look: they were all in the local language, Valencian. Although he didn't speak it, he'd been in the city long enough to pick some up, and it was close enough to his native Castilian Spanish to be able to understand without too much difficulty. The problem came when there was a play on words or the use of some dialect or archaic words that most Valencian-speakers understood, even if they didn't use regularly. The doggerel that was written on the *fallas* was almost invariably of that kind.

He scanned three or four of them, and while the specific meaning was elusive, the general sense was quite clear: bull-fighting, the national fiesta, was, according to this *falla* artist, in crisis. And the bulls themselves – representing the pure spirit of the corrida – were soon going to rise up and rebel if the art form was cheapened with ever more lacklustre performances. Hence the effeminate matador, Cámara thought.

Cámara looked for a reference to Jorge Blanco in there. If anyone had been bucking this perceived trend it had been he, surely. But he couldn't see anything.

One of the *ninots* caught his attention as he took a last look: a man in a suit, with grey hair combed back, a hooked, aquiline nose parked on the front of his long, slender and ageing face. Cámara glanced down at the verse painted at his feet. Whoever had composed the lines was convinced that the man caricatured above was very much a part of the present crisis in bullfighting.

Cámara flipped open his phone and put a call in. After a few minutes he was given an address, which he memorised. Heading back down the avenue he turned left and started to cross town.

The house was a 1930s villa set back from the road, with a large wall and wrought-iron fencing surrounding the garden. It stood near the top end of Blasco Ibáñez Avenue, just across the road from the Viveros park, the university quarter and one of the most exclusive parts of the city.

The gate was slightly ajar. Cámara pushed and the hinges gave a low groan as it swung open. A stone pathway led through the rose bushes to the steps and the front door. In a couple of moments he was standing under the porch, raising the large brass knocker.

Francisco Ramírez was already washed and shaved and wearing a fine woollen suit and silk tie when he answered the door.

'Chief Inspector Max Cámara of the *Policía Nacional*,' Cámara said as soon as he appeared, placing a hand on the door to insist that Ramírez let him in.

Ramírez looked bemused for a moment.

'Are you still—?'

'Yes, very much so,' Cámara interrupted him.

Ramírez moved away from the door and Cámara stepped inside.

If on the outside the house had a slightly Modernist, avant-garde appearance, with rounded lines and large, circular windows, inside it was decorated in a much more traditional style. Dark rugs were thrown over the flagstone floor, the walls were painted white, while the furniture was of the heavy 'Castilian' style – carved oak tables and throne-like chairs painted in thick, almost black varnish. A Valencian family might have given the place a lighter touch – some colourful tile work, perhaps, or curtains in bright pinks or orange. But the Ramírez family had brought their tastes down to the coast with them from further inland and although he had never lived in houses like this himself, it was very familiar to Cámara.

Ramírez led him through to a living room. A large mirror with an ornate gilt frame hung from the wall above the fireplace and Cámara caught a glimpse of himself as he walked past. His hair was ruffled, bags developing under his eyes from the lack of sleep. He'd barely taken any care of himself over the past few days.

Cámara studied Ramírez as they sat down. The man he'd seen back at the Bar Los Toros the night of Blanco's murder had had an air of defiance, even anger about him. But this Ramírez, the one sitting in front of him now, had lost that hardness. Grief had broken something inside him, despite his appearance of normality.

'I would offer you some coffee,' Ramírez said. 'But Mari-Luz, my maid, is having the morning off. It didn't seem fair to keep her here all the time when the rest of the city is having so much fun.'

Without asking permission first, Cámara pulled out his packet of Ducados and lit a cigarette.

'I wanted to ask you about your son,' he said, breathing out a trail of smoke.

'Paco?' Ramírez said. 'Yes, he told me you'd been up to

the farm. I take it your leg is fine now. Oh, and by the way, there's an ashtray on the table next to you.'

'No, I wasn't referring to Paco,' Cámara said. 'I mean Jorge Blanco.'

Ramírez's face remained perfectly still. Cámara pulled on his cigarette, glanced down at the table to locate the ashtray, then looked up again. The silence, the lack of response, told him he'd hit his mark. For a moment it was as if Ramírez had been paralysed.

'He wasn't just *like* a son for you, was he?' Cámara said.

A new shine had come into Ramírez's eyes, and in the reflection a slight tremor was just visible.

Cámara thought to himself of the details that had given the secret away: the photo of Señora Blanco in a colourful summer dress – not traditional mourning – with her teenage son; of how she'd spoken of his father in the present tense. Then there was her surname – Blanco had exactly the same as hers, not that of his supposed father – a sure sign of an illegitimate birth.

'Did she tell you?' Ramírez blurted out. He'd been holding himself in. Now that he spoke a spray of saliva showered from his mouth; his voice trembled.

'No, she didn't,' Cámara said.

'*Zorra!*' Ramírez spat. 'Bitch.'

There was a pause. Ramírez wiped his mouth, breathing heavily through his nose. The fingers of his left hand tapped on the armrest of the chair. He looked up and glanced around the room, as though searching for something to hang on to, but could find nothing. Avoiding Cámara's gaze, he turned his attention to the empty black space of the fireplace and stared at it. Then with a gulp of air he suddenly leaned forward and wrapped his hands around his face. His body shuddered as emotion erupted and streamed through him.

'I've lost a son,' he said, his words barely audible through his hands. 'I've lost a son.'

His body continued shaking as he struggled to compose himself, wiping at his eyes and trying to clear his throat. With a jerk he sat up straight in his chair, still partially covering his face. His tie was stained.

'I hope to God you never have to go through the same,' he said. 'No man deserves this, no matter what he's done, what sins he's committed. Children are life, your sons are your own life. No one should be able to take them away from you.'

Cámara sucked hard on his cigarette. Opposite him, Ramírez had managed to locate a handkerchief from a pocket and was wiping his eyes.

'You can't understand. It was different then. I couldn't have acknowledged him. His mother was . . .' He paused, eyes pulling away to the side as he seemed to recall something from the past. 'What happened, happened,' he said at last. 'We tried to fix it, in the only way we could. You have to remember what things were like back then. And in a rural environment . . .' He tailed off again.

'And did you fix it so that the groom had his accident so soon after marrying your mistress?' Cámara asked.

Ramírez gave him a look of horror.

'No. That was an accident. Really. He was one of my best farmhands. He knew, of course, about the situation, and agreed to marry her, but . . . No.' He closed his eyes and shook his head. 'He got thrown by his horse. It was a stupid thing. Might have happened to him a dozen times or more, and, well, you just picked yourself up, got back on the horse and carried on. But the way he fell. He . . . he broke his neck. Dead on the spot. There was nothing we could do.'

He gave Cámara a look.

'You and I deal with death more than the ordinary person, I suspect,' he said. 'Sometimes the weakest seem to be the longest to hold on, while at others it's the strongest among us, the ones you think will carry on for ever, that seem to slip away. I've seen it all my life with bulls, and eventually you develop an eye for the ones that look to be *bravo*, but which you know will let you down. With people it's more complicated.'

'Blanco went up to visit you at the farm just a couple of weeks before his death,' Cámara said. 'What did you talk about?'

Ramírez raised his hands and started stroking his eyebrows, as though trying to ease out a knot developing in his brow.

'I know that he was upset, afterwards,' Cámara added. 'Angry, even. There was an argument, wasn't there? What did Blanco say, Señor Ramírez?'

Cámara waited for a second, then added: 'Something about the farm?'

'Something about the farm,' Ramírez repeated under his breath. For a moment it seemed as if he was elsewhere, his imagination returning to that day.

'We . . . There were raised voices,' he said at last. His eyes darted from side to side. Cámara made an effort to make as little movement as possible, as though to reduce his presence in the room. Talk, make gestures, or advertise yourself in some way, and people were reminded of who they were talking to. Disappear, vanish or draw a veil over yourself, and they opened up more.

'Jorge knew,' Ramírez said at last. 'It may be that he always knew. Or that finally his mother had let it slip. I don't know.'

He closed his eyes in concentration.

'The fact is,' he went on, 'he wanted a share of the farm. He thought it was his right, as a Ramírez, as my son, that he should have a share. I don't expect to be leaving this world in the near future. But the question of inheritance is clearly one that is crossing other people's minds, given my age. It has always been the assumption that Paco was the one who would take over the farm. Roberto, my second son, as perhaps you know, is less interested in our world. But suddenly . . . well, there was Jorge saying that he should have a stake as well. That he *had* a stake in it all. He was a Ramírez, as a top bullfighter he had championed our name . . .'

He sat back in his armchair, his hands resting on his lap.

'I still don't know quite what he expected. That we would agree on the spot? Perhaps we should have. There was rarely any room for doubt in Jorge's mind. Once he'd decided on something . . . Did he get that from me?'

His eyes shone fiercely with repressed tears as a resigned smile formed on his mouth.

'I have denied myself the pleasure of wondering aloud about such matters for all these years,' he said. 'About which characteristics he may or may not have inherited from my side. And now it's too late.'

He stared Cámara hard in the face, then closed his eyes

again. Cámara waited for a few moments to see if there was any more information forthcoming, but the old man remained silent.

He stood up from his chair and at the sound Ramírez opened his eyes again. After a pause, as though he needed time to understand what was happening, he got up himself and moved to show his visitor to the door. The sound of firecrackers welcomed them from outside.

'You hear rumours,' Cámara said, 'about malpractices among bull breeders. Doctoring the bulls and that kind of thing. Obviously I don't know that much about it, not being an aficionado.'

'It must be a difficult case for you,' Ramírez said, the sharpness returning to him.

'And you've never been tempted?' Cámara asked. 'There are a lot of bullfighters out there much happier fighting safer bulls. And happier bullfighters means more corridas.'

Ramírez forced a smile.

'You know of our reputation, I'm sure,' he said. 'We couldn't betray that.'

'I see,' Cámara said, raising his voice as another *traca* string of firecracker explosions was let off only yards away. 'Only, it was quite useful having Blanco there as your champion, wasn't it? The defender of pure bullfighting. It gave you a perfect disguise.'

Ramírez remained silent, but moved to close the door on him.

'Things are going to be a bit more difficult from now on, I'd say,' Cámara insisted.

The door shut.

Turning on his heel, he skipped down the steps and out

the gate, back into the street. A couple of teenage girls in *fallera* costumes ran past him, giggling in the sunshine. From somewhere nearby he could hear the sound of a paso doble blaring out as another local street party got underway.

Valencia, tus mujeres todas tienen de las rosas el color . . .

Pacing the car-free avenue in the direction of the Jefatura, he started whistling along to the tune.

A call on his mobile broke him off: Torres.

'We've got the data in from Carmen Luna's phone.' Torres had to shout to make himself heard against the background of *falla* noise. 'Last calls made and received on the day leading up to her death.'

'Good work,' Cámara shouted back. 'What've you got? Who made the last call to her?'

There was a pause.

'You're not going to believe this,' Torres said.

'Try me.'

'The last call to Carmen Luna,' Torres said, 'came from a mobile phone. I've had the number checked. It's one of three that are billed to the Town Hall.'

'Which department?' Cámara said.

'Central office. That means—'

'Yes, I know what that means,' Cámara said. 'Find Flores. I want him hauling in.'

'Chief, tomorrow's the election. Today's the Day of Reflection. There's no way Caballero's going to agree to that. If we go around arresting politicians—'

'Just do it!'

'On what grounds?'

'I'll think of something.'

*   *   *

287

He knew the press would still be camped outside the front door of the Jefatura, so he took a different route in order to get to the back entrance.

Checking the time on his mobile, he decided to stop off and get an early bite to eat now before the *falla* crowds started occupying every available place. Around the next corner he spotted a small bar with aluminium windows and faded yellow-and-orange striped blinds. Doubtless they'd have some paella already prepared for lunchtime: he could have something to eat while he thought about how to play things with Flores.

There was already a considerable crowd inside when he walked in. From the bags under their eyes most of them looked to have fallen straight out of bed and into here, picking up from where they'd left off sometime around dawn. Without paying much attention, Cámara found an empty corner of the bar and sat down on a hard metal stool. He noticed they had Mahou on tap and ordered a *doble*. He took his mobile out and left it on the top of the bar: if Torres was going to ring it was the only way he was going to hear it against the din.

The beer was cool and sharp. In three gulps he finished it and brought the glass down with a tap, catching the barman's eye to order another one.

'And give me a plate of paella to go with it as well,' he said.

He felt a hand on his shoulder. Spinning round, he saw a familiar, if unexpected face.

'Chief Inspector. I thought it was you.'

Alejandro Cano looked as though he'd recently stepped out of the shower; his chin was freshly shaved and he was wearing a neatly ironed white shirt.

'I have friends who live in this area,' Cano said. He pulled up the stool next to Cámara's and sat down. 'I always come during *Fallas* and spend a day with them, hand out prizes to the kids, that kind of thing. Helps get them mentioned in the papers.'

'You're here so that the photographers come,' Cámara said.

'That's the idea,' Cano smiled. 'But that's all later. We're just having a few drinks right now.' He indicated a group of men on the other side of the bar. 'You want to join us?'

'I'm fine. Thanks.'

'As you wish.'

He made no move to go. The barman placed a fresh glass of beer in front of Cámara.

'You all right there?' the barman said to Cano.

'Give me another glass of the *sangría*.'

The barman reached for a jug and filled a wine glass with pink sweet liquid, fishing out a few pieces of fruit to float on top, then handed it to the bullfighter.

'Thanks,' Cano said. He raised his glass and turned to Cámara.

'To the successful conclusion of your case,' he said. After a pause, Cámara lifted his beer and made a half-hearted toasting gesture.

'I've read the papers,' Cano said. 'There was no call for that article. Really.'

'Thanks,' Cámara said.

'Look.' Cano reached out and placed his hand on Cámara's shoulder. 'It's the last bullfight of the fiesta tomorrow. I'd like to invite you to come along.'

Cámara's face remained impassive.

'As my guest,' Cano said. 'I'm not fighting tomorrow, but, well, I'm sure you can imagine, they give me good seats, that kind of thing.'

Cámara took another gulp of beer, then pulled out his Ducados.

'It would be an honour for me,' Cano said. 'I know a good man when I see one, Chief Inspector. And if there are any problems with this investigation at the moment, I know they are nothing to do with you, not your fault at all. It would be a gesture of solidarity. You'll see: come with me to the bullfight, as my guest, and those journos will come round. Don't underestimate the power of celebrity.'

He held out his hand. Cámara lit his cigarette, put his lighter back in his pocket, and then reached out and shook it. Cano smiled.

'You working today?' he asked. Cámara nodded.

'All the more reason to take tomorrow off, then. Or at least the afternoon.'

'I'll see what I can do,' Cámara said.

'You might not believe it, but we have our own problems, our own power battles and crises in the world of bullfighting as well.'

Cano took a sip of his *sangría*, then pushed a hand through his hair. For the second time that day, Cámara reflected, it looked as though someone was about to open up to him.

'Is that what happened between you and Ruiz Pastor in the end?' Cámara asked.

Cano sighed. 'Poor old Juanma. He was all right. We had our problems, yes, it's true, but, well, mustn't speak ill of the dead.'

Cámara waited.

'I suppose you've looked into it?' Cano said at last. 'At the time everyone assumed it was because of Jorge, the new bullfighting star, and that Juanma dropped me to become his *apoderado*.'

'That's what I've heard,' Cámara said.

Cano reached over and picked up Cámara's packet of Ducados. 'May I?'

Cámara held up his lighter and lit him one.

'The truth is,' Cano said, 'that things were going badly before all that. Juanma was only ever interested in money, getting as much money as he could. Don't get me wrong, I'm interested in making money as well. Or at least I was.'

He stroked a finger down one of his sideburns.

'You reach a point where that's no longer the motivation. But for him it just never stopped; he needed more. Always more money.'

'And that caused problems between you?' Cámara said.

'After a while.' Cano pulled on his cigarette lovingly in the way of someone who doesn't smoke regularly, savouring the taste of the tobacco. 'He was angling for a bigger percentage. Said he was doing more than just the ordinary work of an *apoderado* for me.' He smiled.

'The scandals?' Cámara asked.

'A lot of it's made up,' Cano said. 'But, yes, there have been a few occasions . . . Women you thought you could trust at the time but then decided to tell their story. The kind of thing that fills the gossip programmes. They need material of that sort to keep going; it's an industry.'

He waved a hand dismissively.

'Anyway, Juanma ended up having to deal with a lot of this kind of thing, paying off girls to keep them quiet. Listen, it doesn't matter if I tell you now; it was all years ago. And I never did anything wrong. But Juanma got it into his head that he was owed more money, a bigger cut. Said he was going to tell everything – and more – if I didn't cough up.'

'What did you do?' Cámara said.

'I gave him his money,' Cano said. 'And then waited. When Jorge showed up I could see Juanma wanted him. It was the money again. Thought he could make a fortune with the guy. So I just nudged him on his way. It was a relief, believe me, even if I was a bit worried for what Jorge was getting in for.'

'You never said anything to him?'

Cano shook his head. 'We didn't socialise. Rivals in the bullring? Yes, of course. Jorge had his style; I have mine. And then there were a few things said that probably shouldn't have been. Got into the papers. But I only ever had the greatest respect for him.'

He tossed the cigarette on to the floor and stubbed it out.

'And I like to think he had the same for me.'

He got up from his chair and downed the last of his *sangría*.

'One thing,' Cámara said. 'The rumours I hear about malpractices among bull breeders, shaving their horns down, doping them, that kind of thing . . . Is that really going on?'

Cano looked him straight in the eye, his face set, unmoving. Then finally he reached out and put his hand on Cámara's shoulder.

'I'll see you tomorrow afternoon,' he said.

*   *   *

Cámara walked out into the sunshine. The outdoor disco opposite was in full swing, and a heavy bass from the enormous speakers was making the windows in the nearby blocks of flats vibrate in time to the beat. There had been no call from Torres yet, but it had given him more time to eat his paella slowly. You should never hurry a good rice dish.

As he drew away from the fiesta down a side street in the direction of the Jefatura, the mobile in his hand buzzed once, then stopped. A text message. He lifted it up and shaded the screen with his hand from the sun to get a better look.

Quiero verte, he read. I want to see you.

He smiled: he hadn't expected Alicia to be the type.

Putting the phone back in his pocket, however, he sensed that something wasn't right. He pulled out the phone again, and this time stepped into the shade of a doorway to get a proper look.

The same words stared back at him from the green-blue screen. Hitting a button, he looked to see who it was from. He hadn't memorised Alicia's number yet, but he now saw that the message wasn't from her.

It was from Almudena.

TWENTY

May God save me from a manso *bull; from a*
bravo *one I'll save myself*
Traditional

Flores's dress sense hadn't improved over the course of the election campaign. Cámara walked into the interrogation room to find his overweight body clad in a shiny dark blue suit, a lime green shirt and red-and-yellow vertically striped tie. Sitting in the chair on the opposite side of the stuffy little room, he leaned forwards, his elbows on the table, hands clasped in front of him, shoulders hunched, a confident smirk settling on his face.

'Oh, we're going to have so much fun with this,' he said as Cámara sat down. Torres stayed on his feet, hovering near the door.

'If you wondered if it was over for you before this, Cámara, then you are now doubly dead. Do you get that?'

His forehead glistened under the strip light hanging a couple of feet above them. The acidic, putrid smell that had quickly established itself in these new police facilities – as though it had managed to transport itself over along with all the paperwork and office furniture – seemed to match the disturbing colour coordination of his attire.

'Arresting a Town Hall official on the Day of Reflection. Do you know how many laws you're breaking here? The Constitutional Tribunal in Madrid are going to be crawling up your fucking arse over this one. We're not just talking about a slap on the wrist, or a demotion, for fuck's sake. You're probably going to end up in the dock yourself. And I for one will be standing there cheering all the way. So let's just stop playing at cops and robbers, shall we? The game's over. I'm calling my lawyer now. And you are finished.'

A swollen index finger was flicked out and pointed in Cámara's direction.

'You seem to be under some kind of misunderstanding,' Cámara said after a pause. 'You must forgive Inspector Torres here. He might have got a bit carried away. It is *Fallas* after all. Did you say you were arresting Señor Flores, Torres?' He turned to look behind him. Torres shook his head.

'There, you see,' Cámara said. 'No one's talking about arresting anyone. No, Señor Flores, you're here to – what's the phrase they use on those English cop shows on TV? Helping police with their inquiries, yes, that's it.'

'I never did think much of the English sense of humour,' Flores said.

'No, I don't imagine you did.'

'Well, if there's no fucking arrest then,' he said getting out of his chair, 'I've got an election campaign to run. Oh, and your career to destroy.'

'Of course you can leave if you wish,' Cámara said. 'But there's the rest of the day to go before the polls open. Your campaign could still be lost. Especially if some of the stuff that we've discovered gets out.'

'There's no campaigning now, Cámara. Day of Reflection. No one's allowed to even fucking talk about the election. So whatever it is, it's too late for you.'

He stepped away from the table and made a move towards the door. Torres stood still, barring his way.

'This isn't campaign material,' Cámara said. 'It's a perfectly legitimate news story. But I wonder how it will affect voters to discover that the Town Hall was directly linked with Carmen Luna's suicide.'

'What?' Flores laughed.

'It would be on the radio in a couple of hours. Be on the front pages of all the newspapers tomorrow morning. Just as people are going out to vote.'

Flores was still standing, but had fallen silent.

'We've got the records of who called Carmen just before she died,' Cámara said. 'We know it was you.'

Flores's eyes widened.

'You wouldn't dare,' he said at last.

'You yourself were insisting that my career is over, Señor Flores. What have I got to lose? A few phone calls and the story's out there. What's to stop me? Once you're doubly dead, as you say, it might as well be triply dead, or whatever.'

Flores was breathing heavily, his puffy face flushing deep red around tight, white lips.

'I'll get you,' he said under his breath. 'I'm going to fucking get you so badly.'

'Let's leave that for later, shall we?' Cámara said. 'In the meantime I think you should sit down.'

Slowly, sulkily, like a child, Flores returned to his seat.

'I've got so much shit on you, Cámara,' he said. 'You think a little game like this is going to save you?'

'I know about your arrangement with my colleague Maldonado,' Cámara said. Flores gave a start.

'Really, Señor Flores,' he laughed. 'I mean, come on. Did you think I was so stupid?'

For the first time since they had been in the room together, Cámara felt the beginnings of a crack develop. It was rare for a middle-class, successful man like this to be on the other side of the table. On the whole, in Cámara's experience, the more someone had – the more money, fortune, fame – the more they had to lose. And the easier it was to break them just by giving the slightest whisper of what you could do to them. Would Flores be like them? He was a politician, probably had a tougher skin than most.

'What I'm really interested to know,' Cámara said, 'is why you called Carmen Luna that night. Knowing what I know, many would say there's blood on your hands. Your call comes in – you're the last person she spoke to on this earth, effectively. And then a couple of hours later she's tying weights to her wrist and throwing herself in the pool.'

'I hope you don't have that effect on all the women you speak to,' Torres said from his post at the door.

'What is this?' Flores said. 'A comedy double act?'

'It doesn't look good,' Cámara said. 'You've got a very big question to answer.'

'Which is?'

'What did you tell Carmen that made her take her own life?'

'You can't make me responsible.' Flores tilted his head to one side, the smirk reappearing.

'What do you reckon people are going to think if they find out?' Cámara said. 'We're not talking about a court of law, Señor Flores. We're talking about voters. Carmen Luna had a lot of fans. You might almost say she was a bit of a national icon. Even if it can't be proved, no one's going to take too kindly to the person who pushed her to suicide.'

'What the fuck,' Flores said under his breath. 'She's dead.'

'What did you tell her?' Cámara smashed his hand down on the table.

'Don't you think she deserved to know the truth?' Flores said with a trembling laugh. 'Everyone else knew.'

His eyes had taken on a more desperate shine. The crack was beginning to widen.

'Her bullfighting boyfriend was a fucking bender. A screaming *maricón*.'

'You rang her up just to tell her that?'

'He was using her,' Flores said. His breath was getting shorter. 'She was just a cover for him.'

'So, what? You were doing her a favour by letting her know?' Torres barked. 'Doing your public duty?'

'She didn't know. The guy had a fucking boyfriend in the background – and God knows what else – and he was using her, talking about getting married and all that shit.'

'And she believed it,' Cámara said.

'That's it,' Flores said. 'She didn't have a clue. Didn't know she was being used by that son of a bitch. She thought they were going to have kids together and all that. Fairy-tale stuff.'

'So you call her up and tell her,' Cámara said.

'Yeah.'

'Tell her that her whole life, the relationship she's in, the future she's planning, that it's all a lie.'

Flores shrugged. 'Yeah, I told you.'

'Why should she believe you?' Torres asked.

Flores's eyes darted back and forth between Cámara and Torres, but he remained silent.

Torres leaned in over him.

'What did you tell her?' Torres went on. 'She wouldn't just believe you because she trusted you. You had something, didn't you? Some kind of proof.'

Flores shrugged.

'Perhaps Señor Flores had some pretty pictures to show her,' Cámara said. Flores looked him in the eye. 'People can be quite indiscreet. All he had to do was send the photos to her in a phone message. Easier than the old way, when you had to go to the trouble of smashing someone's car window and leaving the prints on the dashboard.'

Flores didn't flinch, but Torres gave Cámara a puzzled look.

'I'll get Huerta to check Carmen's phone,' he said.

'That can wait,' Cámara said. 'What I want to know,' he added more slowly and staring at Flores, 'was what was in it for you?'

Flores coughed. 'What?'

'What were you thinking?' Cámara said. 'Get Carmen Luna out supporting Mayoress Delgado?'

'Not much use to you now she's dead, is she?' Torres said.

'Does he have to be here?' Flores said, pointing at Torres.

'I'm here for your sake more than his,' Torres said. 'Chief Inspector Cámara has a reputation for being, ah, very rigorous in some of his interviews.'

'I'm sure that was in Maldonado's notes,' Cámara said. 'But what you're not telling me is why you made that call to Carmen in the first place.'

Flores spread his hands on the table.

'This hasn't been the easiest campaign,' he said with a sigh. 'Blanco's demise made sure of that.'

'Should have made things easier, shouldn't it?' Cámara said. 'Running on an anti-bullfighting ticket?'

'The polls show there's been a rebound,' Flores said. 'Bullfighting is suddenly more popular again. It's the sympathy, I suppose.'

'You mean more than when Blanco was around.'

'Yeah,' Flores said. 'This comeback of his made an impact, it's true. But you should have seen the figures in the days after he was murdered. Went through the roof. There's nothing people like more than a martyr figure.'

'None of which can have done your campaign much good,' Torres said.

'They've got the media pretty much on their side,' Cámara said. 'Isn't that right?' He turned to Flores. 'Putting your own people in charge of local TV – even though it is paid for by public money. Then there's the radio. And you seem to have *El Diario*'s full backing. You and Gallego are quite close, I hear.'

'Likes to pass on information every now and again, does he?' Torres said.

'You're a bit naive to be a policeman, aren't you?' Flores said to Torres. 'Of course we do each other favours. It's how the fucking world works.'

'Ever say anything about Blanco?'

Flores grinned.

'We found out that Blanco was going to tell some big story. Before he got it in the neck. Probably the first to know.'

'Who did you tell?' Cámara said.

'Usual lot – the mayoress, election managers, our financiers.'

'What the fuck did you care about Blanco talking to the press?' Torres asked.

'It's about media management,' Flores said, rolling his eyes. 'We have to know what's going to be said before it's said – anything that might have a bearing on the campaign.'

'So what was Blanco going to talk about that was so important?' Torres said.

There was a silence as Cámara's eyes met with Flores's. Neither man spoke for a moment.

'No one knows,' Cámara said eventually. 'At least not for sure.'

'But you're that worried about losing this election that you've got to spy on newspaper reporters and bullfighters.' Torres was incredulous.

'We like to think Mayoress Delgado's record will see her through,' Flores said.

'Oh, give us a break,' Torres roared. 'You built the whole thing on banning bullfighting in the city. Don't start bullshitting us.'

Flores glared at Cámara.

'My colleague does have a point,' Cámara said.

'Yeah, all right,' Flores said. 'It wasn't good. Blanco got turned into a saint.'

'So you thought you'd tarnish things,' Cámara said, 'by bringing up all the stuff about him being gay.'

'Look,' Flores said. 'The bullfighting world's traditional, right? I mean, honestly I don't really care if the guy was fucking donkeys. But you let all those bastards know that

301

their hero was a *maricón* and believe me, there'll be no more talk about building statues of him. They like their bullfighters straight, the way God made them. Blanco's reputation would be mud. I don't care how many ears and tails he's been awarded over the years. The only thing people would remember is that he was queer.'

'Which makes things easier for you.'

'Well, yeah. To be honest.'

'So you thought Carmen was going to go public,' Cámara said. 'You thought you could tell her all this, about Blanco being gay, about him using her – as you say. And then, what? She'd go running to the press? Tell the story herself? That would have made quite an impact, right? Big, public scandal. The hero's reputation quickly brought down to earth.'

He stopped. Flores was nodding.

'But she didn't, did she?' Cámara said. 'Instead she went and killed herself.'

The nodding stopped.

'That fucked things up for you a bit, didn't it?' Cámara said.

Flores's voice was barely audible.

'Yeah, it did a bit.'

'What? I can't hear you,' Cámara said.

'I said, yes, it fucking did,' Flores shouted.

'So who do you turn to now?' Torres said. 'Who's going to help you now? The *Anti-Taurino* League?'

'Fucking amateurs,' Flores said.

'Oh, what? So you have been cosying up with them?' Cámara said. 'Things must be pretty bad.'

'Forget it, Cámara,' Flores said. 'You're out of your fucking depth. You really are. You want to make the League responsible for Carmen's death now? They're a bunch of losers. Haven't got two pesetas to rub together. But go ahead. Haul them in as well.'

He sat up in his chair, leaning in towards the table, his shirt pressing tightly against his chest.

'I mean, shit. Why not get the mayoress in here while you're at it. She's a bit busy with the election right now, but I'm sure she'd be delighted to – what was it? – help you with your inquiries.'

He laughed. The smirk was back.

'If you're looking for those extra nails in your coffin, Cámara, I'm your man.'

'You're not being very nice about your fellow anti-bullfight campaigners,' Cámara said.

'Most of them are fucking hippies and dope-smokers,' Flores said. 'The only one with any spark is that Moreno kid. But all he's ever after is money.'

'But you don't want to give him any.'

'In case you haven't noticed, Cámara, running an election campaign is an expensive business.'

'But you've got backers.'

'Yeah, thanks for your concern. We're all right. But don't let me stop you if you were thinking of making a contribution.'

'Perhaps you should put them and Moreno together,' Torres said.

'He's a sharp one, isn't he?' Flores said. 'Don't think I won't forget you as well. I can bring down two of you just as easily as one.'

'The thing is,' Cámara said. 'In all of this there's one thing you haven't told us.'

'I'm all fucking ears,' Flores said.

'You see, it took me a while to find out about Blanco being gay. Proof, I mean. And what's niggling me is how you discovered it.'

Flores closed his eyes and threw his head back.

'Paco Ramírez told me,' he said.

'Go on,' Cámara said.

'Look, when someone gives you something like that on a plate you don't ask too many questions.'

'Paco Ramírez came to talk to you?' Torres took a step closer to the table. 'What's a bull breeder doing talking to an anti-bullfight campaigner like you?'

'As I said, I didn't like to ask too many questions.'

'And you believed him, of course,' Cámara said.

'He showed me photographs.'

Cámara looked him in the eye, but Flores was staring down at the table.

'Compromising ones?' Cámara said.

'Yeah. You could say that.'

'Ones you then sent to Carmen Luna on her mobile.'

'So let's just get this straight,' Torres said. 'You're asking us to believe that Paco Ramírez suddenly calls you out of the blue talking about Blanco being gay, and then – what? – comes round to the Town Hall with a bunch of photos to prove his point?'

Flores shrugged.

'That was more or less it, yeah.'

'Why?' Torres said. 'Why the fuck would he do that?'

'Let me guess,' Flores said. 'You're the stupid one, right? Look, I've already said I didn't ask him. I just took it. It was a fucking godsend.'

Torres stood back from the table, crossing his arms.

'I don't know,' Flores said. 'I just assumed there'd been a bust-up or something. Paco wanted to get back at Blanco for something.'

'And he was going to use you to do it,' Torres said.

'Well, he wasn't going to do it himself, was he?' Flores sneered. 'In general you try and get other people to do your dirty work for you.'

'A bit like you and Carmen.'

Flores's eyes bulged.

'Look, I am not responsible for her death.' Tiny bubbles of spit were flying from his lips. 'Let's get that straight.'

'Tell me,' Cámara said. 'When exactly did Paco Ramírez approach you with the information about Blanco?'

Flores fell silent and looked down at his fingers where they were clasped over the table. Cámara waited. Next to him, Torres uncrossed his hands and placed them on his hips.

'Señor Flores,' Cámara said. 'I need to know when you spoke to Paco.'

'Yeah, I heard you,' Flores said, raising his head.

'So when was it?'

'The afternoon before Blanco was killed.'

Torres jumped.

'What?'

'He called around lunchtime,' Flores said. 'Said he wanted to meet. Then came round to the office, told me the story and showed me the photos.'

'And then hours later Blanco is found in the middle of the bullring with an *estoque* in his back,' Torres said.

'You've sat on this all this time,' Cámara said. 'Didn't

think to tell the police, obviously. Nor did you tell Carmen Luna straight away.'

'Withholding evidence,' Torres said. 'We could do him right now just for that.'

'Perhaps it just slipped my mind,' Flores said. 'You'd never make that stick.'

'Slipped your mind?' Torres turned away in disgust.

'You were saving it,' Cámara said. 'Waiting until the last days before the election. Then you made the call to Carmen, thinking that it would be all over the news the next day, just in time to swing a whole bunch of votes back your way as Blanco's reputation got ripped apart for him having a secret life.'

Flores raised his eyebrows and gave a smile.

'As plans go,' he said, 'even if you disagree with it, you have to admit it was pretty fucking good.'

'Brilliant,' Cámara said. 'Just a shame Carmen went and fucked it up for you.'

'So what do we do?' Torres said. 'Get a warrant for Paco's arrest?'

Torres's voice brought Cámara back from thoughts about Almudena. The text message: somewhere inside him it had been circling around and he'd been trying to work out what to do. Text her back? Give her a call? He'd decide later; right now there was too much else going on.

'We've got a motive. This argument over whether Blanco got a share in the farm. And the guy was clearly out to get him.'

After the episode with the alarm they'd returned to their usual spot outside the emergency exit at the back for a smoke.

'You yourself said he wasn't there the whole time at the Bar Los Toros. Could have bumped off Blanco then come round after.'

Cámara bit on the filter of his cigarette.

'How does Ruiz Pastor fit in?' he said.

'Cano told you he was always after more cash, right?'

Cámara nodded.

'From the sounds of it he was virtually blackmailing the guy.'

'So?'

'Let's say Ruiz Pastor knew about Blanco being Ramírez's son, and that there'd been a row over who inherited the farm and all that.'

Cámara remembered Carmen Luna talking about Blanco and Ruiz Pastor, of how they often spoke on the phone, and had done so the night Blanco returned from the farm.

'He was a chancer, I reckon. His big bullfighting star has just been done in and that's his meal ticket gone, but he thinks, I know, I can make a bit of dosh out of this.'

Torres was getting excited as the theory grew inside his mind, almost skipping from foot to foot.

'So he calls the Ramírez family and says he's going to spill the beans, say that they killed Blanco, and he knows why. But they can buy his silence for, oh, I don't know, a million euros. So he arranges a meeting with them, and that's when Paco bumps him off too.'

Cámara wondered silently about Margarita de la Fuente's theory about there being two killers. Was that a false trail? Was it Paco all along?

He felt a vibration in his pocket and placed his hand down to flick open his mobile.

Stub it out and come and see me in my office. Immediately.

'Time to go,' he said to Torres as he placed it back in his jacket.

'Pardo?'

Cámara took a deep drag on his Ducados, then flicked it out onto the waste ground next to a thousand other cigarette butts.

Pardo was facing the door when Cámara walked in.

'Sit down,' he said without moving.

'Let me guess,' Cámara said. 'You've had a chat with Flores.'

Pardo glared at him.

'Flores? I've had the mayoress herself on the phone. And I've only just managed to persuade her not to get the Ministry in Madrid on my case.'

'What do you want me to do?' Cámara said. 'Suspend the investigation just because it's election day tomorrow?'

'You hauled in the mayoress's campaign manager on the Day of Reflection,' Pardo said, as though his sin were self-evident. 'Short of buggering the mayoress herself, there isn't much worse you could have done.'

'Sadly, I don't have the pleasure of knowing Emilia that well.'

'Shut the fuck up, Cámara.'

Pardo stroked his tie, then sat down.

'This investigation has been a disaster from the start,' he said.

Cámara's eyes wandered towards the window, and the view over the city.

'As of Monday you're off this case, whether Mayoress

Delgado wins the election or not. I was going to give you that grace at least – wait and see if she got back into office. But there are plenty of people who'd be happy to see you shunted somewhere a little less embarrassing, Cámara. For the Ministry you're a disturbing little statistic, something they'd rather forget about.'

Cámara stood up and turned to go.

'Get out of here, Cámara,' Pardo shouted after him. 'And don't you dare think about coming in tomorrow.'

Alicia made to kiss him when they met, but she caught some of the hardness that was still wrapped around him.

'Oh,' she said as she backed off a little. 'Should I be taking this personally?'

'Let's get a drink,' Cámara said.

'It's *Fallas*,' Alicia laughed. 'We won't have to go far.'

It was the penultimate night of *Fallas* – the *Nit de Foc*, the Night of Fire, when one of the world's largest firework displays was set off over the city sky. By now the night air seemed to be filled with one continuous explosion as the streets were crammed with people walking in groups, shouting and singing, some carrying plastic cups filled with whisky and cola, others clutching paper bags of freshly fried *buñuelos*. The *fallera* queens had lost their freshly painted look, the golden combs in the backs of their heads coming loose where they'd been jostled in the crowd, stains and creases appearing on their full, embroidered silk dresses. Costumes that had cost thousands to make and several months in the sewing were now close to getting trashed in the carnival atmosphere. The smell of gunpowder was omnipresent as child after child threw his *petardos* to the ground with a wild look in his eye, their crashing only drowned out as spontaneous *mascletaes* hammered out from somewhere nearby, shaking the cobblestones beneath their feet. In the sky above, flashes of reds and yellows and greens grinned at them from the squibs overhead. Was this what hell was like, Cámara wondered? To live an eternal, never-ending *Fallas* fiesta, forced never to sleep and have your eardrums rocked again and again by an entire city of heaving, hysterical drunken partygoers?

Perhaps his time in the city was coming to an end, he thought to himself. On Monday he'd find out which forgotten corner of the force they'd be relegating him to. The *Depósito*? Perhaps he should resign. And do what? Go back to Albacete? Whichever way he looked around him, caught as he was in the crowd, there seemed to be nothing but emptiness ahead of him.

He felt a pull on his arm. Alicia was drawing him away from the fiestas and down an alleyway. He had no idea where to. Was she the answer? This latest fling? Something to hang on to in the vacuum? He felt so far removed from anything going on around him that his senses had fallen numb. Who was this woman? They'd slept together, that much he could remember. But he barely knew anything about her. Yet here she was, as though at the end of a dark, spiralling tunnel, pulling him along, past jeering piss-heads and gutters filled with pulped red-and-white paper cups as though she had a plan, as though she knew where they had to go, where she wanted him to go, to be. Away from all this, yes, away from the noise, and the crowds and the crass labyrinth of a crashing, chaotic world. An Ariadne come to save him, to lead him out, away from the bloodthirsty beast, half-man half-bull, that had been waiting to consume him inside.

He stopped dead in his tracks.

She pulled on his arm, but he wasn't moving.

'Come on, *cariño*,' she said. 'I know a place just a bit further on. It'll be quieter. Trust me.'

They were in a dark narrow street near the Na Jordana Gate. One of the biggest *falla* statues in the city was just around the corner. Beyond that there was only the empty river bed. Not even the *chaperos* and pushers would be down there tonight.

'Where are we going?'

He wanted nothing of this, not the banging, the crowds, the flashing fireworks, this woman dragging him through the streets. His brain felt sodden with noise and emotion, as though a dank black web had been cast over him, slowly weakening and exhausting him, as though waiting for him finally to give up before some hidden, invisible tormentor moved in for a kill.

'What is it?' Alicia said. 'Worried I might be taking you to some dark corner somewhere?'

But what tormentor? Who, exactly? Pardo? He didn't care enough about him. Flores? He'd had worse, and seen them off. Perhaps it was the case itself; it had got into him, stirring something, some undiscovered part of himself. The bloodlust, the anger. Was that it? He liked to think he could control them: his fighting skills could stand him in good stead sometimes. It was useful, a tool. But was he really master of himself, as he liked to imagine? Didn't he actually enjoy it, if he was honest with himself? What had Margarita said about bulls? They kept going, kept charging at the matador, and the person who would eventually kill them. Unless . . . unless they managed to get him first. That fighting urge was inside him, that need for violence, for blood. He hated bullfighting not for what it did to the bull, but for what it did to him, for showing him what he was. The would-be killer inside him was on display there in the middle of the ring. Wasn't that why he had run crying as a child? Not because of the bull. Not because of his sister. But because for a moment, for the briefest of moments when he saw the torero murdering the bull, he could understand his sister's killer, flirting with her, tormenting her, violating her, before finally slaughtering her. That was why he couldn't bear to watch the corrida. It was violence transformed, made something subtler, transcendent. But his own violence was raw, lay deep within him, sleeping most of the time, waking when he least expected it. Wasn't that it? A kind of magical thinking that by refusing to acknowledge its existence it might simply vanish, cease to exist. That was the best way to deal with violence, with one's own bloodlust. Deny it. That was the way of the modern world. A modern world that was then surprised at the violence of its young people, at football matches, in joining thuggish political parties, attacking beggars, old people, other children.

Alicia had stopped and was looking at him with an expression of concern.

'Max,' she said. 'Are you all right?'

'That day,' he said. 'The day Blanco was killed. He called you.'

In the gloom of the narrow alleyway where they stood, she looked into his eyes as though trying to understand what was going on in his mind.

'Still thinking about the case,' she said. 'Maybe I remind you too much of it.' She tried a smile, but Cámara didn't seem to notice.

A crowd of revellers had burst into the alleyway from the top end and was beginning to make its way down towards them. Soon it would be too noisy to talk.

He grabbed her arms and shook her.

'What did he say? What did Blanco say?'

The smile was quickly wiped from her mouth.

'I told you,' she said. 'He just said he wanted to talk. I assumed it was for an interview.'

She tried to wriggle free.

'Steady on.'

'There was more,' Cámara raised his voice. 'There was more.'

'No, really,' she said, 'I swear.' But he couldn't hear her.

'He told you about being Ramírez's son, didn't he? He was going to give you the whole story – about wanting a stake in the farm, about wanting to inherit.'

'What are you talking about?' she said.

'He was going to blow the whistle on what they're up to at the Ramírez farm,' Cámara went on. Bangs and crashes grew louder, reverberating in the narrow space off the stone walls of the houses nearby, as the crowd grew nearer.

'That was the threat he held against them. Give me my share of the farm as a son of Ramírez, or I'll tell the whole world what's going on. Doctoring the bulls, making them tamer for bullfights.'

Alicia's eyes widened in shock.

'Ramírez?' she stuttered.

'That's what the phone call was about.' Cámara was

shouting now, blood rushing to his head. 'Ramírez said no. So Blanco was going to carry out his threat. And you were going to tell the world for him.'

'But I didn't—'

'You mentioned it to your husband,' Cámara said. 'You told me you'd said something to him at the newspaper.'

'What?' Alicia held her hand up to her face, as though hiding her eyes. 'What are you saying? That Javier is somehow linked to Blanco's—?

'Not Javier. But who did he tell? Who did he pass it on to? Haven't you always said he was best friends with Flores?'

'I don't . . . really.' Alicia's voice was inaudible as the crowd suddenly surged past them. A body jerked sharply towards them and Alicia was pushed forwards with a jolt. Instinctively, Cámara reached out his hands and caught her, pulling her up close towards him. She looked into his eyes, fear and disbelief on her face. And with a surging, aching need, he leaned down to kiss her. Her mouth received him coldly, but as his hands tightened around her waist he felt the warmth in her begin to flow.

The crackling-patter sound of a dozen high-pitched blasts in quick succession brought his concentration back to the street around them. With his mouth still pressed to hers, he opened his eyes momentarily at the street party that had been brought to their own still, dark corner. A group of five young men were laughing and staggering next to them, pointing at the one who had clearly just let off the explosions at the feet of the kissing couple. At least a dozen other people – both men and women – were standing around, perhaps part of the same group. The smoke from the firecrackers caught in the pale pink street light, clouding them partially from sight.

A pair of eyes was staring at him, eyes that he had looked into so many thousands of times. They had pleaded with him, laughed with him, cried with him, chastised him, loved him. And now, glassy and bloodshot, they reached out to him once more.

I want to see you, the text had read.

He pulled his mouth away from Alicia's, breathing in sharply.

'What is it?'

The hand wrapped around Almudena's waist, the same one he had seen in her office window, was still there, still making a claim on her flesh. Cámara didn't look – didn't care – who it belonged to. He took a step, Alicia's arms drawing away from him.

There was a smash, the sound of breaking glass. In an instant the dim light in the alleyway was extinguished. A roar of laughter accompanied the darkness, then a cheer. Whoever it was had hit his mark. There was a scream, a screeching sound, like dogs. Cámara felt for the wall behind him to steady himself. The crowd surged past in the narrow space. Bodies pulled and pressed, a hand reached and grabbed his arm, then was released and slipped away. He felt a tugging, like waves trying to pull him out to sea. He gripped the pavement with his feet, his fingers digging into the cracks and creases of the stonework at his back.

In a moment they had all gone. He hung his head. The carnival, the party, had swept past and cavorted towards the far end of the alley. Turning the corner into a main street it was nothing more than an echo.

Cámara stood where he was, exhausted, weeping. Alone.

PART THREE

TERCIO DE MUERTE

TWENTY-ONE

The way you fight a bull reveals who you are
Juan Belmonte

Sunday 19th March

He was woken by the silence. The backdrop of *Fallas* had reverberated through his morning dreams, but in an unexpected hiatus the thick bass of the disco speakers outside in the street below his flat were turned off, and not even a single exploding firecracker filled the void. The emptiness came as a shock, and he sat bolt upright in bed, confused, wondering what was wrong. Had he slept through the entire day and into Monday? Had the fiesta come to an end without him realising? He took a deep breath, then reached for his mobile phone by the bed to check the time. It showed ten past two. Lunchtime. The *falleros* below were simply turning down the music while they tucked into another plate of paella. A string of *petardos* going off in a parallel street told him he was right. Still Sunday, still *Fallas*.

He climbed out of bed and headed to the bathroom, pushing his hair off his face. His brain felt stuffed, clouded, as though the usual grey matter had been surgically removed during the night and replaced with dirty cotton wool.

He looked down at his cock as he pissed, limp and life-less in his fingers. It seemed like an age had passed since that night with Alicia. Pulling on the chain, he let the lid down and walked out into his small living room. Apart from the heaviness, the fuzziness in his brain, there was a different feeling about that morning. He'd slept deeply, it felt. Perhaps for the first time in months. But now, battered and stripped down, he felt like the survivor of a shipwreck. Or at least what he imagined a survivor of a shipwreck would feel like. Actually, perhaps that was a silly analogy, he thought. Here he was in his flat, placing the coffee pot on the hob, four walls and a roof over his head, food of some description in the fridge – a loose description, admittedly. It wasn't as though he'd been cast on some desert island, hungry, lost, destitute. But still, he understood: much of what he had, of what he thought he was, had gone, had been taken away from him. He felt lonely, destroyed. Free.

The coffee bubbled up in its little metal pot, and he poured it into the nearest cup he could find – a chipped, handle-less mug that still had some grinds in it from a few mornings before. God knew how long it had been there, but no matter. *Lo que no mata, engorda*, as the proverb went. That which doesn't kill you makes you fat. It wasn't quite Nietzsche, but it got the message across.

He flopped on to the sofa with a soft, reassuring thud. Reaching towards the table, he pulled out his box and his fingers automatically began fiddling to make the first joint of the day. A stream of sunlight cut through the motes in the air above him and shone strongly on to his face. A new ricocheting echo of firecrackers was belting out from somewhere. There was a party going on right outside his door and he was hiding from it, trying to pretend it didn't exist.

His fingers stopped their work. The sound of *Fallas* still filtered through the walls and windows of his flat, but it was as if a pause button had been pressed inside him. There he was, Max Cámara, a dope-smoking, *Fallas*-hating, proverb-quoting, flamenco-loving, Valencia-based murder detective with the *Policía Nacional*, with a complicated, shattered love life, no social life to speak of, and a career lying in tatters. But in that instant he felt removed from all of that, from the person he normally was. For the first time in his life he felt he could see himself with total clarity, as though observing someone quite other than himself.

He pinched the skin on his arm. Was this one of those out-of-body experiences people talked about? Perhaps he was having a heart attack or something. What came next? A long tunnel with a light at the end? But the pain in his skin felt strong enough; he was where he thought he was. The experience was neither ecstatic nor depressing; there was no sense of madness or craziness. In fact he felt saner than he could ever remember. Clear thought, and with it possibility, seemed to have become a part of him.

He dropped the half-rolled joint back into the little pile of marihuana and closed the box. Still savouring the new state of mind, he walked back into the bedroom and got dressed, leaving his service weapon very deliberately in a drawer with his socks and underwear. He wouldn't be needing it: outside, the vast street party that had been going on all around him for the past ten days was moving into its final, most exciting phase. It was, he decided with a smile, time he joined the fun.

The same boys who had been outside his front door most of the past week were at their usual spot. Black stains on the pavement bore witness to the hundreds of mini, deafening explosions they had let off there each day. As always they gave no sign of registering Cámara's presence as he stepped out into the street, tiptoeing his way around them while they crouched over their box of *petardos*, a hot cigarette-lighter being passed from grubby hand to grubby hand.

'Hello,' he said as he managed to get past them.

No reply. But it didn't matter; it was time he went for a stroll around the neighbourhood, to see what he could see.

'*¿Señor?*'

He turned around. One of the young boys had stood up and was looking at him.

'Our *mechero* won't work any more.'

Cámara held out his hand and the boy placed a pink plastic lighter into it. When he flicked it, it gave off a spark but it was clear it had run out of gas.

'It's finished,' he said.

He put his hand into his pocket and felt for his own lighter, tucked away inside his packet of Ducados, then handed it to the boy.

'Take mine,' he said.

The boy grinned.

'*Gracias*,' he said, and he crouched down to join the others.

'*¡Ostias! ¡Qué guay!* Cool! A new one.'

He headed over towards the main avenue. On the other side the local school had been turned into a polling station for the elections, and a big notice to the effect had been placed beside the door. Few people appeared to be entering or leaving, however.

Usually when he reached this crossroads he bore left, heading into the centre of the city, or else went straight towards the river bed when he had time for a stroll among the pine trees and eucalyptus down there. For some reason he almost never turned right, heading south. Not unless he was driving, that was, and was going to the beach. Today, as part of his experiment at being someone else, or at least not being the person he usually was, he decided to break his habit.

As soon as he turned the corner he wondered why he hadn't done so before. This was all part of his neighbourhood, and he must have walked around here a few times before, or at least passed by in the car searching for an elusive parking space, but now, as he looked into unfamiliar bars and shop windows, it was as if he were in a new and exciting city. There was a place selling Japanese food he couldn't remember seeing before, a French creperie on the corner, an old-fashioned-looking place with heavy green-painted shutters that sold picture frames. Nothing was particularly extraordinary, but the novelty of it seemed to have an invigorating effect on him. All this had been right outside his door. All he needed to do was face the other way and walk.

What else would he try out? He remembered Cano's invitation to go to the bullfight as his guest. There was no reason for Cámara the policeman to go now. He was out of all that. Besides, the old Cámara didn't like bullfighting. He hated it. But the new Cámara? He wondered. Perhaps he should give it a try.

A large, colourful *falla* statue, six or seven metres high, dominated the next crossroads. Towering over the minor *ninots* was a grotesque caricature of Mayoress Delgado, a glass of whisky in one hand and a cigarette in the other. At her feet were three *fallera* beauty queens with broad grins. In front of this group was a smaller figure of a fat man wearing a bright green suit and pink shirt. Cámara looked more closely and smiled. It was Flores. In the figure's hand was a small flattened bull with a look of horror on its face and a large 'X' marked on its side, as though it were a voting slip. The Flores statue was in the act of placing the bull into a large ballot box in front of him.

He began to chuckle. The satire, the fun-poking, had always been one of the characteristics he most loved about Valencians. For all their other faults, they could always be relied on to find someone's weak spot and work on it doggedly. Especially when it came to their leaders.

Next to the *falla*, a bar had been set up in the middle of what was normally the main avenue. A crowd of people was already there, drinking and swaying to the Caribbean music blaring from the speakers of the disco behind. Cámara ambled over. He'd only had a coffee since he'd got up, and he couldn't remember the last time something solid had passed his lips. He thought about having a beer, or a brandy perhaps. But then checked himself. Those were old Cámara drinks. He'd have something he didn't usually order.

'A rum and Coke,' he heard himself say to the barman when he caught his eye. Perhaps it was the Merengue rhythm filling the air that gave him the idea. '*Ron añejo*,' he added. 'Got any of that seven-year-old stuff?'

His hips began to rock in time to the beat as he looked

around at the growing crowd. He'd never been to Salsa classes or anything of that sort. Never had time. Or perhaps not the inclination. But it was good, happy music, this, he thought. Upbeat, life-affirming. There was more to life than flamenco.

He felt a warmth, a body pressing close, and looked round to see a face gazing up at him with a broad smile. He tried to make way to allow the young woman to get closer to the bar, but there was little room.

'I've seen you round here sometimes,' the girl said, still smiling. From her accent he guessed she was Argentinian, black straight hair cascading over her shoulders and down into her cleavage.

'Don't you think *Fallas* is just wonderful?'

A few hours later, after showering and changing, and with a plate of pasta inside him to help soak up some of the drink, he grabbed his jacket and walked out of the flat once more, this time heading towards the city centre. A few other small groups of people were walking in the same direction, pushing past the *Fallas* crowds where necessary; all of them, he could sense, going to the bullfight as well, as though they were connected in some subtle way through shared intention.

And he was vaguely aware of a presence shadowing him as he walked along; a *Policía Local, the Policía Local.* Was it really him again? He chose to assume that it wasn't. It was over for him, finished. There was no point following a man like today's Cámara.

Outside the bullring the usual pre-fight bustle had taken over the small square. Men dressed in fine clothes, women with fur coats clinging to their arms. A *buñuelos* van parked in the road nearby was doing a brisk trade as people filled themselves with something hot and sweet to keep them going for the next couple of hours.

He wove his way through the crowd. An elderly man with long, yellowing teeth was telling his friends – and anyone else who wanted to listen – that today's might well be the very last bullfight ever to take place at the city bull-ring.

'*Hombre*, if Emilia wins the election today, that's it,' he said in a loud voice and waving his hands in the air. 'Finished.'

A few bystanders muttered.

'This is an infamous day,' the man continued. 'A dark day for bullfighting, and for Spain.'

'*Inaceptable*,' came a comment from one of the others.

'I didn't vote for her,' came a reply.

'They should leave our national fiesta alone.'

'And what's more,' the man with the teeth went on, warming to his theme as he sensed a small crowd gathering around him, 'as soon as this corrida is over they're going to take the bullring over for a victory party.'

There was a collective groan.

'Yes, my friends,' cried the man. 'Not only do they have to destroy our culture, but they want to rub salt in the wounds as well. And their arrogance is such that they will stop at nothing to humiliate us! As if we hadn't suffered enough from the recent death of our beloved Jorge Blanco.'

Again, Cámara sensed the hand of Flores: what better place to celebrate their election victory than in the very building that had come to symbolise their campaign?

As he stepped away from the fledgling orator, he could hear others start to assert themselves in the debate: bull-fighting was an integral part of Spain, someone was insisting. It could never die . . .

Cano had told him to meet at the main gate. It wasn't hard to spot him: the flashes of the photographers' cameras gave him a good enough clue. This time, however, there was no girl on his arm. He greeted Cámara like an old friend, embracing him as soon as he caught sight of him and making a public show of inviting him into the bullring himself.

'*¡Hombre!* Chief Inspector,' he cried. 'Finally they let you have a day off.'

Cámara smiled, and remained silent. Best to ride it through.

He felt a hand squeezing him tenderly on the shoulder as they passed through and into the outer corridor of the bullring. The photographers clicked away. Cámara felt like telling them not to waste their batteries, but it was too late. Not that his picture was newsworthy enough to appear in any paper.

The scrum that had seemed to surround Cano outside stayed with them once they were under the shade of the bullring arches. Men and women headed for the famous torero to salute and congratulate him for one thing and another. Cano handled it all very well, Cámara could see. Being the focus of a lot of people's attention was clearly a skill, and he had had a lot of practice.

Making his excuses for a moment – he could rejoin them to take his seat when the fight started – he pulled away from the Cano cloud and paced up the passageway, observing the people as they stood and talked and smoked and drank.

Through an archway he caught a glimpse of the sandy bullring at the centre of the building, the scene of the bloodshed to come. Did he feel sick at the thought? He couldn't tell. It had been an automatic response before. Now he seemed to exist in a state of suspended judgement.

The spectators were already beginning to stream into the seating area, taking their places. A sharp shadow cut across the open space, marking a clear dividing line between those in *Sol* and the others in *Sombra*. The air was still cool, however, and although the sunlight was intense, he felt that the social division at this early time of year should be reversed. Let people pay more to sit in the sun in early spring – at least it would keep them warm.

People began to shuffle towards their seats as the hour of the bullfight approached. He lingered a moment longer, watching the faces in the crowd passing by. It was only after a minute or two had passed that he realised he was looking out for Alicia. Would she be there somewhere? Of course. How could she not come to the last bullfight of the fiesta? He was less certain, though, if he wanted her to see him. He'd screwed things up the night before.

The passageways were emptying and it was time to go in. Something else was bothering him, beyond the bullfight and Alicia. A doubt, a niggling, nagging thought at the back of his mind, but which he couldn't identify clearly or put his finger on. It felt almost like a siren, a warning signal, as though a red light were flashing. But still he couldn't make out what it was about. Nothing to do with the past. Something to do with what was happening now, or was about to happen.

His phone rattled in his pocket and he flipped it open.

'We've arrested Paco.' It was Torres's voice.

'Just thought you'd want to know. Caballero issued a warrant.'

Cámara said nothing.

'Picked him up at the Ramírez place. That house of theirs near the top of Blasco Ibáñez.'

'Yes, I know it,' Cámara said.

'And you'll never guess what?'

Cámara sniffed.

'Go on. Tell me.'

'He's admitting he stayed behind after the bullfight that day. He was waiting for Blanco.'

Cámara paused. 'What for?' he said at length.

'I hit him with what Flores told us, that he was threatening to out Blanco as gay. That's when it came out. He said it was true, and that he waited for Blanco after the bullfight. Said he wanted to talk to him in private, to give him a final chance to back down before he went ahead with his threat.'

Cámara could feel his old life clawing at him.

'He says he saw him,' Torres went on. 'Says they had their confrontation. But that Blanco refused to give in.'

'Then what?' Cámara said.

'He says he just walked away. Went off to the Bar Los Toros for the award ceremony. Which was why he was a bit late getting there.'

Cámara knew what would be going through everyone's minds: that Paco was telling a partial truth in order to cover up a greater one. Yes, admit to being there, even to having a motive, but step back from final admission of guilt in the hope that they wouldn't quite be able to pin it on him.

They'd been there a hundred times before in other cases, and usually it just took another little push to bring the whole case home.

'And another thing,' Torres added. 'He doesn't have an alibi for the Ruiz Pastor murder. Said he left the Ramírez house early that morning to drive back to the farm. He could have been there, chief. He could have done it.'

'Why are you telling me this?' Cámara said. 'You know I'm off the case. Pardo fired me last night.'

'Not until tomorrow,' Torres said. 'Come in now, help me break Paco. We'll get a confession out of him. He's virtually admitted it as it is. We'll do it, we'll make this case. And you can save your arse. It's still only the eleventh hour. There's time yet to keep you in *Homicidios.*'

Cámara held the phone against his ear. He was virtually on his own now in the passageway. The bullfight was about to begin.

'*Jefe*, I need you,' Torres said. 'We've got a rhythm going in interrogations. I don't know if I can do this on my own.'

'Thanks, Torres,' Cámara said. 'I appreciate the call. I really do. But you can do this yourself. You'll be fine.'

'Chief!'

'It's too late.'

Cámara flipped the phone shut and put it back in his pocket. It was time to find his seat next to Cano and watch the bullfight. Tomorrow he'd think about what his future life was going to be.

He heard footsteps and the sound of someone clearing his throat. Spinning on his heel he turned and saw two unexpected faces.

'Shouldn't you be at the Jefatura interrogating my son?'

Any remaining strength seemed to have left Francisco Ramírez since their last encounter: a slight stoop had developed in his shoulders, while the power or shine in his eyes appeared to have dulled. He was dressed, as ever, in an elegant suit, but the knot in his cravat was loosening and his hair, usually slicked back, appeared less than neatly combed.

Propping him up with a hand under his arm was Roberto. He seemed attentive to his father, watching his step as though wary that the old man might stumble. And although he was dressed in a dark blue suit with white shirt and blood red tie, he too looked less than at his best: there was a slight colouring under one eye, and red marks near the top of his collar.

'Are you trying to humiliate me?' Ramírez said. 'First the interrogation at my home and now arresting my son?'

His face blushed as he spoke.

'It's all right, father,' Roberto said to him. 'Paco will be fine.'

Then turning to Cámara he said, 'This has all come as a shock.'

'Yes,' Cámara said. 'I'm sorry we only ever seem to meet when there's a crisis in the family.'

Roberto frowned.

'I'm as surprised to see you here,' Cámara said. 'I thought you hated bullfighting.'

'These are tough times for the family,' Roberto said with a pointed look. 'We have to stick together.'

The two men took a step forward and Cámara moved to the side to let them pass. Ramírez looked at him with hatred as he shuffled along, his bottom lip trembling. Roberto kept his eyes on his father, guiding him as best he could.

'Looks like you've been in an accident,' Cámara said as they drew closer. And he nodded at the marks on Roberto's neck and lower face.

'Those New York girls,' Roberto said with a wink. 'They can get a bit rough sometimes.'

The two men turned the corner and headed into the bullring area. Cámara watched them disappear then turned to take his own seat with Cano. The first fight had already started.

TWENTY-TWO

He who walks with bulls learns how to fight them
Traditional

As far as he could tell there was no magic that afternoon, nothing of the spark that had sent a shiver through him the day Cano had fought. He didn't recall having heard the names of any of the bullfighters appearing in the ring, and when, after the third bull had been killed with little art or skill, and there was a slightly longer gap before the next one came on, he decided to get up and stretch his legs a little.

'Does anyone want anything?' he asked Cano's group. A couple of orders came in: a whisky with ice and a beer.

'I'll be back in a minute.'

Cano smiled at him.

'Don't be long,' he said. 'You don't want to miss anything.'

Cámara headed out into the passageway and strolled in the direction of the nearest bar. He'd scanned the public inside several times already, watching for a sign of Alicia, but he hadn't seen her. Still, there was a chance that she, too, would be out at one of the bars during the break. He realised now that he really did want to see her again. Should he apologise if he did? He'd wait and see.

The bar had brought its shutters down, so Cámara carried on walking, looking to find another. He watched for shadows behind him but could see nothing. If he was being followed it seemed his pursuer had either lost him or lost interest.

A guard in brown uniform with a yellow stripe on the shoulder was standing at a gate that seemed to lead into a different section of the bullring. Cámara was wearing his usual jacket, with his ID tucked into the inside pocket. He showed it to the guard, who allowed him through.

Cámara immediately recognised it from his previous visits as the preparation area for the bulls and bullfighters. Horse shit lay spattered on the cobblestone floor as a couple of picadors and their mounts readied themselves to go into the ring. Apart from a group of *mayorales* keeping an eye on the next bulls to come through, the area was virtually deserted.

In front of him, just to the right, was the chapel. A chain and padlock had been wrapped around the doors, he noticed. No one was to go in there; whereas the bullring itself could somehow be cleansed of Blanco's murder through more bloodshed, for this place there was perhaps little chance of redemption. Cámara frowned. It was as if the building itself were seen as responsible for what had happened there, its doors locked firmly shut as punishment.

He thought of Paco Ramírez. He'd be in the interrogation room now with Torres. How far had they got, he wondered. A confession, perhaps? It would help Torres's career, that was for sure. Perhaps get him an early promotion. If his name wasn't stained by being associated with him, that was. Pardo was usually all right about that, though. Happy to bask in the glory himself but he didn't forget you if you did a good job. For all his faults he had to give him that.

Perhaps by the morning's papers it would all be wrapped up. Even in time for the news tonight, just as the election results were coming in. But Cámara felt strangely empty at the thought. Not because he wouldn't be there to see it happen – he was involved enough in the case – even now – to experience some kind of satisfaction at the thought that it was all about to be resolved. No, it wasn't that. Perhaps . . . He couldn't say. There were plenty of reasons to suspect Paco: an intimate knowledge of bulls and bullfighting – that would explain the symbolism of Blanco's murder, perhaps. But then the killing of Blanco's *apoderado*? Ruiz Pastor had been trying to blackmail the Ramírez family, Torres was probably right there. He'd known something about the whole affair and thought he could get them to pay for his silence. But he'd gone to his death instead. Had Paco done them both? He was fit for a man of his age. He could easily have climbed in and out of the bullring up the drainpipe. Stealing a boat and crossing the Albufera for a rendezvous with Ruiz Pastor a couple of days later would have posed few difficulties for him. Then the motive: Blanco hustling for a share of the farm as Ramírez's illegitimate son, threatening to expose their new, less principled approach to bull breeding. Paco had been prepared to out him as gay to try to shut him up. Blanco was hotheaded, obstinate. Perhaps he'd refused to stand down. Reason enough to kill him instead.

And Paco had no alibi. Cámara tried to cast his mind back to the night of Blanco's murder, when Paco had arrived late for the ceremony. Had he really looked like someone who had just killed a man? Did his face fit? On paper he looked guilty as hell. But he couldn't say. He just couldn't say.

Cámara walked out into an open space that formed a

triangle between the chapel, the outer edge of the bullring, and the open gate that led to the street outside. A truck had been parked there, with its back ramp open and sloping down to the floor. The truck itself was painted mostly white, but there was a stripe running low around the edge: deep burgundy.

He circled around it. The cab was empty, but the door was open and the keys were swaying in the ignition. Whoever was driving was probably just about to leave and would be returning shortly. Moving to the back, he poked his head in and saw an empty, metallic shell with straw and piles of dung heaped in the corners. Running around the top was an open space with bars – something to let in light and air for the bulls while they were travelling, he assumed. More bars crossed the box from one side to the other, as though to reinforce the structure, or perhaps to tie the bulls on to. There were dents and scratches aplenty on the sides, testament, no doubt, to the struggle to get the bulls in and out during transportation.

He climbed up the ramp to get a closer look. The smell of piss and dung mixed in with the straw underfoot seemed to speak of panic and fear, anger and rage. He kicked at a ball of gunk that had glued itself to his shoe. Treading in dog shit, they always told you, brought good luck. He wasn't quite sure what kind of luck treading in bull shit would bring.

Something caught his eye as he moved his foot from side to side, trying to shake it clean, something partially hidden by the straw. Flicking at it with his foot he saw a metal ring in the floor, as though for a trapdoor. He pushed at it again with his toe, reluctant to get his hands covered in whatever mixture of excrement was down there obscuring it from view. But there was only so much he could do. Bending down he took a deep breath and started to poke around. The ring lifted up. Sliding his finger underneath it he pulled.

As he had thought, it was a kind of door for a compartment in the floor. He knelt down again. Some thick blue material had been placed at the top. Cámara pulled on it and drew up some workers' overalls. They had been well used by the looks of it, with brown stains on the legs and what looked like bloodstains around the body. He placed them to one side on the floor. Beneath the overalls were a couple of brown cardboard boxes wrapped in transparent plastic bags. He lifted one up, and placing his hand inside the bag pulled out a box. It rattled as he did so, a sound very much like glass bottles. Lifting the lid he stared down at a dozen phials. Each one had the same label. Cámara lifted one up and tried to read it, but could make nothing of it. The writing was in a foreign language he didn't understand, perhaps German. There was what looked like a company name – Fischer und Hauptmann – and then a list of chemicals with percentages next to them: 2%, 4.1%. It was almost like reading the ingredients on a packet of biscuits in the supermarket trying to work out what was actually in them. Except that he understood even less than usual. Only the brand name, printed in bolder letters across the front of the label, seemed to be written in any language other than Chinese: Ketakom. There was something about it, something that—

A blackness invaded his thoughts: a sharp, invasive nothingness. Then silence.

*   *   *

Consciousness returned to him in circling waves, washing over him, dragging him down, before coughing him out and spitting him on to the shore. Pain announced itself from the back of his skull as he lay curled in a ball on the floor, and he gave out a cry. Or at least he tried. His voice appeared to have left him, and all he could hear issuing from his mouth was colour: blues, purple, mauve.

He fell back into non-being, all-encompassing blackness once again.

When he came to, his eyes opened on to darkness. He tasted it for a while, sucking on it, rolling it on his tongue. It was different: not the blackness of before, this was something outside himself, something he felt he might understand.

Motion returned to a finger, and he twitched it once, then again. Nothing happened. No sound. No sense of another being there with him. He tried again, this time flexing his hand, wrapping it into a fist-ball before opening each finger, stretching them. Still no reaction from outside. He tried lifting his head, and with it came a rustling sound as he brushed what he understood to be clothes wrapped around his body. But still nothing. He concluded that he was alone, and raised his head higher, pulling his weight on to his elbows. The darkness, which had been constant until that point, shifted. There was a window.

He got to his feet, breathing strength back into his flesh. The walls were close around him, and by the touch and sound of his feet on the floor he made it out to be a simple concrete and breeze-block structure. There was a dampness about the smell, as well. Was this a basement? No, the window made that clear. And another thing: the lack of noise. There were no cars, no trucks. Thoughts of the city, of his life there, reminded him of his phone. What time was it? How long had he been here? Perhaps, at least, he could call someone to come out and find him. He was less than surprised, though, when he reached into his pocket and found that it wasn't there. He double-checked in his trousers, but it had gone. He would have to work this one out on his own.

He stepped over to the window. It was dark outside as well, yet a faint gloom, like shadows, seemed to register in his sight: the shift in the darkness he had perceived earlier. The glass felt thin against his hand as he pressed it up to strain at whatever lay out there. He could break it easily. And escape? From where, exactly?

There was a flash, far away in the sky, bright green and white. A firework had been let off, and suddenly the shadows were silhouetted in sharp contrast: a sight he'd seen a hundred times before. He was in the middle of the *huerta* – the vast market-gardening area that circled Valencia, and these were orange trees in front of him. At that moment, as though in confirmation, a draft pushed its way through the window frame, carrying with it a heady, sweet scent of orange blossom on the night air.

The smell seemed to bring a necessary sharpening back to his senses. The pain of earlier remained at the back of his head where he assumed he had been hit, but his immediate thought now was of escape. If, as he thought, he was in some farmer's shed in the middle of an orange grove, there would probably be a way out somewhere. He slid his fingers along the wall away from the window, and after only a few centimetres felt the cool metallic touch of the door.

There was no sign of his captor. He certainly wasn't inside with him now, but it was possible he was standing guard outside. Groping around, he found a plastic handle, gripped it and then lowered it as slowly as he could. When it could go no further, he gave the door a pull. It didn't move. He tried again. Nothing, it wouldn't budge. Whoever had placed him in here had locked him in.

Returning to the window, with every intention of smashing it open, he heard a sound from outside: footsteps in the dirt. They were soft at first, but gradually intensified as they drew closer. There was a jangle of keys. Cámara threw himself against the wall just as the door was unlocked and a shadow appeared in the doorway.

A sharp, piercing howl split the air as Cámara pulled and twisted on the man's arm, locking the elbow and forcing it back on itself. As his captor screamed in pain, momentarily immobilised by the shock, Cámara planted a foot into where he guessed his stomach would be. The scream turned into a deep groan and the man fell to the floor, retching.

Still grappling his wrist, Cámara reached for the man's gun in his holster, threw it to the ground, then dragged him outside on to a dirt track that led to the shed. In the occasional flashes from fireworks, and the reflection of the distant city lights, he could make out more orange trees all around them – they were deep in the middle of the *huerta*, as he had guessed. A car was parked a few yards away.

The man was vomiting, but was already trying to wriggle free of Cámara's grip. Cámara wrenched on his arm again to make him keep still, then leaned over, grabbed a handful of his hair and pulled his head back. In the pale flickering lights he saw a face that had become engrained on his consciousness and a deep, swelling, animal loathing came over him.

'You,' he spat. And almost before he knew what he was doing his fist had landed square on the man's chest, sending him heavily and painfully to the ground.

Cámara took a step forward. He had been brought here so as to be far away from prying eyes: no one would see what they would do to him here. What was the plan? Just keep him locked up? Or something more sinister? He could turn what had been their advantage to his own, though. No one would see or even hear what every sinew in him now wanted to do to the man who had been the agent of torment over the past days. He felt the cold rush through his veins, a giddy sickness in his stomach as the excitement of impending violence took its hold over him.

'No. *Por favor.*'

The *Municipal* was looking up at him with raw fear, trying to edge away from the beating he knew he was about to receive. Cámara lifted a foot and brought it down on his groin to keep him still.

'Please?' he said as the man doubled up in pain once more. 'Please? Why didn't you think of that when you attacked me in the street? Or when you followed me to take smutty photographs? Or when you smashed the window of my car?'

The *Municipal* had rolled on to his side and was curling up into a ball, giving off a faint, high-pitched whine. The neck brace of a few days ago had gone.

'You've had so many opportunities to say please in the past,' Cámara continued. 'Why should I listen to you now?'

The man was crying in fear and pain, shivering as though

341

he were lying on frozen ground. Looking down, Cámara felt
disgust. Couldn't he at least make a stand, rather than capit-
ulate so easily? Was it even worth the effort with him? But
he'd seen types like this before: collapsing into a useless wreck
one minute only to get up the next when they thought they
were out of danger to carry on where they had left off. No,
this man needed to understand where he had gone wrong.

'It wasn't my idea!' the *Municipal* shouted as Cámara went
to haul him up. 'None of it was my idea.'

Cámara let him drop back down to the ground.

'You think I'm stupid, or something?' he said. 'I know
perfectly well you work for Flores.'

'Flores,' the *Municipal* breathed. 'It was all Flores.'

'I'm glad you don't work for me,' Cámara mumbled to
himself, 'if that's your idea of loyalty.'

'Flores said I should attack you,' the other man went on,
clinging to the idea that a full confession would somehow
save him.

'Who were the other two?' Cámara asked.

'They're not police,' he said. 'Just a couple of guys I
know.'

'You use them regularly for this kind of thing, then?'
Cámara said. The *Municipal* was silent. Cámara leaned
forwards and grabbed his wrist, wrenching it behind his
back again.

'No, no,' the *Municipal* said. 'I mean yes, sometimes.
They're ex-prisoners. Just a couple of thieves. I use them
sometimes when Flores wants—'

'When Flores wants some dirty work doing,' Cámara
finished the sentence for him. He softened the pressure on
the man's arm, but held on to it.

'Yeah, that's it,' the *Municipal* said. His head was bowed, his face staring at the floor.

'And the other stuff?'

'That was all me,' the man said.

'You with the camera?'

He nodded.

'And I smashed the window of your car to leave the photos there. Flores even had me deliver them by hand to your girlfriend's office. He didn't like it when you hauled him in. You shouldn't have done that.'

Cámara's eyes rolled. He should flatten the man's nose against his face, but the comment about Almudena threw him for a second. So she had seen the photos. It was to be expected, but until that moment there had been a faint hope within him that they hadn't reached her. Not that it mattered, though. She'd seen him with Alicia in the street.

His concentration lapsed and in that moment the *Municipal* pulled his wrist free and moved to run away. He scrambled to his feet and darted in the direction of the shed, and his gun lying on the floor. Cámara launched himself after him, stumbling on the loose dirt underfoot as he tried to catch him. The two men passed through the doorway almost simultaneously, but the *Municipal* was just able to reach down and pick up his gun. As he did so, Cámara hurled himself on top of him, throwing him to the ground. There was a loud CRACK as the revolver went off, but already one of Cámara's hands was reaching down to hold the gun away while the other was pressed against the man's throat. At once the *Municipal* went limp and the gun fell with a clatter to the cement floor.

'Still hurt, does it?' Cámara said as he pressed hard on

his trachea. A cold thrill passed through his hands, his jaw, his eyes, as he felt life beating in desperation against his fingers. 'Still a bit sore from last time?'

The man was choking, his chest rising off the ground as he struggled for air, paralysed by the pain. Sitting over his abdomen to gain more control, Cámara could hear his legs thrashing against the floor as he fought to stay alive, his eyes like swelling bulges in his head. His grip tightened around his neck, and the *Municipal*'s body grew tauter. It's coming now, he thought to himself: the point where I could kill him. Like flicking a light switch. Or slaughtering a bull.

He released the pressure and got to his feet. On the floor the man was panting for breath, his body immobile except for the rising and sinking of his ribs. Reaching for the revolver on the floor, Cámara slipped it into the back of his trousers. Then he grabbed the man by the shoulders and dragged him back outside. As they were passing through the doorway he saw a coil of rope hanging from a nail in the wall. He grabbed it and started tying the *Municipal*'s hands behind his back, bringing the remainder down and tying his feet together as well. Then he sat him with his back against the wall.

The other man was silent, passive, his hands like ice.

'There's one more thing before we finish here,' Cámara said.

'If you kill me,' the *Municipal* said, struggling to talk, 'they'll know it was you.'

Cámara crouched down to come face to face with him.

'If I was going to kill you you'd be dead already,' he said, and placed his hand firmly but gently against the man's throat again.

'Besides,' he said, '*Por la boca muere el pez* – A fish dies through its mouth. What I need from you is more information.'

Tears glistened at the corners of the man's eyes.

'What did Flores want?' Cámara said. 'Why did he get you to attack me?'

The *Municipal* remained silent. Cámara took his hand off his throat and pulled his head up straight to look him in the face.

'Why?'

A sneer began to form on the man's lip.

'You're useful,' he said at last. 'This investigation is useful.'

Cámara pulled harder on the man's hair and he winced.

'What are you talking about?' he said. 'Useful?'

'It distracts people,' the *Municipal* said.

'Distracts them?' Cámara said. 'Flores wanted the thing clearing up as quickly as possible. He made that very clear. Said that Blanco's death had made bullfighting more popular. It was bad for him, bad for the election campaign.'

The sneer on the man's face was turning into a grin.

'What the fuck are you smiling at?' Cámara said. Still holding a bunch of his hair, he smacked the man's head against the wall behind him. The grin disappeared.

'It was a smokescreen,' the *Municipal* said at last. 'Flores needed it to go on as long as possible. Until after the elections were over.'

Cámara dropped his hand from the man's head.

'Everyone was watching the case,' the *Municipal* continued. 'It just got better and better. Releasing your only suspect, Ruiz Pastor's murder. It was in danger of dying down but then Carmen Luna came to the rescue.'

Cámara slapped him around the face.

'Flores was behind that!' he shouted.

'Flores didn't know the woman was going to top herself. He just wanted her to break the story about Blanco being gay. The suicide was a bonus.'

Cámara's hand was at the man's throat again and he saw the pain swell up in his eyes.

'What in God's name are you talking about?' he said.

Unable to speak, the *Municipal* glanced down at Cámara's hand wrapped around his neck. Cámara pulled it away slightly, just enough to let him talk.

'The Town Hall campaign is all about banning bull-fighting.'

'I know all that,' Cámara said.

'But constitutionally the Town Hall doesn't have the power to do that.'

Cámara dropped his hand from around the man's neck.

'They all know this,' the *Municipal* said. 'They've known it from the start. But they're betting on the fact that no one else does. Or if they do no one's listening to them.'

'The whole thing's a lie,' Cámara said.

'They're campaigning against bullfighting because the only way Emilia's going to get re-elected this time is if young people vote. So they went for banning bullfighting. They even had journalists from abroad calling up.'

'All part of the new international image,' Cámara said.

'Fitted with having Formula 1 here, the America's Cup. Big, money-making events. But one of the opposition parties had discovered the flaw, saying the Town Hall couldn't ban bullfighting in the city even if it wanted to. Some of the others were picking up on it.'

The *Municipal* started coughing, bringing up a ball of phlegm from the pit of his stomach, which he spat out on to the ground.

'But then Blanco was murdered and suddenly no one was talking about anything else.'

'The smokescreen,' Cámara said. He stood up. He desperately needed a cigarette, but his pockets were empty.

'Why not just let it run its course, though,' he said. 'Why attack me?'

'You were in charge of the case,' the *Municipal* said. 'Flores wanted to make sure it dragged on. So he sent me round.'

Cámara spun round to stare the man in the face.

'What? To soften me up?'

'To slow you down a bit,' the man said. 'Give you something else to think about. Perhaps even lead you down a few false trails. Flores had some dirt on you, some scandal.'

'Yes, I know about that,' Cámara said.

'Thought he could use it against you as well.'

'Was that it, then?' Cámara said. 'He just wanted to feel he could control me?'

'Part of it.'

Cámara knelt down again in front of the man.

'But why today?' he said. 'You've been following me ever since I left my flat. Didn't Flores know I was off the case? Didn't he know I'd been sacked?'

The *Municipal*'s eyes widened.

'Someone's managed to be discreet for a change,' Cámara said.

Over towards the city, the fireworks were intensifying, the sound of their explosions reverberating in the night air. In front of him Cámara could see the *Municipal* was quivering again, perhaps through cold or fear. He looked him in the face, though, and was disturbed to see him laughing.

'What's so fucking funny?'

The *Municipal* stared at him with a manic grin.

'Flores always said this case would be your last,' he said. 'And he was right. I've spent all day following an ex-policeman, getting the shit kicked out of me. What for? It's fucking stupid.'

He started laughing again as the fireworks spluttered blues and reds.

'That's your career, then,' he said. 'All gone up in smoke.' He opened his eyes wide. 'Bang!'

His head fell back as he laughed again.

'Bang!'

Cámara fell back on to his feet then stood up. Something had shifted inside him.

'What did you say?'

'I said that's it. You're finished. Why did I even waste a whole day following you . . . Hey, what are you doing?'

Cámara had leaned forward and after flipping the man on to his front was pulling on his arm again, tied up behind his back. Fearing he was about to wrench it out of its socket once more, the *Municipal* screamed. Cámara stared hard at the hands of the watch on his wrist in the gloom, then put him back upright.

'It's all right,' he said. 'I just needed to know what the time was.'

He reached inside the *Municipal*'s pockets and found some keys.

'I'll be needing these as well,' he said.

He looked up at the sky as the machinery continued to click in his head. And the nagging doubt that had been with him since earlier that afternoon, the piece that had refused to fit, clunked into place.

'What's happening tonight?' He pulled the *Municipal* up to his face. 'After the bullfight. They were talking about it. What's going to happen?'

'The party,' the *Municipal* whimpered. 'They're holding a victory party at the bullring for when the first results come in. Symbolic. Kind of putting the boot into the bullfight people.'

But Cámara had stopped listening. He dropped him on the ground and started running to the car.

A veces caza quien no amenaza – Sometimes the one least threatening is doing the hunting.

'Wait! You can't leave me here!'

Cámara ignored the pleas of the *Municipal* as he put his car – a Renault Mégane – into reverse and sped up the dirt track to a place where he could turn around. Following the lights in the sky he should be able to make it back to the city.

There was no time to lose.

TWENTY-THREE

A dead bull is a cow
Traditional

It had gone ten thirty by the time Cámara made it to the outskirts of the city centre. He drove the car in as far as he could, then parked it in the middle of a road where the barricades for *Fallas* made it impossible to continue. He was still another five minutes away from the bullring if he ran from there.

The streets were crammed with people, hundreds of thousands all pouring out for this, the final night of the fiesta. Cámara pushed through as best he could against the tide of bodies, crushing toes and barging shoulders as he struggled through, barely registering the voices of complaint and indignation. He had to get to the bullring. If he could just make it in the next few minutes there might still be time. A hand reached out to try and pull him back.

'Police!' he shouted, and reluctantly the grip was loosened and he was allowed to continue.

Minutes later, panting and sweating, he reached the square in front of the bullring. He double-checked: a handful of *Policías Nacionales* in dark blue uniforms and black jackboots were standing around, chatting and watching the people flowing past; groups of party activists were stepping through the bullring entrance; a party banner had been draped over one of the balconies. But there was no panic, no crime scene. Not yet.

With his badge in his hand, he walked up to the group of policemen and identified himself.

'I need to use your mobile phone,' he said, addressing the sergeant.

It was an unusual request, but you didn't argue with a chief inspector from *Homicidios*.

'Here, sir,' the sergeant said.

Thankfully Torres's number was one of the few Cámara had memorised. He couldn't even recall Almudena's once he'd set it to the phone's memory. He dialled 616 459830 and heard the familiar tone at the other end.

'Who's this?' Torres's voice came on.

'It's me,' Cámara said.

'Paco's still silent on us,' Torres said. 'No sign of any confession. I told you, I can't do it alone—'

'I know,' Cámara interrupted him.

'What?'

'Listen,' Cámara said. 'Officially I'm off this case. You need to find Roberto Ramírez.'

'Roberto?'

'It's important,' Cámara said. 'He needs to be located quickly.'

'You want to arrest him?' Torres said.

'That can come later. For one thing, he needs to explain what phials of dope from one of his companies were doing inside one of the Ramírez trucks at the bullring. But for the moment he needs shadowing.'

'Right,' Torres said. 'Any idea where he might be?'

'They've planned a victory rally at the bullring for tonight,' Cámara said. 'As one of the party's top fundraisers I suspect he'll be coming along.'

'Got it. No arrest, just shadow. I'll reach you on this number if I need to. Anything else?'

'You need good men on this, Torres,' Cámara said. 'Discreet but sharp. I've got a feeling Roberto is in danger.'

The patter of firecrackers heralding the start of another *mascletà* cut them off. Cámara hung up and signalled that he wanted to hang on to the phone. The sergeant nodded. There were five policemen there, their ears pricking up.

'I need all of you to come with me,' Cámara shouted above the din.

They passed through the entrance and into the passageway of the bullring.

The sergeant took the matter in hand as soon as Cámara explained.

'You two stand on the door and watch everyone coming in or out,' he said, pointing to the two nearest to him. 'You two get inside there now and start looking around.'

The four men immediately went to their places. Cámara and the sergeant walked into the arena. Down on the sand there was no sign now of the bullfight that had taken place only hours before. A small metal stage was being set up, spotlights shining and a PA system being wired in. The preparations for Mayoress Delgado's victory party were already well underway. It was coming up to eleven o'clock. At midnight the *Fallas* celebrations would reach their climax and the first statues would be set alight.

'What time is the rally set to take place here?' Cámara asked.

'They're burning the statue in the Plaza del Ayuntamiento at one o'clock, as always, sir,' the sergeant said. 'Then they're coming round here. Reckon the first election results would be in by then.'

Meanwhile there were already dozens – perhaps even a hundred or more – party activists and technicians setting the thing up now. He needed more men – groups scouring the roofs, checking the windows of nearby buildings, scanning the faces of the people coming and going. It would be another ten or fifteen minutes at least before Torres could get his first teams in. He couldn't pull in more ordinary policemen from the street; they could only do so much. Rely on them too heavily and they'd end up losing not only Roberto, but Blanco's killer as well.

The sergeant accompanied him as he headed out of the arena and back towards the passageway. Streams of people were passing through: party activists – the men in suits and women in Burberry coats – smiling at the thought of victory they felt so certain was theirs. Cámara stood to one side to let them pass. A technician laying a coil of cable bumped into him as he came down the slope.

'*Perdona*,' Cámara said, allowing the young man to get through.

He looked up: something back down in the arena had caught his attention: a head of closely cropped black hair contrasting against the bright white of a shirt collar. The man's face was turned the other way, but his height, the slope of his shoulders, the clothes, all fitted. Cámara took a step and joined the crowd heading towards the sand; the sergeant followed closely behind.

Roberto Ramírez was chatting to an older man to one

side of the main arena. Cámara looked at the sergeant and gave a slight nod. Immediately the policeman pulled up his radio and, looking straight towards Roberto, started putting out a call to his colleagues. Cámara just had time to pull him by the shoulder and spin him round to face the other way before the sergeant informed them that they'd found their man, giving his description and current location.

But Roberto wasn't keeping still. Patting his friend on the shoulder, he looked at his watch, made his goodbye and then started to cross towards the opposite side of the arena. Cámara waited a couple of moments and then made to follow, the sergeant still stuck to him. Keeping a close watch on where Roberto was heading, Cámara glanced about the rest of the bullring, looking, searching, but seeing nothing untoward. A woman with red hair approached Roberto, stopping him for a moment with a broad grin. He kissed her on the cheeks and then made to go, apologising that he couldn't stop. Eventually he managed to pull away from the increasing numbers of people and started heading up a side exit.

Back in the passageway, the milling crowds kept Cámara relatively camouflaged, but less so the uniformed policeman beside him. It wasn't so much that Roberto might realise he was being followed than that someone else might. Someone he felt sure was already close at hand. He glanced out at the street through the arches – still no sign of Torres's men.

He looked back to find Roberto, but he had disappeared.

'¿Qué cojones . . . ?'

'Up the stairs, sir,' the sergeant nodded at the staircase leading to the upper floor. He was already reaching for his radio to inform his men, but Cámara grabbed his arm, then lifted a finger to his lips. The sergeant nodded.

Keeping close to the wall, they climbed the stairs. The upper floor had far fewer people on it: a technician was peering down through an archway to his colleagues in the arena, while a young woman was smoking a cigarette and watching the fiesta-goers below. Cámara glanced from side to side: there was no sign of Roberto, but moving away to his right, he caught sight of a shadow cast by one of the street lamps.

Blood pulsed swiftly through him as he realised where Roberto was heading. There was no need for Blanco's killer to wander in openly, or try to blend in with the others. There was another entrance. One that had worked well in the past.

He stayed as close to the inner wall as possible as he circled the passageway. There was no time to wait for Torres now. Trying to stay in the shadows, he moved slowly, crouching low. At least he needn't worry about being heard – the fiesta would take care of drowning out his footsteps – but the street lamps could betray him just as they had Roberto.

Ahead of them, cast against the side of one of the arches, the shadow had stopped. Cámara halted, waving behind him for the sergeant to keep still. A barrage of firecrackers went off down in the street and Cámara took advantage of the sudden crescendo to take a couple more steps forward. From here he could just see Roberto, standing to the side of the passageway, pushing his hand through his hair. He was speaking, but the person he was talking to was just out of vision.

'. . . about more money?'

Cámara could just make out Roberto's words as the sound of explosions died down.

There was no reply, or at least none that Cámara could make out. Roberto waited for a moment.

'Well?' he said.

From behind, Cámara could sense the sergeant drawing closer. He turned and saw the policeman reaching down to unholster his pistol. Cámara held out a hand to stop him, but it was too late: their own shadows were being cast against a wall and the sharp, jerky movement had already been spotted.

Cámara froze. For a moment Roberto remained still, then turning he made to check behind him, as though being told to do so by the other person. The sergeant was already standing up straight, holding out the gun with both hands.

There was a cheer from down in the street as another *traca* of firecrackers was let off. Roberto took another step and came fully into view, a look of shock on his face as he saw the policeman pointing his weapon at him.

BANG BANG BANG went the blasts outside.

Roberto fell to the ground.

Blood was already soaking through his clothes and trickling along the floor by the time they reached him. Cámara felt for a pulse: he was still alive; a bullet appeared to have hit him in the shoulder. The sergeant was speaking into his radio, calling for an ambulance.

Cámara got up and sprinted down the passageway. When he reached the end, it was empty. He leaned over the edge of the balustrade. A movement caught his eye, an incongruity in the crush of people below. A young man had just reached the bottom of the drainpipe running along the side of the Enfermería building. Skipping the last couple of feet to land on the ground, he looked up.

Cámara watched as Angel Moreno grinned at him momentarily, and then darted into the crowds. He waited for a couple of seconds to see where he was heading: it was difficult to make him out from the mass of people but he could detect a pattern of someone pushing their way through, heading towards Marqués de Sotelo Avenue and the Plaza del Ayuntamiento, deep into the heart of the city.

Keeping an eye on Moreno for as long as he could through the archways, Cámara dashed back along the passageway. The sergeant was still by Roberto's side, pressing against his shoulder to stem the bleeding.

'Backup's on its way,' he said as Cámara ran past.

Cámara threw himself down the steps. Plain-clothed officers were streaming in: Torres's team had arrived.

Cámara ran past them and out into the crowds milling around the entrance to the bullring. He stopped, staring at the press of humanity standing between him and his prey.

'Put out a call,' Cámara said, turning round to face the officer nearest him. 'We're looking for a young man, athletic build, short blond hair.'

The policeman pulled out his radio.

'He's wearing light-coloured trousers and a dark tank top,' Camara continued. 'Last seen heading away from the bull-ring towards the Plaza del Ayuntamiento.'

The radio buzzed.

'He's armed and very, very dangerous,' Cámara added.

He looked around. Two armed officers were standing nearby, controlling the gate.

'You two,' Cámara said. 'Come with me.'

The men followed in Cámara's wake as he started forcing his way through the crowds towards Marqués de Sotelo, and

357

the last spot where he'd seen Moreno disappear into the throng.

Again the crushing weight of people. The policemen started blowing on their whistles, but in the party atmosphere no one paid them any notice, imagining they were simply adding to the festival spirit. Only when they came face to face with people and shoved them to one side did anyone realise what was really happening.

Painfully, so painfully slowly, the three of them inched their way through. Occasionally a small gap would appear and a few precious feet could be gained in a second or less, only for the multitude to close in on them once more. And all the while Moreno was getting further away. The children were the worst: too small to be pushed past, too slow in understanding that they had to make way. Cámara listened out for the crackle of the policemen's radios, news coming through that someone further up had caught sight of their man. But they obstinately refused to give any signs of life.

'Are those things switched on?' he shouted at them. They could barely hear him as they made their way through into the giggling, screaming horde in the Plaza del Ayuntamiento.

And then . . . something, a movement, a head bobbing up against the backdrop of people. Was that him? Cámara darted to the side, suddenly changing direction as he caught a quicker movement dashing along the road in front of the Town Hall. Willing himself on he broke through only to see a young man holding out his arms and wrapping them around his girlfriend. Not Moreno. Not their man.

The great Ayuntamiento *falla* statue towered over him as the crowd continued to surge around them. Above the din he heard bells chiming and looked up at the clock on the tower of the Town Hall: half past eleven. Within half an hour the first big statues would be being set alight to the sound of massive explosions. What had Moreno said to him that day? Perfect for shooting someone – no one would hear the gunfire.

BANG.

He grabbed one of the policemen accompanying him and nodded down at his radio. The man shook his head. No news.

'Call up and find out if the medical team have reached the bullring,' he said.

He waited as the officer put the call in, his eyes rapidly glancing around him, looking for anything, any unusual movement, a commotion of some sort, anything at all. Perhaps even a pair of eyes looking back at him. Would he be doing that? Moreno? The normal thing would be to get away as far as possible. But he hadn't done anything normal since the beginning. He'd even had the nerve to show up that very night at the Bar Los Toros. Fresh from murdering Blanco. Right under Cámara's nose. How could he have not seen it before? How else would the *anti-toro* demonstration have wound up for the day immediately afterwards 'out of respect for Blanco' when the rest of the world still didn't know he was dead? Why hadn't he spotted it sooner? Just as he had done now, that night Moreno had managed to climb out of the bullring over the iron spikes and down the drainpipe, dumped Blanco's *traje de luces* and slipped back into the crowd, back among his fellow demonstrators. Had anyone in the march that night even noticed he had been gone for a while? Perhaps Marta Díaz. They'd have to find her later.

Right now he needed to find Moreno; he was armed and ruthless. One shot had already been fired from his gun that night. How many more people was he prepared to take down with him?

He turned to the policeman, who was finishing his conversation on the radio.

'Anything?'

'The medics are there, sir,' the policeman said.

Cámara nodded.

Roberto Ramírez, providing the dope for the very bullfights he purported to have nothing to do with. All his *anti-toro* talk, giving money to Mayoress Delgado's campaign. Discovery of his visit to the Ramírez farm had cast a different light on that. At first he'd assumed that Blanco's mother had confused him with Paco: now he realised there had been no confusion at all. Was it all a complete lie? Had he ever really been against bullfighting? Perhaps it had started that way: the younger son breaking away from the family tradition to form his own life. But later, as he got older? Perhaps it was useful for the Ramírez family to have one of their own in the enemy camp. Tomorrow, perhaps, once he was sorted, they could talk it through with him. Tomorrow the police would check his phone records, his bank statements, his movements back here in Spain, his DNA. Tomorrow they would get him. He'd known Blanco was about to go public. Flores had told him after he got it from Gallego. '*Our financiers.*' Would there be evidence there of a call made to Moreno? Perhaps, if he hadn't been careful enough. What would it have been? A code word? A green light from New York? Or just a simple order? Do it. Go ahead and do it. Kill Blanco. Kill my half-brother. Moreno wanted money, and Roberto wanted Blanco dead, just as Paco did. But he had even more at stake – his true involvement in the world of bullfighting when he professed to hate it, drugs from one of his own companies being used to dull the famously aggressive and *bravo* Ramírez bulls: information he couldn't allow to get out, not for himself, not for the family. Blanco would have to die. Hadn't they all said how stubborn he was? Once he got an idea into his head there was no letting go.

Except that killing Blanco hadn't been enough. Blanco must have talked, or let something out. Enough for Ruiz Pastor to suspect that the Ramírez family were in some way responsible for his death. And so with an eye for a pay day, he'd tried to blackmail them. What had he done? He'd talked to Roberto at the funeral. Alicia had mentioned it. Perhaps he thought he was dealing with an intermediary, someone who could negotiate with the family. But he'd ended up talking to the person who was behind Blanco's murder in the first place. And so he'd brought death upon himself, agreeing to a meeting in the Albufera. What had he expected? A handover of money and a promise to keep his mouth shut. He'd certainly been silenced. Roberto had seen to that, trying to make it look as though Blanco's killer had committed the same murder. Except that he hadn't. The very act of trying to copy Moreno's M.O. had made that clear. Eventually, at least. Those scratches still disfiguring Roberto's neck and lower face: Ruiz Pastor was a big man; he would have put up a fight.

And now . . . BANG. Moreno had come after him. He should never have stolen Moreno's ideas: the *estoque*, the *banderillas*, the mutilation. He may have been just a hired killer in Roberto's mind, a useful tool, a young man set to destroy the bullfighting world. But Moreno didn't like that. He was an artist proud of his work, and would brook no imitators. Not even Marta with her anti-bullfighting leaflets. And once he held a grudge against you . . . Moreno's former maestro at the bullfighting school had discovered that.

Cámara turned to the two policemen.

'Stay in this area and keep looking,' he said. 'I'm going to scout around.'

He walked slowly up the elongated square towards the top end where it joined with Calle San Vicente, finding gaps in the crowd and squeezing himself through as best he could, neither rushing nor forcing his way past.

By now his eyes seemed to do the looking for him while other parts of him, other senses, scoured his environment. And still he walked forwards. Eventually, when he reached the top of the square, he stopped. Keep going? Which way? Left down to the market? Or straight on towards the cathedral? The crowd seemed to make the decision for him and in an instant he was being swept along as a surge of people caught him up and he was carried along for a few yards, suddenly and unwittingly part of a large group enjoying its own mini fiesta within the fiesta.

Before long he was approaching the Abbey of San Martín. A group of *fallera* beauty queens was standing on the steps absorbing the admiring stares from the crowd. One of them, one of the older ones, caught his eye. There was something about her that reminded him of Alicia. Something about her nose, perhaps. He couldn't say exactly. But he found himself gazing at her for a few moments. Alicia. Where had she been today?

A movement to his left. Something different, a different rhythm, a different kind of motion. And he knew at once that Moreno had seen him. His head spun to look across the street. A figure, barely visible, was darting down an alleyway on the other side. Short blond hair, a black top. With a start he launched himself after him, crashing into the crowd.

'Police!' he shouted. 'Police!'

The beginnings of a pathway were opened up for him. Crossing the street he managed to break his way through to the top of the alleyway and looked down. The figure had disappeared. He pressed on, squeezing along a tiny gap between the people and the buildings down one side and into the Plaza Redonda. A group of teenagers was splashing water from the marble fountain at the centre, laughing. Cámara lifted his foot on to an iron bollard near the edge of the square and stood up to get a better look.

There it was again. The same figure, the same, different movement, like a flash, passing through one of the arches around the square and out into the Carmen district on the other side. And its labyrinth of alleys.

Cámara jumped off the bollard. Moreno was playing with him, flirting with him, almost like a matador with a bull. And still Cámara kept charging. He had no means with which to call for backup. There was just him and Moreno. And what felt like the whole world standing in between them.

He heaved his way through the archway in pursuit and out behind the Santa Catalina church. Reaching a crossroads he glanced right, then left, just in time to see his prey vanish behind a corner.

A group of seven-year-olds in *fallero* costumes was tripping up the alleyway towards him, throwing the last of their firecrackers to the ground, their crashing sound splitting the air and amplifying as it bounced off the buildings on either side of the narrow space. Cámara did his best to run through and round them, but he mistimed his step and fell over as he pulled himself away to avoid crashing into a little girl.

The others giggled as he picked himself up, but the little girl looked frightened.

'Are you all right?' Cámara asked. She stared at him with open eyes, not responding for a moment, before finally nodding.

He surged forwards, heart beating faster now, cold adrenalin speeding through his veins. Ahead, the Plaza Collado was the sight of another *falla* statue and the crowd was pouring in from all the alleyways and streets that fed into it to watch the ceremony for setting it alight. Just a few minutes to go. The press of people was getting tighter and tighter and there was hardly anywhere to move. He had to find a gap somewhere, a place to catch sight of his prey once again, otherwise he would get trapped.

There was a small newspaper kiosk to one side of the square. Hooking a toe on to a narrow ledge, he hauled himself up, out of the crowd, to get a better view. The kids he had crashed into in the alleyway moments before saw what he was doing and decided to copy him, clambering up with him, and over him, before eventually settling on the roof. If any more came up, Cámara thought, the cheap metal structure might collapse.

He waved his badge at them; they crowded round to hear him.

'I'm looking for a man in his early twenties,' he said. And he gave them a description of Moreno.

The boys on the roof looked down at him and frowned.

'Dunno,' said one.

'Haven't seen him,' said another.

'Just look around, will you,' Cámara said. 'See if you can see him from where you are up there.'

A young voice chirped up from the other side – the girl he had almost knocked over.

'There's a bloke over there trying to get out of the square,' she said.

'What's that?' said Cámara.

'Is it blond hair, you said?' one of the other boys asked, looking down at Cámara.

'Yes.'

'Short?'

'Yes, yes.'

'Well, there's someone like that just left. Pushing past everyone to get out of the square.'

'Where?'

Cámara jumped down from the ledge and back on the ground. The boy pointed over his back.

'Just charged up towards Caballeros,' he said.

Again the crowds in his way, once again having to push and force his way past. It was getting worse now, thicker, denser, tighter.

'Police!' he shouted. 'Police!'

The crowds just seemed to move in closer.

Fighting his way through to the edge of the square he looked up the alleyway where the kids said they had seen Moreno leaving, and saw a tide of bodies moving against him. He'll be slowed up as well, he thought to himself. He'll be being held back as well.

Then he saw: Moreno's head, clearly and deliberately turning to look for him as he broke away from the mass of people and paused, before darting to the left down a side street. He'd seen him, seen that he was still being chased, and he was drawing his pursuer on and on.

Cámara waded forwards, his head spinning now from having to jump from side to side as he sought the gaps in the crowd and edged his way closer. If he could just get to the alleyway there might be an opening there, a chance. He reached into the back of his trousers and pulled out the *Municipal*'s revolver, quickly checking it was loaded.

He broke through. But no sign of Moreno. It was calmer here, fewer people, but there was no end of side streets and other alleyways where Moreno could have disappeared. He looked up: some of these buildings had been abandoned. It wouldn't take much for someone like Moreno to reach up and climb into them through the first-floor balconies.

He stopped: there was an infinity of possibilities. Should he turn right? Left? Or just clamber into one of these old buildings himself and have a look around? Ahead of him the way was clear.

He sprinted forwards, appearing in a small passageway in time to hear footsteps breaking out at the far end: the sound of someone running away. He was closing in.

The passageway brought him to the edge of the larger Plaza del Tossal, where a crowd was waiting for the burning of the *falla* statue. A couple near the edge were breaking away, the man with his arm over the girl's shoulder, looking down at her with concern. The girl was holding her foot as she hopped, before leaning against the wall of a nearby building.

'*Hijo de puta*,' she swore. 'Bastard's probably broken my toe.'

The man glanced up in anger, as though looking for someone.

Cámara took a step forwards and identified himself.

'What happened?' he said.

'Some prick just pushed right through to get in,' the man said. 'Fucking lunatic, pushing people away. Trod on my girlfriend's foot.'

'Stamped on it, more like,' the girl said, looking up at them.

'Young guy? Short blond hair?' Cámara asked.

'Think so,' the man said.

'Which way did he go?'

'Just pushed straight through. Here, are you going to arrest him?'

Cámara was already breaking through the crowd.

Policía, Policía.

This time people seemed to know instinctively what he was about, and edged out of his way as best they could. He was there to get the arsehole who had just pushed past them all so aggressively. At last, a policeman doing his job.

He didn't see her, but one of the pair of eyes now resting on him from a few feet away belonged to Almudena. She pursed her lips as she recognised him, hesitated, and then pushed forwards to try and converge with him as he made his way through the throng. There were still some things that needed to be said.

A splitting, cracking sound roared out as the first fireworks for the *falla* were let off: a handful of colourful explosions in the air above them at the start of an elaborate chain of firecrackers and more fireworks which in a few seconds would culminate in the *falla* statue itself being set alight. As the bright lights lit up the faces staring up, Cámara caught sight of one head bobbing up and down ahead of him, not bothering to watch the spectacle.

'Stop!' he shouted. 'Stop!'

But his words were lost in the barrage of noise from the aerial blasts above. The *petardos* had started now and were spitting and flaring along a string before they gave an enormous, deep-sounding boom at the foot of the *falla* statue and the first flames began to lick the sides of the brightly painted wood-and-foam structure.

There was a scream. Moreno was almost in reach, pushing towards the front of the crowd at the foot of the *falla* statue.

'Out of my way!'

The crowd melted before him. Ahead, just a few yards from him, Moreno had stopped and turned to face him through the growing gap in the throng. But he wasn't alone. Pressed against him, immobilised by a tight headlock, and with Moreno's gun pushed against her temple, was Almudena.

Cámara stopped in his tracks, unable to move. Moreno was grinning at him, his eyes flashing with a manic stare, his lips trembling. Beside him, Almudena was ashen faced, too frightened to make a sound, struggling to keep herself upright as Moreno pulled her from one side to the next.

The revolver was still in Cámara's hand but it was too late to raise it. Moreno spotted it and pressed his own pistol harder against Almudena's head.

'Drop it!' he screamed. 'Drop it or she's dead!'

Cámara raised his other hand slowly, as though to show he'd understood, and then started to bend at the knee in order to place the revolver on the ground.

'Hurry up!' Moreno barked.

Cámara knew that without a gun there was no way he could confront Moreno, no way he could resolve this. Yet even with one in his hand there was little he could do: a clean head shot was almost impossible with a weapon like that, but even if he was lucky with his aim the bullet would cause Moreno's body to spasm, making his hand squeeze and so pulling the trigger. There was only one place he could be hit: straight between the eyes. That way he would fall down dead instantly, with no spasm, no pulling the trigger. But only a top marksman could even attempt such a shot.

He knelt down further, keeping his eyes on Moreno as his hand reached the ground and he unwrapped his fingers from the revolver. Almudena stared at him with incredulity. Was he going to abandon her now like this?

And then it happened – so suddenly that it left him breathless. A splash of red and Moreno slumped to the floor, a dead weight. His lifeless arms were still hooked around Almudena, and she was dragged down with him.

There was a scream. In an instant Cámara was lurching forwards, his arms reaching for Almudena, to raise her up from Moreno. He turned her over; her face was bloodied from the mess ebbing from the hole in the centre of Moreno's forehead. Her body felt limp in his arms. He checked; she was unharmed.

As the flames of the *falla* statue intensified, the crowd moved in around them, the moment of immediate danger apparently gone. He looked up, then back at Almudena;

her eyes were resting on his, unblinking. Her mouth opened; she seemed about to speak to him.

'Almudena!'

A man's voice was heard shouting in panic close by.

'Almudena!'

She moved. Feeling appeared to be returning to her. Yet still she kept her gaze on Cámara.

Someone pushed through from behind them. A pair of arms thrust through and suddenly she was hauled away. Cámara let her go without any resistance. From the corner of his eye he could see her resting her head on the other man's chest, her body shaking as the fright and shock took hold.

A hand was placed on his shoulder as he crouched by the wreckage of Moreno's body. Cámara turned to look: it was Beltrán, with a Sako sniper rifle hanging from a strap over his arm.

'Good job you ducked like that,' Beltrán grinned.

'Thank God it was you,' Cámara said.

TWENTY-FOUR

The bull that horned me sent me to a better place
Traditional

Monday 20th March

His feet felt swollen, beating the polished red marble pavement with a heavy clomp as he took each step. He had to be careful not to slip – the surface had only just been washed clean and he felt his toes curling instinctively as he tried to keep his balance. Around the corner he could hear the sound of high-powered water hoses being used to wash away the fiesta. The first light of dawn was beginning to break out towards the sea, but already it was as if *Fallas* had never taken place. As was the case every year, after the final bonfire had burnt to the ground, and long before the *falleros* had stumbled home for the last time, a cleaning operation had got underway, transforming the city, under the guise of darkness, from the party capital of Spain into just another Mediterranean port town.

An army of sweepers and rubbish collectors worked like bees in a seemingly chaotic fashion, but always managing – miraculously, it seemed – to get the job done by the next morning, so that after more than a week of paralysis Valencia once again became the nervy, semi-functioning city it usually was. All that remained from the fiesta were a few metal barriers stacked away to one side awaiting removal, or the marks on the tarmac where the *fallas* had burnt to the ground. A few nearby buildings might bear their own personal souvenirs – cracked windows and scorched facades from their proximity to the flames: scars that had to be healed and repaired.

Cámara circled around the Plaza del Ayuntamiento and then headed down towards the baroque, brightly painted building of the Banco de Valencia. The first of the street lamps were beginning to dim as the daylight increased. Across the road a group of tourists – they looked German – was standing outside the front door of a hotel next to their luggage, with every air of waiting for a taxi or bus to take them to the airport. They'd come and witnessed *Fallas*, probably drunk vast quantities of Agua de Valencia cocktails and were now heading home. Probably still half-pissed by the looks of them.

A voice inside wondered why he didn't go home himself. Perhaps if he tried now he might be able to get some rest. But he dismissed the idea. As soon as his eyes closed all he could see was Moreno's face glaring at him, the hole in the centre of his face, and Almudena's ashen features. There would be no rest. Not tonight, perhaps not for a while.

He walked on, as he had done all night, heading down past the old university building towards the Parterre. A group of young people, still clinging on to the party spirit, screeched past him in an open-top sports car, metallic disco music blaring at full volume, a blonde girl in the back seat waving at him drunkenly as they went past. They'd have enough cocaine on them to keep going for another couple of hours, then a quick shower, another line and back into work, fresher than the rest of them in most cases.

He dropped his head and carried on walking. Under a gigantic rubber tree a truck was pulling up to hitch a shuttered *buñuelos* stall on to the back and wheel it away. Even the smell of frying sweet batter – second only to gunpowder in the air during *Fallas* – was being cleansed from the city.

There was a beep: still sitting in his pocket, the sergeant's phone was trying to tell him something. A text message, probably. At this time? He put his hand down, felt for the phone and pulled it out, flipping it open with his thumb.

The text was from Torres: *Roberto is in the Nou d'Octubre hospital. Medics have given leave for questioning.*

Cámara closed it shut and put it back in his pocket.

There was a park nearby and he found himself wandering towards it. A handful of bright yellow freesias shone up, catching the first rays of light as the sun started to rise above the rooftops. Cámara had always liked these flowers. He had bought bunches of them for Almudena on occasion, surprising her at the office with them as he passed through the centre.

As he stood in front of them, staring down at their light, happy faces, he heard a sound. After a brief splutter a sprinkler system coughed into life, casting an arc of droplets into the air, rainbows bursting above his head as they glinted in the sun. He took a deep breath and let the water wash over him, first moving across him one way then another as the machine swept in a semicircle over its patch of garden. In a few moments the droplets had formed streams of water on his scalp, cascading down his neck and soaking into his shirt. Water. Water to wash away the fire, the dirt. Everything.

He listened, straining to hear. And for the briefest of moments the city was silent.

'Maldonado's seriously pissed off. He had a bet running that the Blanco case would still be unresolved by the end of today. He's going to lose a lot of money.'

Torres met him round the back door.

'It's a weird one, this. Yesterday we spent most of the time trying to get Paco to confess. Today we're questioning little brother Roberto instead.'

Cámara was reluctant to show his face, and strolling in through the main entrance would have broadcast his presence in the loudest of terms. He was suspended, pending transfer to another section. His career in *Homicidios* was over. But still he found himself back at the Jefatura.

Torres pressed on the metal bar of the emergency exit to let Cámara in. He held a cigarette out to him and lit it as Cámara put it in his mouth, his body craving the extra nicotine of Torres's Habanos that morning.

'Have you spoken to him yet?' Cámara asked.

'No.' Torres lit his own cigarette and inhaled deeply. 'We're going down to the hospital in a minute.'

He looked Cámara in the eye.

'Thought I might try and persuade you to come along.'

Cámara shook his head, rubbing a hand over his unshaved chin as though trying to bring feeling back to his numbed self.

'Besides, we do something irregular like that and the courts will be all over it,' he said. 'The guy would die a natural death before anyone got round to banging him up.'

Torres nodded. For some reason the technological

revolution had bypassed the Spanish judicial system, and cases were still dealt with on bits of paper. Some could take anything up to ten years to be resolved, and it wasn't unheard of for documents to go 'missing'. Television news cameramen often lingered over the piles of folders and box files that littered the offices of every lawyer, prosecutor and magistrate in the land – a nineteenth-century anomaly in a supposedly hi-tech age.

Torres filled him in on the morning's work: a team was looking into the paperwork linking Roberto's German drug company with the Ramírez bull farm. By the looks of it they hadn't been overly careful to hide anything: sales, if they could call it that, had been carried out through a third party based in Rome. What was difficult to prove was that any money had actually changed hands for the drugs. They could trace them reaching Spain and then the farm, but there was nothing to show any payment for them.

'Perhaps there was no money in it,' Cámara said. 'Family thing. Roberto kept things quiet at the drug company and they were simply handed over as a gift. In the end it was in his interests to keep the family business going as well, despite all that talk of being *anti-toro*.'

There were other links to Roberto. Huerta had analysed Moreno's phone, which they'd picked up along with several other items from the corpse. Moreno had erased the memory, but his phone company had already given them a detailed breakdown of all calls made and received by the number over the previous two weeks. A New York number had rung the night before Blanco was killed. It was almost certainly from a public phone, but it tied in exactly with Roberto's business trip to the city.

'The green light,' Cámara said.

'Probably.'

'Roberto heard it from Flores, who'd got it from the editor of *El Diario*,' he said. 'Blanco's got a big story to tell. That's when he knew.'

'And triggered Moreno to act,' Torres said.

Cámara flicked his cigarette out on to the waste ground. At least they could smoke in relative peace now – no kids hurling firecrackers about the place. He almost missed them.

Torres took a final drag and they turned to head inside.

'Any sign of Roberto's phone?' Cámara asked as they walked down the steps to the basement.

'Claims not to have one,' Torres said.

'You might want to look into it anyway,' Cámara said. 'Check the phone companies. You need something to link Roberto to Ruiz Pastor's murder.'

'Oh, I think we might be all right on that score,' Torres said. 'Caballero gave the go-ahead for a DNA sample. Quintero is checking it out right now. If it comes back the same as the stuff he scraped from under Ruiz Pastor's nails . . .'

'The scratches on Roberto's face,' Cámara said.

'Ruiz Pastor was a big man. We know he put up a fight.'

'I just hope to God . . .'

They reached the bottom of the stairs and started walking down the corridor.

'Another thing,' he said. 'I had a quick look at Roberto's bank accounts. Well, his Spanish ones at least – looks like the guy's got money all over the world. Anyway, the day after Blanco was killed, the day he flew back for the funeral and all that, he took a large amount out in cash.'

'How much?'

'Ten thousand euros.'

Cámara pursed his lips.

'Says it was to buy his mother a present. Being away and all that.'

Cámara gave him a look.

'Yeah. Didn't exactly ring true for me, either.'

'Money for Moreno,' Cámara said. 'Payment for his hired assassin.'

'But how are we going to prove that?'

Cámara remembered the new leaflets at the *Anti-Taurino* League's stall.

'No sign of Marta Díaz?' he asked.

'We've got everyone looking for her,' Torres said. 'And by everyone I mean a couple of squad cars for now.'

'Right,' Cámara said. 'Bloody *Fallas*.'

'Anyway,' Torres said. 'You better get going, before someone finds you're in the building.'

Footsteps came from the other end of the corridor. Torres looked at Cámara. There was still time to disappear if he hurried. Cámara reached out and put a hand on his chest. There was no point. He was finished here. How much worse could they make it for him?

The footsteps grew louder until finally a face appeared under the strip lights.

It was Pardo.

'You,' he said to Cámara. 'Come with me.'

'Torres has nothing—' Cámara tried to say, but Pardo butted in.

'And shut up!'

*   *   *

377

Pardo stood and looked out at the city through the smoked glass of his window. It was a clear sunny day outside, and the first sounds of a city slowly waking up after the fiesta came drifting up from the streets below.

'For fuck's sake, Cámara.'

Cámara shuffled in his seat and closed his eyes for a moment, trying to appear composed.

'Sir?'

Pardo spun on his heels and bashed into the side of the desk. Cámara opened his eyes with a start and saw Pardo glaring at him.

'Don't try it on,' he bellowed. He checked himself, as though conscious that he was in danger of losing control, and moved to sit down on the other side of the desk.

'Do you have any idea,' he said, tapping the tips of his fingers against each other, 'how many people want to see you disappeared? I mean, not just transferred out of *Homicidios*, but really just out of the fucking police force altogether. Booted out, sent away for good. Never to come back.'

Cámara gave a shrug.

'The Town Hall wants you out because you've been harassing their staff. I take it you heard, did you? Emilia got back in. Only just, mind.'

'Did you expect a different result?'

'It doesn't make things any easier for you. Meanwhile, the Ministry in Madrid is calling up wanting your head for interfering in constitutional affairs, asking what this guy's doing arresting politicians on the Day of Reflection.'

Pardo had started counting all of Cámara's enemies on the fingers of one hand.

'My boss wants you gone because he reckons you're the

most incompetent chief inspector on his staff, who can't even obey a direct order. Even the head of personnel wants you out because you caused an evacuation of the entire building by lighting a fucking cigarette right under the fucking smoke alarm.'

Cámara sniffed. It's coming now, he thought.

Pardo leaned forwards, placing his palms together over the desk.

'You haven't slept for days, have you?' he said with a change in tone.

Cámara frowned.

'Moreno, eh?' Pardo said. 'That must have been tough.'

Cámara fought back the images of the impact of the bullet, the blood spatters on Almudena's face.

'The DNA test?' he said.

'On Roberto? Still waiting to come through. Everyone's pulling out the stops for this one. Full backup.'

'About time,' Cámara said.

'Look, this hasn't been our finest moment, I admit that.'

Here it comes, Cámara thought: the moment of self-flagellation. But the shit only ever flies in one direction.

'We all fucked up a bit here,' Pardo said. 'We've just got to live with that.'

He sat down in his chair and swivelled it from side to side for a moment.

'How did you know it was Moreno?' he asked at last.

Cámara looked up with a raised eyebrow.

'The rally,' he said. 'The night Blanco was killed. They came round to the Bar Los Toros. Once they'd left I later found out they'd packed in for the day there and then rather than carrying on. Said it was out of respect for Blanco.'

'So?' Pardo said.

'No one knew then that Blanco was dead. Only the *Municipal* who came to fetch me, and I was with him the whole time.'

Cámara placed his hands on his thighs.

'And Moreno?' Pardo asked.

'It would have been easy enough for him to break away from the rest of the demonstrators for a while,' Cámara said. 'No one would have noticed. Hid himself in the chapel, strangled Blanco, carried his body out to the middle of the ring, mutilated it, then escaped out down the drainpipe of the Enfermería and slipped back into the crowd, joining the others just as they passed that way heading down to the Bar Los Toros.'

'So Marta Díaz was in on it as well.'

'It would have helped for her to manoeuvre the demonstration round to where Moreno needed it just at the right time, but it might be hard to prove unless you've got material evidence against her.'

'Or a confession,' Pardo said.

'Someone's got to find her first.'

Pardo waved a hand.

'Just a matter of time,' he said. 'She can't hide for too long.' He paused.

'The mutilation, though. What . . . ?'

'Moreno trained as a bullfighter when he was a kid,' Cámara said. 'Never made it, though. They threw him out of bullfighting school.'

'So he knew all about it, about making it look authentic,' Pardo said. 'Revenge as well of some sort, perhaps. But why try to murder Roberto? Weren't they working together?'

Cámara carried on with his explanation. Perhaps if he told Pardo all this now he'd save himself the bother of having to write it all down in a *minuta*. Or would that end up being his final act in *Homicidios*?

'Roberto tried to make Ruiz Pastor's murder look like Blanco's – as though it was the same person. But Moreno didn't like that. Vanity, I reckon. He was a touchy sort, proud of his technique. He didn't like someone else copying him. I doubt he liked the fact that Roberto knew he was Blanco's murderer, either. He'd taken Roberto's money, he'd got what he wanted. Perhaps he thought it would make things easier in the future to get rid of him now.'

'The girlfriend can help confirm all this.'

Cámara was silent.

'You don't think we're going to catch her, do you?' Pardo said.

'I don't know,' said Cámara. 'There are plenty of groups abroad willing to help out a leader of the Spanish anti-bullfighting league. Push it too hard and before you know it we'll have a diplomatic incident on our hands, the French or the Germans or whoever refusing to hand her over in the name of humanity.'

Pardo looked at him.

'You've changed your tune a bit. A week or so ago I'd have said you'd be the first helping her over the border. Don't tell me you've become an aficionado overnight.'

Cámara shrugged.

'All right. None of my business,' Pardo said. 'Still, if you ever want tickets just give me a nod. Right?'

Cámara was alarmed to see that the man was actually smiling at him. What was this? Some sweetener to soften the blow of demotion? Or of being fired completely? It wasn't easy for them: he was a civil servant, after all, guaranteed a job for life. But he'd disobeyed a direct order. They could push it to that if they wanted. He wouldn't get in their way.

Pardo leaned in again, a look of seriousness on his face this time.

'You're not the brightest officer on my staff, Cámara,' he said. 'In fact, I've sometimes wondered if the top floor was fully furnished in your case.'

Cámara kept a straight face.

'But you've got a good instinct,' Pardo continued.

Here we go, Cámara thought to himself. A good instinct for which corner of the warehouse to store some stolen goods no one was ever going to reclaim. Bye bye *Homicidios*, hello *Depósito*.

'You showed that over Roberto.' He raised a hand. 'Don't worry. I'm confident we'll nail him. Quintero's coming back soon with the DNA test. And if that doesn't get him, something else will. You're right on this one. I know you are. His size forty-three shoes, the fact that his plane back to New York didn't leave till the afternoon on the day Ruiz Pastor was killed. He had the time and motive to do it; there's more than enough pointing at him to convince me, at least. What's more, officially the *Guardia Civil* should have pulled him in – Ruiz Pastor's murder was their case. Makes us look doubly good.'

He turned in his chair and stared out the window again.

'Of course, none of us should have been fooled by all that *anti-toro* stuff he's been spouting over the years. What do they say about blood ties, families, that kind of thing?'

'*Nada mejor en la vida que una familia unida*,' said Cámara. There's nothing better than a united family. Although this clearly didn't always extend to half-siblings, he thought to himself.

'Yes. Thought you'd know that one. Perhaps that's what put you on to it in the first place. All that old wives' stuff might not be such bollocks after all.'

'They're as traditional in this country as bullfighting,' Cámara said. Pardo grinned.

'Look, the point is I'm keeping you on,' Pardo said. 'You solved this case. That's what counts. I don't care who wants you gone. You've done good police work. Messy as fuck, and a huge amount of crap to clear up. But you got there.'

'The transfer . . .' Cámara started.

'Bollocks to the transfer. You're staying. And they're going to have to get rid of me first if they want you out of here. Don't worry, Cámara. Today you're a hero. You got Blanco's killers. All right, so one of them's in the morgue. But we've got the other one, and he's a big fish, a big player. Not the usual junkies and pimps we have to deal with most of the time. That counts, Cámara. Looks good. Looks like we're not afraid to go after the criminals whoever they are. The public like that.'

Cámara was silent, too stunned to say anything.

'I'm not going to give you a fucking medal,' Pardo said. 'Go on, you can fuck off now.'

He nodded at the door, and somehow Cámara found himself rising to his feet and making his way out.

'One other thing,' Pardo said as Cámara leaned out to reach the door handle. 'All that Bautista business.'

Cámara felt the hairs tingle on the back of his neck. Here

it came, the final, subtle stabbing. Demotion to inspector?
He turned round to face Pardo.

'You can forget about it,' Pardo said. 'You're clean.'

Cámara blinked.

'The report's gone missing,' Pardo said with half a smile.
'Bit of a mystery, really.'

EPILOGUE

It was the first truly hot day of the year, and Cámara was glad he'd left his jacket at the office. His service weapon was back in a drawer in his desk. No need to bring it for this. Although what was it going to be, exactly? A social thing? Perhaps there was a work angle to it. She hadn't said on the phone.

Crossing the Plaza del Ayuntamiento, he rolled up his sleeves and felt the cooling air circulate around his wrists. *No te quites el sayo hasta el cuarenta de mayo*: Don't take off your smock till the fortieth of May. They were still a few days short, but already spring felt it was giving way to summer. The nights were still cool, but soon he'd be having to sleep with all the windows open. It would be like that until almost the end of September.

The square was back to normal, the madness of *Fallas* barely a memory from almost a couple of months back. The florists' stalls were bright with richly coloured blooms, traffic flowed in its usual jerky and aggressive fashion. A bus was honking its horn at some motorcyclist for getting in its way, the sound like a thousand mules braying in unison. Someone had once told him that in parts of France – was it Montpellier? – the local buses were fitted with tinkling little bells instead of horns, giving off a gentle peal whenever they needed to make their presence felt. Not here, not in Valencia. That could never catch on.

He thought about stopping for a quick beer at one of the touristy bars at the side of the square, quenching his thirst in the heat before his meeting, but the clock tower on the Town Hall told him he didn't have time. If he went straight there he would only be a few minutes late. A couple of posters of Emilia's grinning face stared back at him as he raced past. Not content with having won the election, the mayoress felt the need to remind her fellow Valencians of the fact weeks, even months after the event. What struck him most was that none of the images had been defaced. Only a few years back some politicised graffiti artist would have carefully doctored each one. But no one seemed to go in for that kind of thing these days; everyone was too busy worrying about their mortgage repayments, or finding a job.

He crossed Xàtiva in front of the train station and worked his way past the bullring towards Calle Castellón, glancing up at the Enfermería and its rogue drainpipe. The same old useless spikes were there at the top, still failing to prevent anyone getting in and out. Perhaps in the nineteenth century, when they'd built the place, that had been enough to deter any would-be trespassers. But now? After all that had happened? In his mind he could hear the bullring officials justifying to themselves why there was no need to change anything, or make it more difficult to get in and out by that route. It was a one-off, a freak incident. There weren't going to be any more attempts on bullfighters' lives like there had been on Blanco. So just leave it as it is.

They were probably right. If anything, Blanco's death had taught the country to value its bullfighters even more. The wave of sympathy for *los toros* hadn't been enough to dethrone Emilia, but there was no sign of the increased interest in bullfighting falling off. Not yet, at least. Perhaps next year would be different, but for now matadors were appearing in unexpected places, writing articles for leading newspapers, appearing in cultural programmes on television. According to rumour, a couple of bullfighters had parts in films that were about to go into production. Having seen its most precious son martyred, the country as a whole appeared to have fallen in love once again with its 'national fiesta'.

The Town Hall's attempt to jump on an *anti-toro* band-wagon now seemed badly misjudged. The fact was, though, that as the *Municipal* had told Cámara, there was never any chance that the local city authorities could ban the event. Soon after the election results were announced, and the celebration parties had ended, a brief communiqué was made stating that while Emilia stood firm in her stance against bullfights, there was little she could do as her hands had been tied by the government in Madrid. It was bullshit, as everyone knew. But she'd won another four years; that was all that mattered. People gave their usual shrug on hearing the news and then got on with things. Politicians lied and got rich; it's what they did. Wouldn't everyone do the same in their position?

The Bar Los Toros was empty. The TV was blaring from its usual corner while the cigarette machine flashed from the opposite wall. Cámara walked over, placed a few coins in the slot and hooked out a fresh packet of Ducados from the shelf at the bottom. Clearly the barman had found a way to override the lock designed to stop children from buying cigarettes. He heard a rattle of bottles as he lit a cigarette: the barman was out at the back clearing away crates of empties.

'*Hombre*,' he said when he caught sight of Cámara. 'Didn't hear you come in.'

'That's all right,' Cámara said. He checked the time on his new mobile. 'No one else turn up?' he said. The barman raised a quizzical eyebrow. 'A woman?' Cámara added.

'Nah,' the barman said. 'Believe me, if a woman had come in I would definitely have noticed.'

He wiped the bar in front of him and then reached for a glass.

'You'll be wanting one of these,' he said, pouring Cámara a Mahou from the tap. 'It's getting hot.'

'Yes,' said Cámara. 'Came on quite suddenly.'

'I prefer it like this,' said the barman. 'Don't like the cold, me.'

Cámara accepted the beer, but kept his eye on the door, expecting it to open at any moment. And with something of a surprise he realised he was feeling slightly nervous. Why had she said here, of all places? He laughed to himself. Where else would she have said?

At that moment he heard the click of the door and spun round before the barman could say any more.

'*Hola*,' he said.

There was a pause.

'Oh,' she said at last. 'You're already here.'

He leaned down and felt Alicia's face brushing against his

as she gave him a kiss on either cheek. A brief sense of disappointment passed through him. What had he expected? Part of him had had some dream of a more passionate reunion than this, perhaps. But the feeling passed; a more professional side switched on: whatever her motives were for meeting him, reigniting a sexual spark didn't appear to be one of them.

He picked up his glass and they walked across to a table near the window. In the light from the street he tried to get a better look at her, but her hair, slightly longer now, was hanging over her face as she fumbled with her bag and squeezed into the tiny space between the table and the chair. He could tell that there was something changed in her, less centred, somehow.

Finally she sat up straight, pushing her hair behind one ear and smiling at him.

'It's been a very long time,' she said.

He nodded.

'Too long,' she said. 'It's just that I was . . .'

'It's all right,' he said. 'What do you want to drink?'

'Red wine,' she said without a pause. 'Shall we get a bottle?'

A few moments later the barman placed a Rioja in front of them with a couple of plates of nuts.

'We've run out of anything more elaborate,' he said, pointing at the tapas. 'Unless you want me to heat up some chorizo.'

'That's all right,' Alicia said. 'This will do.'

He went back behind the bar and started rattling his crates again, giving them a sense of privacy.

'I knew we'd be virtually alone here,' she said. 'That's why I chose it.'

Something fluttered inside Cámara at her words.

'How are things at the newspaper?' he said.

'Oh, you know, busy,' she said. 'There was all the fallout from Roberto's arrest to cover, stuff on Angel Moreno; people wanted to know who had actually killed Blanco, what kind of a person he was. All that stuff about him being kicked out of bullfighting school, his relationship with Marta Díaz. That kind of thing. They needed a Satan character, or something; a Judas. Roberto is more difficult, more complicated. But Moreno? I'm almost glad he died, because if you'd got him alive they'd be ripping him to pieces right now.'

She checked herself.

'All right, I don't mean that,' she said. 'You were there, weren't you?'

Cámara shrugged.

'It was bad, eh?' she said. 'Yeah, I can imagine so.'

She lifted the bottle of wine and poured.

'It's good to see you again,' she said, raising a glass. Cámara raised his and they clinked together.

'You too,' he said.

'Anyway,' she continued, 'they put me on to cover the court case as well, the whole prosecution thing. I don't know anything about legal reporting, but because I knew Blanco they thought I was the right person to follow the story right to the end.'

'I hear proceedings are going to start against Roberto soon,' Cámara said. 'I'm out of it now, as you know. But occasionally we hear things. I could give you a ring if I get wind of anything interesting, if you like.'

She gave a half-smile.

'You gave me the thread,' he said. 'The connection from Gallego to Flores to Roberto.'

'I'm not sure if that makes me feel better,' she said. 'If I hadn't said anything to Javier, Blanco might still be alive today.'

Cámara took a sip of his wine.

'You think they'll get a conviction?' she asked.

'I heard that Caballero was fairly confident,' Cámara said. 'But the judge who's presiding over the court case is one of the tougher ones. He's thrown out watertight cases before because of some spelling mistake or other.'

Alicia laughed, and for a second there was a hint of a connection.

'You don't care, do you?' she said.

'About whether Roberto gets banged up?' He put his glass back down on the table.

'I did my bit. He's guilty. I know that. Everyone knows that. Even if he walks free at the end of this, everyone knows he was behind Blanco's murder. And that he killed Ruiz Pastor himself. For Christ's sake, Ruiz Pastor had Roberto's DNA under his fingernails from scratching at him when he was being attacked.'

'Roberto claims that's just because they shook hands a few hours before at Blanco's funeral.'

Cámara gave her a look.

'Listen,' he said, 'if the judge buys that . . .'

He waved his hand.

'I'm a policeman,' he said. 'My job ends the moment I hand over a suspect to the investigating judge. If he, or one of his colleagues screws it up afterwards . . . It's not that I don't care. I just can't afford to care too much.'

'It's all right,' she said. 'I understand. Still no word on Marta Díaz?'

Cámara shook his head.

'There was a report of a sighting in France, a couple of weeks after Moreno died. But nothing came of it. Since then it's gone cold.'

He grabbed the bottle and refilled their glasses. The question of why Alicia had asked to meet up with him still hadn't arisen. Just to have a chat about the case? She'd already appeared to brush aside his offer of information.

'How have things been for the Ramírez family?' he asked, trying to keep the conversation going. She'd get to it eventually, whatever it was.

She gave a long sigh. 'Not good,' she said. 'Not good at all.'

'I bet the mother took it badly,' Cámara said.

'She hasn't been seen since before Roberto's arrest. Staying at the farm up in Albacete. Hasn't left once, by all accounts. Just gone to ground.'

'The others?' Cámara said.

'From what I can gather, Ramírez has effectively handed everything over to Paco. He's broken; everyone says so. First losing Blanco, and now this.'

'What about the drugs?' Cámara said.

'I'd say they've taken a knock from it. Bookings are down. They'd built their reputation on providing the best bulls, as you know. And the denials only carry so much weight.'

They both knew that after Cámara had found the phials of dope in the Ramírez truck – later positively identified by Huerta as a variant of ketamine that left almost no traces in the bull, and was undetectable by the vets at the bullring

– searches had been made of the Ramírez farm, but no other samples had been found. The family had denied all knowledge, claiming the drugs had been planted to stain their reputation.

'People start looking back at previous bulls they've produced, trying to detect a trend there, to see if they really were doping them. They probably aren't doing it any more, but it's possibly too late for them. The doubt is there, and the crowds might react badly to seeing Ramírez bulls on the card now.'

'You think they might close down?' Cámara asked.

'They'll probably limp on for a year or two more,' Alicia said. 'But after that?' She frowned.

'Anyway,' she said, suddenly changing the tone. 'How are you?'

'All right,' he said.

'Flores been giving you any more problems?'

He grinned.

'I get parking fines from streets I've never even driven down,' he said. 'Not every day, but occasionally. Then there's a demand for some non-existent arrears on my council tax. That kind of thing.' He laughed; it seemed even Maldonado had eased off recently after getting stung with his little gamble; rumour in the Jefatura was that he'd lost almost five thousand euros.

'Nothing I can't cope with. It's good. Shows I really had him rattled.'

'He doesn't give up,' she said.

'Do any of us?'

She seemed embarrassed for a moment and stared down at the table.

'And your girlfriend?' she asked. 'Did that . . . ?'

'End?' he said. 'Yes, it ended. Ended a long time back. It just had to go through the motions of dying. You know how it is.'

Almudena. Would he ever be able to think of her without images of that night coming to mind, of her pallid face, Moreno's arm wrapped tight around her neck? To bring her up now seemed strange, almost as if it put the conversation out of kilter. He'd never talked about her with Alicia. It had been so brief there had barely been time.

'She started a relationship with her business partner,' he said. Just as I'd ended up in bed with someone else, he thought to himself. Why hadn't he called Alicia himself over these past weeks? Sitting here with her now he realised how much he felt for her. They'd had fun, a lot of fun. There was no reason why they shouldn't carry it on for a bit, see what happened. Did every relationship have to have 'for ever' stamped all over it, and if not be rejected? It was crazy. Yet he had to admit to himself that he'd just let things drift. It would get picked up, he'd thought to himself. A moment would come when it would feel like the right thing to do, to lift up the phone and give her a call. But the weeks had gone by and he'd done nothing. And yet still he couldn't explain why.

'Have you met someone else?' Alicia asked.

'No,' he said, slightly taken aback. 'No, I haven't. Look, I'm sorry I didn't call. It's just, I—'

'I'm leaving,' she said, breaking him off. 'I'm leaving Valencia.'

Their eyes met and locked for a moment, then broke away.

'Oh,' Cámara said. He reached for his wine glass and took a mouthful.

'I've got a job on one of the nationals in Madrid,' she said. 'Bullfights, crime. More of the same, really.'

'But better, hopefully,' he said. 'All this Blanco stuff, it must have caught someone's eye.'

'The truth is I've been trying to get out for a while,' she said.

'Your ex-husband,' he said.

'That, and . . . well, that, really. After the divorce I felt I should take off and try somewhere new. It's not easy working with someone you've been so intimate with.'

'And then there's the benefit of getting out of this city,' Cámara said with half a smile.

'Yeah,' she said with a laugh. 'There's that as well. It's great, Valencia. Got a lot going for it.'

'It's just that sometimes you need something else,' he said.

'Something like that.'

She poured some more wine into both their glasses. Cámara pulled out his cigarettes and offered her one.

'I wish you luck,' he said. 'I hope it goes well for you there.'

'Thanks.'

'Who knows,' he said. 'I might suddenly get promoted and sent off to Madrid myself.'

She smiled.

'It was fun,' he said. 'I had a lot of fun.'

That was all he said, nothing more. And he didn't quite know what he expected her to say, perhaps just 'Me too,' or something to that effect. And that would be it: she'd go off to Madrid, and he'd go back to *Homicidios*, and they'd have some fond memories of each other. And perhaps in a few months' time they might give each other a call, just to see how the other was getting on, perhaps even meet up for another drink like this if ever they could. But she didn't react like that. Not the same resigned but joyful farewell. Her eyes betrayed a completely different emotion, one much stronger than he was expecting, but which he struggled to identify.

'There's something else I need to tell you,' she said.

He watched her closely: her bottom lip seemed to tremble.

'I wasn't sure if I should tell you this. It's all over, all settled,' she said. 'But I thought it only fair.'

Her head had dropped and she was staring at the table again.

'What are you talking about?' Cámara asked as delicately as he could. There was a sudden fragility in her he felt he didn't recognise.

She paused.

'I got pregnant,' she said at last, looking up with reddening eyes.

'That night . . .' she said. 'We didn't . . . You said you were . . .'

Cámara was motionless, as though unable to withstand the weight of his own body.

'Don't look like that,' she said. 'Please.'

Her eyes were brimming with tears now.

'I . . . Look,' she said. 'I just . . . I wasn't sure what to do, whether to tell you. Of course I had an abortion. Just last week.'

'You . . .' Cámara started.

'But you told me you were infertile, see? Said you couldn't have kids.'

'I . . .'

'So I thought you should know.'

Her eyes seemed to plead with him.

'It's better that way. Don't you think?'

Cámara walked in the afternoon shadows cast by the train station as he passed back up the Calle Castellón. The pavement seemed to move of its own accord beneath his feet, sensations from his body as though in suspension. He felt as if he were floating, a bubble of limited consciousness cut off from the world around it, travelling slowly, obscurely in a place he knew that he knew, but felt removed from. People walked past him, or struggled to squeeze by, other bubbles locked in their own worlds. Were they as unseeing as he? In some part of himself he felt sure he had not always been like this, that this was exceptional – not his ordinary way of being. He tried to cling on to the thought: it was the only thing to hold on to, to prevent him from simply drifting away, getting lost on some passing breeze.

He clenched his hands, as though trying to retrieve physical sensation as an experience he could recognise, that could tell him when, where and who he was.

There had been the beginnings of a child: a promise, a potential. Now it was gone, but for a moment, a few weeks perhaps, it had existed. And it was him, and part of him. Almudena had been wrong. The doctor had been wrong. So convinced had he been that he'd never got round to doing the test. What point had there been? Just to learn what he thought he already knew? Almudena was fine, wasn't that what she'd said? So it had to be his fault. And then when the relationship ended there was even less reason to have it confirmed.

And he'd thought that deep down he didn't really care. Things had gone wrong with Almudena. What were the chances they wouldn't do so with anyone else sooner or later? Was that the best way to bring a kid into the world? Certainly his own family and childhood were useless as a training ground for parenthood. Besides, he was forty-two: a bit old, perhaps, to be thinking about starting a family. Not that there was any biological clock for him as there had been for Almudena, but he didn't want to be an old dad, complaining that he couldn't play football with his son because of a bad back. Not that he liked football anyway, but that was the kind of thing dads were expected to do, wasn't it? What could he teach any future children, anyway? Old proverbs? How to cultivate marihuana? (He'd have to learn himself from Hilario first.) How to catch murderers? He wasn't even sure he was any good at that.

And so he'd given up on the idea. Let others have kids. He wasn't cut out for them in the first place. You had to live with what you got. And all he had was a *masclet* hanging between his legs: all bang and no power.

But they'd all been wrong. He was as potent and fertile as any man, any of the other males now streaming past him as they burst out of the train station and dodged the traffic to get across the road. He felt as though some primitive side to him, some cave-inhabiting being that existed within him somewhere, was picking up an essential missing portion of itself and putting it back in place. And a sense of wholeness – one that he had been unaware of before all this had happened – returned to him. He could have children. Whether he chose to or not was another matter, and at some level Alicia's abortion stung him – that had been part of him that had been snuffed out as well. He understood it; it had been necessary, even if it did hurt. But the point was that the potential for him to have children had been returned to him. That mattered; it gave the future a different hue.

For the first time in what felt like the entire day he was aware of himself breathing again, warm air rushing in and out of his lungs. He blinked, trying to engage with his surroundings. He was standing still, facing away from the road. In front of him a circular colonnaded brick building rose up into the blue, cloudless sky: a heavy, solid presence that seemed to bellow its existence at him. He rubbed his face with his hands and then opened his eyes again. People were tutting and moaning as they pushed past his motionless form in the middle of the pavement: this wasn't a place for lingering: either you moved or got out of the way. But he continued to stare up at the bullring regardless, smiling to himself that he should find himself here once again.

He turned and started walking away.

ACKNOWLEDGEMENTS

Particular thanks go to Jesús Herrero of the *Cuerpo Nacional de Policía* and Judge Víctor Gómez for giving me invaluable insights into the complex workings of the Spanish police and judicial systems. I have tried to reflect what I learned from them as accurately as possible.

My understanding of bullfighting benefited enormously from conversations and contact with Lorena Pardo, Jesús Morcillo, the bull-rearer Antonio López, the matador Alvaro Amores, the retired bullfighter Rafael Ataide 'Rafaelillo', Pascual Esteller, Enrique Aguilar, and other members of the *Asociación de la Prensa Taurina de Castellón*. Special thanks, however, go to Montse Arribas, who opened so many doors for me.

Much of the information on the symbolism and mythology of bullfighting came from the excellent book *El Simbolismo del Toro* by Mariate Cobaleda, with additional details from *Ritos y Juegos del Toro*, by Angel Alvarez de Miranda.

Miles and Ingrid Roddis have an encyclopaedic knowledge of Valencia and were kind enough to pass on their comments and offer much valued support. Gisela Dombek helped with a number of details, while Vicky gave much assistance at home.

Alex, Vicentín, Txarli and Tiziano of the *Grupo Chiau* filled me in on the finer points of *Fallas* and firecracker appreciation. *Muchas gracias, chicos.*

Thanks also to Mariajo Soriano and José Crespo; to Mike Ivey, for his encouragement and generosity; and to Rob, for reading an early draft and passing on much appreciated advice.

My agent, Peter Robinson, has been a stalwart throughout, supportive, generous and thoughtful, and this book owes much to him.

Thanks to Alison Samuel at Chatto & Windus, to Mary Chamberlain, for her excellent copy-editing and to Sandra Oakins for the map. Once again, it has been an enormous privilege and pleasure to work with Jenny Uglow; her contribution, not only to the book but to my own development as a writer, has been inestimable.

Lastly, thanks to Salud, for so much that cannot be expressed here.

GLOSSARY

Alamares – Adornments on a *traje de luces* (q.v.)
Albufera – Wetland area and beauty spot south of Valencia
Anti-taurino – Anti-bullfighting
Apoderado – A matador's manager

Banderillas – Colourful darts used in bullfighting
Barraca – A traditional thatched house in the Albufera (q.v.)
Bravo – 'Brave', a bull with fighting spirit
Burladero – Entrance/exit into the bullring and safety barrier

Cabrón – Slang insult, 'bastard'
Callejón – Passageway around the bullring, separating the
   bulls from the spectators
Capote – Large, usually pink and yellow, cape used by bull-
   fighters
Carajillo – Coffee laced with liquor
Chapero – Slang for male prostitute
Chicuela – A bullfighting move
Chino – A small firecracker
Copla – Traditional Spanish folk song
Cremà – The mass burning of the Valencia *Falla* (q.v.)
   statues on the night of 19th March
Criminalistas – *Guardia Civil* (q.v.) crime scene investigators
Cuadrilla – A matador's team of bullfighters and assistants

Cuerpo Nacional de Policía – Spanish National Police (Max Cámara's police force)
  Un Nacional – a member of the national police

Depósito – Impounded goods depot

Embarcadero – Jetty
Estoque – Matador's sword

Fallas – The main fiesta in Valencia, held in March
  Una falla – a statue made of wood and papier-mâché for *Fallas* which is burnt down on 19th March
Fallero – An active member of the *Fallas* fiesta
Feria – Fair, bullfighting fiesta/meeting
Fiambre – Slang for 'corpse'

GEO – *Grupo Especial de Operaciones* – Elite police force (SWAT team)
Gilipollas – Slang insult – 'prick'
Golfo – A hedonistic rogue
Grupo de Homicidios – Homicides unit
Guardia Civil – Civil Guard – Paramilitary police force
  Un Guardia – A member of the Civil Guard

Huerta – Market gardening area around the city of Valencia

Instituto de Medicina Legal – Forensic laboratory

Juez de Guardia – Duty investigating judge

La Puerta Grande – 'The Main Gate' of a bullring

Manso – 'Docile, a bull with no fighting spirit
María – Slang for marihuana
Maricón – Slang for homosexual
Marrón – Slang for 'corpse'
Masclet – A kind of fire-cracker
Mascletà – A fire-cracker display held every afternoon during *Fallas*
Mayoral – A herdsman
Mechero – A cigarette lighter
Médico Forense – Medical examiner
Montera – A bullfighter's hat
Muleta – Red cape used by matador

Ninot – One of the figures making up a *Falla* statue
Novillero – Apprentice bullfighter

Petardo – A kind of fire-cracker
Policía Científica – Criminalists, crime scene investigators – part of the national police
Policía Judicial – 'Judicial' police, policemen working under the orders of an investigating judge
Policía Local/Municipal – Local police force, controlled by the Town Hall
 - *Un Municipal* – A member of the local police
Porro – A joint (marihuana, not meat)
Prensa Rosa – The gossip press

Sangría – Oh, come on, you know what sangría is
Secretaria judicial – Court clerk
Seguirilla – A kind of song, or style, in Flamenco
Sol – lit. 'sun' – the sunny, cheaper seats in a bullring

Sombra – lit. 'shade' – the shady, more expensive seats in a bullring

Tercio – 'Third', a section of the bullfight

Tertulia – A discussion, often held by aficionados after a bullfight

Torero – A bullfighter

Toro – A bull

  Los Toros – Bullfighting

  Toro de lidia – A bullfighting bull

Traje de Luces – 'Suit of Lights', a matador's outfit

Tricornio – Traditional hat worn by members of the *Guardia Civil* (q.v.)

Verónica – A bullfighting move

www.vintage-books.co.uk